SOME RISE BY SIN

Siôn Scott-Wilson

Deixis Press

For my wife, Siân

PROLOGUE

There is a sudden jerk as the horse strains at the traces and we are away. I see Mutton through the window, marooned on the pavement in an agony of indecision. Rosamund, still shrouded and hunched, totters away without a second glance, vanishing utterly into the mists. As we trot past, Mutton finally turns, races up the steps and begins to haul frantically on the Glendale bell-pull. Kak John leans against the iron railings, raising a hand in stealthy salute. Even through the haze I can detect the gleam of his delighted grin.

Edward is already drooling and snoring, head lolling against Poppy's shoulder as Poppy reaches to pull down the leather window blind. The cab is now almost pitch black, though I can see the glint in Poppy's eyes as he turns his attention to me and I realise that this young Mohock is not quite so drunk as I had supposed. 'Well now, it seems that the Hack is mine and so you must ride along with us for the moment.'

'So it would seem, your honour.'

'You say your master is a gentleman, and so I should not like to have turned him out on such a night, abandoning him to the tender mercies of such a man as that. I did not much like the cut of him, nor his bugger's grips, the wretch.'

'Oh, sir, you have the right of it. That rogue and his confederate have tonight plied my young master with strong drink and carried him to this residence with the intention, I believe, of fleecing him at cards. It is a blessing that my master has no head for liquor and was made utterly insensible by it. Elsewise, who can say what calamity might have occurred?'

Poppy considers this for a moment, eyeing Bobby shrewdly, who, despite my firm grip on her arm, rolls with the motion of the cab, giving, for the moment at least, the illusion of life. 'I had supposed as much. And so, who, precisely, is your gentleman?'

It is a question I cannot, for the life of me, answer.

CHAPTER I

Too bad about old Sausages; I was fond of that dog. He had character.

I got him off a ratting cove down Bermondsey way, cheap for the price of a pint. He was only going to knock old Sausages on the head anyhow on account of he wouldn't go. Some dogs just won't—no killer instinct nor no taste for it. That was old Sausages, he preferred his grub hot, greasy and out of a frying pan, which is why I called him Sausages. Do anything for a snag, he would.

Not much for ratting, but good company all the same. Funny-looking bugger with his hair all sticking out, like he'd read a Penny Blood and got the frighteners on. Looked a bit like a sausage and all, which gave me a chuckle. All body, stubby little legs and only a morsel of a head. He shared my scran and kept me warm some nights.

Facey never took to him much. Then again Facey doesn't take to anyone much. 'Look after number one', says Facey. Then he shoots me his look and says, 'and maybe number two. But never no more 'an that, as you well know, Sammy Boy, since two is company but three is one too many a mouth.' That's Facey for you.

I suppose Facey always reckoned Sausages was one too many a mouth and good for nothing but he was my pal. So, I was sorry when they hanged him. But they had him bang to rights, the Kent Street lot. One of them youngsters had come by a few rashers in a nice parcel when Sausages caught the scent of it. He could move when he wanted to all right. Before you could say 'knife' Sausages had them rashers in his teeth and was off. They cornered him down by the canal, gammon gone, and not even a scrap of greasy newspaper left from the wrappings. Well, of course, after a big dinner like that Sausages was no trouble to catch. He always did like people. Too trusting by half.

Fair play, they gave him a proper trial, with evidence called and a beak appointed and all the trimmings. One of them youngsters even came on for the defence. But poor old Sausages never stood a chance, what with him all trussed up, shame-faced and whimpering every time the beak asked him why he done the crime.

They hanged him from one of them new lampposts on the canal. And I'm sorry for it but you can't go round stealing people's dinners, even if you are the kind of ratter what prefers a fry-up.

We buried Sausages this afternoon at the brick fields over Haggerston way and Facey said some words, which I'm appreciative for: 'Sausages. You and me were never friends. But Sammy liked you right enough, so I suppose that's something.' Or some such.

That shows class in my book.

CHAPTER II

'Now, Sammy Boy, pocket that twine,' orders Facey. 'Waste no time on thems that ain't a coming back, for there ain't no profit in it. You of all people should know that.'

Woolgathering. That's what I'm doing. Took me a moment to realise I was running old Sausages' string through my fingers. Should have kept him on that lead a bit more often. If I had of done he'd still be above ground.

'Make a hole in that.' Facey aims a meaty finger at my glass of shrub. 'Be proper dark soon.'

I ram the twine back into the long greasy inner pocket of my overcoat where I feel the cold touch of the short iron crowbar. In my other pocket I sense the reassuring weight of its business partner, the broad chisel, along with a small tin box of freshly made up mortar. I have a good stout rope triple-wrapped around my waist. These are the tools of our trade. Mine, at any rate. Facey keeps other articles about his person, which carry the greater risk should we be searched by the Crushers.

Of a sudden Facey quivers like Sausages used to when he smelled viands cooking in the pan. Facey misses nothing.

'Now then, Mrs Pigeon,' he bellows over the noisy throng, 'a little something to warm the cockles.'

Though Mrs Pigeon is only four feet and some few inches, Facey has been quick to spot the small black pudding of a figure across the busy wine vault cram-packed with bodies.

The woman trundles over to us like a skittle ball. 'Oooh, Mr Facey, you're a sight for sore eyes. I'm no tippler as all hereabouts can testify, but just this once I will take a bracer of something to keep the chill from me bones.'

'Geneva?'

'Well, gents, unaccustomed to spirituous liquors as I am, but seeing as how the melancholia must needs be kept at bay, I'll break the habit of a lifetime and join you in a glass of something reviving. Geneva, just as you say, Mr Facey.'

Facey raps a coin on the counter to summon Fearon. Though there are plenty of customers in the vicinity who, in all honesty, have a prior claim to the man's attention, Facey is not a man to be ignored or kept waiting. 'A glass of your tuppenny best, Fearon. None of your sulphuric adulterations, if you please.'

'Don't be coming down on a man for making a living, Mr Facey. There's plenty as prefers their concoction that way.' Fearon expertly twists the stopcock of a small black barrel to release a crystal stream into his less than crystal receptacle.

Facey slaps his two coppers on the counter in exchange for the brimful beaker of gin.

He drops a shilling from under his palm into the beaker before extending it to Mrs Pigeon. 'Well, Mrs Pigeon. This is, as you say, the good spirit what drives away the bad spirits of that melancholia, which you was just now mentioning. And if anyone is more deserving of the contents of this glass, I can't think of them.'

She reaches for it with a trembling hand; Facey dangles it just out of her reach.

'But first we need to know on what grounds these melancholic spirits have arisen and on account of who?'

'Well, my dear Mr Facey, didn't my aunt Pikelet get carried off with an ague just two days previous and isn't she in the ground already this day? Who is to know the vill of God in this wicked vorld?'

'Crepe?'

'Certainly, Mr Facey, a quantity of black crepe has been worn today in respect of my great aunt Pikelet, God rest her.'

Crepe is cant for the aged ones, denoting wrinkles. If the deceased party is young, Mrs Pigeon knows to say silk. Should some nosey party happen to stick his great flappers where they're not wanted he would rate the conversation quite innocent, concerning only mourning garb.

Facey grimaces. There's not so much profit in the old 'uns. Our customers like the merchandise young, smooth and in good health, notwithstanding they're dead, of course. Silk is what we'd prefer to hear.

'Age catches up with us all.' Mrs Pigeon knuckles her eyes. 'But I do take solace in the notion that my dear aunt Pieclott, is now gathered up and safe and sound in the arms of our Lord, having first been laid to rest most beautiful, inside the Shoreditch. God bless 'er.'

Shit.

This is not good. Mrs Pigeon is telling us that the best she's got is an oldster inside St Leonard's rather than outside in the churchyard. Inside is always more risky. Takes longer on account of we've got to break in first.

I wait and see what Facey decides.

He allows Mrs Pigeon her glass of Geneva at any rate.

'I thank you, gents. There's not many that understand what it is on the nerves to be out there day in and day out, observin' all them aspects of humanity put into the ground. It do make you feel a touch of maudlin. It do, Mr Facey. And that's all I got for you today,' she shrugs. 'Middlin' weather, you see, gents. 'T'ain't sufficient hot for the murdering miasmas of summer nor chill enough for them winter killing frosts what bring on the deadly croup.'

'Well, you just take a bracer, Mrs Pigeon and no one can say you han't earned it.'

Facey tips me the wink.

Fuck.

He wants to do it. I hate these churchy pulls.

Facey summons us closer. As we huddle, surrounding drinkers shuffle back a ways, allowing us a private word or two. There's due respect here when business is being discussed.

'The late Ma Pieclott, you say?'

'Some 'at as like. Must of popped her clogs pretty sharp as they ain't yet had time to carve a name into the memorial stone. But you'll feature it, never fear. Blank slab, elm coffin.' Mrs Pigeon tosses off the gin in one and gives us a wink.

'Did you just drink off your perquisite, my love?' asks Facey, grinning.

'Fuck, I did an' all. I've gone an' dranked that shillin' what you slipped into my glass',' belches Mrs Pigeon by way of reply. 'The specie is already repeatin' on me. I'm tasting the King's silver here.'

'Well then, Mrs Pigeon, you must go forth and meet the world arsey-versey.'

'How so, Mr Facey?'

'Why, you must shit before you can eat and not t'other way round.'

I snort my drink. Facey is not what you might call a wit under normal circumstances so this squib is something of a triumph for him. It shows he's in a good mood, which is always welcome.

Mrs Pigeon is not amused. She scowls. 'Funny, Mr Facey, funny. I hear there's an opening for a warm-up man over at the Adelphi, which a man of your gifts might comfortably fill.'

Mrs Pigeon freezes. She's overstepped and knows it. Facey's upper lip is stretched tight across his front teeth. Not a pretty sight. Facey can dish it out all right but is never comfortable as the butt of another's wit. I do take liberties myself but Facey and I have known each other since we were snotty street arabs in Portsmouth.

'Now, now, Mr Facey, don't take offence at an old woman's poor attempt at fun. You've paid me well in both liquor and specie, even though I've dranked the money by mistake, it will keep, and I will have it to spend tomorrow, bowels and the Lord permitting. Like the goose what laid a golden guinea, I daresay. Only silver, and a shillin' in this case.'

Facey's lip relaxes. A moist, rumbling chuckle escapes from deep inside his chest. He produces another couple of coppers for Mrs Pigeon. 'Pieclott then?'

'Pieclott, Piecrust, something of that order. Don't signify really. Won't be of no help. Like I said, the slab were blank as yet.'

Facey grins. 'Remember what old Pounds used to say, Sammy Boy. Life is but a blank slate what is waiting for you to write something worthy on it. Or words to that effect.'

'Or words to that effect,' I murmur. Actually, what Pounds used to say was this: 'Life is but a blank page, waiting for you to fill it with your dreams.' But I'm not about to bandy words with Facey. Doesn't like me parroting John Pounds. Never did.

Facey casts around for Michael Shields. The Feathers is Shields' second home of an evening and, sure enough, we clock his dial over by the fireplace, yarning with Jack Stirabout, a pudding maker of dubious reputation. Facey tips him the wink. Shields nods and slips away. Jack Stirabout turns and warms his bum, but really he's watching us, hooded eyes, black as printer's ink, over his leather mug.

'Best have the pins then,' announces Facey, rubbing his hands. Facey keeps a set of pins at the Feathers and another at the Fortune of War up Smithfield way.

He raps a penny on the counter, 'Penny for our pins, Mr Fearon.'

Fearon reaches under the counter and hands over two stout rolling pins. 'No rest for the wicked then, Mr Facey.' He pockets the penny.

Facey slips the pins into specially sewn pockets down the inside of each trouser leg. 'The pastry won't make itself overnight, Mr Fearon. And if Sammy and me are not there to do it, there's many will go hungry without their breakfast bite tomorrow morning.'

'You're a pair of shire horses, Mr Facey: an example to us all. If every man adopted suchlike virtues of honest labour the world would be a better place. Truly it would.' This is rich, coming from Fearon, whose establishment, the Feathers of Shoreditch, is famous for accommodating pretty well every vice known to mankind.

Facey beams. The pins are an absolute stroke, performing as they do no fewer than three different functions. A legacy of Facey's less than glorious naval service, they are, in fact, belaying pins: teak, and hard as iron. Facey has simply carved a handle on the other end of each. In consequence, there are some few of our acquaintance who still believe us to be relatively honest bakers, a trade which accounts for our odd hours. Some nights, we even pat our hair and faces down with a little flour to gild the lily. In reality the pins are for slabwork. And they make a handy pair of cudgels should we have to resort to brute physicality, which, on occasion, we do.

By the time we exit the Feathers, Shields is ready outside with his handcart. He nods once and settles his chin into the turned up collars of his overcoat though the night is barely chill.

We set off at a brisk pace, staggering a little up Shoreditch High Street. As yet we are a perfectly reputable trio of working men on the way home after a hard day on the market. From our unsteady gait it might appear that we have overindulged somewhat in the spirituous liquors. We bob and weave across the pavement taking care to avoid exposing ourselves to the glare of the gas lamps, which have lately sprouted here, all the while keeping a wary eye out for the Crushers.

We slip down Cock Lane, which, mercifully, is as dark as a Gypsy's curse. Before us is the low wall surmounted by a high railing enclosing St Leonard's churchyard: The Shoreditch.

Facey is up and over the spiked iron railings before you can blink twice. To his credit he has never lost the strength and flexibility he developed on the old Billy Ruffian with all that climbing about in the rigging, even if he did run in the end.

I sling my rope over the railings while Facey hauls me up like a mackerel on a line. Behind us Shields waits in the lane, merging with the black mass of his cart.

I land feet-first in the churchyard and hunch in the cover of a nearby tombstone as Facey creeps towards the church.

Within minutes he's back. 'Skelly-keys won't open the side-door,' he whispers. Then he's off again into the night.

I kick my heels against the stone for what seems like an age, so long that I'm actually beginning to see in the dark. I can make out the words cut into the stone I'm hunched against:

TAKE YE HEED, WATCH AND PRAY
FOR YE KNOW NOT WHEN THE TIME IS. 1787.
IN MEMORY OF
MR JOHN ONELY
WHO DIED MARCH 24TH 1777.
AGED 36 YEARS.

I'm still considering this sage advice when finally Facey reappears. 'I've had to cut the padlock on the lobby door. It's done, but the snatch will need to be disguised.'

I follow him up a set of stairs on the south side of the church where there's a side door into a lobby of some kind. We enter, carefully closing the door behind us. Though it's blacker than the Earl of Hell's riding boots in here, I can hear him fiddling with a heavy latch. There's a breath of stale, frozen air as he opens the side door into the church.

I remain in the anteroom, carefully casting about in the dark. By touch alone I discover a cloth-covered table, which I explore. My scuttling fingers encounter a glass object; a bottle or decanter of communion wine by my reckoning. I take a pull. Good fortified red wine. I take another swig and retreat back through the lobby door into the churchyard where I empty the contents onto a mound. I hope the recipient is duly grateful. Though I doubt it. I leave the decanter propped up on whomever's memorial it happens to be. In the morning the empty will be found and, with luck, will account for the broken padlock on the lobby door.

Task complete, I flit back up the stairs, ease through the anteroom, stepping softly as a mouser, and slip silently into the icy church. Light sputters to my left. Facey, holding a stub of candle, which he fits carefully into a small tin shade designed to mask the glare.

Without a word he works his fingers around a blank slab, searching for joints. Finally, he produces a thin blade and sinks it into the soft mortar around the edges. 'This is the one all right, Sammy.' He pronounces.

Facey produces a small bottle of vinegar from his coat, which he pours around the edges of the slab. After a minute or so he works his blade back into the mortar, running it to and fro, followed by more vinegar, then more blade. Finally, he looks over, satisfied with his endeavours, and hisses. 'Go on then, Sam. Have at it.'

I widen the gap first with my chisel, taking care not to damage the stone. Next, I heft the short crowbar from my coat, shove it into the edge of the slab and ease my weight onto it. As the slab rises an inch or two Facey slips in a couple of wooden wedges. I push down again. My partner deftly pops in another couple more wedges.

I insert the crowbar a little further. This time there's enough space for Facey to shove one of the teak rollers under, canting the slab.

I slowly withdraw the crowbar allowing the slab's weight to settle firmly onto the roller and move to the other side where we begin the process again. Facey inserts his wedges and slips in the second pin. The heavy stone slab is now raised a couple of inches, sitting handsomely on the twin rollers. We give it a push and slide it to one side. It moves like it's on wheels, exposing the earth floor beneath through the dim glow of the tin lamp.

'Well?' I ask.

'Blank slab. Fresh earth, Sammy Boy. Gotta be right.'

Facey scrapes away a thin layer of soil to reveal the pale yellow wood of a coffin lid. It looks brand new. Just to be sure, he removes a long thin flexible rod and jams it through the wood. He withdraws the rod and runs it across his tongue. 'Elm, new, lined in black cloth,' he pronounces.

I never know how he does this. Elm, yes, I understand. But I don't see how anyone can taste black cloth, even someone as good as Facey.

It's the work of minutes to dig away the dust and loose earth around the coffin and pass my rope underneath. Facey and I haul it up. He levers the lid with my crowbar and surveys the prize. Sure enough, the coffin is lined with black cloth. Inside, an elderly woman, freshly passed within a day or so. Her waxy countenance further jaundiced by the flickering candlelight.

Our task now is to remove every stitch of clothing. We do this because the legal penalties for theft of property, including shrouds and clothing, far outweigh the penalties for bodysnatching. Facey and I are not thieves. We're better than that. We're Resurrection Men.

We bundle the shift and sundry articles of clothing into the coffin before lowering it back into the hole and replacing the loose earth. Now we roll back the slab, reversing the excavation process. I take a little tin box from my cly and begin to fill the joints with fresh mortar. Finally, to give the impression of age, I dust the edges with a little brown powder from a tiny bag I keep around my neck. Facey gives the slab a quick polish with a soft rag, flicking loose dust from around the joints. It's a fine job, as always, and will stand all but the very closest of inspections. Pity it's only crêpe for our efforts.

The stiffness of rigor has passed, the body is slack and surprisingly heavy. Between us we lug the corpse through the churchyard and drop it over the railings. The carcass slaps to the cobblestones with a wet, meaty sound.

'Tom's,' Facey hisses into the night.

'That is a fair distance, Mr Facey, sir, and London Bridge is likely still busy even at this time. A fair distance is a fair risk. Five bob is not worth the candle. What say seven?' comes back at us from the dark.

'Don't play with me now, Shields.'

'Sure as a shilling, I am not playing with you, Mr Facey. But that is many a mile to be carting a object that I would not be able to vouch for. The risk is uncommon severe.'

'Do not use my name. And do not presume to bargain with me while I am on the other side of an iron railing.'

'Certainly, I will wait for you at Saint Tom's but I hope you will take my labours into account when it comes to a reckoning.'

'I will, Shields, be sure of it.'

Shields creaks away with his burden while Facey and me clamber back over the railings, cut back down Cock Lane and head south towards Norton Folgate. Facey is still simmering with rage. Shields has pushed his luck here. There are only a few destinations for goods such as ours, as Shields well knows. St Thomas's Hospital is usually first port of call, then St Giles' and occasionally King's College School of Anatomy in the Strand. From time to time with an especially young or fresh corpse, we might venture over to the West End to sell direct to the toffs; amateurs or those with private anatomy studios. It is quite wrong of Shields to quibble with us over price while we are at a disadvantage like that and to my mind shows a want of character. At any rate, sooner or later there will be a reckoning and if I'm any judge of Facey's mood, it will not be to Shields's advantage.

Facey has still not uttered a word by the time we reach Bishopsgate.

From the shadows of a doorway I spy the gaslight glimmer reflecting off a row of brass buttons. Instantly I cast my arm round Facey's shoulders and stagger, throwing in a dry retch or two for good measure.

The Bobby steps out, barring our way. A most imposing figure, he must be well over six feet in his boots, maybe seven if you count the reinforced stovepipe hat. We stand, arms round one another, swaying slightly, playing it lushy as he raises his bulls-eye lantern to better inspect us.

'Now then, men. It is some six hours past the hour of sunset. How do you account for yourselves here in the street at this time?'

'I have already given a good account of myself at the Feathers in Shoreditch, sir,' belches Facey thickly.

'How so?'

'I have stood a round or three of good Geneva in the company of honest friends tonight, as many a man can testify.'

'Well then, where do you go now?'

'To our place of work, sir. For we are bakers and must prepare our crusts for the morning pies.'

'I have no doubt you come from consuming spirituous liquors tonight. No doubt on that account, since your breath is sufficient testimony. As to your profession and destination, can you offer proof? If not, I must take you before a Magistrate.' With that, the Crusher unsheathes his baton.

'For what, cocky?'

'Being abroad after the hour of sunset without a good account as to your purpose. And making riotous assembly.'

'But there are only two of us here.' Facey untangles my arm, looks me up and down, cross-eyed and swaying slightly. 'Or is it three?'

'Loitering with intent also.' The Bobby grips my arm and raises his baton. 'Now, show me the tools you have about your person before I am forced to chastise your accomplice.'

'A moment, sir, a moment.' Facey rummages in his long trouser pocket for one of the pins. 'Here is my rolling pin.'

The Bobby releases my arm and raises the lantern for closer examination.

Facey cracks him a colossal blow across the temple, sending his topper clattering into the gutter. The Bobby releases his grip on me, staggers back a step but somehow remains upright. He flings the lantern at Facey, who is for a moment distracted, and strikes out with his own truncheon catching Facey a solid blow across the left eye. I leap onto the Bobby's back and manage to get my arms around his throat.

Facey is on his knees, both hands cupping his injured eye. The Bobby bellows and whirls round in an effort to dislodge me. I'm hanging on for dear life, trying to choke the man, but I cannot bring any real pressure to bear on account of the stiff leather stock he wears around his throttle. With one immensely strong hand the Bobby begins to prise my arms open, with the other he reaches for the wooden rattle at his belt. Mercifully, Facey is now back on his feet. He brings the pin hard down on the Peeler's unprotected crown and I feel the fight leak out of him. We sink to the kerb in a tangle of limbs.

Facey stands over us, pin raised for a killing blow, but I'm in the way.

Instead, Facey lowers the pin, points it at the unconscious Bobby and says, 'Consider yourself chastised.'

From what I can make out in the gloom, Facey's left eye is a bloody mess, resembling something off a Smithfield butcher's barrow. Though now is not the time for a full investigation.

Together, we set off at the trot down Bishopsgate, slowing to a brisk walk at new London Bridge, which we cross without incident. Shields is already waiting for us at the hospital side entrance in Thomas Street. He nods and hangs back in the shadows on the other side of the road with his cart while we rouse the porter.

The porter knows us and our business here, and is quick to alert Eddie Barber. Though young and not yet a proper surgeon, Barber has considerable status at St Thomas's, being understudy, so to speak, to the famous Mr Green. Eddie is what they call an anatomical dresser, which means his job is to tickle up the bits and pieces ready for the surgeon's work.

I'm fond of young Eddie; he's a decent gent, gives no trouble and a fair price. His appearance, though, is somewhat dishevelled at this hour, most likely on account of his still being hard at the grindstone. Unlike most folk, who have a healthy respect for, or even fear of, the dead, Eddie is what I would call an enthusiast. Without taking a moment to fix his stock or smooth his hair he grabs one of the spare lanterns from the porter's lodge and dashes across the road. He can barely wait to lift the tarpaulin but as he directs the beam over our offering his expression crumples. 'Oh dear. An old 'un. Singularly ancient indeed.'

'She's but a young slip of thing, Eddie. Not three days previous this one was dancing a jig over at the Phoenix. I observed her kicking up a storm with these very eyes, I swear,' objects Facey.

'If so, it can only have been with the left one, Mr Facey, which, if you don't mind me saying, is something of a shambles. I don't like the look of it even in this Stygian gloom. When our business is concluded here, I will examine it properly if you will let me.'

'I will, sir. And very kind in you it is.'

Eddie grimaces and pinches the flesh of the woman's forearm. 'Sixty-eight, seventy years, if she's a day. Specimens of this antiquity are of little value to us, gentlemen. The veins are thin and weak and difficult to mount. No, I cannot give you much for it.'

'Have a heart, Mr Barber, it has been a long and arduous hoist tonight,' I plead.

Eddie shakes his head. 'I cannot help that, Sammy. What were you hoping for?'

'Twelve guineas,' I say without hesitation.

'Seven sovereigns.'

'Nine.'

Facey and I have long ago agreed that I take charge of financial negotiations in our partnership, having the superior temperament for it.

'Eight sovs, and we will shake hands on it.'

'Done,' I say. And we do.

Barber waves his lamp at the porter who strides over and takes possession of the corpse, hoisting it over his broad shoulders before disappearing into the bowels of the hospital.

Facey counts coins into Shield's eager hand. 'Five Shillings, Shields. Not a penny more.' Shields has marked the shocking state of Facey's eye and perhaps it is this memento of violence which pacifies him. At any rate, he pockets the coins without objection, nods once, tucks his chin into his collars and slinks away into the night, leaving us only the softly diminishing sound of his creaking wheels.

Eddie ushers us through the porter's cubby across Edward Square, through Clayton Square and into the dispensary. At this time of night it is quiet but a hospital is never entirely without activity. One or two functionaries, stewards, nurses and, strangely enough, bakers, pass us in the squares with a nod, a brief acknowledgment, but only to Eddie.

In the glare of the dispensary gas lamp, the damage to Facey's eye is obvious even to me as Eddie swabs away the blood. 'How do you see with this eye, Mr Facey?'

'I just peers out of it. Thank you for asking.'

Eddie sighs. 'Is there anything over and above the usual?'

'I see flashes of light here and there but, trust me, Mr Barber, this is pretty run of the mill for a mill of this nature.'

'A mill, sir, is our way of describing a bit of a rough up,' I interject. Eddie Barber is doing his best for Facey and I do not approve of Facey making light of his efforts.

'I see.'

'As do I,' retorts Facey.

'And is there anything else out of the ordinary? Black dots for example?'

'Certainly black dots. They swarm about me glim like tadpoles in a pond.'

Eddie grimaces before smearing a greasy orange salve across Facey's peeper. 'This will help a little but I fear there has been damage to the internal workings of the eye itself. The eye, like any other organ of the body, is a delicate mechanism designed for purpose, like a watch. I believe that there has been trauma here, which has tipped the workings out of true. I could not, and neither could the great Mr Green, surgically enter the inner workings of the orb to remedy the situation. Rest may help. I can only advise that you remain prone, on your back, for at least one week. And apply this salve from time to time, along with this material for a bandage.'

Facey accepts the pot of salve and the brown linen strip, thankfully with a certain graciousness. On the whole, he's fond of Eddie too, in his own way.

'I will grease the glimmer every day, but you might recall that me and Sammy Boy are scarcely gents of leisure. A week on my back would be a fine thing. But I cannot have it. It cannot be done.'

'Well then, keep the bandage over for as long as you can. At least for tonight you and Sammy will remain here and rest?'

Facey nods. 'We will at that. And thank you for it.'

'I cannot admit you to the wards as I do not wish there to be a connection made between us. But you may doss in the Treasurer's Stable where you will not be disturbed since he is presently out of town.'

'Fine by me,' says Facey.

As always, I go along.

The sun is long since up by the time we emerge; someone has left bread and a pitcher of milk for us at the stable doors. We wolf it down and skedaddle. Facey seems his old self this morning, aside from the brown bandage across his eye.

One part of London is usually as good as another since we do not keep a permanent crib these days. Today, south of the river suits us very well as we have business in Stockwell. Besides, I always look forward to seeing Rosamund.

Rosamund is not the name she was born with but is the only one she will answer to. Someone, no doubt some species of divine, has assured her that rosa is Latin for rose, while mundus stands for world. It delights her to imagine an entire world full of blooms, and so Rosamund it is. And who am I to say that such a moniker is inferior to Sammy, Facey, or even Sausages come to that?

Rosamund works a tiny stretch of kerb at the Vauxhall end of Kennington Lane. In the past many have tried to steal her patch but she is resolute and has always returned. This little scrap of ground has become Rosamund's kingdom by right of occupation and, these days, she is rarely troubled by pretenders to her throne. In the evenings, she will shift to a spot on Vauxhall Walk in order to catch the Pleasure Garden strollers.

Rosamund is hard at it, cross-legged, head down, scraping away with her blocks of chalk.

I know she's aware of my presence by the shadow I cast across her landscapes. But without even looking up she says, 'I've not seen you in a monkey's age, Sammy. Where've you been at?'

I shrug. 'Here and there. How do you do that, Rosamund? How can you tell it's me without even looking?'

'The boots, glocky. Spend all day kerbside and you'll get to know a pair of boots a sight quicker than you recognise a face.'

Rosamund adds a bold stroke of light grey chalk to the skyline above a range of hills and rubs it in with her thumb, smudging colours, yet somehow creating the illusion of morning light. I love watching her work. It's like a conjuring trick with sunshine.

Finally, she peers up at me through slitted eyes. 'So, what do you reckon?'

'Beautiful, as always.'

Rosamund nods at the compliment, taking it as her due and turns her attention to Facey. 'Well?'

Of course Facey has neither my patience nor my partiality. 'They're just fucking chalk daubs on the pavement. For two pins I'd kick your carcass out of the highway only, for some reason, Sammy Boy reckons I ought to be appreciative. I'm appreciating your art by not booting you up the arse.'

Rosamund nods. 'Good, it is quite sufficient to have tamed the savage beast. The savage beast doesn't have to love the work.'

'I don't love the work,' retorts Facey. 'And we have business to attend. It is a blessed nuisance but what with one thing and another we find so little time these days for outings to the Royal Academy nor even to take the waters at Bath, more's the pity. Is that not so, Sammy Boy?'

I gaze down at my boots, having no desire to encourage him.

'Perhaps you should. I am in favour of any activity of a self-improving nature, although in your case, Mr Facey, it'd be difficult to know where to begin.'

It takes a moment for Facey to comprehend the barb but when he does I'm relieved to find that his response is only a deep rumbling chuckle. 'You've got spirit, girl. I'll grant you that.'

Instead of acknowledging the reprieve, Rosamund simply ignores him and returns to her landscapes.

Facey considers her for a moment. 'Why not stay here a while, Sammy? Our business with "The man they couldn't hang" will not require us both.'

'I will, and thank you for it, Facey.' With that, I hunker down beside Rosamund, cross-legged on the kerb.

George Spicer, "The man they couldn't hang", keeps a Dollyshop in Stockwell high street, though his true calling is as a fence of hoisted property. A large, slow-moving, greasy cove, Spicer is known in our world as "The man they couldn't hang" on account of his having no neck to speak of.

Spicer and others of our acquaintance are putting together a Rig, a house-clearance racket to which Facey and me are contributing five hampers of chinaware. Spicer has purchased our contribution from a dealer in Lambeth and the stuff is snide rather than hoisted. With the Rig, everything on sale must be above board and regular to keep us all on the right side of the law—just. For the house-clearance racket is nothing more than a bit of fleecing. The principals have taken a short lease on one of the big villas off Russell Square; a notice of demise has been inserted in Lloyds Weekly and will be followed by advertisement of a House Clearance auction to take place this Tuesday coming, catalogues duly printed and circulated with no reserve prices. Events such as these draw folk from all corners of the metropolis on the lookout for bargains; linens, crockery, knockdown silverware and such like. In short, flats hoping to benefit from the misfortune of others.

The goods we lay out are all quite genuine, bought and paid for, but of a certainty have never graced the rooms of any grand household. It's all just cheap, showy, gimcrack stuff. Come the auction, members of the Rig, like Facey and me, will be present to drive up the bidding in the expectation of taking double, or even treble what we paid for our tat.

Aside from the eight sovereigns we took last night and the few odd shillings to go along, we've sunk all our ready capital into this. It's high time we moved on from the resurrection game and we've had our eye for a while now on a nice little boozing-ken in Stepney, which to my mind, is a far better end for Facey and me than the prison hulks or scragged.

Facey should be in Stockwell by now, checking the hampers, running through our inventory to be sure that Spicer hasn't fiddled us along the way.

'Penny for 'em,' says Rosamund softly.

'I was thinking on our tavern. We're not so far off now.'

'Good for you, Sammy.'

'You are to be our official artist in residence, you know. Your pictures will hang on the walls, seeing as it will be quite a respectable establishment.'

'They're not meant for walls, glocky. They're pavement pictures. Besides, how am I meant to shift a huge slab of granite like this?'

'I could shift it for you,' I say. I could too.

'No. Pavement chalks are for the pavement. What would my pictures be doing on somebody's walls in great fancy gilt frames like chunks of gingerbread?'

'I like them.'

'So does everyone. It's why they throw me these coppers,' she replies, indicating an old linen bonnet holding a few meagre coins, 'which accounts for my fame and great wealth.'

I sigh and look up at the sky, which is, as so often in London, grey and brooding. 'Be coming on to rain soon.'

Rosamund sweeps a layer of dark green chalk across a forest canopy, instantly the quality of her images changes as though a cloud has moved across the sun.

'Rosamund?' I say.

'What is it, Sammy?' she continues to add layers, rubbing and smudging, never taking her eyes off the work.

'A thing I've been meaning to ask you.'

'Go on.'

'Some—actually pretty well most—of the pavement artists I've seen, work their pictures on a scrap of paper or canvas or a bit of old tarp.'

'Yes.'

'So's they can take them away at night, then lay them out again each morning.'

Rosamund turns and looks me full in the face with her strange unblinking grey eyes. 'What would be the point of that?'

'It would save you having to do them all again every day.'

Rosamund sighs. 'You think I should ask money for doing nothing?'

'No. It's just—.'

'They're different each time, Sammy. They might be the same views but every time I do the work there's a twist—in the light or the sky or the colours.'

'But that doesn't mean you ... '

'Do you think them beautiful?'

A droplet of rain lands on her Scotch hillside, a tiny crushed spider-smudge of black. Rosamund rubs it vigorously with her thumb. More drops begin to patter around us. She runs her hands across the landscape working in the splashes, turning bright colours to mud, smudging and befouling. 'How about now?'

For some reason I'm enraged at her wanton destruction. I don't have the words to explain the anger and sadness I feel, so I haul myself to my feet. 'It's raining,' I say.

Rosamund reaches up, grips the tail of my coat. 'Stay.'

'Why?'

'I want to show you something.' She gazes up at me with a peculiar, lopsided smile. So I sit once again, turning up the collars of my overcoat against the cloudburst. By contrast Rosamund turns her face to the sky, revelling in the rain. 'I do believe that the heart must ache for there to be true beauty.'

The rain comes on heavier now, dark fat blotches exploding across the granite. Rosamund gazes down at her chalks where the images are beginning to run and spoil without the aid of her hand.

'Knowing that a thing cannot last is the element which renders it more beautiful in our eyes. It is what makes a thing bittersweet and achingly sad, yet even more magnificent. True beauty reflects the impermanence of life, Sammy.'

'I believe you may have a touch of the vapours.' I take off my overcoat to protect her, laying it over her thin shawl.

'Don't be such a numbskull.' She shrugs it off. 'Look.' Rosamund remains transfixed by her own pictures. Rivulets of colour run and merge across the pavement, hours and hours of craft melting into a multi-hued channel of wet chalk. It's heartbreaking, and yet I can detect a beauty in it.

'Do you see it?'

'I do.'

'Well then.'

The cloudburst passes, thinning to a more delicate patter now.

'Take a rose or a butterfly. We understand that they will not be with us long. They disappear so soon, yet the sadness of knowing that they are so ephemeral is what makes them so beautiful. Because we too will fade.'

Rosamund brushes a stray lock of hair from her brow. 'Now you know why I will only work my chalks on a pavement.'

'Aaah, Lady Rosamund, the fucken rain's gone an' fucken ruined your lovely pitchers.'

Kak John.

He could be anywhere from fifteen to eighteen. Hard to say with all the muck on him. Kak John is the occasional street sweeper hereabouts. It's not a particularly profitable patch and I suspect he only stays this side of the river so's he can keep an eye on Rosamund. A young lad with his spunk could be doing very well for himself over in the West End by now.

In point of fact Kak John makes his real income selling pure to the Bermondsey tanners. Any kind of shit. Horse, dog, human. Doesn't signify to Kak John. Which is why we call him Kak John. That and the fact that he's always covered in it. Truth be told, apart from the stench, I'm quite partial to Kak John. He's always looked after Rosamund for a starter and he's a straight arrow; Facey and I have even used him as a crow to keep a lookout on occasion.

'All right, Mr Samuel?'

He also calls me Mister, which is peachy in my book.

'How's business?'

'Shit mostly, Mr Samuel.'

'I'm sorry to hear that.'

'No, it's right enough, but it's mainly shit. The street sweeping business is not what I would 'zactly call thriving round these parts. Not enough tin hereabouts. How's your good self?'

'Thriving, John. I have learned another word today.'

'Ah, we all needs constantly to try elevate ourselves, Mr Samuel, else what are we put on this earth for to do? What is this new word, if I may be so bold?'

'Don't exactly know, John, as I have not properly learned it yet. Rosamund will tell you as she just finished the saying of it. Elephant, sounds like.'

'Ephemeral,' says Rosamund.

Kak John deliberates, mouthing the word a few times before nodding approval like some grave academic. 'That is a rare and mighty word. What's it mean, your ladyship?'

Rosamund grins. 'Lasting for only a very short while. Like your promises, John.'

'No,' objects Kak John. 'I never broken a ...'

'Ah, John, you promised to take me to the Gardens only last week.'

'I will, your ladyship, any one of these evenings now.'

Kak John is not likely to take Rosamund to Vauxhall Gardens any time soon as she well knows and, much as I enjoy their banter, I expect Facey back at any time. 'Rosamund, let me have that elephant word again please. It shall be my word of today.'

Ever since I was at John Pounds' little school, I have always sought to extend my vocabulary. Indeed, upon my departure from that humble site of education it was Pounds who exhorted me to be sure to learn one new word each day. And this I endeavour to do.

As it happens, there are three quite rare and mighty words in those very sentences.

'Ephemeral,' she repeats.

'Efferamal.'

'Effingmill,' echoes Kak John.

'Remember it as though you would a set of initials—F. M. R.—a fine gentleman, an aristocrat no less, holding the rank of earl.'

'F.M.R.'

'F.M.R. Earl. A noble quality present in so much of what we find to be beautiful.'

'F.M.R. Earl.'

I catch the distinct, rhythmic clump of Facey's advancing boots and reluctantly haul myself to my feet, brushing damp chalk from my hands and keks. 'I will try to remember that. Thank you, Rosamund.'

'I will quiz you on it next time we meet. Now, here is your Mister Facey, who goeth about seeking whom he may devour,' Rosamund remarks, noting the sour expression on Facey's mug.

He arrives nursing a package. 'Kak John,' he nods briskly.

'Mr Facey, sir.'

'From the looks of you, I should say that business is good.'

'Can't complain, sir.'

Facey grimaces. 'We shall never be short of shit in the metropolis.'

'Just as well, sir. Else we should all have to make do without good shoe leather.'

'Good shoe leather which I have willingly expended today for the sake of business only to find that "The man they couldn't hang" rates me a pigeon to be plucked.'

'I seldom do business with "The man they couldn't hang", Mr Facey, unless dire need and vile circumstance leave me no choice. I cannot vouch for his nature.'

'Nor I,' growls Facey.

My heart sinks. If Spicer has rooked us, our savings are gone and my dream of a little boozing-ken is over.

Facey catches sight of my face. 'Cheer up, Sammy Boy. It ain't as bad as all that.' He begins to unwrap his parcel. 'Besides, I have bought you a couple of pies, still hot and hot.'

'I cannot manage two.'

'Then you must do as you wish with the other, chuck it or save it for later, for I have eaten my share at the shop.'

This is kind of Facey. I know he has bought the extra pie for Rosamund but he'll be damned before he gives it to her. 'Rosamund, John, help me here. I am not such a swell as I can bear to throw away a good hot pie.'

'Always ready to see a good man out of a spot of bother. Known for it, I am,' announces Kak John.

I hand him the extra pie and note that, on breaking it in two, he donates the bigger chunk to Rosamund, whereupon he crams his own portion into his mouth without ceremony, heedless of the meat gravy trickling down in his chin.

Rosamund produces a threadbare but clean fogle from her sleeve, carefully wraps her share and places the little bundle on the pavement for later. She will not allow anyone to see her eating.

'And where is Pure John today?' inquires Facey.

'My brother has a new station, running for Lieutenant Trench,' announces Kak John, proudly.

Pure John, a filthy, impudent street urchin of about eight or nine years, is Kak John's younger brother. Although he has always assisted with the collection of pure, we call him "Pure" on account of his being a good deal more fragrant than his elder sibling. Which, it has to be owned, is not saying much.

Facey nods sagely. 'It is good for a young lad to find an honest trade and I am happy for him, Kak John.'

'It is a few more pennies each day to put between ourselves and the picking of oakum, Mr Facey.'

'Trench is a spinner; no officer, and certainly no gentleman, but I daresay there are worse men to be grafting for.' With that Facey throws a curt nod in Kak John's direction and we are away.

'You are vexed, I can tell,' I say, as we head towards Regent Bridge.

'Calm yourself, Sammy Boy. There is no real harm done, other than to Spicer's conk. I am vexed only because "The man they couldn't hang" took us for a pair of flats.'

'He did not deliver then?'

'There are five hampers, certainly. All shipshape and Bristol fashion. But I took it upon myself to tally the contents, each and every piece from creamer to tureen. And, as you well know, Sammy, reckoning is not my strong suit.'

'Pass beyond the digits of your hands and you are all at sea,' I agree, perhaps a little too readily, as Facey throws me one of his dark looks.

'To cut a long story short, after some deliberation, it appeared to me that the contents of but four hampers had been spread around to fill five. Giving voice to my suspicion, "The man they couldn't hang" made no attempt to dispute the fact, merely shifting blame onto the shoulders of his disreputable vendor, blackguarding that absent individual in a multitude of ways, whilst asserting to his own spotless conduct in the matter.'

By now we have crossed Regent Bridge and find ourselves north of the river once again.

'How are your boots, Sammy?' asks Facey, inspecting the sky, where a watery sun is battling to elbow its way through the overcast.

'Sound, for the moment.'

'Well, then, what say we take the towpath to the Palace of Westminster? A spot of mud will not hurt two gentlemen in stout boots such as we.'

'To what end?'

'There is to be sport at the Cockpit.'

'Ah.'

Facey enjoys his ratting and has a keen eye for a capable dog. One of the reasons he and Sausages never saw eye to eye, I shouldn't wonder.

'And don't you waste no sleep over our missing inventory, Sammy Boy. Come Tuesday, the shortfall will be made good by "The man they couldn't hang". Every last piece.'

'Surely not from the goodness of his heart?'

'I was forced to chastise him a little.'

'You should not have. Another mill is the last thing you need, given the condition of your eye. Perhaps you should follow Eddie Barber's prescription and rest up. We could try Bridewell Sal's, she'll take us in for a day or two.'

'It was scarcely a mill, Sammy. Spicer is a mumping great jelly of a man, with no skill at throwing the raws. Besides, it was only a love tap I gave him; a gentle swipe across the jaw and one in the razzo. As for resting up, there'll be plenty of time for that when I'm a dead 'un. Besides, we have yet to catch the scent of this Templeton cove.'

'That pursuit can surely wait.'

'It is a simple task and a good piece of tin for old rope.'

'I suppose a few civil enquiries at the Cockpit could not harm,' I concede.

Robert Templeton is doubtless typical of his sort: a young man of good family let loose on society with a greater appetite for the temptations of the metropolis than his allowance will accommodate. Inevitably, young rakehells like this Templeton find a source of ready cash amongst the many shys and jerryshops about town. From time to time they find themselves unable, or unwilling, to pay and so take french leave and go to ground. Which is where Facey and me come in. Templeton's debts are now long past due and we have been tasked with finding the absconder by Messrs John Dear, the cent per centers of Three Kings Court, for a bounty of two sovereigns. Tracking down young ne'er do wells like Robert Templeton is a handy way to make a little easy blunt here and there. Easy it may be but I do not like the work overmuch. Mostly our quarry has squandered their tin on fast living, vicious amusements and the cards and so are not to be pitied. On occasion though, the debtor is a hard-working man fallen on hard times who must be taken up and imprisoned in the sponging house until every penny is repaid. Yet by depriving him of his liberty we remove entirely his very livelihood and the means to repay. It is a thing that does not seem right to me, though conversely if all debts were left unpaid how could we trust any man or his promises? After all, what are those scraps of paper, our banknotes, our notes of hand, but emblems of trust? I cannot fathom the rightness of these matters and so am seldom easy in the role of gazehound for shys and lenders; to my mind it is quite a different kettle of fish to the hoisting of the dead. For they are dead and do not care.

'No more mills, Facey. And no more night work until the Rig is done, then we will know where we stand.'

'Just as you say, Sammy Boy. A little sport will put me straight. And who is to say we have not earned a bit of a spree?'

My boots are heavy with mud by the time we clear the boat builder's yards. There must be a leak somewhere as my left foot has been immersed in a slippery soup for a good half a mile now. Mercifully, the changeable weather has finally made up its mind to stay fine for a spell. Mudlarks are out, pecking away down at the waterline, skiffs haul against the current, transporting wares and fares upriver. Patches of late afternoon sunlight wink and glitter across the river and this, along with the promise of sport, has put Facey into a more even temper.

Ahead, the Palace of Westminster looms over us; Facey gazes up at these grand edifices, which are covered in scaffolding. 'Half London goes hungry and yet there is always sufficient tin for fine new buildings should their purpose be the greater comfort and glory of our betters, eh, Sammy Boy?'

'I do not pretend to understand the world. All I know is that we are born to a station in life and there we must remain 'til the day we die. But some few, in the manner of the Fancy, will hazard all they have on a chance or two.' I shrug. 'In so doing they may rise. Or they may fall. If fortune does not favour their endeavours, they will sink to an even lower station, that is for a certainty.'

Facey gazes at me for a moment. 'You always was a deep file. Too much thinking is not good for a man. Take care, lest you fuddle the noggin.' He shakes his head disapprovingly. 'You worry too much, Sammy Boy.'

'It is by no means a perfect philosophy. There are always decent God-fearing folk who are content to remain in their station, bothering no man, yet find themselves slipping nevertheless, towards the lowest rungs of humanity through no fault or hazard of their own making. This, I cannot account for.'

'You are speaking of Rosamund then.'

'I am.'

'For a man to climb out of the steaming pit, there must be the backs of others to climb upon.' Facey grimaces. 'It has always been the way.'

'You have never liked her. Why?'

'I do not have an opinion of Rosamund, one way or t'other. It is disease I do not care for.'

'She is not diseased.'

'And yet her face resembles the skin on a tapioca pudding.'

'You well know they are smallpox scars, and from many years previous.'

'I do not care to catch it from her.'

Sometimes there's just no talking to Facey.

CHAPTER III

We traipse along Great Peter Street in silence before turning into St Anne's Lane. In a matter of moments we have been transported from the lofty grandeur of Westminster Palace to the most squalid poverty imaginable. The distance may be small but the contrast is beyond reckoning. A trickling, stinking sewer runs along the centre of the street; on either side wooden hovels huddle together, canting crazily at all angles like rotting, blackened teeth. A few thin children, filthy and nearly naked, pick through the awful piles of refuse. I flick a few coppers in their direction. It does not seem so very long ago that Facey and me had as much.

Facey shoots me a disapproving look as we turn the corner into Old Pye Street. There is plenty of life here but little joy. Coarse women squabble over bottles, shouting enticements at us, waving slack bubbies and hoisting skirts. The houses here are more substantial although there is still an overwhelming air of decay and the stink of bad meat on the boil. A dust contractor's yard, halfway up the street, seems to have burst its bounds, leaking oyster-shells, cabbage-stalks, and broken china into the open thoroughfare. Children again, sifting through the filth for anything that can be sold. Bullet-headed young men wearing tight corduroy kecks and showy neckerchiefs loiter in doorways, ogling us with hard eyes from under flat caps.

Facey sneers, glaring about him through his one good glim, daring any one of them to chance his arm. None does. These men may be poor and predatory but they are not raving mad.

Between a slop-shop and a threepenny ken is a flaking green door. There is no sign, nor outward manifestation of the activity within, only a door with a pitted brass knocker. But the very fact of a brass knob remaining attached and unmolested in a street such as this tells its own story. Facey gives three sharp raps. The door is opened by a hard-looking ginger cove who, without a word, ushers us along a dark, cramped hallway and down a precarious wooden stairway to the cellars.

The cockpit is, in fact, two cellars knocked together to form one large, noisy space full of fug. The combined stinks of smoke, stale flat beer, rats, dogs and unwashed human beings is almost overpowering. By comparison, Pye Street enjoys wholesome country air.

Gaslights illuminate the centrepiece: a ring enclosed by wooden barriers, not unlike a small arena of those ancient Romanish times. Wooden benches, arranged one over the other, rise stepwise above it nearly to the ceiling. This is the pit for dogfights, cockfights and rat killing.

As yet, the sporting fraternity mill around the outskirts of the pit, swilling bad beer and adulterated liquor, bellowing and hooting. Almost immediately I catch sight of a young man in an exquisitely tailored plum-coloured coat: Frederick Compton, holding forth on the merits or otherwise of one of the ratting dogs. As an occasional student and dabbler in anatomy at Guy's Hospital, Compton has been a profitable customer of ours in the past, but now, surrounded as he is by his sporting cronies, he studiously avoids my eye. Principally for devilment but partly by way of business I make my way towards him. 'Mr Compton,' I say, holding out my hand, 'I am glad to see you here.'

Compton recoils like he's found a toad in his madeira but swiftly recovers his composure and lifts his quizzing glass, feigning to scrutinize me. 'Ah yes. Mr Samuel, and Mr Facey, I believe?' he drawls. He condescends to extend a manicured index finger for me to shake. 'Well, gentlemen, do you perhaps have a mutt you wish to show me?'

'We do not, sir. We have other business here.'

'Then I should not wish to keep you from it.'

'Might I beg just a moment of your time, sir,' I insist with all deference.

Compton swallows nervously, aware of the curious looks from his associates. 'Very well, Mr Samuel,' he says, and, with a wink and a grin at his associates adds loudly, ''Tis some specious ratting tip, I make no doubt.'

Compton steps away, beyond earshot of his companions and hisses in my ear, 'Devil take you, what is the meaning of this familiarity, Mr Samuel?'

'Have a care, Compton. You would do well to keep a civil tongue in your head,' growls Facey, 'for you are in our world now.'

To his credit, Compton stands his ground, glaring at Facey before returning his attention to me. He raises an inquisitive eyebrow. 'Well?' he says, 'what must I do for you to leave me be?'

'We are seeking a certain Robert Templeton. He has outstanding debts.'

'That ain't hardly remarkable 'mongst my acquaintance,' drawls Compton.

'We have been informed that he is a youngish man, a year or two short of twenty and of good family.'

'Templeton, you say? Never heard of him, nor such a family. Tenpole, Trumbull and so forth, not Templeton. Certainly not a sportin' fellow nor one of the Fancy, else he'd be known to me.'

'You have not met with him across the tables?'

'Mr Samuel, you have asked your question. I have answered it. I wish you good day.' Without further acknowledgement,

Compton spins on his heel and heads back to his cronies. 'As I imagined,' he sneers for their benefit, 'naught but a worthless tip.'

Facey and me shove our way through the press in the direction of the counter.

'Ah, Mr Facey and ... and associate.' A sweaty, bleary-eyed, weasel face intercepts us, waving a beaker of gin. 'I see you are acquainted with young Frederick Compton. Now that is a happy coincidence ... '

'What do you want, Mattheson?' grunts Facey.

'Money, tin, shine. Same as all else hereabouts.'

Molly Mattheson, at one time the Honourable Henry Mattheson, is, or was, the son of a baronet. Now known as Molly, for an inclination to sodomy. Disinherited, cut off for numerous vile practices too public to be ignored or covered up, Molly Mattheson is a procurer for wealthy gentlemen of particular tastes and a pipe addict. He is beyond redemption and it is, frankly, a miracle that he remains amongst the living.

He grins through rotting teeth, perspiring face swaying close to mine, so close I can smell his carrion breath. He taps his florid nose. 'I know a thing.'

'Then I wish you joy of it,' snaps Facey, turning away. Likewise, I barge past, making for the counter. But Mattheson is not so easily ignored and has a grip on the tail of my coat, like a drowning man. Facey spins abruptly, grabs the bony white wrist and squeezes hard, almost to breaking point, if Mattheson's squeals are anything to go by. 'Fuck off,' he hisses.

Mattheson backs away, nursing the wounded joint and contents himself with wheedling. 'Come now, gents. No need for the mauleys. We are all friends here.'

'We are not friends, Mattheson, barely even acquaintances and still, there is shame enough in that.'

'Nevertheless, I am in possession of something that men in your line of work will always have need of.'

Facey shoulders his way through to the counter, where he raps a shilling on the wood.

'And what might that be?'

'Why, information, sir. Information,' smirks Mattheson, unabashed.

Facey bellows his order for two beakers of Old Tom. When we turn, drinks in hand, Mattheson is still there, waiting with the patience of a poacher. 'Now, gentlemen, for a small emolument, I could put you in the way of a very advantageous business opportunity, in your line of work as it were.'

'We are bakers, Molly. Have you suddenly come into possession of a stolen beef pie, a quantity of suet perhaps?'

He gives us a sly wink. 'A tasty pudding certainly.'

I sip my Old Tom. The extra sugar in the gin does not quite mask the vile aftertaste of turpentine.

'Out with it then,' snaps Facey.

Mattheson smiles, exposing too much gum and a quantity of saliva, which, along with the turpentine, has pretty well put me off my drink entirely.

'A day or so ago an unfortunate party met their maker.'

'Why should that be our concern?'

'Perhaps it is not. Perhaps you are merely in the business of raising buns. But if you did happen to have an interest in, shall we say, the raising of other, less toothsome, articles from their places of rest, you might find this news considerably to your advantage.' With that he taps his sharp nose twice. It is warmish on account of the press of bodies and lack of ventilation, yet Mattheson perspires like a busted cistern, oily drops leak continually from his hair and face. He mops his brow with a disgraceful rag.

'Folk drop like flies in the metropolis every day. This is scarcely news to us. Nor anyone.'

'Ah, but I have it on good authority that this one is a bit special. A little out of the ordinary and would, I'm certain, attract a fine premium.'

Facey is raring to have a gander at the dogs, but Mattheson has him on the line now. 'In what way special?'

'This one is neither man nor woman, but something in between. A curiosity of nature known as a hermaphrodite. Got to be worth twenty guineas, if a penny.'

Facey sips his gin, considering. His mouth twists in disapproval. I can't tell if it's the drink or Mattheson's foul breath. 'I do not know this word, this … this oddity.'

'Hermaphrodite, a creature, having the parts of both man and woman, most precious rare, and of profound interest to any anatomical gentleman worth his salt.'

Facey throws me a quizzical look. I shake my head. He well knows I'd rather sit tight, at least 'til the Rig is done. Nevertheless he continues to nibble away at Mattheson's bait. 'On what "good authority" does this information come into your possession?'

'Ah,' Mattheson smirks, indicating his threadbare togs, 'I was not always as you see me now. I have fallen low, I admit, and yet I still have honest friends in a higher society than the one to which I am currently consigned by the fickle hand of Dame Fortuna.'

Facey nods philosophically. 'Aye, buggery and the pipe will do that to a man.'

Mattheson starts, somewhat put out by Facey's candour. 'My dear sir, it appears you have quite the wrong impression of me. Cards have been my downfall, along with a foolishly trusting nature.'

'Just as you say, Molly.' Facey smiles, nods briskly and turns his attention to the yelping, baying dogs, which are being held in check by their handlers over by the far wall. He shoulders his way through the sporting crowd in the direction of the din. I stick close behind in the realization that I am mistaken: it is not Facey who has swallowed the bait here, but Mattheson. The man dutifully follows, unwilling to drop a promising prospect, raising his voice now. 'I have particular knowledge of the circumstances, I shall not say how, but it is likely the easiest hoist you will ever make, Mr Facey. None else knows of it. The body is freshly passed but a day previous and is, as yet, not even interred. It lies in a West End tavern cellar waiting for the right men to come a calling.'

Facey swivels with a thunderous countenance. In the violence of his expression the bandage has slipped, revealing a terrifying, blood-gorged eye. 'Never presume to mention the specifics of my trade or the next time you open your foul mouth, it will be full of soil,' he hisses.

Mattheson backs off, cowering in fear for his life. He quickly melts away into the throng.

Facey grins, adjusting his bandage. 'Useful tip there, Sammy Boy, and no push expended for it. Not even the price of a wet.'

'It's not a job for us, Facey, not now with your glim and such. Besides, we might profitably remain on the trail of this Templeton fellow. At least for the while,' I plead.

'Let me think on it,' Facey concedes, elbowing a couple of punters out of the way. He crouches to cup the snout of a likely looking pie-bald Bull Terrier. The ratting-cove is hard-pressed to keep the creature in check on its stout leather lead, such is the animal's enthusiasm for the coming combat. The dog is all muscle, teeth and fury, but for some reason, it permits Facey to maul its bullet head, even fondle its tattered ears. Perhaps it recognizes a kindred spirit. At any rate, Facey rises and makes his pronouncement. 'This is the one for us, Sammy. I like the cut of his jib.'

The contender's name is Billy and he's carried to the pit where his weight is proclaimed to be twenty-six pounds. For some reason, this fact is significant; the sporting crowd nod sagely at one another, odds around the pit are retabulated.

Facey approaches a florid gent in a bottle-green coat, murmurs something in his ear, while dropping heavy gold coin into his upturned palm.

Bulging sacks are emptied into the pit, emitting a squealing, wriggling mass of rats, black and brown bodies thrown into contrast by the stark white surface of the arena.

Now Billy is released. He has no way of knowing this, but Billy has twelve minutes to kill one hundred, else his owner and other members of his syndicate are a good twenty sovereigns out of pocket.

Billy lets loose with all that pent-up rage and enthusiasm of his. The snapping of his jaws can even be heard over the roar of the crowd, crimson spatters across white paint and in a short while his head and snout are covered in gore. I catch sight of Compton and his party nearest the ring, red-faced, howling their support, fists pumping the air. After five minutes the clock is stopped. Billy is given a breather and a bowl of water to lap.

Facey is as jovial as I've seen him in a good while. 'Here we are, Sammy Boy, fifty-eight rats accounted for in under half the allotted time. With our push down at two to one, we are golden. Come on, Billy.'

Billy is cleaned up and dropped back into the pit, where he finishes off the hundred in a total of eleven minutes something, snapping necks and tearing throats, quick as looking. Each of the two umpires checks his timepiece and the feat is confirmed. Facey is delighted, slapping my back repeatedly. 'Good enough, Sammy Boy, I'll collect the tin we are owed and there's an end to hazard. I'm content to watch the rest of the night.'

Facey stops dead, his hand remains on my shoulder and begins to squeeze. I look up, following his point of view, and catch sight of Mattheson, deep in conversation with none other than Teeth.

Teeth is bad news. For the living and the dead. And most especially for other Resurrection Men. You cannot miss Teeth, even across a crowded cellar such as this, since he is two yards high and white as marble. An albino, I've heard tell, is how one should describe such a man. Yet it is not his paleness that marks him out over and above other men, but his teeth. A set of Waterloo dentures, supposedly collected by the man from the very field itself and incorporated into a set of gnashers, way too large and perfect to be convincing. Although he must be approaching his fourth decade, he still carries himself well; ramrod straight in threadbare but well-fitting frogged black coat and trousers. Word is that Teeth was with Blucher back in '15: one of his infamous Black Prussians.

Teeth works with a file known as Mutton and together they make a formidable pair, best avoided. Regrettably, they are in the self-same business as me and Facey, but most of the time we stay well away from one another's turf.

We observe Teeth drop a few silver shillings into Mattheson's outstretched paws.

I can sense Facey's wrathful indignation through the quivering hand on my shoulder. 'Now, now, Facey, let it go. We did not care for the hoist in any event.'

Mattheson, clutching his new wealth, scuttles away up the rickety stairs no doubt in a hurry to clamp his ghastly wet lips around a pipe of some description, clay, flesh, or both.

Teeth surveys the room, with his height advantage it is but a moment before he catches sight of Facey and me. He acknowledges our presence with a slight dip of the head; he grins, treating us to a great horse rictus.

Facey scowls, he cannot bear to lose out to any man but in this case discretion is certainly the better part of valour, so I take his arm and steer him towards the wagering gent in the bottle-green coat. The name, Nicodemus Riley, has been picked out in childish white letters along the flap of his thick leather satchel. He is all smiles and twinkles.

'Ah, Mr Facey, sir. I wish you joy of your success.' Riley nods, winks, claps, bobs and shakes our hands, as though sharing our good fortune with us. In short, everything but hand over our winnings.

Facey, who has less patience than most, can bear it no longer. 'So, Riley, will you produce my tin or are we to stand here all night bobbing about like a set of dumplings?'

Riley huffs and sighs, with an apologetic grin he opens the satchel. It is empty but for a few slips of paper. 'Ah, sir, there is the nub of it. Had you come but a minute or two previous I would have been able to give you satisfaction, but as you see there has been a run on Billy tonight and the mutt has quite cleaned me out. Who would have thought it? Snap. Fifty-eight buzzers gone in six minutes. Snap, snap, snap. The remainder destroyed utterly in eleven something. Unheard of. Ain't natural and that's the truth. You will take my marker, of course.'

'I will take my readies.'

'I have none to give.'

'Then I must take your life. For this is no small sum.'

'Ah, sir. I do not say you could not do it. But how would it profit you to press a suit for twelve sovereigns against a dead man?'

'Sixteen.'

'Sixteen. Just so. I stand corrected. How would you then recover—'

Without warning Facey's left hand shoots out, grips the man's greasy neck stock and twists. He cocks his right fist back, poised to snuff the man's lights, if not his life.

Riley drops the satchel, goggles and gasps for breath as Facey slowly hoists him off his feet. If Riley had been relying on the public nature of our disagreement for his safety then he was much mistaken. The fracas barely attracts attention from the sporting fraternity, other than what I imagine to be a few swift wagers here and there on Riley's chances of survival.

Riley squirms and manages to gasp, 'Now that I think on it, there may be a little travelling money about my person.'

Facey releases the man. With one hand Riley frantically claws at his tightly twisted stock, with the other he rummages in his pocket for a couple of sovereigns and a silver shilling, along with a cloth button. 'Take it,' he croaks.

Facey takes the money, expression darkening by the second. Riley now rootles in his satchel for one of the paper slips and, with a stub of pencil, laboriously letters an IOU for sixteen sovereigns, using the satchel for a writing surface. He offers it up. 'Never fear, my trade is underwritten by Messrs Pimlott and Chuffington, no less. You will see that these slips are endorsed by those well-regarded gentlemen. In consequence my markers are safe as any banknote signed by the governor of the Bank of England himself. Safer even.'

I examine it. Sure enough, it has been ready printed with the simple header P&C, and Riley's lettering is in order. It is something I suppose.

'This is a mere scrap of paper, whereas I gave you eight sovereigns in hard cash money,' objects Facey, with that wolfish grimace of his.

'That is true,' explains Riley, 'but—'

We'll never know what he was going to say next as Facey's massive fist crashes into his dial. Riley is lifted off his feet by the force and thumps quite forcibly into the whitewashed cellar wall where he collapses in an untidy heap, leaking claret from a pulped razzo. Facey stands over him. 'You have until tomorrow to obtain my tin, Riley, or by God I will find you and administer further chastisement.' A pointless exercise since the man is quite unconscious, and will remain so for some time by the looks of him. There are a few half-hearted cheers and whistles from around the room but otherwise little response to the violence, which is more or less commonplace hereabouts. In any case, for most folk there is far more important business afoot. The dogs are about to go in again. This time a pair: Towser and Ajax, matched against one another for the most kills in a minute. We make our way to the arena and watch as the canines set to with a will.

Facey has the hump, and even though the dogs are exemplary, a couple of whirling dervishes, accounting for no fewer than two-dozen vermin in sixty seconds, they fail to cheer him. I expect this black countenance to last the remainder of the evening.

'Sir, sir. Mr Samuel, sir.' A tiny, grubby hand plucks at my sleeve.

'Why, it is Pure John.' My heart sinks. 'What has occurred, is Rosamund well?'

'Calm yourself on that account, Mr Samuel. All is tip-top in Vauxhall, or was, when I last looked in, which was not so very long ago. I remind you that it is my brother what stands sentinel over that turf, keeping all mischance and villainy at bay.'

'I do not need reminding of that, Pure John, as I myself have met with your brother only some few hours previous.'

'All the more reason then not to let your inexpressibles bunch so tight about the parts. Trust me, you will enjoy a more contented existence.'

Facey guffaws at this impudent retort.

Pure John has a good heart. No doubt of it. But he is insolent and most infuriatingly contrary. I let it pass though since he appears to have put Facey into a good humour.

'Now then, Pure John. Tell us your business. Be quick, for we are busy men.'

'I see that, sir. Keeping an eye on them ratters whilst supping on Old Tom can be awful hard graft.'

I gaze down at Pure John, his innocent grimy face beams back up at me. Facey emits a wet, throaty chuckle. 'Well?'

'Haven't I been across half London on the hunt for you gents tonight though?' Pure John begins to enumerate the destinations on his stubby fingers: 'One, the Fortune of War, Smithfield—not there. Two, the Feathers in Shoreditch—never to be found. Three, Weller's, Drury-Lane—nary a sign of you gents and no one seen you all night. Four. The Rising Sun in—'

'That is because we are here, Pure John.'

'I see that now a course. And do not need informing of it after the fact, since it is me what discovered you and not the other way round.' Pure John looks at me as though I am a half-wit. 'I am quite run off my feet and could use a port wine with a bit of sugar myself.'

We lead Pure John to the counter where Facey orders his reviver, though I do suspect the boy of having already enjoyed a bracer or two at some of those aforementioned establishments.

Facey grins as the boy attempts to cock an elbow on the counter in imitation of his elders. Failing, on account of his diminutive stature, Pure John is content to stir a broken lump of sugar into his hot port wine. 'Now, gentlemen, I have an important commission from the good offices of Lieutenant Trench's Messenger Service and no time to waste about it,' he announces importantly. 'You are urgently summoned to the residence of one mister Joshua Brookes of Great Marlborough Street.' With that, he downs his port wine and begins to pat at the pockets of his tight jacket. 'Mister Brookes insists that you waste not a moment and will kindly avail yourselves of a Hack to which end I have been entrusted with a purse of—shit…'

He pats himself furiously once more, though it is clear that his pockets are quite empty. 'Oh, Mother of Christ, some bastard's only gone an' buzzed me.'

Facey is wheezing with mirth by now, but I can see that the boy is close to tears. 'Oh, sirs, you won't peach me to Lieutenant Trench, will you? 'Tis only my second week an' I've already gone an' bollixed it. Ah no, wait.' He drops to a crouch and fiddles with his left shoe before popping back up holding aloft a soft purse. 'Garn, what a muttonhead I am. Here we are, gents, six shillin' and you will be pleased to take a cabriolet at your earliest convenience and to keep the change.'

I take the purse and sift through the coin before handing the boy one of the silver shillings. 'For your trouble, Pure John. Take it home now, to your brother's safekeeping.'

'Thank you kindly, Mr Samuel. And I wish you gents good fortune.' Pure John treats us to a formal little bow as we depart.

Heading towards the stairs, we hear his shrill piping voice over the hubbub. 'I'll take a ceegar and sixpen'orth of brandy, your finest mind, and none of that watered-down horsepiss neither.'

CHAPTER IV

'You know what will come of this,' says Facey. 'There will be a commission here.'

'I know it,' I reply, 'but what choice do we have?'

What choice indeed? Joshua Brookes is one of London's most respected anatomists and a favoured customer of ours. In the past we have carried out a number of specific commissions on his behalf and always with considerable profit.

We are ushered from the establishment by the same ginger cove who brought us in. 'Here is a lantern for you, sir. Our boy waits at Victoria Street, where you will be so kind as to pass it into his care along with a ha'penny for the lease.' I take the lantern and drop tuppence into his palm as we emerge into the brooding darkness of Pye Street.

A few candles waver here and there in the rookery windows, a pathetic challenge to the supremacy of the night. Without the lantern we would be utterly lost. We step out; this is not a place to linger, even for men like us.

On Victoria Street we duly relinquish the lantern to a slothful young snot-nose along with his ha'penny. A few yards along is a stand where the Hackneys wait. Our driver is surly and resentful but after some back and forth agrees to a fare of three shillings, which leaves us two deaners in the purse.

We are whisked up St James', Piccadilly and Regent Street like a couple of West End swells before heading east on Oxford Street.

'Never fret now, Sammy,' says Facey, lounging back in his seat as though born to it. 'We can always decline should the task prove not to our taste.'

'We decline and Brookes will offer his trade to others of our calling.'

'That is a consideration, certainly,' agrees Facey, adjusting his stained bandage.

The cab halts before an imposing sandstone villa. 'At any rate, let us hear him out and give the thing due thought. We have birds in bushes aplenty, but this may be a fine bird in hand for the nonce.'

I hand the surly cabby three shillings in full settlement, but he balks at this. 'No extra then? No perquisite for a swift, safe and comfortable journey?'

I'm keen to hold back as much of the purse as possible, given our current shortage of the readies. 'I cannot deny your skills with whip and rein, but what remains in this purse is our only means. We are but working men like yourself, sir.'

The cabby spits. 'Garn, you scabby fellow. This is what comes of allowing dregs to ride, when by rights you should employ Shanks' Pony, 'stead of mine. You and Pirate Conrad there.'

'What do you say, cocky?' inquires Facey, approaching the driver. 'Dregs, is it?' The driver shifts away, the altitude of his perch precludes Facey having at him. 'Pirate Conrad, is it?' Facey paces around the vehicle seeking an opportunity to score a blow.

From his vantage point, the cabby retorts, 'Dregs, I say. Men of your sort ought not be allowed to ride a cabriolet. I knewed it when I took your fare. I sha'nt make that mistake again. Gee'on!' With that he flicks his whip at the pony.

Facey's huge fist whips out catching the beast just above its eyes. The pony staggers, forelegs buckling to the cobbles.

'You just punched my fucken' hoss, you cunt.'

'I did, and if you come down from that perch I will apply the selfsame treatment to you.'

The pony struggles to its feet as the cabby flails away frantically. 'I will have the law on you for this.'

Facey shrugs. 'Then you must quit the metropolis and ply your trade elsewhere, for if the law and me ever exchange words at your behest, I will seek you out you and murder you in your bed. Then after, I will punch your horse as many times as I please.'

The pony, as though aware of the threat, staggers away into the night under the whip of his chastened master.

Facey hauls on the gleaming brass bell pull.

We are admitted by an elderly, liveried servant who, expecting our arrival, ushers us up a flight of stairs into sizeable but crowded rooms.

There are suspended skeletons aplenty here of course, as befits a man of anatomy. Facey and me have no fear of such objects, but the multitude of shelves surrounding us are crammed with glass jars containing a variety of strange, gelatinous objects, which give me a sense of unease. It is full as an egg and difficult to move about in such a space without endangering some article of preserved flesh or bone. Facey and me squeeze ourselves into a small window seat, maintaining a state of rigidity for fear of breakage or incident.

It is not long before Brookes arrives in a state of undress, wiping his hands on a towel.

'Ah, Mr Facey and Mr Samuel, my thanks for attending this summons. I am most grateful.'

'Think nothing of it, sir. You were most generous in your disbursement of expenses. It is not every day that Sammy Boy and me are treated to a clop through the West End in a cabriolet.'

'This is not an every day commission. You will not have been in this part of the house before, I think?'

'No, sir. Never.'

We have only ever been given our commissions at the dead of night and at the tradesmen's entrance. It is quite something to have been admitted into the bowels of the house. It must be important to Brookes for him to take such a chance.

'Here is my museum, or what remains of it. I have lately sold off a good deal of my collection but this is yet the best of it. Now that you are here, you may look around if you wish. It should interest gentlemen of your calling. Ordinarily it would cost you two shillings but since we are friends, I will not charge you.'

'Much obliged,' says Facey, rising carefully, 'I will take a gander.'

I get to my feet and examine the jars on the shelf nearest. To my horror a twisted double baby peers back at me from inside the glass.

'Encephalitic conjoined twins. An aborted foetus,' explains Brookes.

I have no idea what he's talking about but in the neighbouring jar floats a terrible six-fingered hand.

I recoil, take a deep breath and retreat to the soothing familiarity of a stuffed, striped horse.

'Now that is a Quagga. From the continent of Africa and quite rare.'

Rarer still, I imagine, should there be an African Facey over there treating them as he does their European cousins.

On another shelf is what appears to be a human heart, mounted on a wooden block. The heart has a complicated network of red and blue pipes leading away, tapering off to ever more tiny filaments.

'Beautiful, is it not, Mr Samuel?'

'It is indeed, sir. I know this to be a heart but I do not recognise the streams and rivulets here.'

'It is not a true thing of flesh but taken from life all the same. Those are the veins and arteries, which attach to any man's heart, feeding into a gossamer net of capillaries. We fill them with coloured wax and mount them, so. It is not our design which renders them beautiful, but God's own work.'

'And by rendering with wax, you will make them last, forever?'

Brookes shakes his head, sadly.

'No, Mr Samuel. Nothing here is permanent. Though I would wish it otherwise. In time, the wax dries out and becomes friable. The structure cracks and wilts and becomes quite meaningless. And so the work must be done again. Even my jars filled with a potent preservative cannot protect the unique flesh contained within from time, and ultimately its decay.'

'I have an acquaintance who has pondered long and deep on this very subject.'

'Indeed?'

'Whose endeavours, like your own, are fated to melt and muddle into flux until they are quite disappeared. But she is content with her condition since she believes that the beautiful things in this world are eph … ephemeral in nature. To perceive an object as truly beautiful, it must be framed by impermanence.'

Brookes gazes at me for a moment or two, astonished. 'Why, Mr Samuel, I am quite taken aback. You have given me something to think on. And not a small idea, neither. May I shake your hand?'

'You may, sir. Though as I say, it is not my own philosophy.'

There is a clatter from the far room. Facey reappears clutching shattered porcelain relics. 'I hope this figurine was not worth so much, Mr Brookes. I am too big and clumsy a fellow for rooms of this kind.'

'No matter, Mr Facey. The time has come to discuss our business.'

We take our seats at the window. Brookes pulls up a spindly straight-backed chair and settles himself, facing us. 'In the early hours of Wednesday morning a body was discovered in a Bentinck Street doorway. Accordingly, the corpse was carried with all speed to the Coach and Horses tavern on the corner of Poland Street, where a coroner's inquest was assembled by dusk of the same day. As a householder of good standing in this locality, I was summoned to attend.

'Though attired in the style of a well-bred young man of fashion, the face and physique of the corpse were of indeterminate sex. Additionally, the hair was long and lustrous and bore the signs of the curling tongs. On closer examination, the breasts were unremarkable, but upon removal of the nether garments the body was found to be what a man of science would term an hermaphrodite.'

'I know this word,' blurts Facey. 'Neither man nor woman but a half an' halfer. Offering a bit of both worlds, as it were, down there.'

'Great heavens,' exclaims Brookes, jolting back in his chair, 'you gentlemen are full of surprises tonight.'

'Education is the ticket, Mr Brookes. Sammy and me endeavour to better ourselves daily. Why, only this morning I was required to render my opinion upon some fine art pieces.'

I presume by this he means not booting Rosamund up the arse. But I keep my own counsel on the subject, allowing the art critic and man of culture his moment of glory.

'Indeed?' nods Brookes, courteously.

'Please continue,' I insist.

'Since there were no outward signs of foul play, no significant marks on the body and suchlike, the inquest has returned an open verdict. I have my own suspicions but there is unlikely to be further investigation. There were no identifying documents, so the body will remain at the Coach and Horses until it is claimed. It will not be, I am sure of it. In consequence, it will be collected by the parish to be buried in an unmarked pauper's grave, two days hence.'

'Then the hoist must be from the Coach and Horses?'

'Precisely. You are familiar with the tavern?'

'I am.' Facey sucks his teeth. 'But I must tell you that this is not a resurrection matter, sir, but something far more hazardous. For this is no mere churchyard disturbance, it is housebreaking, no less: a serious offence carrying heavy penalties under the law. We are not the fellows for this task. You require cracksmen, sir.'

Brookes raises a hand. 'I cannot. I am not acquainted with men of that stamp and have no wish to be. I understand your reluctance, but I promise you will be well compensated. You have no idea what a prize this is for an anatomist, what a rara avis. Such a specimen might come along only once in a generation, if at all. Gentlemen, I must have this body at any cost.'

Facey rubs his hands along his greasy keks before moistening anxious lips. He screws his face, rubs his hair and tugs at his ears as though gripped by strongly conflicting desires. Frankly, he's laying it on a bit thick in my opinion but old Brookes seems to be eating it up. The man leans in, a desperate expression on his countenance.

'Well, sir,' announces Facey. 'We will do it, on account of you always having been a decent, fair-minded gent to us.'

Brookes leans back in his chair and sighs in relief as though divested of some heavy burden. 'I thank you. You have no idea what this means to me.'

'I do hope it means a good few sovereigns to you, sir,' replies Facey.

'How does one hundred sound?'

'Holy Mother of Christ,' somebody whispers. Then I realize it was me.

'We will do it thrice over for such a sum,' says Facey, 'the raree aviary is as good as yours, sir.'

Brookes stamps two times sharply with his heel to summon the servant before rising to his feet. We shake hands.

'I hope you will not be offended if my man shows you out through the tradesmen's portal. I cannot have suspicion thrown on me, since I have already been party to the inquest and my interest in such curiosities is well-known.'

'Indeed not, sir. Front door, side-door, tradesmen's, it is all one to us.' Facey has become quite breezy at the promise of an easy hundred sovereigns.

We follow the servant who shows us out of a side entrance into a pitch-black alley before softly closing the door behind us.

'Well, Sammy Boy, the wheel of fortune has turned tonight and no mistake,' announces Facey, rubbing his hands. I detect the gleam of his teeth through the gloom.

'Round and round, like some strange fairground ride. I do not care for such diversions, they have always made me hurl the cat.'

We exit the alley onto Great Marlborough Street, which is well furnished with gas lamps as befits a thoroughfare full of grand villas.

'Listen, Sammy, I do believe I can hear the beautiful sound of one hundred golden sovereigns calling out to me,' he begins to croon in horrible falsetto. 'Come, Facey, I have kept myself pure for your hands alone. A hundred sovs, not a penny less. Here am I awaiting your caress…' He chuckles and picks up the pace. I am forced to trot to keep up with his long, eager strides. In double quick time we cover the few hundred yards or so and arrive at the Coach and Horses on the corner of Poland Street.

CHAPTER V

Facey throws open the doors and shoves his way to the counter. It is very late but the place is still crowded, mainly sporting types and a few of the younger West End toffs. But there is still a sprinkling of the disreputable: cyprians and mollishers by my reckoning, discreetly touting for a little trade. On the whole though, the Coach and Horses is a good house, and tolerates very little in the way of lewd or low behaviour. This is the kind of establishment I dream of. The counter is formed from polished dark wood with brass railings, well-upholstered chairs with button backs have been furnished for the comfort of patrons, while sporting prints adorn the dark green papered walls. A fire burns brightly and I detect the welcoming aroma of good cigar smoke and brandy fumes.

For once, mindful of its gleaming surface, Facey does not rap the counter with the edge of a coin. Instead, he waits respectfully for the attentions of our host, a man of middle age, but well-muscled and thickset. From behind, his left ear resembles a cauliflower and when he turns to face us it is evident that his nose has been broken more than a few times. Few enough would need to be told that this man has been a pugilist.

The hammered countenance erupts into a monumental grin as he catches sight of us. 'Now, there's a sight for sore eyes,' he announces in a deep bass voice. He unfastens his apron and addresses the can. 'Be so good as to fetch the hot fixings, Ned, quick as you like. I have here a couple of old and dear friends to attend.'

Without further comment he ushers us, still grinning, into a private room. The place is modest without frippery or ornamentation as befits Tom's character, but it is every bit as comfortable as the public. We settle ourselves into a trio of leather armchairs round a small table. Our host gazes at Facey, appraising the stained bandage before shaking his head in mild disapproval. 'Speaking of sore eyes, I see you've been letting your left drop again, young man. It always was a failing in you.'

Facey grins sheepishly. 'Ah, Tom. You know that reprimands never did much service with me.'

Tom Canon sighs. 'I know it. But it is good to see you, nevertheless.' With that he extends a paw; the two of them shake hands vigorously, exhibiting their power. Tom's grip is still firm and I note that his fist is quite as large as Facey's own.

Tom turns to me grinning. 'And young Sammy, you have not been able to train him better?'

We shake, mercifully, with less robustness on Tom's part as he would otherwise have had my arm off. 'He is a stubborn ox and will not be yoked by any man, sir. As I think you well know.'

Tom laughs. The can appears bearing a tray of cut lemons, sugar, hot water, brandy, spices, a small mixing bowl and three glass tumblers.

We sit in companionable silence while the can mixes our toddy. We nod and smile, well pleased with one another. And why should we not be? After all, Tom Canon has been a good friend to us over the years.

Canon is a pugilistic legend, having at one time held the heavyweight bare-knuckle champion's belt, losing it but seven years ago to Jem Ward, the Black Diamond. Canon was himself brought on by those two greats, Tom Spring and Tom Cribb. And, at one time, might have made Facey his heir in the ring but it was not to be.

The can bows and returns to his duties while Tom ladles out the hot mixture. We touch glasses.

Tom indicates Facey's bandage. 'You have not left off throwing the raws entirely then?'

'Only in the way of business, Tom. I am, on occasion, obliged to offer chastisement to men of less honest virtue than yourself. I have not come up to scratch for some years now.'

'Since last night, he has knocked on his back a Peeler, a Dollyman, a book making cove and a horse,' I add, not without a touch of pride.

'A horse?'

'Knocked him flat,' I affirm, feeling the toddy spread its warm, pleasant glow to my belly.

'You always did have a right hook on you, young man. Best I ever saw, including mine. Cribb's even. Could have made something of that, you know.'

'I know it, sir.'

'You got beat in the end though, by your own self. That terrible rage of yours. You never would learn the science and I'm sorry for it.'

'As am I, sir. Heartily sorry. But when the fury comes upon me I cannot think straight and consequences are of no concern.'

'Never fret. Not all men are born to perfect form for knuckling. You had the mauleys,' Canon taps his head, 'alas, not the noggin.'

Facey nods, subdued. Harsh words were exchanged on this subject when we last had dealings with Canon. I am thankful that sufficient water has passed under that bridge to avoid the revival of a quarrel.

Canon sips thoughtfully. 'A horse, eh? I have never fought a horse. Though come to think on it there was a fighter back in '23, one Billy Harrison. "Horse" Harrison they called him, on account of him having a punch like a mule's kick. Horse's arse more like. Punch of a kitten and a jaw of glass.'

We chuckle, prompting the ladling of more toddy. Tom gazes into his glass. 'What a precious pair of rogues you were, to be sure.'

He'll be thinking on our flowers, I'll wager. Back before Tom owned his own place, between bouts he worked as the can over at the Lamb and Flag, Shoreditch. Facey and me were only youngsters at the time and made our living selling any old thing we could get our hands on, fruit and vegetables that had fallen off the market barrows. As well as plenty that hadn't.

For a while we had a nice bit of fakery going with the blooms from the market. Ones that hadn't sold all day and were starting to wilt, we'd buy the lot for a song then tickle them up by sticking them in a bit of sugar-water overnight. By morning, with a lick of paint, clipping and crimping, mostly they were good as new, fresh as a daisy, so to speak. We tried to sell a bunch to Tom, but he was too fly and up to all the tricks of the street. He gave us the old heave-ho along with a good kick in the kecks for our trouble.

In time though he took a shine to us and threw us a bit of work as potboys and hauling the barrels.

In truth, it was Facey he liked the cut of. Tom rated Facey as a comer and set to train him up for the scratch, with me as second. Of course, Facey being Facey would never take to being told, nor would he learn the science of the thing and so we parted company. Some hard words were spoke but to look at the pair now you would not think it.

Facey grins and raises his glass. 'Tom, you have done very well without us about your neck. A fine living you have got for yourself.'

'Aye, I cannot deny it. And so as to yours, gents.' He coughs delicately, 'What is your own living these days?'

Facey downs his toddy. 'Tom, if it were any man but you I would say, "this and that and a bit of the other". But you are the honestest cove I ever came across, so I will tell you straight that we are in the main, resurrection men.'

Tom Canon nods, sips his toddy and says, 'I am a taverner, not a beak. It is not for me to sit in judgment on any man for his livelihood.'

'Thank you, Tom. I take that very kindly,' says Facey offering his hand.

Tom shakes and makes a wry face. 'Well then, I expect you are here to see what I have in my cellar.'

'Indeed we are.'

Tom picks up candle and sconce from a nearby table and ushers us down a set of whitewashed stairs into his tavern cellars.

Barrels of all sizes line the walls down here. A small trestle to one side boasts a collection of cellarman's tools: wooden mallet; bungs; stopcocks and the like. The air is chilled and the sharp odour of strong spirits fills the air. The irregular light from Tom's candle illuminates a single empty table in the centre of the room.

'What have you done, Tom? Bundled the body into a barrel of brandy, like old Lord Nelson?'

'I have done no such thing,' replies Tom, turning towards us with his candle. 'The body is neither preserved nor concealed; I wished you to see with your own eyes. It is gone.'

CHAPTER VI

'If you are done, I will have that cracklin' off your plate, Sammy Boy, for I am sharp set,' announces Facey, before pronging the fatty remains of the bacon on my plate. His left eye now covered with a fresh linen bandage, dispensed by Tom who is well schooled in such matters. The flesh around it glistens with Eddie's greasy salve.

We have passed the night on truckle beds in an attic room. Tom sits with us in the snug while we make short work of a hearty breakfast. 'Fill up now, lads. Bellies and pockets both,' orders our host. I am full to bursting but with Tom's encouragement I cram a few heels of bread and a wedge of cheese into my pockets. 'You'll take a dish of tea?'

'No, Tom, small beer will suffice for us working folk.'

Our host pours himself a dish of steaming tea while we help ourselves to the small beer jug.

'You have become quite the swell,' remarks Facey.

Canon chuckles. 'I cannot deny it. I am become used to a life of indolence and luxury as my belly will attest.' He indicates his barely noticeable paunch. 'The habit of taking tea at all hours of the day has crept up on me and now I cannot help it, ruinously expensive as it is. I find it sharpens the mind and stimulates the digestion and so I cannot believe it to be a vice. Much like the effects of tobacco. Now surely you will at least take a cigar with me?'

'I will, Tom,' announces Facey, working away at a morsel of gristle in his teeth with a fork prong. 'Seeing as how a breath of tobacco is not only one of mankind's greatest pleasures but is a sovereign remedy against any ill, if taken regularly and without stinting.'

'Likewise,' I say.

Tom hands round cigars and lucifers from a leather caddy, which we gratefully accept before settling to the business at hand.

'Night before last, it went, in the small hours. It would appear that your commission has been frustrated and I am sorry for it.' Clouds of blue grey smoke punctuate the words as Tom fires up his cigar.

'No ordinary commission,' I explain. 'For this was no ordinary corpse, but an anatomical rarity, worthy of a fine premium.'

Canon puffs away philosophically. 'Doubtless it is others in your trade who have made away with it then. Were they kin they would have come and claimed the body like Christians, 'stead of breaking into my establishment in the dead of night.' He casts a sly glance at Facey. 'It would seem you have been beaten to the punch.'

'Very funny, Tom,' sighs Facey. He gives me a wry look. 'Teeth,' he announces.

I nod.

'What will you do now?' asks Canon.

'Naught,' I say, 'for you have the right of it. We have been beat to the prize by others in our profession, Teeth and Mutton, most like. A dangerous, determined pair. So, we must let the thing slide and onto other business.'

'Two nights ago, by any chance did you catch sight of a long streak of marble-white piss, two yards high wearing a

Blucher coat? You would not have missed him with his great carthorse grin.'

'And a tough-looking cove with mutton-chop whiskers?' I add.

'I did not, for I would have recalled such types. But it don't signify since they had no need to enter my tavern.'

'How so?'

'The trap to the ale cellar has been tampered with. The bolts cut through. Entry was made direct from the street.'

'Impossible,' exclaims Facey, 'you forget that I have spent many an hour hauling barrels for you, even were the barrel trap thrown wide, a grown man could never squeeze down that chute.'

'Never a man of your size, to be sure. The corpse was slim and small in stature, almost that of a child, I believe it would have been possible to bring it out.'

'For the body to come out perhaps, but what of the man to go down that chute and shift it? That would take some brawn. Lest you are saying, Tom, that the body upped and walked on its own account?'

'It is a conundrum, certainly. Perhaps your Mister Mutton is small but mighty.'

'He has strength enough but he is stout. And Teeth is a good yard too long for such a feat.'

'I cannot account for it then, gents.'

Facey puffs thoughtfully on the stub of his cigar. 'Perhaps not Teeth and Mutton then.'

I expel a steady stream of smoke from my own cigar and watch as it billows upwards toward the ornamented plasterwork of Tom's ceiling. It curls round the cornices, softly hanging like a gossamer blanket. I'm mulling on Mattheson's desperate craving for this substance when the realisation comes to me.

'No. Not Teeth and Mutton,' I announce. ''Twas only last night Molly tipped them the wink and the body was took the night before.'

Facey's brow wrinkles. 'You're onto it there, Sammy Boy. Teeth and Mutton are out of it. The question is: who else has Mattheson been opening his yap to?'

'The question is: whether we should not give this up as a bad business and have done with it. In four days we will have our Rig.'

Tom stubs the end of his cigar. 'I will say it, young Facey, though it may rouse you to anger. I have been made uneasy this morning by the state of your glim and so must agree with Sammy. I have seen wounds of this kind. Have a care, young man, or you will lose the use of it entirely. Rest is the only remedy. And to that end you may remain under my roof for as long as it suits.'

Facey gently prods his eye through the bandage. 'Come, Tom, it is naught but a tap and the day I am brought to bed and pap from a blackened eye is the day I put on the hempen cravat and turn myself off.'

'I will not quarrel over what I think best for you. We have been down that road before.'

'Nevertheless it is kind in you, sir.' Facey extends his hand. Once again they shake vigorously like a pair of bedlamites at a broken street pump.

I have to say, I'm disappointed. I could have done with a few days loafing about in the Coach and Horses: good, hot grub, cigars and brandy on tap. In truth, I'm also concerned about the state of Facey's eye. Evidently it's exuding some form of discharge since the new bandage is already beginning to show a small brownish stain. My expression must have revealed these misgivings since Facey punches me lightly on the arm and says, 'Chin up, Sammy, we will go directly and have words with Molly. If all leads to a blind alley, well then, I will give up the thing and lay low 'til Tuesday, just as you say.'

'In that event, you will return here, I hope?' offers Canon.

'We will, sir. With thanks.'

'Though it is no small thing to walk away from a hundred sovs,' mutters Facey, hauling himself to his feet.

Tom Canon whistles. 'One hundred sovereigns, is it? I never heard of such a thing. No ordinary commission to be sure. If I'd a known I'd have sold the bloody thing myself.'

There's a round of good-natured backslapping, which leaves me gasping since I'm half the size of these brutes. Canon produces a small purse, which he throws in my direction. 'If you will not stay and rest, then you will at least save your legs. Here is travelling money for you. A token, but all I can afford since this habit of taking tea has all but ruined me.'

'Now, Tom,—'

Tom raises a huge palm. 'But me no buts, though should you succeed and some of those hundred sovereigns were to find their way across my counter, you would not meet with objection here.'

Facey grins as I pocket the purse. I can tell by the weight and shape of coin that there's a good few shillings in there. We push our way out through the public, where business is already picking up at this mid-morning hour, and out into the street.

'As I recall,' says Facey, 'Molly keeps lodgings in Spitalfields.'

'When he has the tin,' I reply. 'When he is without means, who knows how or where he keeps himself?'

'For the moment he may yet be in funds. Teeth paid out a few shillings last night and will not be best pleased with the worthless pup he has purchased.'

'May he choke on it. So, we will surely find Molly where there is smoke to be had.'

'Chinee George, I should say.'

'Chinee George, to be sure.'

CHAPTER VII

There are no stands on Poland so we head north to Oxford Street. As we walk I glimpse Facey gingerly prodding at his eye. He will not admit to it, but I believe it is beginning to pain him. 'What say we take the horsebus 'stead of a cab and use the balance of our shillings with Doctor Nero?' I ask.

'Nero is a quack and I would not trust him to tell a boil from a bum. I have told you, there is nothing amiss. A day or two and the glim will be as right as rain.'

'What harm would it do to have a little physick put by? Just to be on the safe side? After all, we are heading in that direction and have the tin for it.'

'Very well, Sammy, I can see you will not let the matter rest until I have been poked at and mauled by every sawbones in London. I will take one of Nero's potions if it will have the effect of keeping you silent, which is about the only claim not yet made for his nostrums.'

From the stately elegance of Poland Street we emerge into the shocking noise and bustle of Oxford Street. This is the finest, as well as the longest and straightest, of London's main arteries, extending from Hyde Park to Newgate Street and the City. Though, like the inhabitants, the buildings lining the thoroughfare are a peculiar mixture of wealth and decay, poverty and progress: elegant mansions alongside the Pantheon rub shoulders with ramshackle one-storey tumbledowns. As far as the eye can see barrow and basket women obstruct the footway selling sweet oranges, flowers, oysters or songsheets. Men tout for business every few yards, and if they are not selling goods of their own, they are hawking on behalf of others by means of brightly painted hoardings held aloft or strapped to their bodies.

The road is no less congested, filled with horses, wagons, traps, cabs and conveyances of all description, all competing to reach their destination by the quickest means possible, yet succeeding only in creating a maelstrom of chaos and confusion yielding little forward momentum. Here and there, agile and brazen young street sweepers flit to and fro, guiding patrons through muck and peril for a few coppers.

One of the basket crones grips Facey's sleeve. 'Why, 'tis Admiral Nelson, risen from the dead. Buy a sweet orange, your lordship, do.'

Facey shakes her off with a savage grunt.

'But, sir, 'tis known as the naval orange,' the hag wheedles. Her cronies wheeze with laughter and for a moment I fear that Facey is going to turn back and give her a clump, which would no doubt spell a swift end to the spindly wretch. Thankfully, he grits his teeth and pushes on through the crowds.

Over a surging river of hats and heads I can detect the painted signboard of Nero's stand. NERO. MASTER OF PHYSICK. is picked out in florid capital letters painted white, bordered in red against a light blue background. The words TEETH, LUNGS, EYES, LIGHTS & BONES—A SPECIALITY. attest to his fields of accomplishment, illustrated by the relevant body parts.

Nero's pitch is a portable booth on the footway, consisting of a small stage with just enough room for a restraining chair and the sawbones himself. Nero is in the process of extracting a tooth from a costermonger and has drawn an audience of enthusiastic loafers. They watch with relish as Nero delves into the man's gob, rummages around and after some vigorous shaking and hauling produces a bloody, blackened tripod, pincered between finger and thumb. He holds it aloft. For a moment the air is filled with a terrible stench. 'I have it, ladies and gents, the offending article. A perfect extraction for your satisfaction. A vile and noxious molar abstracted by the ministrations of Doctor Nero, roots an' all. No breakage, shattering, and consequent risk of post-procedural malaise. Ignore the stink, for that is commonplace and merely the release of poisonous fluids built-up under pressure within the jawbone—to be expected in a life-preserving procedure of this nature.'

The costermonger leans forward in the chair so far as the leather restraints on his arms will allow to cough and puke a concoction of blood, drool and pus across the boards.

The crowd applauds, though some of the more refined ladies appear somewhat faint.

'Fuck,' slurs the costermonger, ''tis almost bearable.'

'There,' announces Nero, 'you have heard it from his own lips. A man, so maddened by pain from this masticatory organ, who but an hour hence would have topped himself. Yet within minutes under the ministrations of Doctor Nero, has attested without solicitation that the agony is all but alleviated.'

The crowd bursts into applause as Nero releases the costermonger from his straps. Nero raises his hands. 'A moment, if you please. For the second part of my procedure I will administer the absolute remedy 'gainst pain and infection of the mouth and body: Nero's Sovereign Pancurial Linctus, ultimate paregoric for neuralgia, apoplexy, dropsy, pox, the bloody flux, female hysteria, rickets, whooping cough, blotch, blemish and coarseness of the skin. Many have found prodigious benefit with only a bottle or two, even the greatest in the land, though I am precluded by their elevated status from naming them here.' Nero places thumb and forefinger against his nose to exaggerate size and shape, provoking laughter and catcalls, for we understand by this signal that he refers to First Minister Wellington.

Nero pours a dose of Linctus onto a teaspoon and feeds it to the costermonger, followed swiftly by a second.

In a short while the costermonger rises to his feet, unsteady to be sure, but alive and in good spirits. The loafers whistle and hoot their approval. He gazes about, waving weakly in acknowledgment of the plaudits. 'Ladies and Gents, thank 'ee. I do believe I am hale enough to haul a dozen baskets.' A solicitous wife and daughter hand Nero a few coins and usher him away to his labours. Onlookers surge around the booth, as Nero embarks on a brisk trade in bottles of his Pancurial Linctus.

We wait till the congregation has thinned to a handful of gawkers before stepping forward.

'May I be of service, gentlemen?' asks Nero, pocketing a final shilling.

'You do not know me, sir?'

Nero gives us a shrewd glance, satisfying himself that we are not splitters. 'I do not.'

I raise a leg of my kecks to reveal a small puckered scar.

'Ah, bless me, such beautiful scarification. A ball in the meat of the calf and a most satisfactory extraction, even if I do say so myself. I recall the work, now that you put me in mind of it.'

'Well, sir. I have another such for you here.'

'A ball is it?'

'No.'

'What then?'

'My associate has an injury, which may benefit from your ministrations.'

'I see.'

'So, I would be pleased if you were to minister to him.'

'He seems a big, healthy cove with fine calves.'

'His calves are not the issue.'

'Very well. You must tell me what is amiss and I will inform you if I can be of assistance.'

'You do not mark it?'

Nero looks Facey up and down for a moment.

'I cannot see what ails.'

'His orb, the glim is the problem, I should like your opinion on it.'

Nero considers Facey once again. 'I had thought he was in fancy dress or coming it the dashing gallant with his eye patch. 'Tis all the rage these days.'

'Beneath the bandage is a wound.'

'Well, then I will examine it.'

I sense that Facey is growing irritable, lacking my faith in Nero's skills. 'You agreed to this, have patience,' I hiss, and so he reluctantly allows Nero to take his arm and guide him to the chair. Nero straps him down.

'First, a little of the Pancurial to take an edge off discomfort,' announces Nero, indicating a box containing dozens more bottles and the sparse tools of his trade. Few indeed, since Nero is well known for extracting teeth employing only a prodigiously powerful thumb and forefinger. For more complicated interventions, such as mine, he relies on a simple cutting knife and a sharpened spoon.

Nero administers a couple of spoonfuls of linctus, which Facey dutifully swallows, but not before throwing me a black look.

Nero carefully removes the bandage. The lids are closed, grossly swollen, leaking pus and blood. He prods a little before prising apart the swollen lids. Facey squirms in the chair. The orb itself is clouded and crusted provoking excited muttering from the remaining loafers, titillated by the gory spectacle. I am not a man of qualification or judgment in these matters but what I see does not fill me with optimism.

Nero is of my thinking. 'The orb is much damaged and beginning to fester. It must come out, if this man is to thrive,' he informs me under his breath

Facey shakes his head. "Tis merely a knock, but if it will content you, Sammy, I will take a bottle of the man's paregoric. It is not so bad.'

Nero looks doubtful. 'I fear this is beyond even the powers of my Pancurial.' He shakes his head dolefully at me and whispers, 'I can see that you require proof of my efficacy.'

Nero turns to address his audience, ever the showman and keen to stimulate further trade, he flourishes the spoon. 'Consider the humdrum spoon, Ladies and gentlemen. With this instrument we prolong and sustain our lives by drawing nourishment to the mouth. And yet, how many of you I wonder, have ever regarded this humble instrument as a life saviour?'

Nero pauses, scrutinising the crowd before bellowing, 'Hare. Show yourself, sir.'

A shambling, emaciated creature stumbles through the audience, one of the many beggars who infest the street hereabouts. A thick black bandage over both eyes suggests that he is blind, though it is no surety amongst this sort.

'Here, sir,' he calls, flailing his arms about for direction. A kindly old buffer sucking on an orange, steers him toward the booth.

Nero takes the beggar's hand and hauls him up to the tiny platform. I am forced to relinquish my place to make room, stepping down into the rapidly expanding crowd.

'The gentleman you see before you is none other than the notorious William Hare.' A gasp erupts from the onlookers, quickly becoming an angry buzz. But Nero is master of their moods, raising his huge hands in a placatory gesture. 'Now, now, people. The infamous Burke, prime mover in the foul murders of Mary Paterson, Daft Jamie Wilson and Mrs Docherty, has long since received his reward, rightly scragged at the Scotch Lawnmarket for his heinous deeds. But take pity on this poor miscreant, for you will discover that William Hare did not, after all, evade the Lord's justice.'

Nero prompts the beggar with a jab of the spoon in his ribs. The man swallows nervously and begins to speak in a hoarse voice with a hint of Irish burr. ''Tis as you say, sir. I am William Hare and had imagined that by turning King's evidence I would evade culpability for my part in that horrid work. But no. There was to be a reckoning right enough, swift and sure.'

The crowd is silent now, hanging on his very words.

'Not long after the events, with which you are so familiar, I made my way to County Down of my birth country, intending to live quiet and go about my business. But in a short while I was discovered and beaten senseless by a mob of mechanics and labouring types.' The man pauses to swallow once again, Adam's apple bobbing up and down in his scrawny neck. 'They mauled and pummeled me most grievous and flung me into a pit of lime, leaving me for dead. With some assistance thereafter I made escape and was able to take passage for London where I begged a crust here on the street. But the lime pit had destroyed my eyes, filling them with foulness and corruption at the very risk of my life. It was only through the Christian charity of the good Doctor Nero, with spoon and paregoric that my life was preserved.'

With that the beggar unties his bandage and whips it away to reveal stark, puckered, empty cavities beneath.

The assembly gasps. With impeccable timing Nero raises his spoon aloft like a standard. 'Aye, ladies and gentlemen. With this very spoon, through these very hands was his life conserved. Judge the work and the work alone. Yours is not to pronounce upon the character of the man for I remind you, that likewise joy shall be in heaven over one sinner that repenteth, more than over ninety and nine just persons, which need no repentance. What say you to that, William Hare?'

'Indeed, sir. To be sure, not a day has passed without prayer or regret and repentance for those dreadful deeds. Had it not been for your chirurgical skill and kindness I would for a certainty be a dead man, without hope of redemption.'

The audience is ecstatic. There's nothing the London public enjoys more than grisly spectacle with a deeply satisfying moral conclusion. In that respect Nero's performance is almost as good as a hanging. They show appreciation by flinging coppers onto the stage.

Hare replaces his bandage, drops to his knees and casts about the platform, fluttering hands blindly seeking farthings. Nero gazes down beaming, delighted to see that the crowd has now swollen to a considerable number. He raises the spoon again for silence.

'Ladies and gentlemen, tarry a while. For you are about to witness that self-same procedure: an operation of the laudable spoon.'

The audience cheers. I gaze over at Facey who has been uncharacteristically quiet all this time, most likely under the dampening influence of Nero's nostrum. He scowls down at William Hare, on hands and knees still, scrabbling around for coin. 'William Hare, is it?' he sneers. 'You fool. You sad and cowardly rogue. Bring a fine profession into disrepute, would you?' With that Facey launches a mighty kick from the chair, catching Hare full in the arse of his kecks, sending him tumbling off the platform into the crowd, coppers scattering.

The mob howls with glee, momentarily beyond even Nero's control.

I take the opportunity to step back up into the booth and speak quietly into Nero's ear. 'Surely, you do not intend to spoon out his glim?'

'Indeed I do, sir. I will spoon him to health, sir. Trust me, young man, 'tis the best thing. Sans immediate intervention, poisons drawn to the wound will infuse and corrupt his body. In short, it is mortal.'

'You are certain of this?'

'I have seen it before. Many a time.'

'There is no other remedy?'

''Tis the only thing for it. Besides, the crowd will not have it any other way.'

'I do not care a fig for the wishes of the crowd. But desire only what is best for my partner,' I hiss.

The mob has quieted and waits expectantly. Nero abruptly turns away from me to address Facey, raising his voice for the benefit of the onlookers.

'Sir, I will employ my sharpened spoon to extract your poisoned orb. You may expect to feel pain for the briefest of moments as the optical cord is severed, but only for a second, for I will swiftly fill the cavity with powder of the coca plant, which will banish all feeling. Thereafter, you will require further tinctures of Pancurial Linctus. Let us say, for a week or so at regular intervals.'

'You will go to the devil,' bellows Facey, violently shaking his head, straining against the straps.

'One simple push, a half twist and the offending article will lie on my spoon, sir, never fear.'

A substantial crowd has now gathered, drawn in by the drama of an unwilling victim, and I am caught in an agony of indecision, unable to decide what is to be done for the best.

Facey refuses to keep his head still, frantically shifting from side to side as Nero advances. The spoon is only inches from his eye when he shoots me a look, furious and yet pleading at once.

'No,' I yell, 'you will not take his glim.'

Nero turns on me and, for a moment, I think he might be about to spoon me in the face. Thankfully, he lowers the instrument. I brush past him and unbuckle the leather restraints holding Facey to the chair.

The mob is less than happy with this outcome and, thwarted, begins to fling half-sucked oranges and oyster shells in our direction.

'I am sorry for your wasted efforts, sir, but I cannot permit it,' I bawl into Nero's ear as we crouch to avoid flying fruit and sundry brickbats.

'Think nothing of it, my dear fellow,' grins Nero. 'Never before have I drawn such a prodigious crowd. Only consider the quantity of Pancurial to be sold when they have regained their equilibrium. Besides,' he says, indicating Facey, 'sooner or later, you will come to me again, I have no doubt of it.'

'Well, then. In the meantime we leave you to your trade.'

'You will surely take a few bottles for your trouble, I hope. 'Tis in the main a solution of opium along with potent proprietary infusions, a little arsenic and alcohol flavoured with liquorice. Your friend, I think, will require it.'

Facey and me fill our pockets with bottles and quit the booth, forcing our way through the mob, who are now more interested in brawling with one another than the elevating spectacle of a medical procedure.

We find ourselves kerbside, where we are able to flag the horsebus. It is not full and so we are able to sit side by side. Facey replaces his bandage and with his one good eye examines his boots for a long while before announcing, 'You are fortunate, Sammy Boy, that this Pancurial, in addition to banishing pain, imparts a feeling of wellbeing and a blanket sense of goodwill, elsewise I am all but certain that I would, at this moment, wish to chastise you severely with my fists.'

'Here,' I say, uncorking a bottle, 'have another gobful then.'

CHAPTER VIII

They do say that London is like a man reclining: the West End is his head, the shining face of our metropolis; the City, a great belly—the repository of trade, our sustenance; the East End, his arse.

Certainly no one would mistake Whitechapel for a shining face, not with the combined stink and fume of the tanneries and breweries hereabout, yet there are signs of advancement, like the new Pavilion Theatre, rising above the jumble. Energy too, for it will not be kept down entirely. It will not allow itself to remain forever the bowel of the metropolis without a struggle.

In some ways Whitechapel resembles an individual from my philosophy: the congregation of foul, suffering alleys, pressing in at all sides, weighs on the place with the ballast of despair. Yet it is like one of those men who, born to every disadvantage, strives to elevate himself in spite of all.

Facey and me head north up through Essex Street, giving onto Red Lion Street. There is life and commerce here, mainly rag trade; slop shops and the like; as well, there is the run-off from Spitalfields fruit and vegetable market: vigorous young street arabs, like Facey and me ten years back, hawking pilfered stock. But as we turn into White's Row, the lassitude of poverty quickly overwhelms and begins to sap the spirit. That lifeless, dismal sense intensifies as we approach Dorset Street. If the East End is truly the arse, then here is its product: squalor beyond even the Westminster rookeries. And here is a house we know only too well. For those who frequent this place are the forgotten ones: men and women who have fallen so far that they do not care how they live or even whether they survive at all; whose only desire is for the next pipeful. And, since they are past caring for themselves, they are seldom missed when the smoke claims them, as it inevitably does. Chinee George's smoking ken has always been a fruitful source of merchandise for men in our trade.

The rotting front door stands open, hanging from its hinges. There is no purpose to securing this abode, since there is nothing within of any value, aside, of course, from the tin Chinee George keeps about his person.

The hallway is empty, derelict as always, the upper floor unreachable, the stairway having long since collapsed. And so we descend; a flight of stairs, worn hollow in the centre by the ceaseless footfall of the damned. I know what hell is like, for I have been here many times to collect. Hell is a long, low room lit only by the guttering flame of an oil lamp suspended over the doorway.

The place is filled with cramped and terraced berths, resembling a dormitory or ship's cabin. In each berth is a recumbent figure, head thrown back, limbs in mindless disarray, or hunched, knees to chin, over a pipe. Most lay silent, but some mutter to themselves, others talk together in curious, low, monotonous voices. The air is thick and heavy with the smell of brown opium smoke. Through the gloom appear little circles of red light, now bright, now faint, as the bowls are sucked. A big Chink wearing a stovepipe hat moves silently from berth to berth, checking for signs of life in the bowl and in the breast. From time to time his hand expertly worms its way into coat or trouser pocket of the particularly insensible. Invariably coming up empty.

A moon face looms from out of the shadows.

'It would seem that business is good,' remarks Facey in a half whisper. The crack of doom would not wake half the occupants of this room, yet for some reason, it seems right, in this place, to speak softly.

'Yes,' replies Chinee George, elongating the word to a sibilant hiss.

'We are here for Molly Mattheson; we must speak with him.'

'Yes.'

'He has been here, Chinee George?'

'Yes.' Chinee George's face reveals nothing, not even his age. His skin is perfectly smooth, though oily and somewhat yellow, like butter. Nothing moves in that face but the eyes, which dart about from time to time.

'He is here now?'

Chinee George shakes his head.

We have done business with this Celestial for four years, yet still we know little of him, only that he is protected in this enterprise by shadowy and powerful interests. He favours dirty ship's slops: baggy canvas shirt and trousers cut–off at the calf, though he must surely be a man of considerable means by now. In truth, we do not even know his name. But it is unlikely to be George. We are not his only associates neither. By our reckoning, Chinee George does business with a half-dozen or more resurrection crews across London on a rota system known only to himself. From time to time an oriental messenger-boy appears in the Feathers or the Fortune of War. He says nothing, giving us only a meaningful glare, but we understand by his presence that another pipe-fiend has carked it in this place and Chinee George wishes us to dispose of the corpse. We collect the body and split the proceeds down the middle. We have never tried to rook him, though this is only because we are afeared to:

Facey believes him to possess second sight and a Chink faculty for laying a potent curse.

'Do ee knowee where Molly isee?' Facey enunciates each word carefully in his half-whisper, though I am quite certain that Chinee George has no problem understanding plain English.

'Yes.'

Facey sighs.

'Will you tell us then?' I ask in the same half-whisper.

'Yes.' Chinee George's black eyes flick across at me and I swear I detect the beginnings of a smile.

Reluctantly, I unload a shilling from Tom's purse, which I press into his hands.

Chinee George grins and suddenly is all pidgin prattle: 'Got plenty tin, gone back Spitfield crib. Two hours pass, huh. Half ball took.'

'Thank 'ee kindly, George,' I say, extending my hand.

Chinee George glances down at my hand, immobile as a statue. 'Yes,' he says.

Molly is known to keep irregular lodgings in two places. The most likely being Thrawl Street, which has the advantage of being close by; only a short walk up White's Row, across Fashion Street and down Osborn.

The building is typical of the rookery; a blackened sandstone exterior, three stories high, infested with dippers, vagabonds, drunks, brutes and mollishers, living hand to mouth, sometimes upwards of a dozen to a room.

Naught is safe nor sacred in these places, not even the inhabitants, which is why Facey and me choose not to hold a permanent crib and keep our property portable.

We enter the dank hallway to find a family of seven encamped on the first flight of stairs. The head of the household, a massive cove in labourer's garb stained red with brick dust, is laid out to the sixth step, snoring, dead drunk to the world. His wife, a tiny, bonneted red-haired woman cuts bread and butter for her five hungry-looking children. We step around, giving them a friendly nod: Irish, without a shadow of a doubt.

On the third flight we find a young boot black sitting on the top step with his little box of brushes, piping his eyes and wailing most pitifully. 'What ails, young snot-nose, it cannot be so bad as that?' inquires Facey. I have an idea that his good humour is down to a few extra sips of the Pancurial on the way over.

The youngster wipes his razzo on the sleeve of his tight, threadbare jacket, leaving a glistening slug trail against the dark, greasy wool. 'That's all you know about it, mister.'

'What say I give you a ha'penny if you can tell me where Henry Mattheson resides, sometimes called Molly?'

''Tis why I am here. You will keep your ha'penny and I will inform you, gratis. That Molly bugger is in that there set of rooms 'long with others of his 'quaintance, who are no less buggers and brutes.' The boy snorts a prodigious quantity of snot as he indicates the fourth door along the landing.

'Then what's amiss, boy, that you should be sat here spouting the brine like Nelly Bligh, 'stead of at your trade?' I ask.

'Not half a hour previous that Molly bugger strolls up to my pitch, and I thinks to myself: now here's a down-at-heel gent, what wants his boots revived, but no. He says to me if I was to 'company him to his rooms here I was to receive a silver shilling for pulling at his parts. Well, sirs, a silver shilling is twice what I can take in on a good day and so I says "I will".' The lad pauses to wipe another snot trail across the sleeve. 'For what harm could it do, since to my mind 'tis nothing more than a hauling at the street pump, which I must go at each and every morning to wash the blacking from my face and hands?'

'He rooked you then, is that it?' says Facey, grinning.

'No, sir. Not that Molly hi'self. But t'other gent.'

'Other gent?'

'A swell. Oh, very grand to look at, but still a bugger and a brute for all his airs and fancy togs. For when me and Molly comes up these very stairs he is waiting with his 'complice, another flash-looking cove.

'"Molly, my dear," says the swell, "we have been waiting on you. I could not leave my card, since there was no steward to leave it with. There being naught but a tribe of savages occupying the hallway." And then this gent pulls a brown ball from his pocket, which Molly is very happy to see and which the gent give him.'

The boy rummages in his box for a filthy rag to mop his tears. Boot blacking from the rag spreads dark circles round his eyes, so now the urchin resembles a small but indignant owl. '"Now Molly, leave the youngster alone for we have business with you," says the gent, pulling at his elbow. "But sirs," I protest, all la-di-dah politeness-like, "Excuse me, pray, for I have a prior engagement here." With that, the brute laughs, clumps me round the flapper and kicks me flying down the stairs. Now I have lost a silver shilling, my ear rings like a church bell and I am sore bruised about the ribs.'

The boy's lower lip begins to tremble again. I delve into our purse and produce a silver sixpence. 'Here,' I say, 'take this for your lost trade today. In the future you will avoid men of his stamp, I hope.'

The lad snatches the coin and squirrels it away in his box. 'Oh, thank you, sir. And do you wish for a tug on your truncheon now?'

Facey guffaws.

'No, I do not. Get on with you before I am next to kick you down the stairs.'

The urchin scuttles away clutching his box.

Facey tries the door to Molly's rooms. It is not locked. We push it open to reveal a single, darkened chamber, the only window being stuffed with rags. Originally, this must have been three rooms but the partition walls have been demolished, leaving only empty wooden framework, like some archaeological site.

Rotting straw mattresses lie scattered about the boards, some with stained blankets, most without. At present, Molly and the two swells are the only occupants. Molly lies on a mattress by the window, while the two young men are perched on a couple of seats formed from old packing cases, the only articles of furniture in the room.

One of the young men gazes up at us with distaste. 'We are engaged in private discourse here. Be good enough to conduct your business elsewhere.' He dismisses us with a languid wave.

'We have business here, sir,' replies Facey evenly.

The young man looks up sharply, evidently more accustomed to his commands being obeyed. From what I can see, he is tall and well-made with a full head of jet-black hair, fashionably curled: a strikingly handsome fellow. In his riding togs, hessian boots, calfskin breeches, royal blue cutaway coat and pristine-white choker he is as out of place in this room as a fish is out of water. 'The business of sneak-thievery, no doubt,' he sighs, waving us away once more. 'Well, then you may take whatever you find, and welcome to it. It is none of our concern.'

He returns his attention to Molly, lying there before him, barely conscious, muttering, coughing and groaning softly. Meanwhile, his companion, equally well dressed, though lank-haired and sharp-faced, prepares a pipe, filling the bowl with a large brown chunk of opium. He passes it across to the dark-haired young man, who sparks up a Lucifer and sets it to burning. The weasel-faced cove then crouches at Molly's head, raising him up by the shoulders.

'Come now, Molly. Here is another pipe for you. Smoke up, there's a good fellow,' says the dark gent, pressing the smouldering pipe into Molly's limp hands.

'Our business here is with Mattheson,' says Facey.

The dark-haired young man slowly rises to his feet. He is indeed tall, having perhaps an inch or so on Facey. 'What? You still here?' The languid manner betrayed by anger flaring in his pale blue eyes.

'Still here. And here we will remain 'til we have spoke with Mattheson.'

The young man stands quite still, only his fingers move, twisting the leather braid of his horsewhip. 'Mattheson is at his pipe, as you can plainly see. You will get nothing from him of any substance.'

Mattheson is seized by a fit of coughing. The sharp-faced cove slaps his back repeatedly before feeding him more of the pipe.

'It appears to me that Mattheson has had quite enough pipe.'

'That is not for you to say.'

'But I do say it.'

For a moment I am quite certain that the young man is about to strike out at Facey with the horsewhip. Then abruptly, he favours us with a smile and an ironic little bow. 'Come, Phillip, fetch the horses. We have been here quite long enough. I shall have to burn these togs, for I fear the stink of this place will never come out.' He makes his way to the door. The sharp-faced associate leaves Molly to the smoke and scuttles after.

We step quickly over to the mattress and crouch at Molly's side. His fingers are slack, yet still manage to retain their grip on the pipe. The eyes are open but the lids flutter and I cannot say if there is any recognition in them. 'Molly,' I hiss. 'We are here about the body you talked of.'

'Bobby,' repeats Molly.

'Body. The one you spoke of last night.'

'Night,' he echoes.

'Here,' says Facey, lifting Molly by his scrawny shoulders, 'leave it to me.' He begins shaking Molly so violently that he drops the pipe and I hear his teeth rattle. 'Who … else … knows … of … this … body?'

Molly pouts, reminding me of the little boot black. I fear he is about to burst into tears. 'Poor body.'

I retrieve the pipe holding it just out of reach. 'You may have your pipe, when you have told us what we need to know,' I say.

Facey slaps him hard. The eyes roll back in his head. Facey drops him to the mattress, seemingly insensible.

Of a sudden Molly smiles, the eyes flicker open and appear to focus.

'Molly, listen now. That creature; the Man-Woman. Who else knows of it?'

'Beautiful body. So … badly used.'

'Molly, where is the body?'

'Bob, bob, bob, bobbing back up.' Molly chuckles to himself. 'Should never have come back,' he whispers. 'Never.' Ever so slowly his eyes shut.

CHAPTER IX

Facey raps on the scarred counter for a couple of brown porters.

'Will I take the pins then, Mr Facey?' says Fearon, passing over the bottles.

'You will, for they will not be needed tonight.' Facey slides the pins from his long pockets and hands them across, along with a coin, to Fearon, who dips out of sight to store them somewhere beneath his counter.

Facey and me find empty places on a bench near the wall and broach the porter. I reach down into my own pockets to unload the bread and cheese from Tom's breakfast table. For a while, we gorge ourselves in silence for we are both thirsty and sharp set from the labours of the day.

I take a swig and sigh with pleasure at the strong, malty brew. Facey pops a hunk of cheese into his mouth and drains the last of his bottle. 'Take your ease while you can, Sammy Boy. For there is to be another trek across London, this time on the soles of our own boot leather.'

'To what purpose?'

'Why, we must have our tin and so tonight will renew our acquaintance with Nicodemus Reilly at the cockpit. I cannot allow such a debt to stand.'

'And what of Brookes' commission?'

'What of it?'

'We are abandoning the chase?'

'We have lost the scent. What more is to be done?'

'I do not know but it seems a very hard thing to be bilked of such a bounty.'

'Well, we must take as we find. There are still two sovs to be had from the finding of this Templeton cove. 'Tis a simple matter, since it seems he is not a sporting gent, nor of the Fancy, so I warrant it was the tables that sunk him.' Facey licks a finger and dabs at the remaining crumbs of hard cheese scattered about the table. 'Should he have been fleeced at the gaming hells, they would know of it at Ma Leach's.'

'Two sovs are not one hundred.'

'Two sovs are not to be sniffed at. As for the raree aviary, all we have are the addled ramblings of a smoke-fiend. At the best of times, Molly's words are scarcely to be relied upon, but after so many pipefuls there is no sense left in him at all. No, that trail is gone cold.'

'Molly keeps elevated company these days, it seems.'

'No better than he, for all their flash togs. There is a base, vicious inclination about the tall one, which cannot be concealed from a man such as myself. I have seen it afore at sea and in the ring. A certain savage glee about the eyes, which reveals a taste for inflicting pain. There was a boatswain's mate on the Billy Ruffian who made too free with the rope's end; took overmuch pleasure in starting the men. Disappeared overboard one night off Rochefort and not one soul amongst five hundred saw it happen. The big cove has that selfsame look, for I marked it well as he was standing afore me thinking whether or no to try for a cut with that horsewhip of his.'

I attempt to conceal a smile, cramming the last crust of bread into my mouth.

'I am not blind, Sammy. I see that you take me for a hypocrite.'

'I have said no such thing,' I reply, coughing breadcrumbs.

'I understand it from your smile. I will admit that, on occasion, I am more inclined to fling the mauleys than most, but what is done by me is done in hot blood and not in cold. I take no pleasure in it. There is the difference.'

I make no reply, but deliberately finish off my porter and wipe the crumbs from my kecks.

He sighs, 'Very well then, Sammy. Other than in the case of Spicer.'

I grin. 'So, tonight you will be content to let me to play principal in our dealings with Reilly and keep a tight rein on that hot blood of yours?'

'I will, Sammy Boy.'

'For it seems that Reilly is Pimlott and Chuffington's man and we do not wish to brush up against that pair, howsomever slantendicular.'

Ordinarily, here in the Feathers, men take care not to stray into the space of those in cahoots, lest they overhear something they should not. But for some time now an unfamiliar stocky cove in a long tarp coat has been slowly and quite deliberately inching closer. He keeps his back to us but still, he is overstepping. I am about to object when of a sudden, he turns to face us. It is clear that he is not here to drink, his arms are concealed beneath the voluminous coat, which he wears about his shoulders. 'Forgive me, gents, but I could not help but overhear the tail end of your conversation. And it is wondrous strange that you should happen to mention Messrs Pimlott and Chuffington at the same 'zact moment I am here on their very commission. And stranger still that you pronounce a profound reluctance to have dealings with them since they have so very urgent a desire to meet with you. There, gents, what do you say to that?'

'Bugger off,' snarls Facey.

The man's smile disappears. 'Do not be so disobliging, Mr Facey. You will please to 'company me to the offices of my masters as I have asked.'

Facey rises to his feet and stands over him. Although the man appears to be powerfully built, Facey has a good few inches on him.

'Who says so?'

The interloper allows his coat to fall open, revealing two hexagonal steel barrels aimed at us. 'Why, this pair of barkers do and they will have the final word on the matter. Come now, gents. For I should be just as happy to put a ball in each of your bellies and think naught of it.'

The irons never waver as he withdraws them just sufficiently to benefit again from the concealment of his coat. I tense, ready to jostle his aim but it is evident that the fellow is one who both knows and enjoys his business. 'You are likely nimble enough to evade me in this crowd, Mr Samuel, but should you attempt it, I promise, it will go worse for your partner who, with all his bulk, makes a most handsome target.'

'Easy now,' says Facey, 'we will come quiet, since we have given your masters naught to reproach us for.' There is nothing for it, so Facey and me allow ourselves to be herded out through the public and into the street, where a private growler awaits, along with a driver.

We climb aboard. Our custodian cautiously placing himself on the opposing seat, he shrugs off the coat entirely to reveal a pair of expensive, engraved pistols, still trained at our guts.

'I see you are assessing the firepower, gents. Should you be thinking to rush me in the hope of a hang fire, I will save you the trouble. 'Tis a beautiful pair of matched Galton's. Percussion caps, d'you see? There will be no misfire here, I assure you. Ain't progress a fine thing?'

The man has every advantage over us, so we simply settle back in our seats and wait. We pass down Shoreditch High Street and North Folgate in silence, broken only by the steady, monotonous clip, clopping of the horse.

In a few minutes we are through Bishopsgate and on into Houndsditch; it would appear that we are heading back to the City. I cannot imagine what has provoked these men to reach across half of London in order to pluck us. Like anyone in our world, we know plenty about the doings of Pimlott and Chuffington, but have taken great pains to remain without their sphere of influence. We are beholden to no man, and our trade has always been of too little consequence for men of such preeminence to interfere. I wonder if we are to be punished for Reilly's broken razzo.

I have no time to consider this before the growler pulls up in Aldgate High Street.

The buildings hereabouts are ancient and timber framed, many having been coaching inns, at one time servicing London travellers entering by the ancient Aldgate postern. On this portion of the street there is still the Bull Yard and Black Horse but the remainder have since been converted to warehouses or given over to the practice of commerce: a respectable district, without the grandeur of Leadenhall or Threadneedle.

We are disembarked, under the baleful glare of the Galtons, swiftly ushered into one of the nondescript commercial buildings and prodded up a flight of stairs, where we are led into a place of business on the first floor.

Shelves of legal tomes line the walls; there are Ottoman rugs on the floor and a welcoming fire burns in the grate. The walls are papered in fashionable but discreet stripes and decorated with engravings of London life as well as detailed cartographics.

Two large desks split the room, each almost entirely obscured by books, writing implements, inks and piles of legal documents. At the far end sits an enormously fat cove demolishing a pie of some description, nearest to us, a spry, bespectacled party. They are attired alike in sombre jackets, breeches and Geneva collars like a pair of City clerks or pulpit pounders.

The bespectacled cove jumps to his feet, rubbing his hands. 'Ah, Mr Facey, Mr Samuel, welcome, welcome.'

He cocks his head to peer out of the single window, inspecting the night sky. 'The sun has most evidently set and so I feel that a glass of something might be in order. Yes, indeed I do.'

He gestures to a pair of straight-backed chairs set side-by-side against the wall. 'You gentlemen will be seated, while I see to the refreshments.'

The barkers are still on us, so we obey without objection while the specky gent fusses with a decanter.

He brings across a couple of dainty wine glasses containing a brownish liquid, passing a third to the fat cove.

'Amontillado, gentlemen, is characterized by being darker than Fino but lighter than Oloroso. It is named for the Montilla region of Spain, where it has been a staple for some one hundred years now.'

We have both downed ours in one quick draught, though it is probable that we should not have, especially when we observe the gentleman raise his glass and take a series of delicate sips. 'Ahh, we have had our quarrels with the Spaniard, but no man can say he is not the supreme arbiter when it comes to viniculture.'

The fat cove also takes an appreciative but tiny sip while Facey and me sit uncomfortably in the straight-backed chairs, empty glasses now superfluous in our hands.

'There is some Pound cake if you would—but no, I can tell you are eager to be at the business at hand.'

He slaps his head. 'What is become of my manners? We have the advantage of you gentlemen. And so, first, before all else must come the introductions: I am called Chuffington and that fine figure of a man is Mr Pimlott. Meathook I believe you already know.'

'Meathook, is it?' grunts Facey, sneering at the Galtons.

'Oh, dear me, no, no, no. You must not think any the less of Meathook for employing the barkers. He is neither soft, nor a man of refined sensibility. Quite the contrary. It was I who insisted on these weapons. When occasion demands, they are often tidier and more convenient. Is that not so, Meathook?'

'Right enough, Mr Chuffington.'

'Rest assured, Meathook is quite without remorse or any finer feelings to speak of, having spent twenty years or more at the Smithfield market. Gore is nothing to him, he has bathed in buckets of blood and scaled mountains of offal. To Meathook you are naught but slabs of meat, two carcasses of beef, unless and until we declare that you are worthy of finer consideration. Do you comprehend this? It is so very important that you do.'

We nod vigorously. Meathook grins, the Galtons disappear into his pockets to be replaced by his instrument of preference, a vicious-looking curved iron butcher's hook.

I'm hoping that Facey does not see this as our opportunity to rush him. Our combined force may well prevail but one of us will most likely receive a six-inch barb in the vitals. Me, probably. Mercifully, Facey appears to have no such ambitions, he sits like a stone, quite expressionless.

Chuffington paces the room, almost prancing. 'You will be wondering why we have summoned you here tonight. Pimlott and Chuffington branching out? Moving into the resurrection racket?' He chuckles. 'Rest assured, your livelihood is safe from us, if not your lives.'

Facey sighs. 'With respect, Mr Chuffington, we have never knowingly trespassed on your turf or your concerns. We are but small men, seeking only to go about our trifling affairs.'

'You believe that you are too insignificant to be of concern? That you are unknown to us? You will be amazed, Mr Facey, at our degrees of connection.' With that he nods at Meathook, who turns and makes for the door.

Though we are no longer under gun or hook, fleeing now would be a fruitless exercise. With their reach these men could run us to ground at any time and besides, we have yet to discover what it is that they want.

'The Rig, gentlemen,' pipes Pimlott, in a curious, high-pitched warble for such a substantial man. 'We have a significant stake in George Spicer's impending scheme. Indeed, we have become the prime movers in the affair. Do you imagine then that we would not have taken the trouble to scrutinize our associates in such an undertaking? We have investigated your character and reputation, we know a great deal about you.' With that he crams a hunk of pound cake into his fat, slobbering maw.

'Then you will know that we are straight arrows and quite undeserving of such treatment,' objects Facey.

'Such treatment?' counters Chuffington. 'A glass of amontillado and a slice of Pound cake? If that is deemed harsh, then I truly fear for you, should you ever be taken up.'

'We did not get any cake,' mutters Facey.

The door opens to reveal Meathook now accompanied by George Spicer, the pair of them lugging a large wicker hamper. They are followed by a couple of porters, similarly encumbered. As they deposit their loads on the Ottoman rug, we hear the clink of chinaware, confirming my worst fears.

Three additional hampers are brought in to complete the set. Spicer's lip is still puffed and split but he manages to smirk and leer in our direction before throwing back the lids. It is the chinaware. Our entire fortune.

The porters leave, carefully closing the door behind them but Meathook and Spicer remain, poised over our hampers like carrion crows.

Chuffington selects a small soup bowl and examines it. 'No doubt you will know something of us,' he muses.

'Indeed we do, sir,' affirms Facey, most respectful. 'Plenty enough.'

'Then you will know that we are sincere in what we have to say. Tonight, there are but two outcomes for you gentlemen: one—we find you culpable and you are punished. Two—we are convinced of your innocence, in which case, you will aid us by informing against the guilty party. Either way, it is necessary for you to fully comprehend the matter and its implications.'

Facey nods, as do I.

'We are, both of us, Pimlott and I, men of ingenuity and parts. At one time clerks, articled and apprenticed. Mr Pimlott here laboured in shipping accounts, 'til he struck upon a new and revolutionary method of reckoning, a system of double-entry; in and out, plus and minus. Alas, his master, a man quite lacking in vision, suspected knavery and dismissed him out of hand.

'I, myself was a solicitor's clerk, but had the temerity to make a play for the partner's daughter. And was similarly dismissed. Mr Pimlott and I had the good fortune to meet up in a pie shop on Berners Street; the remainder of our history is as you know it, I am sure.'

We gaze at Chuffington, pantomiming our most sympathetic expressions, nodding and sighing.

'At that time it occurred to me that London is not one world at all, but two quite distinct worlds. A higher and a lower: the one that is reserved for those born to privilege; t'other for those who will make something of it by their own hand.

'If the upper world had no use for a Pimlott and a Chuffington, then it would be to the lower that we would devote our energy and intellect. And as you see,' he indicates the room around us, 'it has borne fruit.

'Our realm, gentlemen, may encompass a baser, coarser sphere but it is not entirely absolved from the principles of order and natural justice. A contract remains a contract. Dictum is yet meum pactum. A solemn undertaking must be honoured. Transgressions punished. For if not, where would we be?'

'Where indeed, sir?' I respond quickly enough, though I do not think he was expecting an answer.

'We are not beasts, commerce cannot thrive amidst chaos. There must be regulation and order amongst us. I insist upon it. Wrongdoing cannot be ignored, punishment must follow, swift and condign.'

'Now we come to it,' pipes Pimlott.

'Indeed we do,' agrees Chuffington. 'Some three days previous, Mr Pimlott's well-regarded and saintly mother passed from this vale of tears.' He flings the soup bowl into the fireplace where it smashes to pieces.

'I am sorry to hear it,' I say.

'A mason, commissioned for the purpose of imprinting the name Agnes Constance Pimlott into the stone of the memorial, this morning at his labours, observed scratches on a corner of the slab, the slightest of abrasions but sufficient to arouse suspicion. On investigation, the slab was removed, the coffin disinterred and found to be empty.'

I make a sympathetic face. 'That is … regrettable.'

'Empty,' pipes Pimlott. 'In short, minus one body.'

'You, or men of your profession, have made away with Mr Pimlott's blessed mama. Pimlott's own flesh and blood, forsooth. Ordinarily, the law would lay a fine upon the perpetrators. But since this is an action which strikes at the very heart of Pimlott and Chuffington, our judgment shall be harsher by some degree.'

'I did not care for her overmuch,' interjects Pimlott.

'That is beside the point,' hisses Chuffington.

Facey shrugs. 'We are a cagey lot in our trade, Mr Chuffington. I do not see how Sammy and me can be of assistance in the matter, knowing little to nothing about the comings and goings of other crews.'

Chuffington nods. 'I see. Then let us begin, as we ought, with the soup.'

Meathook picks out a few of the soup bowls from the first hamper and begins to smash them one at a time, slowly and deliberately with his iron hook.

Spicer, grinning, withdraws another couple and crushes them under his heavy, hob-nailed boots.

'Gentlemen, we are devilish sharp set. Surely you have aught to offer us,' urges Chuffington.

Spicer gleefully selects a couple of our dinner plates, ready to clap them together like cymbals.

Chuffington cocks his head sideways at us, like a curious sparrow. 'Well?'

Facey sighs. 'I have never been much in the peaching line, Mr Chuffington. What you require from us goes very much against the grain, but perhaps you should speak with a pair who go by the name of Teeth and Mutton. You will not mistake Teeth, on account of his teeth. And his very particular alabaster appearance.'

Chuffington tops up his glass and chuckles. 'Oh, that is precious, is it not, Mr Pimlott?'

Pimlott makes a wheezing sound, like a busted church organ. Gigantic head bent over his desk, rocking back and forth. Finally, he composes himself sufficiently to unfurl a pristine fogle from his sleeve and wipe oily tears of mirth from his pig-eyes.

Chuffington smiles fondly at his helpless partner. 'Not one hour ago were those very men in this very room, and you would never credit what was their opinion on the matter.'

Facey sags. 'You do not have to tell us.'

'You are a man of great perception, Mr Facey.'

'You take their word for it?'

'I do not. But men whose word we do trust were able to account for the whereabouts of Teeth and Mutton last night. It is your whereabouts that is in question here.'

Facey remains just as he was, there is no movement, no outward sign and yet I am utterly conscious that he, like me, has just seen our way out of this dilemma.

'The corpse ... I beg your pardon, the late Mrs Pimlott was took last night, you say?'

'According to the mason, the scratches were fresh made and not apparent yesterday. It would appear that the body was took last night,' affirms Chuffington.

Facey indicates his bandage. 'I have an injury, Mr Chuffington, which has precluded work of a physical nature for the major portion of this week. I do not expect you to take that for gospel, nevertheless, we were excluded from our accustomed business this last night, as any number of good men will testify.'

'That is easy for you to say,' replies Chuffington.

'You will accept that a hoist cannot be undertaken outside the hours of eleven and four in the morning, and that is only if the moon is on the wane?'

'We do.'

'Then you will find that Sammy Boy and me was at the Westminster Cockpit 'til perhaps one in the morning. Thereafter at a very great gentleman's place on Great Marlborough Street, having been summoned there by a lad from Lieutenant Trench's Messenger Service. At the hour of two, or thereabouts, did we enter the Coach and Horses Tavern, where we drank off toddies with our host and passed the remainder of the night. All of which can be verified by men of no particular partiality and some degree of rectitude.'

Chuffington strokes his chin, impressed. 'It is a good account, Mr Facey, and, for the moment, I am inclined to believe it.'

At this point Pimlott decides to pipe up. 'There is a hole in them numbers.'

Chuffington smiles. 'Ahh, leave it to Mr Pimlott to find a hole in the numbers. For he always will, you know.'

'Hole? What hole?' demands Facey.

Pimlott scoops the cake crumbs from his plate and scatters them into his great gob. 'The hours from one, postmeridian, onwards, we will, for the sake of argument, take on trust. It is the hours preceding that which I question. Those hours you claim to have passed in the Westminster Cockpit, are the very same hours and at the very same place where Teeth and Mutton was. Yet they made no mention of your presence there. Nor does anyone else that we have questioned. How do you account for this?'

'Do you see it? Do you see how his mind works?' says Chuffington, gleefully. 'Is he not a colossus of logical deduction?'

'Would Teeth and Mutton offer us an alibi, gratis, if it is not in their interest?' I retort.

Chuffington considers this. 'No, you have the right of it. They would not. But there were others in attendance and not one has attested to your presence last night.'

'We were there,' insists Facey.

'So you say,' insists Chuffington, 'but it seems that there is indeed an unsubstantiated period of two hours during which you may have been able to commit this awful crime against my partner. If you are innocent, we are sorry for it, but I must hand you over to the tender mercies of Meathook and others. You will understand, I'm sure, the necessity for your immediate removal to our warehouse cellars.'

Meathook grins, producing the twin barkers once again, indicating with them that we should get to our feet and accompany him.

'We were present when the dog, Billy, took one hundred and so buzzers in under twelve,' asserts Facey.

''Tis a feat much discussed throughout the metropolis today. You will get no credit from that knowledge, Mr Facey,' chuckles Chuffington.

'Your own man, Reilly, took my sovs on the mutt.'

'Reilly is indisposed today. He made no mention of you.'

'Wait,' I say. 'Somewhere about me I have a article, which may convince you.'

Meathook advances, cocking the barkers but Chuffington stays his man with a raised hand. I frantically rummage inside my coat but the scrap of paper eludes me.

Chuffington shrugs. 'We may stand here forever while you claim to have seen this dog or that man, but if you cannot furnish the proof, then you must face the consequences.'

'Please,' I insist, 'but one moment more.'

Between the cold chisel, bits of twine and stale breadcrumbs in the deep pockets of my jacket, my fingers finally close upon a small folded sheet of paper. I pull it out and hand it to Meathook, who delivers it to his master.

Chuffington puts on his specs and unfolds the chit. 'Upon my soul, 'tis our marker, written up by Reilly 'gainst the ratter Billy.'

'And so this "hole" is now filled to your satisfaction?' I say.

Chuffington looks to his partner whose head slowly shifts on its great fleshy pillows affirming his acceptance.

'Very well,' announces Chuffington, 'as for the rest, we will take your word on it, 'til it can be verified. You may go.'

'And what of this?' demands Facey, indicating our hampers.

'We will keep the remaining crockery as surety against your tale,' smiles Chuffington, 'never fear, we shall preserve it as though it were our own.'

CHAPTER X

It is midday at the least by the time we find ourselves on Pye Corner, having passed what remained of the night at a thrupenny ken in Cock Lane. Facey digs at his thick, black hair searching for lice and fleas, unwelcome but inevitable fellow occupants in such quarters. Above us the Golden Boy, memorial to the Great Fire, gazes out across London, impervious to our troubles.

We enter the Fortune of War, which teems with the usual low-life. Facey appears out of sorts today and I cannot say for sure whether it is on account of the turn in our fortunes or the effects of his injury. Either way, he is content to settle himself at a bench and leave me to make my way through the press.

'Let me entreat you, Mr Samuel, not to rap on my counter with the edge of your coin. Though you are on the small side to be sure, I am quite able to see you standing there,' pronounces Ricketts, the burly taverner.

'It is a gold sovereign, Mr Ricketts, and I should be grateful if you would break it in the course of supplying me with a bottle of port wine and some sugar.'

'There will be more than a coin broke, if there is another dent in my counter,' responds Ricketts, biting into my sovereign.

Satisfied with its quality, he doles out a quantity of silver shillings in return.

'And perhaps you will be good enough to send out a boy to fetch a couple of fowl and have them cooked up for Facey and me.'

'It will be done, just as you say, Mr Samuel. And you will forgive me for my abruptness just now. For I'm sure I did not see that Mr Facey was with you.'

It is a wearying fact of life that men such as Ricketts are no respecters of intellect and resource, only brute force.

I join Facey at his table with our bottle of port wine and pour out a couple of tumblers, stirring in the few bits of sugar.

Facey produces a bottle of the Pancurial from his pockets and adds a good dose to the mixture.

'Is that wise?' I ask.

'Wisdom is an overrated virtue,' retorts Facey, downing the concoction. He pours himself another, adulterating it with more of the nostrum. His countenance is pale and the bandage round his eye vile and crusted.

'Have you salved the glim this morning?'

'I cannot bear to touch it,' responds Facey. 'It is become most shocking painful.'

'Then what is to be done, if you will not allow the sawbones to intervene?'

'It will right itself in time, 'tis only the pain that must be accommodated. I find the linctus answers well enough.'

I sift gloomily through the contents of our joint purse. There is little enough for all our labours: one of Reilly's gold sovereigns remains, though there are a good few of Tom's silver shillings and sixpences along with the change from Ricketts.

'Ah, you must not mind me, Sammy Boy,' sighs Facey. 'I am peevish and ill-tempered company for you today.'

'As you have every right to be. It is all gone, even the marker. We are quite smashed and must begin over.'

'Aye,' agrees Facey. 'It is a very great shame that Mrs Pigeon cannot be relied upon to tell a Pimlott from a Piecrust. But never fear, I will have those sixteen sovs from Reilly, marker or no.'

'I wish you would forget Reilly.'

'Why ever so?'

'We are not entirely off the hook, so to speak, in the matter of Ma Pimlott. For if it ever comes to light that the corpse was hoisted a night earlier than this fool of a mason has claimed then it will be but a simple thing to connect us with the enterprise. There is Shields for one.'

'If Shields peaches, he implicates himself.'

'True, but there were plenty of eyes in the Feathers that night, not all of them blind drunk. I think it prudent we steer our course well clear of Pimlott and Chuffington and make ready to quit London. At least until the dust has settled. I should not desire a second interview with those men.'

'And where should we go?'

'Why, to Edinburgh. There are medical schools crying out for what we are able to provide and a good living to be made, though the Scotch are known to be close with their purses.'

A degree of colour has returned to my partner's face and his spirits have lifted, owing, in the main I believe, to the effects of the Linctus. He slaps a meaty fist down onto the table. 'I'll claim Brookes' bounty first.'

'Last night you reckoned it had become a stale line, and you were in the right of it. Most likely by now that corpse is diced into a hundred pieces or more, the flesh in portions, ornamenting the dissecting table of every anatomical student in the city.'

'If so, we will hear of it soon enough,' says Facey gazing about. That is true since the Fortune of War is one of the boozing kens where men of our trade are apt to gather, owing to its proximity to Barts'. Indeed, Teeth and Mutton huddle over by the lead-paned windows engaged in earnest, whispered conversation with a porter. On a bench nearby I spy John Bishop and Thomas

Williams, a young, excitable pair, who have yet to understand the meaning of caution and will intrude upon a churchyard regardless of a waxing moon or the presence of watchmen.

'If we are not to quit the city then surely the discovery of this Templeton is our most likely prospect.'

Facey grunts. 'We will try at Ma Leach's by and by.'

'Here is your fowls, gents.' Our musings are interrupted by the potboy, unloading a couple of roasted ducks on trenchers. I hand the lad a sixpence and we tear into them.

It may be the scent of the roasted duck that draws Bishop to our end of the table. He grins at me, a horrible black-toothed grimace. 'Lord, and don't that smell good,' he says.

'Tastes good, an' all,' confirms Facey, stripping a leg with his teeth.

I keep a stick of liquorice about my person for scraping the molars and sweetening the breath and, from time to time, Facey will deign to give it some use. On the whole though, we are pretty well accustomed to reeking breath and broken, blackened teeth. Bishop, however, is in a class of his own, his teeth are not merely stained but jet-black through and through.

'God in heaven, but what is amiss with your gob?' says Facey, starting.

Bishop grins, a frightful black gash. ''Tis naught but my ebony teeth, gents.'

'Ebony, is it?'

'I am, as you know, a great admirer of Mr Teeth, the Prussian gentleman you will observe over by the window. Seeing as how I had lost, through conflict and decay, the chief allotment of my own gnashers, it occurred to me to follow suit and have a replacement set constructed. You would be quite knocked aback, gentlemen, absolutely flattened, to learn of the cost of a set of genuine enamels fashioned on Waterloo lines. I could not pay it in a year and so determined that my teeth would be constructed from the next best thing, namely wood: hardest and most durable of its kind. And here they are. Which, you will note, they have the particular advantage of not being detectable by moonlight. Though I do wonder if ebony ought to splinter so and taste of boot black to quite such a degree.'

Facey licks the grease from his fingers as he considers Bishop's gob. 'You are not to come anywhere near my duck with those foul articles.'

Bishop, crestfallen, shifts away, back up the bench to be replaced in his spot by Lieutenant Trench.

'Gents, I bid you good day.'

'Trench,' acknowledges Facey, working at a wing.

'I have this morning been interviewed by certain parties with regard to you gentlemen,' remarks Trench, softly.

'And you have answered honestly, I make no doubt,' retorts Facey, spitting gristle.

'I cannot afford to dissemble, nor take sides. You understand that a messaging service must be forthright and accountable at all times, if it is to thrive.'

'I am quite sure of it … Lieutenant,' says Facey, ripping the remains of the carcass apart with his fingers.

'I have affirmed that you was summoned to a gentleman in Great Marlborough Street on the night before last. Nothing more, nor less. I hope that I have not been of disservice to you gents. That is all.'

Facey leaves off eating and appraises the man. 'Well, Trench, you have said what you know to be the case. Whether it is to our advantage or disadvantage don't hardly signify.'

Trench is a gentlemanly sort. A man of enterprise, well turned out in blue coat and passably clean linens. He is affable enough and it is decent in him to share this intelligence. So I cannot comprehend why Facey is coming it so disagreeable.

Trench shrugs and makes to rise. 'I came to be amenable, not to set up a quarrel here, gents.'

'There is no quarrel here, Lieutenant Trench, and we are grateful for your information,' I say quickly.

'And yet, your partner is not so well-disposed, it appears.'

Facey deliberately puts down the duck leg that he has been worrying at before addressing the man. 'Trench, you must know that I was, for a time, ship's boy. As a seafaring man I can say for a certainty that you are no lieutenant. And yet you style yourself so.'

Trench is about to object, but decides better of it. He lowers his head. 'You are in the right of it, Mr Facey. I have no officer's commission. I was but a lowly middy in the service, having failed to pass for Lieutenant on no fewer than six occasions. I simply could not hammer the mathematics of sine or cosine into this thick skull of mine and would never make any sort of navigator. It has been a source of great shame to me and some considerable amusement to my younger comrades. You will pity the sin of pride in me, I'm sure. And perhaps even forgive this lapse? Between men who have served?'

Facey nods, considering Trench for a moment. Finally, he says: 'Since you put it so, I will, sir. Such disclosure takes courage. And that, I can admire in any man, be he waister, middy or admiral of the red.'

Trench lowers his voice to a whisper. 'I have also found that the rank inspires faith in my rectitude, surely an advantage in a confidential messenger. And so, would not wish it known that I have exaggerated my achievements.'

Facey chuckles. 'Rest assured, your patrons will hear naught from me on the subject. You will stay, Lieutenant, and have a glass of wine with us, sir?'

'That is very decent in you, Mr Facey, and I should like it above all things.'

I fill Trench's glass with our port wine.

'On which vessel did you serve, Mr Facey?'

'The Billy Ruffian, sir.'

'A damned fine ship, sir. And we will toast to the Billy Ruffian.'

Trench and Facey touch beakers and take a hearty swallow each.

'And you, sir?'

'I had the honour of serving aboard the Aboukir. Likewise of the line and four and seventy.'

'Then we will drink to it, both victory and vessel.'

'Aboukir. Victory and vessel.'

The bottle is all but empty. Facey raps on the table with the edge of a shilling. 'Ricketts,' he bellows, 'another couple of your port wine and not so near this time with the sugar, you parsimonious bugger.'

It seems that mere landsmen like myself are excluded from all this hale fellow, four-and-seventy Billies, abby dabby sea-doggerel. But I am content for the moment. It is a fine thing to see Facey back in spirits.

Ricketts duly brings the wine along with a good quantity of sugar; I notice that he has nothing to say to Facey on the subject of dents.

'And how is Pure John coming along, Lieutenant Trench?'

'He is an impudent scalawag, Mr Samuel, but resourceful. I believe he has the makings of something about him.'

'I am glad to hear it.'

'But I have no doubt that, at this very moment, he is making a beast of himself, gorging and imbibing far more than is good for him and will be fit for naught the rest of the day.'

'How so?'

'A short while ago a young lady arrived at my place of business on Albemarle Street and begged me give him leave for an hour or two. Though humbly enough attired, she was most gracious and spoke in a manner that belied her outward appearance. Her hope was they might be permitted to regale themselves on the small basket of comestibles she had brung, with some few bottles of porter, on account of it being his elder brother's birthday. I did not see the harm and, being taken with her tender disposition, gave the boy leave to go, though no doubt he will so stuff himself with pastries and so hog the porter that I shall find him insensible at his post upon my return.'

'I believe I may be acquainted with the lady,' I say, 'and your description of her does you credit, Lieutenant.'

'I am gratified to hear it. A Miss Rosamund, I believe.'

Facey cocks an eyebrow in my direction. 'Ah, I warrant you have touched a nerve there, Lieutenant.'

'Indeed? As I say, a most gracious soul.'

Facey reaches for the bottle, fills Trench's beaker and is about to do the same for mine when I shake my head. 'Do you know, I believe I should like some air. What say I pay that visit to Ma Leach's? See if I cannot put us on the trail of this Templeton cove?'

Facey drops a chunk of sugar into his beaker, slowly stirring the mixture with a great blackened finger. Finally, he looks up at me through his one good eye and nods. 'Why not? A little air will do you good.' He shoves a respectable portion of the shillings in my direction. 'Here, Sammy Boy, you will leave the Lieutenant and me to our wine and our belaying and our t'gallant staysails.' A sly smile splits his unshaven face. 'Come to think on it now, old Ma Leach's place would be but three or four streets from Albemarle, if you are quick smart I daresay you might kill two birds with the one stone.'

In truth, it would certainly be wiser for us both to use this time in preparation for quitting the metropolis. But then again, as Facey has observed, wisdom is an overrated virtue.

CHAPTER XI

Having had a deal of practice over the years I make excellent time on my shoe-leather up High Holborn and Oxford Street and so, rather than pressing on to King Street, I turn swiftly down New Bond Street and onto Albemarle as Facey, no doubt, reckoned I would. Trench's place of business is at number forty-eight, a narrow edifice of worn sandstone, five floors high and boasting a pair of imposing jet-black double doors. A multiplicity of small brass plaques affixed to the painted wood attest to the various activities within and, for the sake of my pins, I am gratified to find that Trench's Messenger Service keeps its chambers no higher than the second floor. The front portal is ajar, propped open with a broken chair leg, and so I enter the cramped vestibule. It is poorly-lit and smells of onions but seems lively enough; chamber doors open and shut in quick succession and young men of commerce in various states of dishevelment flit energetically back and forth, in and out of the building on some vital commission or other, papers in hand, fixed determined expressions on their faces. As I ascend the wooden stairs I hear the sounds of high-pitched voices raised in disputation.

It is a simple matter to locate Trench's chambers since it is the source of the bickering. Within, I find a gaggle of messenger boys larking, smoking foul cigars or simply lounging on wooden benches, some with their muddy boots up on stools. Pure John holds court in the centre of the room, red-faced, hands on hips. 'I have sank three bottles of porter easy as kiss my hand and have ate two ices from Gunter's and hang the expense.'

'You never did,' intones a tubby-looking boy mournfully.

'Well now, Dillon, here is proof of the pudding and of the porter,' announces Pure John, with that he emits a shockingly loud belch in the tubby one's direction.

'For shame, Pure John,' I say.

All heads turn in my direction. A tall young man in a half-cut jacket with a good sprinkling of pustules decorating his phizzog leaps to his feet at the sight of me. 'Good day, sir,' he gabbles. 'Lieutenant Trench is not presently on duty but I am his second-in-command as it were. How may I serve you?'

'Mind you do not burst a boil, Cunningham, for 'tis only Mr Samuel and not King Billy hisself.'

'My thanks, Mr Cunningham, but I do not require the services of your lads, only a moment of Pure John's time.'

Cunningham shrugs and slumps back on his stool, a mite chagrined not to have an important commission from me.

'If it is my brother and Miss Rosamund you are after they have already left, Mr Samuel, though if you are sprightly on your pegs you may snag them on St James's.'

'I will Pure John, and so I shall leave you to your edifying philosophical conversations and such.'

Pure John belches deafeningly again for the benefit of the tubby Dillon and to a smattering of applause from his associates.

Ahead of me at the corner of St James's and Jermyn Street I catch sight of two familiar figures. For a moment I am unsure that I have it right since Rosamund is wearing a plaid shawl and a green dress that I have not seen before. I find myself somewhat discomforted to note that they are walking arm in arm, Kak John toting a willow basket in his other hand. Nevertheless, I increase my pace and since they are only strolling, quickly overhaul them.

Kak John becomes aware of me first. 'Why, Mr Samuel, sir. In all this great and mighty metropolis what a stroke of fortune it is that brings you to the 'zact same street as we, at the 'zact same moment. There is a word for it I believe, though I do not right now rec'lect it.'

It is hard to find anything of the dissembler in Kak John's open, honest demeanour though I note that he has not relinquished Rosamund's arm. She gives me a brief bob of acknowledgement, a slight smile playing across her lips. I tip my hat to her like any of the great swells hereabouts.

'It is good to see you, Sammy,' she says softly.

'Though in truth it is no coincidence,' I reply, smugly brandishing the utterance that Kak John lacks.

'That is it,' exclaims Kak John, grinning, 'the very word I was reaching for, Mr Samuel. You have it in one.'

'Indeed he does,' agrees Rosamund, but by her tone I believe she is not quite pleased with my cock o' the walk treatment of him.

'It is on account of lately speaking with Lieutenant Trench at the Fortune of War,' I explain. 'Having business myself in the West End, and being informed that you was to be here to mark Kak John's birth day, had hoped to join the revels. I give you joy of the day, John.'

'Thank you kindly, Mr Samuel, though to be sure 'tis not my 'zact birthing day, since I do not know it. We had resolved some years past to reckon it today, June twenty-fourth, which being as good as any other day and better'n some, makes a respectable date for a spree should fortune allow for it. Though 'tis a pity you were not here earlier since you have missed the porter.' Kak John gives the basket a shake. From under the cloth I hear the clink of empty porter bottles.

'I had it from your brother that there were ices from Gunter's, no less.'

Rosamund gives me one of her lopsided smiles. 'It is true we made a picnic in Berkeley Square, though we were not half so grand as you believe, and dined on humble pastries that I had brought from a Vauxhall pieman. I did not eat my share and you would be most welcome to it now, Sammy.'

Kak John begins rummaging in the basket amongst the cloth-wrapped bundles. I am certain that Rosamund has not partaken since she does not care to be seen eating and will have what is in the basket for her supper. I would not deprive her of it for worlds. 'You are very kind but I have ate afore I set off.'

'I will assert as we did partake of Gunter's ices an' all, Mr Samuel,' announces Kak John proudly.

Rosamund removes her arm from his and taps him on the back of his hand in mock frustration. 'Oh, John, you have made a liar of me.'

'I should certainly hope not, Lady Rosamund, since it is the most honest truth. For you see, Mr Samuel, we set ourselves down under them plane trees in the middle of Berkeley Square like the grand Mucky-Muck hisself. We was stuffin' dainties and quaffin' and generally nanty-narkin'. Then after the porter was gone, mostly to the account of my brother I might add, we set to observin' all the nobs having their ices brought to them in their carriages. Lady Rosamund tells us to close our eyes, which we done. She asks us to choose which is our best flavour that we might like to try—I say, "Pine-apple" and Pure John says "Cherry" and so we go with cherry—then she tells us all about it, how it tastes and feels in your mouth and on your tongue, and Mr Samuel, she weaves the words like she weaves them chalks of hers; before you can help it, there's a picture in your head and you're spoonin' up the best thing you ever ate in your life. And if that weren't better than the real thing then I don't know what is. And though we could none of us never stretch to even one quarter of the cost, that is how we all had ices from Gunter's.'

'Then I can only say I envy you, John.' I do too.

'Quite right, Mr Samuel. Precious toothsome and no mistake,' affirms Kak John, smacking his lips. 'Now, since long experience with the substance has taught me that pure will not collect itself, I must return to my labours. I was intending to escort Lady Rosamund back to Vauxhall but since you are here, Mr Samuel ... ?'

'I should remind you, John, that I am no delicate bloom that must be caressed and cossetted and cannot walk a mile or two across my own city without the aid of an arm,' objects Rosamund.

'Nevertheless, I should like it above all things,' I insist.

'In that case I should be happy to oblige you,' she replies, to my great satisfaction.

Kak John hands over the basket while Rosamund lays a hand on my arm. We say our farewells and set off along St James'. I can feel the slightest pressure of her brown hand through the thick wool of my coat. It is a long-fingered hand and perfectly clean despite her work, though the fingernails have been bitten to the quicks. I am torn between my undertaking to Facey and the pleasure of having Rosamund to myself. We walk in silence until we reach the corner of King Street.

'What is it, Sammy? You are like a frog on a hot rock.'

'Forgive me, Rosamund. It is the small matter of business hereabouts. I have not yet attended to it.'

Rosamund grins. 'A poor excuse, glocky, and you will not drop me so easy as that. It is scarcely worth setting out my chalks for another hour or two, not 'til the Pleasure Gardens open and draw the evening crowds. So for the while, I find I have become a lady of leisure.'

'It is only a trifling matter and will take no more than a moment.'

'Then I shall be sure and keep a good hold on you,' she says, giving my arm a squeeze.

In a short while we find ourselves before the bright red panelled door of number seven, King Street. Door apart, it is a nondescript place with little to indicate its true purpose. But this is Mrs Leach's, London's most notorious gaming hell. There is a brass knocker fashioned like the head of a popinjay, which I use to give a series of short raps. After some minutes' delay, we hear the sound of heavy bolts being withdrawn from within.

The door is opened to reveal a tall, unshaven, handsome cove with a high forehead. Though it is somewhat before three in the afternoon, he is in a state of undress and has on a long, shabby blue velvet robe. He yawns and smiles broadly. 'Why 'tis Mr Samuel Samuel 'companied by a enchanting young lady.' He dips his head in acknowledgement of Rosamund, who returns him a short bob.

It is Charming Geordie, one of the house puffs. Unlike many such monikers, his is not ironical: everyone likes Charming Geordie, even the punters who have had a shocking bad run at cards. And ordinarily, there is no other kind at Mrs Leach's. Geordie's role is to sit at the tables, appearing to win at Hazard or the cards and to make a great show of it for the benefit of the pigeons. By puffing his successes he is able to persuade the gulls to further increase their wagers until they are well and truly fleeced.

'I have not seen you in many a month, Mr Samuel, and you are a welcome sight, to be sure, though I do not believe we have had ourselves a karker.'

By this he means a dead 'un. Facey and me have occasional business here on nights when the cowpees have overstepped: a pigeon has been plucked irredeemably close and the consequence is apoplexy or oftentimes self-murder. It is not good for the house since it discomfits the remaining punters and can draw down the unwanted attentions of the Magistrates and Crushers. On these occasions, men like Facey and me will be called in to spirit the body from the premises at all speed.

'I am not here on business of that nature, Geordie, but a dunning matter and seek a trifle of information concerning a young buck by the name of Robert Templeton. He is none of the Fancy, nor the sporting set, though by his debts is certain to have his share of vices.'

'And so he has, Mr Samuel.' Geordie rubs his stubbled chin twixt thumb and finger, screwing up his eyes as he chases down the memory. 'I recall him. 'Twould have been a touch under two years back now: a well-looking fellow, though very young; callow, boastful and somewhat reckless. A player of Faro, and just our kind of mark, to be sure. We did what plucking we could in course, but it seems he was inclined toward a more particular set—the Mollys, I should say. For a few nights we took his readies all right but then never saw him after. Should I be a betting man, which, as you well know, Mr Samuel, I am most assuredly not, I'd hazard you'll bring him to earth should you seek him amongst the Molly houses of Mayfair.'

I fumble in my pockets for the small cat-skin purse in which I have stored those coins from Facey. 'You are very good, Geordie, and will take a shilling or two for the interruption to your slumber.'

Geordie rubs his eyes. 'Well, I cannot say that I have had much of that but if that meagre purse is your only means, I should not wish to reduce it further.'

'It is, Geordie, for we have lately had a run of ill-luck, Facey and me.'

'Then you may have the wake-me-up and the recollection, gratis. It is my own dictum that no matter the night's run of luck we make every endeavour to leave a man the price of a Hackney home. I shall do no less for you.'

'I take that very kindly, Geordie,' I say, returning the little purse to the depths of my coat pocket.

'Ah, but the condition remains attached, Mr Samuel.' Geordie grins and winks at Rosamund. 'You must employ some of them shillings to pay a Hackney for the benefit of your companion. For I can see she has too much of refinement to be traipsing the streets alongside of you.'

'Indeed she has, Geordie, and I am obliged to you.'

'I too, sir,' adds Rosamund, flushing a little.

It being a nobby district on the whole, there are a good many Hacks plying for trade hereabouts and, before long, the two of us are ensconced in one of the newer two-wheeled horse cabs with the driver up behind. They are less grand but more nimble than the four-wheeled coaches and in consequence of its size, Rosamund and me are squeezed together, somewhat hugger-mugger, me with the basket on my lap. I am conscious that we are both quite rigid, determined not to bump or jostle the other as we are buffeted by the motion of the ride.

'I have your friend Geordie to thank for this rare treat. He is a good sort of man, I believe,' says Rosamund. An inconsequential comment intended, I think, to put us both at ease.

'They call him Charming Geordie, though you might not like him so well had you a few hundreds in your pockets and a hankering for the dice.'

Rosamund sighs before turning her head, giving me a telling look. 'Even good men may find themselves in questionable occupations. We must all live, I suppose.'

'And yet the acquisition of guineas is not all there is, I should say.'

'Indeed it is not, Sammy. Our position in society need not define us. It is not how we are born, nor even the end we make, but how we conduct ourselves in between that matters.'

'You would be amazed to know it, but Facey and me were schooled for a time. Under the ministrations of a gent by the name of John Pounds, a character you would have admired, I am certain, since you are of similar mind.'

'Not so amazed, Sammy, since I know you to be a deeper sort of man.'

'If there is any truth to that, then it is only to the credit of John Pounds. He was not a gent of any particular renown, more's the pity, and yet he has elevated the lives of many—Facey and me notwithstanding.'

Rosamund jabs a sharp elbow into my ribs. 'Oh pish, Sammy. You fish for another compliment, which I have no mind to bestow.'

'No, I am sincere. I believe I disappointed him greatly. As a young boy, Facey went away to sea but did not find it much to his liking and ran. On his return, we took up together again. The two of us could never resist the lure of the metropolis and, with the arrogance of youth, lacking any thought or stratagem, believed we could make great things of ourselves here. And so we quit Portsmouth with little regret and I never saw Pounds since. I hear he passed a year or so back. He well knew what had become of me though, I received a letter from him penned but a few months before he died, directed to the Feathers, which I had from Fearon. I have kept it about my person and have it still.' It is strange that I find myself telling Rosamund this, since I have never told another living soul about the letter, not even Facey.

Rosamund gently places her hand on mine. 'Might I see it, your letter?'

'I have never shown it anyone.'

Rosamund quickly withdraws her hand. 'Forgive me, I am prying.'

'No, no, I should very much like you to read it.' With that I place the basket on the floor between my feet and dig deep into one of the inner pockets of my coat for the flat leather pouch in which I keep this memento. I withdraw the precious letter and open it out with care since the folds have become somewhat fragile with wear. 'He was not a man much given to affection or sentiment and so it is curious that he should write.' I say, as I pass it to her.

'It is a good, clear hand,' remarks Rosamund on the penmanship. 'And a quality paper.' She begins to read out loud. Though I know it by heart, her fine voice and lively rhythm make the words sound a good deal better than the ones in my own head.

My dear Samuel,

Mindful as I am that you are full-grown and do not require the guidance of any man, you will forgive my presumption in bestowing these jottings upon you. Though some time has passed since you left us, it is a peculiar thing, but you have been in my thoughts a good deal lately. Perhaps because I feel the weight of years on me, I cannot help myself but to play the pedagogue one last time.

I have always known you to have the makings of a fine man. But how does a man truly measure his own worth? I know you, Samuel, and am cognizant that you will be tempted to judge yourself harshly, as you were often wont to do. Only pause for a moment, and think on this: there are many who would devote their lives entirely to the acquisition of gold, believing that in consequence, they are better men for the having of it and that the world smiles upon them. But once that gold is spent, what then? When a man parts with his gold it is lost; used up.

What I have tried to teach you is that in truth, there is another way for men to rise, and it is through the acquisition of knowledge and understanding. For knowledge is a currency that may be profitably spent each day and yet may still be owned. It might be given and shared and yet the donor will never be the poorer for it. On the contrary, he will be the richer by far; I have found this to be true every day of my life. Moreover, knowledge and understanding are the specific remedies to hate and confusion. By understanding a thing can blind hatred and oppression be vanquished. Knowledge is truly golden while understanding is the path to compassion.

But do not be like one of those cold, calculating men who know much and in consequence, believe others to be of lesser worth. Acquire knowledge and understanding of the world and also of your neighbour, not for what it may bring in worldly goods, but for its own end.

Do not be too hard on yourself when you fail, Samuel, as you will from time to time. There is no need to aspire to perfection. There is grace enough in the endeavour. Remember, in seeking knowledge we better ourselves and so rise.

Indulge an old man in his canting ways, Samuel, and know that these words are meant kindly and with all humility from

Your most affectionate servant,
John Pounds

Rosamund carefully refolds the letter. 'You are right in supposing that I would admire him. These sentiments are much in accord with my own. It is a fine letter.'

'He well knew what I had become,' I say, 'so, you see, I did not live up to his good opinion of me.'

'Nevertheless, he believed you to have potential, Sammy.'

'I do not know this word.'

'It means the makings of something, a possibility. Your desire to know its meaning is testament to the truth of it.'

CHAPTER XII

Nine Elms Lane is a low, swampy district of osier beds and mean cottages. Pollarded trees line the road: skeletal sketches against the sky, like a regiment of the dead. In the distance is the remnant of Red House Mill, sails long gone, reduced to a defiant, broken peg. In the main, the modest cottages hereabouts are home to the labouring man. But there is a neglected, vacant feeling to many, no doubt owing to the regular flooding of the river.

We pull up outside a two-storey abode, brick-built and in better repair than most. A good number of the panes have retained their glass and reflect the gentle glow of the late afternoon sun. In front there is even a tiny garden of sorts.

I step down from the Hack, extending an arm for Rosamund. But she simply hops from the bench in a billow of skirts.

I pay the driver the agreed fare taking care to add a couple of pennies, which I can ill afford, but have no wish to repeat the disagreeable episode of two nights previous in Rosamund's company. Thankfully the cabbie gives a brusque nod and whips on without comment or objection to the paucity of the tip.

'I am much obliged to you, Sammy. If you have no pressing business should you care to step inside and take some tea?'

I have no great liking for tea and would be prudent to return to the Fortune of War at all speed with my news of Robert Templeton. 'I should like it very much,' I say.

Rosamund carefully unlocks the front door. I remove my hat as I step across the threshold and the moment we enter the hallway, a side-chamber door opens a crack; an oldish, reddish head in mob cap emerges. The woman peers out at us, owlishly, through small round spectacles. 'Miss Rosamund, you have been out and about then and without your chalks?'

'I have, Mrs Buttle. I have been at a picnic party in Hanover Square, which was most edifying.'

'I am happy to hear it. You know I cannot see so well and have no notion of the time. Is it late?'

'It is not, Mrs Buttle.'

'I am not one of those to discourage company, Rosamund,' she says, appraising me.

'I know it, Mrs Buttle.'

'Unlike some, I do not frown on gentlemen callers of the right sort, I'm sure.'

'This is Mr Samuel, who has brought me safe home. I would offer him tea in my rooms, though it would not be proper. Perhaps you will stand chaperone and join us?'

'I cannot; I have bacon charring on the skillet.' She considers me carefully through her thick lenses. I run the brim of my old hat round and round through my fingers as I am scrutinized. 'Well, well, he seems respectable enough and may 'company you to your door.'

'My thanks, Mrs Buttle. I will bid you a good day.'

Mrs Buttle glares at me before reluctantly closing her door.

Rosamund takes my hand and leads me up a flight of stairs to the first floor. She produces a second key and unlocks the door to her rooms, quickly pulling me inside. The curtains are drawn and the room is dark despite the late afternoon sun outside. 'Mrs Buttle is a bulldog,' she explains, 'with a bark, to be sure, but no bite at all. She was a good to my pa and remains a dear friend to me. Near-sighted only when she desires to be. Which is to say, when I am short on the rent money, she will refuse to notice it. Or when I do have it, will perceive only half the coin, leaving the remainder. It was she who nursed my father and me through our illness. My pa, of course, could not be saved,' she says sadly, 'but I do believe my own recovery is somewhat owed to her ministrations.'

She steps away, a lucifer flares in the dark room as she lights a candle.

I gaze around, too stupefied to respond. It is only a small room, containing a stove, bed, table, washstand, a few articles of folded clothing and a box of blocky chalks. But almost every surface is covered with flowers.

Rosamund has created for herself a world of roses.

She fusses with the tiny pot-bellied stove, adding a couple of sticks to revive the embers and putting an old black kettle to boil. 'Tea. It is Bohea and there is strength in the leaves for one last brew, I hope,' she says. 'It will not take long.'

'I am a simple man, your tea would be wasted on me,' I reply, wishing to spare her precious store.

'Oh, I don't believe you are a simple man, Sammy,' she chuckles, appraising me. 'You put me in mind of my grandpa on my mother's side.'

'How so?'

'He was a soldier and fought in the Americas. I saw him only twice as a child and though terrifying to look upon, with his whiskers and tobacco smell, he was very gentle with me. I've always felt that he was a good man at heart. Children can sense these things.'

'And that is how you think of me?'

'In a way,' she smiles. 'A good man in a bad occupation. Strange is it not, that we revere our soldiery, make idols and first ministers of men whose trade is to cause the death of thousands. And yet look down on the Resurrectionist?'

'You do not wholly despise my profession then?'

'I cannot say I admire it.'

'Then what?'

'You are not the cause of a life lost but only profit from what remains. No worse than a mudlark to my way of thinking.'

'You are not aghast at the anatomist's work?'

'Why should I be? When an article of no purpose is put to use for the furtherance of knowledge then it is no bad thing. To my mind the body is not sacred of itself, being only the repository of the soul for a short while. And, as for the Day of Judgment, when some say we are to be reunited with our earthly remains, why should anyone desire such an outcome?'

'I cannot say.'

'If we have already achieved a state of perfection and are sat at the right hand of God, why then should we wish to return to our mortal vessels, once more prone to the ravages of age; of frailty and disease? No, Sammy, we set too much store in the receptacle, perhaps too little in the spirit.'

'I think it is you who are not so simple, Rosamund.'

She smiles at this. 'I'm simple-minded to desire that the world might be other than it is, that is all.'

'You wish for a world of blooms and have already begun the work,' I say, indicating the blossoms surrounding us.

'That work is long over.' Rosamund reaches for one of the blooms and holds it out for me. 'You see, Sammy, paper. Nothing more.'

I observe now that it has indeed been artfully fashioned from pink and white paper.

'It is quite beautiful.'

'At one time I thought so. I've lived amongst them so long that I scarcely notice them at all. They stand memento to what I have lost.'

'Your pa?'

Rosamund shakes her head. 'Happier times. I could make hundreds of these blooms in a day before the contagion stole the deftness from my fingers. Now they are too clumsy for such fine work and only good for clasping at my blocks of chalk.'

'I am sorry for it, Rosamund.'

'It's no matter, I've come to understand the true beauty of life. While it blossoms, we must celebrate.' She blows a little dust from the rose and replaces it on the table. 'I was insensible with the sickness when my pa succumbed. He was took by the parish with all haste for fear of further contagion, and so I do not know where they laid him. In a pauper's grave, most like. But it's of no consequence, I would not mourn the husk, for I keep the bloom of him here.' She taps her head. 'Safe in my memories.'

With that she turns abruptly to the stove where the kettle is boiling.

In a short while she brings me a delicate little cup containing a steaming, brackish brew and indicates the hard-backed chair. 'You are to sit on my chair and drink. Tea is reviving to the faculties and will help fortify you for the walk back to wherever it is you must go.'

'The Fortune of War in Smithfield, since Facey is doubtless there still,' I reply, settling myself and accepting the cup with both hands. I gasp as the heat of the vessel scalds my skin.

'What are you about, glocky? You must put a finger through the handle, else your hands will blister.'

I do as she advises, wedging my finger into the tiny space with some difficulty.

'I am no great drinker of tea. I believe I should have done better with your porter and ices,' I say.

'Oh, to be sure, you missed a rare treat, Sammy. Those ices were quite delicious, though I shouldn't be the one to say so. Nevertheless, I believe I have a way to make it up to you.'

'How so?'

'Why, there is a travelling fair at Clapham Common. Tomorrow being Sunday, I should not object to your company, if you've a mind to it.'

'I have always loved the fair,' I say, lying through my teeth.

Rosamund smiles. 'Now, you must turn your face away whilst I put on my old gown. The Pleasure Gardens open shortly and, after a day of leisure I must exercise my chalks for the evening strollers if I am not for the poor house.'

I sip gingerly at the tea, which, as I suspected, is an insipid, bitter concoction, like hot marsh water. I should much prefer a bottle of porter but there are only empty bottles in the basket. Besides, I must keep my eyes fixed firmly on the cup for fear of them straying towards the sound of rustling garments.

'There,' she says after a while, 'all done.' She is back to the frayed brown gown, which she wears for her work on the streets.

I get to my feet and take a final mouthful of the foul tea to avoid giving offence. The tiny handle however, remains attached round my finger and will not come away.

'I see you have been apprehended by my cup then.' She laughs, for once revealing her teeth, which are only a tad chipped in the front and, to my mind, none the worse for it.

'My fingers are too big and clumsy for the handling of delicate stuff,' I say.

She takes my hand and guides me to the window, where a pan sits on the sill. There is a coating of lard around the edge, which she uses to grease my trapped finger, carefully releasing it without further catastrophe. Smiling, she keeps a hold of my fingers. I attempt to pull away, for I do not wish her to see my black, broken fingernails and callused palms. 'You've fine, gentle hands, Sammy; I've always thought so, though they could use a scrub.'

She releases me and turns abruptly, presenting her back to me. 'Perhaps you will now put those hands to work and hook me together.'

I have no idea what this means and stand like a dumpling until I notice her gown is still a little way open at the back, a row of tiny hooks set to one side. I flex my fingers for the task but the sight of her bare shoulders gives me pause. Ordinarily concealed by her shawl, I have never seen them before. But now in the moonlight the skin there gleams, white and perfectly unblemished. An inkling of what she once was. For the length of a heartbeat, Rosamund is utterly motionless, intensely aware of what I have observed.

Without a word I set to the task and am quickly done. Rosamund turns to face me, moving closer she reaches out and, with the back of her hand, softly touches my face. 'I think, glocky, you are not so clumsy as all that.' With that she picks up her old shawl and throws it round her shoulders.

CHAPTER XIII

I accompany Rosamund to her evening patch outside the Pleasure Gardens, parting at New Bridge Street where Rosamund gives me that strange half smile of hers and briefly brushes my hand with her fingertips. "Til tomorrow then, glocky.'

It is a considerable distance to Smithfield but I cannot stretch to the price of another Hack if I am to conserve what tin remains for tomorrow. Nevertheless, I am in excellent spirits as I cross the river at Vauxhall Bridge: it seems that Rosamund does not entirely despise my company and, indeed, rates me a man of potential.

❧

It is black as pitch by the time I catch the glint of the Golden Boy on Pie Corner; I navigate the remaining yards guided by the flickering glare of twin gas beacons set above the entrance.

The Fortune of War is packed to the gunwales with the usual assortment of rogues and brutish trulls, but a curious air has infused the place since I was earlier here, a kind of fevered eagerness, which pervades all. Flushed, grinning faces leer at me as I shoulder my way through the crowd. There is little sign of the usual steady drinking. Tonight, all here seem determined to swill as much as they are able in as short a time as possible.

Bishop's bleary face looms out at me from the crush, porter leaking from his blackened gob. 'Why, Mr Samuel, you have timed your appearance to perfection for a swell is amongst us and has been standing drinks for all.' He upends his mug, tipping a good deal of the contents down his chin. ''Tis Liberty Hall tonight. Come, I'll claim another fill, and one for you an' all.'

I grip his sleeve urgently. 'Have you seen Mr Facey?'

'Not since one or two hours, I reckon. Him having passed a most agreeable afternoon in company with Lieutenant Trench along with a bottle or two. Misfortunately, they left together a while ago and have missed the spree.'

'Where, Bishop, where did they go?'

'Alas, Mr Facey don't see fit to include me in his plans,' replies Bishop, swaying a little. He draws me closer, clasping both of my arms as though about to impart some confidence. ''Tween you and me, I don't believe your Mr Facey cares for me overmuch.'

'Do not be dismayed by it, Bishop, he does not care for anyone overmuch.'

'I am in the selfsame trade and only desire a morsel of respect from a man I admire greatly. Is it too much to ask, Mr Samuel? Is it, sir?' His voice cracks, I do believe Bishop is about to pipe his eye and so disentangle myself in short order.

'You must not let me keep you from your ration, Bishop.'

'I'll not, Mr Samuel, and next will take a two-penneth of Geneva to keep the London air from my bones. You're certain you'll have naught?'

'I am.'

I turn to leave when Bishop says, 'And you'll be sure to inform Mr Facey of our achievements when Tom Williams and me prevail in this most valuable commission?'

'What commission?'

'Why the open-handed swell has made it known that he'll stump thirty gold sovs for a dead-'un.'

'He is an anatomical gent then?'

'Who can say? Though 'tis not any old corpse, but a most particular one, else we should all be out at the churchyards even now, excavatin' for our great grandmamas.'

'What corpse, in particular?' I ask, already knowing the answer.

''Tis some oddity of interest to philosophic coves. Called a "her-oddity", having both cock and cunny to boot. But never despair, Mr Samuel, Tom Williams and me'll secure it and mayhap you'll see this marvel afore we turn it over for the bounty.'

'I am more curious to see the kind of gent who will pay thirty sovs for a corpse, howsoever particular. Will you show him to me, Bishop?'

'Certainly, though he ain't so very hard to clock, being as he is a proper gent and a rather a longish cove with a stink of lavender flowers about him. You'll find him alongside Ricketts, clasping a open purse, I hope.'

We are interrupted by a series of sharp, insistent raps from the region of the counter. I follow Bishop as he lurches ahead, barging his way through the throng. Slowly the revellers begin to hush for the speechifying. 'Well, well, gentlemen and ladies, and so I will bid you goodnight,' announces a strong baritone voice in clipped tones. 'And you will drink my health in these remaining shillings.'

He is familiar to me and, at first, I endeavour to place him amongst the wealthy young dabblers in anatomy we have serviced in the past. With a start of recognition I realize that it is the tall young swell from Molly's crib. He now stands with Ricketts as the patrons give him a raucous cheer, raising tankards, bottles and mugs. I doubt he recognizes me but, having no desire to reacquaint myself, lower my head as he gazes about him with a complacent air.

I note that Teeth and Mutton are still present and appear markedly sober, holding themselves apart from the revels. I sense Teeth's lofty scrutiny and momentarily meet his eye. He turns swiftly without acknowledgement and, as the young man leaves, he and Mutton follow close behind, doubtless eager to press their suit as the only crew worthy of this commission. I do not care overmuch, my only pressing concern being the discovery of Facey.

Bishop grips my coat. 'Mr Samuel, should you and Mr Facey be going after the her-oddity, seeing as how famous it will be for the victorious crew?'

'I do not think so, Bishop,' I reply.

''Tis a freak and a most prodigious creature, I have heard.'

'Then I wish you joy of it.'

Bishop grins blackly and taps his nose. ''Tis not a simple matter, Mr Samuel. By all accounts the corpse was not even properly buried afore it was spirited away, no doubt to confound the anatomical gentlemen; its whereabouts are unknown, though I have my suspicions. What is your opinion?' he asks with a sly, knowing look.

'I do not care to hazard,' I shrug, 'for in any event Facey and me have other fish to fry.'

Bishop grins before upending his tankard and, finding it empty, examines the interior with a perplexed expression. 'Now, Mr Samuel, I believe I should take another fill while the porter yet flows from Liberty Hall. And you will let Mr Facey know that I was the one to give you this news?'

'I will, Bishop, though, as I have said, this commission is not for us.'

He leers, a great murky chasm, and taps his nose once again before I turn and shove my way back through the mob. I reach the doors without further incident and make my way out onto the street. Standing kerbside, instantly immersed in the surrounding darkness, it takes me a moment or two to secure my bearings before I step out.

I notice a hefty, weather-beaten, bristle-faced cove in a triple-caped Garrick lounging against the wall a few yards away. He appears to take no particular interest in me and so I give him a wary nod as I bustle past. Of a sudden, I feel a great meaty arm encompass my neck from behind, squeezing on my throat. A rough, gravelly voice rumbles in my ear. 'Calm yourself, sir. I am no footpad. All I ask is a little compliance and you will avoid a grave coshing.'

A thrill of terror courses through me. Like a fool I dallied, knowing full well we ought to have quit the metropolis when we had the chance. No doubt we have been peached and I shall not survive another meeting with Pimlott and Chuffington. I feel the arm relax for a moment and instantly twist away but he is shocking quick, his great mitt snakes out again and grips me by the throat almost lifting me off the ground. With his other hand he raises a small leather sandbag. To my relief he does not strike.

'Now, Mr Samuel,' he rumbles, 'I prefer you do not make a quarrel with me since you seem to me a decent enough cove.' He jerks his head, indicating the shadowy outline of a vehicle on the far side of the road. 'Besides, I should only beg a moment of your time.'

Since Facey is not with me, there is nothing for it and so I allow myself to be marched across the road, the brute's giant mitt clamped firmly round the back of my neck.

As we close on the carriage, I perceive that it is one of those roomy vehicles of the style known as a Berlin and painted a dark shade of blue, all but blending with the gloaming. Given the cut of his coat, I take my escort to be the jarvey.

The door opens and a set of fold-out steps are released from within by an unseen hand. I clamber up into the shadowy compartment, propelled sharply on my way by a swift shove from the jarvey and find myself caught in a tangle of knees and feet. One of the occupants lashes out with his boot, catching me a good dunt in the face. Eyes watering, I stagger backwards, slumping to the bench as the door is slammed to.

I have already caught the powerful fragrance of lavender and so, despite the pain, am marvellously relieved to find it to be the tall young gent on the bench facing me. It is one of his elegantly burnished Hessians, which has just connected with my nose.

I feel the blood beginning to trickle from my nostrils but am reluctant to treat it, or indeed make any move at all. It is not the young man who has put the fear of God into me, nor his companion—the sharp-faced toad eater we clocked at Molly's crib—but the monstrous wolfhound perched on the bench beside him. The beast growls, low and threatening, never once taking its eyes from me, which are the selfsame piercing, icy-blue as its owner's.

'Steady Brus,' orders the young swell, smiling. 'The sight and scent of your claret has him excited, I fear. You are quite right to keep so still, for if he decides to have at you, I would not give much for your chances.'

'I shall do nothing to antagonize him, I assure you, sir.'

'Excellent, then we shall enjoy a fine, productive interview. Am I correct in thinking you to be Mr Samuel Samuel?'

'I am, sir.'

'The most curious names you people go by. What is that? A drunken father stuttering at the font?'

'I was never baptized, sir, but called Samuel Samuel after my pa, since it was the first and only name my ma knew him by.'

The young swell chuckles, 'Did you hear that, Phillip?'

Phillip lounges back on the bench beside me, a sulky pout on his dial. 'I could scarcely fail to, Harry, since the creature speaks quite tolerable English.'

'Indeed he does, Phillip. You have some learning then, Mr Samuel Samuel?'

'I have, sir, I can tally and know my letters, which stands me as well as any man, I hope.'

'There, you see it, Phillip?' the young gent's expression twists into an angry sneer. 'A little learning and this wretched double-bastard believes himself to be the equal of any man. Well, sir, it will not do. For men of your station learning only imparts a corroded sense of self and a disdain for the natural order and will most likely see you hanged. No, sir. A man's standing may be judged on blood, breeding and property alone. Why, even my hound, Cerberus, possesses two of those advantages. Two more than you, which being so you will address him as "sir", since he is your superior in every respect.'

'Yes, sir,' I reply, still exceedingly wary of the well-bred beast, which has begun to slaver all over the upholstered seat.

'Firstly, I am Henry Liston, and that gentleman seated next to you is Phillip Trubshaw.'

I nod twice by way of acknowledgement.

He pauses, giving me a searching look. 'I have seen you before, have I not?'

'I do not believe so, sir.'

'Ah, but I have. I do not forget a face so easily, even one so smeared with filth and hog-bristle. Wait, I have it. Matheson's pit. You are partner to the impudent Cyclops brute.'

'My associate has an injury to his glim,' I concede, unwilling to let the man to think me an ignoramus.

'That would be Mr Facey then, I take it?'

I nod warily, careful not to startle the quivering hound.

'And what was your business with Matheson?'

'No great thing, the matter of a trifling sum owed to us,' I lie.

Liston considers this for a moment. 'You and many others, I daresay. Well, you may put it down to experience and close that account, eh, Phillip?'

Trubshaw chuckles throatily by way of reply.

'How so?'

'Matheson has had his last pipeful. He is expired from the smoke. And good riddance to him,' snarls Liston.

'Then doubtless the Chink-ball you pressed on him was the finisher,' I reply without thinking.

The carriage is silent but for the regular panting of the hound.

Liston narrows his eyes dangerously. 'Have a care, Mr Samuel. You must know I am well protected from reckless accusations by the laws of slander for one, and for another, there is Brus.'

Hearing its name, the hound's ears twitch; baring its teeth, it lurches at me. Liston hauls it back, patting the wiry head affectionately. 'Even should you, a filthy, degraded stump of a man, stand before a Justice and say your piece, how would you be regarded? Should I give my friend Phillip here the gift of a horse and it kick him to death in the stalls, would I be held to account for it? No. Matheson died by his own hand and indeed, the world is no worse a place for it.'

'Harry, I grow tired and this…' Trubshaw waves a petulant hand at me, '…this creature reeks prodigiously and is precious vexing.'

'You are in the right of it, sir,' I say, 'I take back my ill-advised words and you will never hear them again from me.'

Liston smiles. 'And you will apologise to Cerberus, who you have also offended.'

'I'm right sorry, Brus.'

The smile instantly disappears; the blue eyes flare with a cold anger. 'I have told you, my hound is your better in all respects and you will address him as such.'

'I apologise, sir,' I say to the hound, bobbing my head for good measure. Curiously, Cerberus settles at this, easing its awful growling.

'Good. You are commonly amalgamated in your trade with this Facey?'

'He is my partner of many years, sir.'

'And where is your Facey at this time?'

'I do not know, sir. I am come to seek him out.'

The young man shrugs, idly fondling his wolfhound's ear. 'No matter. I have heard it said that you pair are amongst the most proficient in London at the lifting of a corpse and I am here with a particular commission for you.'

'Then you have been misinformed, sir, for we are honest bakers, nothing more. I do not understand why you have chosen to single me out, nor how you came by my name.'

'Do not take me for a flat, Samuel. Honest bakers do not frequent such houses as the Fortune of War. And, in return for a modest emolument, it is your own associates who have named you. You should thank them, for it is, I suppose, a recommendation of sorts.'

'Well, sir, you may think what you will but I cannot help you unless it is a good crusty pie that you require.'

'Look at him, Phillip, ain't he priceless? He twists and turns like a damned weasel when I am intent on doing him a service.'

'Lay out your proposal, Harry, and be done with it. It will take an age to Glendale and I am sharp set.'

'Well, Samuel,' Liston turns his cold blue eyes on me once again, 'somewhere in this metropolis is a cadaver, only recently passed. A young man of seventeen years, slight of build, being called a hermaphrodite. You have heard of such a thing?'

'I have, sir.'

'Have you indeed?' Liston appraises me shrewdly.

'I have had the news only now from one John Bishop.'

'So you are aware that I offer a bounty of thirty sovereigns for this object?'

'I am, sir.'

'And why then should an honest baker concern himself with such information, I wonder?'

I curse myself for my foolish tongue; before I can come upon a plausible answer, Liston raises his hand. 'No matter, Samuel, you may present yourself as butcher, baker or candlestick maker for all I care. What you may not know is that this corpse was removed from its lawful resting place some two or three nights previous. Perhaps you or your associate have heard something of this?'

'Not a whit, sir.'

'I should like to see it given a Christian burial and so have no wish for it to fall into the hands of any other man but mine. Is that clear? I must have it, one way or t'other. When they have swilled their way through the last of my shillings, every resurrectionist and rogue in London will be on the scent and since you come so highly recommended, I desire that you and your associate will do your part. Should you succeed you will come to me most discreetly at Glendale in Poland Street where you will receive thirty sovs on the nail, and not a question asked. Now, what do you say, Mr Samuel?'

'By all means, we will endeavour to keep an ear to the ground but tonight there are the crusts to prepare for the—'

Liston sighs heavily. 'Secure him, Phillip,' he orders.

With that, Trubshaw throws his arm across my windpipe, choking me, at the same time wrenching my right arm up behind my back.

'You persist in making a game of me, Samuel. Thirty sovs is carrot enough for any man but you, it seems. Since you will not run for the carrot I must employ the stick.'

Trubshaw rams my arm higher up my back, almost to the point of dislocation, causing me to yelp with agony.

'Twist him, Phillip, twist him,' Liston hisses, eyes gleaming with excitement. Trubshaw lays on with a will, increasing the pressure on my arm and shoulder socket. The pain is unbearable; I swear I can almost feel the gristle tearing.

Liston reaches into his pocket for something before leaning towards me. With one swift lunge he catches hold of my ear. Cerberus has sprung upright, now standing on the bench, snarling and quivering. Pain aside, I'm in mortal terror that the beast will lose all control and launch itself at me.

'Steady, Brus,' snaps Liston, 'down, boy.' To my relief the monster drops, settling back on its haunches, though grumbling still.

Liston savagely screws the loose flesh at the base of my ear, adding a further layer of pain. There is a flash of something bright, a snick and my ear is released.

Trubshaw relaxes his grip and there is nothing for a moment until a sudden searing pain lances my ear. As I blink back tears, I see that Liston holds a razor in one hand, in the other, the gobbet of bloody flesh that was a portion of my earlobe.

I feel the blood cascade across my jaw and down my neck and Liston smiles at the sight of me. 'An ear to the ground, is it, Samuel? You will have to do better than that, I think.'

With that he turns to his hound, tossing my living flesh like a table scrap. With a flick of its head the beast snaps it from the air and it is gone.

'There, he has had the meat of you yet and will be eager for more. Perhaps you will see now that I am in deadly earnest.'

Having tasted my substance the hound eyes me fixedly with the same cold blue gaze as his master; I cannot say which is the more predatory.

'I will do as you ask, sir. Should you allow me to leave now and collect my partner, if it is in my power, you shall have your cadaver.'

'You see, Phillip, should you desire compliance from these creatures, it ain't any use coddlin' 'em. You must thrash 'em; beat the obstinacy out of them. The stick's the only thing they apprehend.'

'I had already thought it so, Harry. And thirty sovs is a deuced amount of coddlin' too. I would have said half the sum too rich since they would only fritter it on whores and drinking themselves insensible, the animals. And now that you have your tame corpse-stalker, may we go? I cannot bear the sight nor stink of him longer. And if I ain't to have a bite and a bottle soon, I swear I shall quite expire.'

'Very well, Samuel Samuel,' announces Liston, flinging open the door. 'You may go about your business, though when next we meet, you would be wise not to appear empty-handed.'

As I rise from the bench I rummage in my pockets for a fogle, which I put to my leaking ear. I have already set my foot on the carriage step when Liston places a hand on my shoulder.

'But you have not thanked Cerberus,' he says, 'for the service he has rendered in disposal of your scrap. Had your gore befouled the floor of my carriage I would have made you eat it yourself.'

To my shame, I whisper, 'Thank you kindly, sir,' with a deferential nod to his hellhound.

CHAPTER XIV

Oxford Street remains busy on a Saturday night with many of the street traders still touting for business. Gas lighting illuminates young bucks and respectable couples mingled together with beggars, dippers and buttoners along with the usual sprinkling of cyprians and loafers. Not one of them spares me a second glance despite the sheet of claret decorating my jaw and neck from the recent wound. Church clocks begin to strike the hour of nine when I turn south off the great thoroughfare and down Poland.

Odd though it may seem, I feel fortunate to have been plucked by this Liston: the scare has served to remind me of the danger we are in. Consequently the most pressing matter tonight is that of Facey's whereabouts, which is what brings me to this vicinity of the Coach and Horses. For the moment, it is the most likely sanctuary, being a place we might lie low for a night or two, and one which we are not known to frequent.

A brisk walk along Great Marlborough Street and I am in through the doors of Tom's establishment where I am greeted by the friendly fug of good tobacco smoke combined with the soft, rich fumes of spirituous liquors. It is well attended tonight, though unlike the Fortune, Tom's patrons are more or less sober and respectable: merchants mostly, and the better class of tradesmen with their heads together or in the newssheets, a bracer of good port wine or brandy at their elbows.

There is no connection here to Pimlott and Chuffington's affairs and so my presence arouses little curiosity from the benches other than the odd raised eyebrow at the state of me. I keep the old fogle clamped to my ear, serving to staunch the blood and masking the worst of my gory appearance. At the counter though, it is a different matter: the young can, Ned, acknowledges me with a sly wink, followed by a frenzied tapping at his long, sharp razzo and many a curious grimace. He casts a thumb up at the ceiling and places a finger to his lips with a meaningful stare.

I am in no mood for dumb show and so cut short this vexing performance. 'Is your master at home?' I enquire.

'Certainly, sir,' hisses Ned. 'He is above.'

'Is it a state secret then that Tom Canon is present in his own house?'

'No, sir,' he whispers, 'but I have been sworn to silence over the whereabouts of the one-eyed gent who is most certainly absent should anyone come enquirin' but yourself,' with that he folds his arms and winks again, looking mighty pleased with himself.

'Am I to take it then that the one-eyed gent is within?'

'I did not say such a thing, but you may take yourself to the spare chamber on the upper floor.' He winks again before bellowing for the benefit of all: 'And you will find neither hide nor hair of a one-eyed gent. Not in this house.'

Before this muttonhead can alert the entire parish I quit the public rooms and swiftly make my way to the modest staircase leading up to the private portions of the house.

It is but one short flight to Tom's domain on the upper floor. The first door to the right is that which leads to the spare bedchamber, and so I give a short rap before entering.

For an instant I rejoice to see Facey in just his shirt, sprawled and muttering on the bed. Tom Canon sits at the bedside but my happiness is short-lived when I catch sight of his grim countenance. Frowning somewhat at my appearance, he beckons me over with a gesture.

Tom occupies the only chair so I set myself down gently at the end of the bed, careful not to disturb Facey, who though insensible, is evidently in some distress, groaning, perspiring and breathing heavily. A fresh bandage covers his eye, but already there is a darkish spot beginning to stain the linen.

'What has occurred, Tom?'

Tom sighs. 'It is as you find, Sammy. Your partner has been brought low by a grave malady of the flesh.'

'What ails him?'

''Tis the glim, some contagion has set in. I have ministered to it this past hour, salving, applying poultices and brown paper but the corruption is far beyond my meagre skills, which being only good for fresh cuts and contusions of the ring. Young Facey's wound has been allowed to fester and mortify; I believe that the poison has brung on a fever.'

I reach out my hand to touch Facey's damp forehead. Sure enough, his flesh is damp and burning hot to the touch.

Tom indicates the empty bottles of Pancurial scattered about the floor. 'Those Specifics were about his pockets and since they had the effect of relieving the pain, I have let him drink them off. I believe them to be opiates of some kind.'

'You have done right by him, Tom. We have ever been fortunate to count you friend. But how is it that Facey came to be in your care?'

'You do not know?'

'I do not.'

'He was brung here earlier this evening with some difficulty by a companion, a naval sort of fellow.'

'Lieutenant Trench?'

'Aye, the very one: a decent, competent sort of cove for all his stiff-necked airs. He has dispatched runners to all the houses you are known to frequent; to deliver a warning, Sammy. It seems you are in some danger.'

'I had reasoned as much, Tom. I believe we must flee the metropolis, for a while at least.'

Tom shakes his head. 'It cannot be done soon, Sammy. Facey will not be moved, surely you see that? Even in these favourable conditions his recovery is by no means a certainty.'

'I see it plain, Tom,' I say, lost for a counter argument.

'Listen, Sammy, you are safe whilst under my roof, and may remain so for as long as needs be. The entire of London may wish you to the devil but will have to pass me first; though the mauleys are not what they once were, my old right hook is still due a sensible portion of respect.'

'I am grateful for it, Tom.'

'Now lad, what of yourself? How is it you come in off the streets like an old mutt with half an ear gone?'

'Hard to credit, but 'twas a toff, Tom. Took a razor's edge to it and fed it to his dog. It is but a trifle though and only worse to look at on account of the gore.'

Tom shakes his head sadly. 'What a world we live in. Airs n' graces, fine manners and a bit of blunt ain't what make the man, Sammy. Some of the truest gentlemen I ever knew were to be found at the scratch. At any rate, let's wash and salve the wound and you'll be right as rain in a day or two. Though should the pair of you remain here much longer I shall be forced to hire a nursemaid.'

I remove my old coat and submit to Tom's ministrations. The items he has used on Facey sit atop the small bedside chest. There is a bowl of clear water and rags along with a quantity of brown paper and a small jar of ointment. Tom dips one of the rags and scrubs away the dried claret on my face and neck. As he dabs at my ear I can feel that the wound is setting to bleed again.

Tom gently salves it with a thick dollop of ointment causing me to gasp at the sting. 'Smarts, don't it?' says Tom. 'Never mind that. Best thing for a gusher, as most face wounds tend to be. 'Tis a concoction from my pugilistic days and has never failed to stop up the claret.' With that, Tom tears off a small strip of the brown paper and slaps it over the wound.

As though aware of my pain Facey suddenly cries out and begins to thrash, flinging aside the bed linen. 'Handsomely now, handsomely, you great baboon. Over the side with him,' he roars in his delirium.

Tom grips his shoulder and gently presses him to the mattress. Facey kicks out with his legs. 'He must lay still, Sammy. Secure his limbs,' orders Tom.

I take a hold of Facey's ankles but restraint only drives him to further exertions. His one good eye flicks open, gleaming with a terrible purpose; the delirious bellowing increases in volume as he attempts to raise himself. 'Bobbies is it now? Primped up watchmen, more like. Peelers, you say? Come, and I will peel you like a basket of fucken oranges.'

Tom now presses on my partner's shoulders with all his power and weight as I lie across Facey's legs. Although in a much weakened condition, and quite out of his wits, Facey is still a formidable adversary. But ever so slowly I begin to feel the strength ebbing from him and, with a heartbreaking groan, he finally submits. 'I will see you all in hell first,' he mutters, sinking back onto the mattress, fresh blood, sweat and stinking brown matter oozing out from under the bandage.

Tom releases his hold. 'I believe he approaches a crisis, Sammy. These opiates are finished and I have naught but brandy to administer. I do not say this lightly, but the glim is in any case destroyed and to my way of thinking a medical man would most likely choose to remove the article if his life is to be saved.'

'That choice was offered, Tom, a day since. But he would not have it at any price.'

'The price now, I believe, is his life. We are beyond Facey's objections, Sammy. You are his partner and bosom friend; it is for you to make the decision.'

'I must think, Tom,' I say. 'Is there no hope of recovery else?'

'How can I know, Sammy? I cannot give you any such assurance.'

I find myself twisting a corner of the damp bed sheet while Tom eyes me intently. I am caught, frozen by the fear of either outcome until I realize that with my silence I have inadvertently made a choice. It is the coward's way: to do nothing.

'Courage, Sammy,' says Tom softly.

I try to control my breath, exhaling slowly before I say the words, when there is a gentle knock on the door.

Tom tenses. 'Who is there?'

'Lieutenant Trench,' answers a voice from without.

'Come in, Lieutenant.'

The man enters, removing his Chimney Pot, accompanied by Pure John. Trench ministers a sharp dig to the youngster's back whereupon the boy remembers to take off his own battered cap.

'Bugger me, sir, here is Mr Samuel large as life, who is not ever to be found where he is 'spected to be,' announces Pure John with some irritation.

'Whisht, Pure John, have some respect now,' says Trench, advancing to the bed. 'Now then, Mr Samuel, I am relieved to see you here, though I regret the circumstances of it.'

I rise to take his outstretched hand. 'Well met, Lieutenant. It seems I am obliged to you for your consideration of Mr Facey.'

'It is what any man would have done, Mr Samuel.' Trench nods before extending his hand to Tom. 'Mr Canon,' he says, 'how does he fare?'

'Ever worse, Trench,' replies Tom with a meaningful glance at me.

I smile at Pure John who inches closer to the bed. 'And Pure John, how do you do this evening?'

'There is a precious thick head on me, obliged to you for asking. And is there brandy in them bottles for I should feel a deal better once I have taken a little hair from the dog what has bit me?'

'You have duties still, my boy, meegrims or no,' chides Trench gently before turning to me.

'Lieutenant Trench. You have already done us a great service and now I must beg another.'

'Name it, Mr Samuel.'

I glance back at Tom who watches over Facey like a mother hen. 'I should like to send for a fellow of some experience in these matters. I believe he may still be summoned at this hour,' I say. 'The gentleman in question is known as Nero, and has a mastery of chirurgery.'

Trench nods. 'You are convinced a procedure is required then?'

'I do not know for a certainty, but must abide by the opinions of a man of learning.'

'Quite right, Mr Samuel.' Trench turns to address Pure John who is now investigating the empty bottles surrounding the bed for heeltaps. 'Belay that fossicking, Pure John, here is an urgent commission for you.'

Pure John reluctantly relinquishes his task, fixing his bright eyes on me. 'Well, Mr Samuel, do not trouble yourself that I have already worn myself to a nubbin this evening, chasing you half across Shoreditch and the Spitalfields with a canister full of rags an' feathers and all to no account.'

'I am sorry for it, Pure John. Be assured, there will be a reviver for you on your return.'

'Before I depart, for my druthers.'

'You will attend to the matter in hand, Pure John. There may be a life in the balance here,' warns Trench.

'As you say, sir,' concedes the boy, looking down at his boots.

'Then you will fetch Nero at all speed.'

'I will, sir.'

Tom produces a gold half-sovereign, handing it to Pure John. 'You will show him this but do not give it him. You may inform him that it shall be his when his business here is at an end.'

'Consider it done, sir,' replies Pure John, slipping the coin into his shoe.

'Well then, Pure John, off with you. Run like the wind.'

'I will, Mr Samuel.'

'There is not a moment to be lost.'

'Indeed not, Mr Samuel.'

'What do you still do here, Pure John?'

Pure John gives me a sideways look. 'You will perhaps let me know where your gent is to be found. It is a small matter, I know, but 'less you wish me to scour the entire of London for this Neery cove, it may speed my purpose some to have a destination in mind afore I set off.'

Trench cuffs him across the back of his head before addressing Tom and me: 'You will forgive him, sirs, for his saucy tongue. No doubt it will see him hanged one of these days.'

'The fault is mine,' I say, 'I am all at sixes and sevens here. Nero keeps a booth on Oxford Street less than a quarter mile from here. His name is writ large on the signboard for all to see.'

'Oh,' sighs Pure John, once again eyeing his boots. 'Only, I ain't so handy with my letters, Mr Samuel.'

'There is no shame in that, Pure John; you will find hawkers aplenty thereabouts who know him.'

'Then I will be back afore you can say knife,' he grins, the smile disappearing almost as quickly as it arrived. 'Ah, bollix, I did not mean to—'

'Never fret, if 'tis the knife he must face then so be it, though 'tis more like to be a spoon,' I mutter.

'Then I am away, Mr Samuel.' With that, he is off like a tiny comet, leaving us with the sound of his running feet clattering down the wooden staircase.

Tom slowly hauls himself from his seat. 'Now then, you will stay for some refreshment, Lieutenant?'

'I will, sir. Much obliged.'

'I will send up hot shrub, leaving you, for the moment, to discuss your affairs.'

'My thanks,' I say, as he heads for the door. Tom is unusually heavy on his feet and I perceive lines of fatigue etched into his face. He is not so young as he once was and I am certain that he has been without rest since Facey was brought here. 'For all you have done, Tom.'

He stops for a moment and turns to face me. There is grief there too. 'He was like a son to me, Sammy. You will have courage when the time comes? You will do whatever is called for?'

'I will, Tom.'

He gently shuts the door behind him.

Facey moans softly.

I take my place at the corner of Facey's mattress, leaving Tom's chair free for Trench. He sets himself down, though remaining stiff-backed, rigidly perched on the edge of the seat. 'A good sort, your Tom Canon,' he observes.

'He is a true friend, Lieutenant Trench. Just as I have discovered others of similar high character and integrity amongst our acquaintance.'

'It is often when you face a lee shore with the wind against you that a man's true nature reveals itself.'

'Well, sir, I hope you will count yourself not least amongst that number.'

'I'm obliged, Mr Samuel. Once your Mister Facey and me had settled a trivial misunderstanding with regard to my naval service, we passed a most pleasant afternoon over a few bottles. He is somewhat like a oyster, I find: a man of estimable qualities for all his hard shell.'

'Very like,' I nod.

'Though not all your associates would agree. I take it, Mr Samuel, that you have been informed as to the danger you are in?'

'I have not, though I have a sensible notion as to its cause.'

'I do not have the specifics, Mr Samuel, but will tell you all I know. It would have been somewhere about two bells into the First Dog Watch, that is to say the later part of the afternoon; we had already seen off a good few bottles in the Fortune when a curious old tabby hove to, insistent on speaking privately with Mr Facey. Though attired for a funeral, she was somewhat dishevelled and trembling like a half-drowned rat. I reckoned her already three sheets to the wind but the woman could not be brought to converse like a Christian until she had drank off an entire bumper of Geneva.'

'Mrs Pigeon,' I sigh.

'I did not catch a name, though your Mr Facey seemed to know her well enough. Forgive me if I intrude on a private matter but from what little I overheard it seems you are urgently sought.'

'And it will not be to our advantage, I make no doubt.'

'I should say not, Mr Samuel. There were signs and frantic gestures from which I was able to take the urgency of her meaning right enough.' Trench runs the flat of his hand across his throat. 'Unmistakable in any language.'

'And what of Mr Facey, how did he take it?'

'Well, sir, we was both by then a trifle swipey to be sure, but your man Facey was the worst by far. At least that's what I reckoned. There was a rage on him at the news but it soon became clear that it was more than just the grog at work, him being by now on the verge of a delirium, white-faced and sweating, his one good eye rolling about in his head like a dismounted gun on deck. I reckoned it might be best to get him gone from that place, quick smart. Mr Facey would be safe enough in my rooms for the night, but he would not hear of it. Nothing but Tom Canon's Coach and Horses would do for him. Since he was raving and is a man of considerable power and will, I conveyed him here with some difficulty, though grateful for the dusk, which served to mask our passage across town.'

'You could not have done him a better service, Lieutenant Trench. Our connection with Tom is an ancient one and unknown to most. For the moment, there is nowhere safer.'

'You should also know that in the pauses between delirium Mr Facey's prime concern was for your safety, insistent that I return to my place of business and dispatch messengers to your most likely haunts and induce you here at all speed.'

Facey moans softly, tossing his head from side to side.

There is a brief silence and I take the opportunity to collect my thoughts. It is probable that Pimlott and Chuffington have somehow twigged to the truth of our unfortunate hoist and we must quit London the moment Facey is hale. The difficulty is that we have so little tin to speak of. Our stake in the Rig is utterly lost, while Brookes' commission has become a stale line, moreover, half the crews in London are now on that trail. All that remains is the Templeton business and that is only half done.

'Lieutenant Trench, our purses are light enough, to be sure, but might I offer you some compensation for your labours?'

Trench bristles, rocking backwards on his chair as though I had just struck him. 'You mistake me, Mr Samuel, if you think I would share a bottle with a man and call him friend only to top it the mercenary after serving him a half-decent turn.'

'Forgive me, it is only that that you have, this night, been put to some trouble and expense, dispatching runners to all parts on my behalf.'

'Well, Mr Samuel, though he is a scalawag, there is one amongst my small crew who would never have let the matter rest until you were accounted for. He has some affection for you, sir, the more so, since he exhibits such a very low opinion on the rest of us.'

'Pure John,' I smile.

'The very one. I should say that he is most put out that his service was not after all required. And now, Mr Samuel, if all is in order I shall—'

Trench is interrupted by Tom's reappearance at the door bearing a steaming pitcher and glasses. 'Here is fortification for the trials ahead. Lieutenant Trench, you will stay for the proceedings, I hope? I reckon it will take our combined efforts to see it through.'

'In that case, I will, Mr Canon. I have some experience in matters of the orlop from my service days.'

'Good man.' Tom pours the steaming shrub into the tumblers and passes them round. 'I should take it kinder, Lieutenant, were you to call me Tom, since we are to be comrades in arms.'

'Thank 'ee, Tom,' replies Trench, raising his glass.

'Likewise, it is Sammy, if you please,' I add.

'Since we are on terms of intimacy, I will tell you, my baptismal name is … is … Boniface, but it will never lend itself to any kind of dignified or agreeable modification. In my early days of service I was called Bun Face and worse by the snottys. I should not wish it wider known.'

'It shall never be heard from my lips,' announces Tom.

'Lieutenant, then,' I say, raising my own tumbler to him, 'to your service.'

Trench eyes us warily for signs of mirth at his expense, detecting none, he smiles, straightens, returns the salutation and drinks off his shrub.

There is a clatter of booted feet on the stairs outside. The door bursts open to reveal Pure John. The boy whips off his cap with a flourish, bows, and taking a moment to catch his breath, announces, 'Here is your Neery cove, gents, with his quitment bag an' all.'

Behind him appears the shambling figure of Doctor Nero, bushy hair awry, he enters, casting an indignant glance at Pure

John. 'That is to say, Doctor Nero, gentlemen. Nero, chirurgeon and master of physick is arrived and at your service.'

CHAPTER XV

'Y ou will forgive my discomposure,' says Nero, removing his coat before bowing briefly, 'but I am given to understand that the matter here is most pressing.' In a few short strides he is at the bedside, where he takes a firm hold of Facey's wrists. There, he appears to await some form of divine inspiration, his gaze, all the while, flitting about the ceiling.

He releases the wrists before leaning in, snuffling at my partner like a truffle hog. Next, he drapes his large, ham-like palm across Facey's brow, muttering to himself, pursing fleshy lips. At length, he straightens and turns. 'And has he made stool?'

'He has,' replies Tom, 'though he had not the wits to use the pot.'

'You have not retained the substance then?'

'It is not my practice, sir.'

'Pity.' Nero shrugs. 'Well, 'tis all one. His breath is foul and tainted; the currents of his blood, sluggish, indicating obstruction. Moreover, there is a particular and excessive humour at work in him; black bile I should say. At any rate, he must first be let and right swiftly too.' So saying, he begins to unstrap his leather case. 'You will be good enough to provide a receptacle.'

We are all caught up in the wonder of Nero's perspicacity and skill and so it takes Tom a moment to respond. 'Would the po serve, sir? Since it has not been employed for—'

Nero frowns. 'It will have to do, for there is not a moment to be lost.' With that, he produces a stubby instrument from the bowels of his satchel, which he holds aloft for our inspection. It appears to be a nail buffer of the sort popular with ladies of quality: thick, ornate ivory handle set with a short flat blade tapering to a triangular point. 'A memorial lancet, given me by none other than the great Crichton hisself, as a token of small services past. Gentlemen, you will oblige me by securing the patient. You, sirs,' he says, levelling the instrument at Trench and then Tom, 'will take a shoulder apiece. You, sir,' he points it at me, 'will secure his left arm. The boy will manage the receptacle.'

Tom fetches the empty chamber pot, handing it to Pure John who accepts with great solemnity, eyes wide, thrilled to be playing such a vital role in the enterprise.

We each of us, set about our appointed tasks, I take ahold of Facey's arm while Nero arranges his shirt sleeve. Facey is limp and silent other than the long, rattling, bellows-to-mend, exhalations of his breath. Away from the streets, Nero is less of the showman, his movements deft and economic. He jabs the point of his instrument into the arm just below the elbow, whereupon Facey whimpers and attempts to roll. But we have him fast, our combined weight pressing down, and so he settles. Darkish blood begins to trickle out from under the blade, the crimson ribbon shocking against the whiteness of his flesh. 'Catch it, boy, catch it,' orders Nero, arranging the crook of Facey's limp arm above the rim of the po.

We remain in this manner until Nero is satisfied with the quantity of blood drawn off. 'About five ounces, more or less,' he announces, sniffing at the po. 'As I thought, it is clotted and sour, adulterated with an excess of black bile.'

Nero clamps the incision with the ball of his thumb and applies pressure, stemming the flow of blood. After a minute or so he retrieves a strip of stained linen from the pocket of his coat, which he employs to bind the tiny wound. 'For the moment, he is sound enough.' Nero nods at the empty bottles scattered about. 'You have ministered the Pancurial, I observe.'

'We have found it efficacious against the pain, sir,' affirms Tom.

'In course you have. It is my own sovereign remedy.'

'But no curative,' I add.

Nero gazes at me with a calm, fixed expression. 'You imagine me a crocus, sir? You will recall that I did entreat you to allow me to redact the orb some days past now. The Pancurial will cure only that which may be cured, sans intervention.'

'So you did,' I concede.

'There is a dead dog in this ditch, sir.'

'Forgive me, I do not take your meaning.'

'The greatest in the land have begged for the secret of my Pancurial, but I will not part with it at any price. Not for a hundred guineas. No, sir, not for a thousand. Pray, do not mistake my specific for a sarsaparilla; no sassafras and burnt sugar here, my friends. Pancurial is the ultimate and proven paregoric for neuralgia, apoplexy, rheumatiz, dropsy, pox, the bloody flux, rickets, whooping cough, whitlows and fever; it will purify the blood and balance the humours. It would cause even the waters of the Fleet to run sweet. But there is an obstruction in this stream, a foul and putrescent dam tainting all it touches. Just as carrion draws flies, a mortifying organ will draw to itself all ill-humours and noxious miasmas from the air. Such a circumstance is beyond even the powers of my Pancurial. And should a dead dog befoul your spring sir, what would you?'

'Haul it out, I imagine.'

'By all means, sir. "Haul it out." We shall make a medical man of you yet. An intervention certes, the obstruction removed with all speed for the sake of the whole.' Nero steps to the bed once again. Leaning over Facey, he slips the damp, stained bandage upwards to the hairline, exposing the injury. The glim is vilely discoloured and swollen, no longer resembling human flesh; a dark vermillion fright, crusted and oozing gleaming viscous fluids, forcing back the lids like some foul grub eager to emerge from its chrysalis. 'Behold your contagion, gentlemen. A Moloch, a carbuncle, no longer a true part of the corpus sanus. I tell you, it must be plucked forthwith and consigned to the midden.'

Nero reaches into the leather satchel and withdraws his sharpened spoon. 'Gentlemen, consider, I beg you, the laudable spoon. With such I shall shortly endeavour to preserve the life of this man. But I must tell you, that once begun, celerity is all. Digging about won't serve, no, not at all, and may do for him as surely as a knife to the breast. It must be speed or nothing: insert; sever; extract. And so you must each play your part. To your stations now and let no entreaties nor cries, howsomever dreadful, dissuade you from your resolve.'

'But is there truly naught else for it, sir?' I make one last appeal.

'Why certainly. There is slow, lingering, agonizing death for him should you so choose.'

At his signal we make ready, Trench assigns himself to Facey's legs, whilst Tom and me take a good hold of the arms and shoulders. Tom gives me an almost imperceptible nod of encouragement as he gently brings his weight to bear. Nero himself presses down on Facey's forehead with his powerful left hand, holding it steady.

Facey's one good eye flicks open. 'What's this?' he cries. 'Set upon as I sleep, you villains. Sammy Boy, where are you, Sammy?'

'Hold hard, gentlemen,' bellows Nero, prising further apart the swollen eyelids with powerful thumb and forefinger before plunging in with the spoon. A spurt of stinking matter is released as the instrument sinks into the soft, yielding cavity, popping out the orb. Facey arches and convulses, roaring blue murther, his sweat-slick head twisting from side to side under

Nero's grip. The organ, still connected by its bloody threads, flaps about, bouncing against his cheekbone like some frightful bob-for-apple on a string. We all of us push down to the limits of our strength, pinning him to the mattress. Facey subsides, grimacing; his good eye meets mine, a single teardrop glistening in the corner. 'Sammy Boy, what are you about?' he whispers sadly before fainting clean away.

Nero delicately reinserts the spoon deep into the cavity of the eye and twists, severing the glim with its sharpened edge. The bloody, misshapen gobbet tumbles away. The chirurgeon deftly scoops it into the palm of his free hand before depositing the awful object with a flick into the waiting pot. Pure John gazes down, white-faced and stunned at the contents of the vessel in his hands.

'Come, boy,' chides Nero, wiping his hands on a soiled fogle, 'compose yourself. Yours is now the pressing task, to dispose of the afflicted part at all speed, on the dust heap or the gutter or where you will. Certes, it must not be permitted to linger here in the room with us, being a repository of foul humours and malaise. Even now it has the capacity to draw down upon itself vile currents and miasmas of disease. Off with you. Run like the wind.'

Pure John nods grimly and, holding the pot as far away from himself as he is able, makes swiftly for the door.

From the recesses of his satchel Nero now produces a small paper packet, which he unfolds to reveal a fine greyish powder. He takes a large pinch of the substance and, teasing apart the sagging flaps of Facey's eyelids, sprinkles it into the gory chasm beneath. Facey shudders but, mercifully, remains insensate. 'Powdered coca leaf will deaden the agony of the wound. I will leave you the remainder. You will also administer the Pancurial from time to time, which you will find most efficacious in the healing process.' He gives me a meaningful glare. 'In a moment, when the powder has taken effect, I will apply a salve: Arabian

Nine Oils, a rare and wonderful commodity, which promotes the formation of a healthy scarification.'

'Is he ... is he cured?' I say.

Nero smiles, extracting from his satchel a half-dozen or so fresh bottles of the Pancurial. 'You are a great one for your miracle cures, sir. I am a doctor, not a mountebank and so shy away from unwarranted claims and exaggerated prognostication. The next four and twenty hours or so will be the test. Should your man survive 'til Monday, you will begin to note swift improvement thereafter.'

'And if he should not?'

'Then he will not.' Nero shrugs as he prepares a small funnel of waxed paper. Placing the narrower end to Facey's open mouth, he carefully administers his specific. Though Facey is yet insensible, he will not suffer himself to be choked. He coughs, spraying syrup before the majority is swallowed off in a series of gasping, convulsive gulps. 'There is almost one half a bottle given: a very considerable quantity. Mark me, from here on it must be half as much, administered once or twice daily. Though the temptation is great, it would not do to give more. Even with a substance as beneficial as the Pancurial, too much is a dangerous over-sufficiency.'

'Doctor Nero, at sea I have seen men endure the amputation of a limb at the surgeon's hand, cheerful and robust, whereupon a few hours after, will suddenly decline and expire,' observes Trench.

'True enough,' replies Nero, uncapping a jar of greasy ointment. 'I will warrant my handiwork, but not its outcome. The work you have observed here is very fine: under twelve seconds, I shouldn't wonder, from ingress to extraction. A promising beginning, to be sure. But all men are different. Some may thrive while others wither for no cause perceptible to us poor mortals. Yet, take heart: this one is no wilting violet, but a precious great ox of a fellow, and so, with the judicious application of my nostrum, and God willing, he will be up and about in a day or two. The wound, right as a trivet within a week.'

Nero gathers a gob of the greasy brown salve on the end of his thumb and smears it into the empty socket, provoking neither objection nor response from his patient. He slips the stained bandage back down to cover the wound and collects his satchel from the floor. 'Well, sirs, I have done all I can for him. He has been in Nero's hands and now he is in God's. There is no better combination, to be sure.'

'I can attest to it, sir,' agrees Tom, pouring a glass of the tepid shrub. 'You will take a glass before you leave? You have earned it and more besides.'

'Since you are so obliging, then I will, sir,' replies Nero, taking the glass. 'To the good health of your confederate.' He downs it in one and smiles with great complacency. 'And now, to the matter of the reckoning: the piper has played and must be paid. I believe it was to be a half-sovereign?'

'Indeed, and not a wit begrudged. The coin was entrusted to the boy and so you will have the goodness to await his return.'

Nero rolls his eyes. 'In my experience, boys and specie mix like oil and water, sir. That is to say, not at all. You will find they invariably part; the tin frittered away on sweetmeats and fripperies, candied apples and the like. You have a trusting nature, sir.'

'You do the lad a great dis—' Trench's objection is cut off by the breathless reappearance of Pure John, giving the lie to Nero's assessment of him.

The youngster clatters into the room brandishing his bloodstained pot. 'Oh, sirs, you will never credit it,' he gabbles, 'I did as you asked and made for the dust heap on the corner of Portland where—'

Trench places a gentle hand on his shoulder. 'Now Pure John, do you still have the coin, the gold half-sov that was entrusted you?'

'Why, yes, sir.' Pure John lays the pot on the floor and fumbles briefly about his shoe. He solemnly returns the coin to Tom.

'I am most particular to select my lads for their rectitude and virtue,' announces Trench with a degree of pride. 'Mine is the trusting nature, but only because my young fellows have never given me reason to be otherwise.'

'Just so, sir.' Nero accepts his bounty with good grace, slipping the specie into an already heavy purse. 'My thanks to you, gentlemen. Should you require more of the Pancurial, you know where it is to be had for a shilling a bottle. You may send this miraculous young paragon if you so choose.' With that, Nero fastens his satchel and takes his leave.

Pure John is still quivering; eyes round with wonder, bursting with his news.

'Now, lad, what is it you wish to tell us?' says Tom.

'I dinged the mollick, sirs, as you required. And you would never credit it.'

'Out with it then, lad,' says Trench.

'I had chucked it far as I was able, blood, gore an' all into the pile when from out of nowhere comes a mangy, vicious piebald mutt and, quick as you like, went and ate it up for his dinner.'

There is an awful silence in the room.

'And good luck to him, the glocky bugger,' says Pure John, hugging himself with glee.

Tom clears his throat. 'Best there is never a word of this to Facey,' he announces gravely.

CHAPTER XVI

I pass an uneasy night under Tom's roof, discomfited by my own whirling thoughts and the occasional bouts of Facey's ravings. From time to time, Tom looks in and fusses with the bedclothes or bandages. Somewhere about dawn I must have fallen into a deep slumber since I do not wake 'til near enough midday.

Facey's bedclothes are all awry and damp from the fever but I am gratified to see that he is more settled now, breathing shallow but regular. I wonder if Tom has slept at all, since at some while earlier this morning he has left out on the bedside table a full pitcher, clean rags and his grooming accouterments. Once I have made use of the piss pot, I give the gnashers a going over with my liquorice root and set to work scrubbing my face and neck, taking care to work around the wounded ear. After a good, close shave, I examine my appearance in the black-spotted hand mirror. With a run of Tom's comb through my hair I manage to cover up the brown paper doings with my longish locks and clap my hat down over all. A second glance in the mirror now confirms to my satisfaction that, rather than resembling a wretched one-eared tomcat, I present a tolerably clean and respectable figure.

I find Tom downstairs in his private room, a small glass of brandy before him. Impossibly, he looks a deal more cheerful and spry than when I last saw him.

'Sit yourself, Sammy,' he says, indicating one of the chairs. 'There is bread, cold pork chops and a hunk of cheese here for you. Should you join me in a glass of brandy? I am not ordinarily a great tippler, but today I feel the need of a bracer.'

'You have earned it, Tom, if any man has.' I pour myself a small glass and cut a little of the bread and cheese for myself. 'He is peaceful as of now.'

'Aye, but you should know we are not out of the woods. The next day or so will be the decider.'

'What more can be done?'

Tom takes a small sip at his brandy. 'There is naught to be done, other than administer the Pancurial from time to time. Sleep is the great healer and so he ought not be disturbed. He will mend. Or he will not. Though I am of a mind with your Nero: a great beast like Facey will surely be up to scratch soon enough.'

'Then I can do nothing?'

'You have already done the very best thing for him, Sammy. No easy matter and a test of any man's mettle. Well done, lad.' Tom smiles and raises his glass.

I dip my head in acknowledgement, knowing myself to be the most infamous fraud.

Tom indicates the bottle. 'You'll take another?'

'My thanks, Tom. I will not. Since there is naught I can do here I have another matter to attend to and am already late,' I say, rising and collecting my hat.

'Is it prudent to venture abroad, Sammy?'

I stare at my boots seeking inspiration. 'It concerns an acquaintance who is … who I have … who means a good deal to me. I could not flee the city without … '

'Ah,' says Tom, twigging it. 'Then you must go and with all speed.'

At length, the crowded horsebus halts at Clapham High Street where I alight, along with the full complement of my fellow passengers. We merge with cheerful hordes of pedestrians heading toward the Common; excited men and women, some still in working clothes, hurrying, drawn by the sound of the steam trumpet and the scent of roasting meats.

We turn north up Rookery Road, where a dozen or more canvas pavilions have been erected around a flattish expanse of scrub grass a short distance from Long Pond.

The outer perimeter consists of barrows and stalls, vending consumables of all description: meats, roasted, baked and boiled; tobacco hangs in reddish brown braids or can be had as snuff from small paper packets; there is fruit and gingerbread for sale and, of course, beer, at every turn.

The inner circle is formed by a labyrinth of tents, painted and lettered, gaudily illustrating the wonders within. At the heart of it all an arena, marked out by ropes and staves. A white-faced cove in a baggy suit and curious conical hat holds the crowd spellbound, standing upright on a horse, as it canters around.

I search the crowd and spy a pack of boisterous youngsters over by one of the beer vendors, Pure John amongst them.

'Why, 'tis Mr Samuel,' pipes Pure John, swigging from a bottle of porter. 'You have missed out on the whelks, but that aside, could not have come at a better moment, for we are to have three more of porter. Each. We will take some gingerbread and a little baccy and I intend to inspect the marvellous Aphrodite.' He jerks a thumb over his shoulder, indicating the arrangement of tents housing the curiosities. 'You may join us, if you like.'

'Ain't it prime, sir?' pronounces a very tiny fellow, gripping my sleeve and leaning upon me in a desperate effort to remain standing.

'It is good to see you in such spirits, Pure John.' I grip the tiny fellow by the collar of his jacket, holding him upright as he pukes over my boot. 'Your brother is here also?'

'Oh, come along, Crabshells, there is more porter to be drunk and you are already three sheets to the wind.' Pure John sighs. 'John is somewhere hereabouts in company with Rosamund Pitface. I did not think she would care to see the marvellous Aphrodite and so we have parted for the time being.'

The young Crabshells steadies himself and attempts to bring me into focus. 'Ain't it prime, though,' he murmurs, before toppling forward, flat on his face.

Pure John grimaces. 'He has almost ten years on him, sir, and cannot hold one or two of porter and some few of gin without coming it swipey and puking his guts.'

'I will see him home, never fear,' announces another of the messenger lads. 'For we are close neighbours and I am not well myself.'

Pure John smiles. 'You must have a cart then, Jemmy. For I know you are situated in Lambeth, which is a long haul for lugging such a dead weight.' He reaches into the pocket of his jacket.

'I will pay the fee,' I say, producing my purse.

'You will not, for I have been at the Under and Over and have already taken four shillings off these fairground dumplings. There is nothing so simple, Mr Samuel, as the skinning of a skinner,' he says proudly, handing a few coppers to his young associate.

'You are a good lad, Pure John,' I say, 'but I would beg you not to refer to Rosamund as "Pitface".'

'I see as I find, Mr Samuel. But since it is you that is asking, that name will never be said again.'

'I take that most kindly, Pure John.'

'And now you will 'company me to the tent of the marvellous Aphrodite?'

'I will not, for I hope to meet shortly with your brother and Rosamund.'

'Oh, sir. I wish you would. These others are pitiful and will not do it,' he indicates the remaining messenger boys around him in their various states of staggering inebriation. 'She is said to be the most beautiful lady alive, and only the merest wisp of gossamer veil to conceal her tits. I would do the thing on my own, Mr Samuel, only—' he beckons me closer and whispers, 'I am somewhat anxious.'

I sigh. 'Very well, Pure John, since you are in funds you will pay the entrance. But you must know that I am well accustomed to such sights.'

'Oh, I expect you are notorious for your killing airs and devilish good-looks 'mongst the ladies, Mr Samuel.'

I cuff him lightly round the ear as we make our way past the yellow curtained tent of the Conjurer to the pavilions.

The entrance is attended by a sly-looking barker in a brown Derby and ill-fitting, black-and-white chequered suit.

'Pa and son, is it? What a treat in store.' says the showman. 'And what father would not wish to hedify his offspring with the remarkable gentleman glass-blower, his hair all of glass? Or the spectacle of Pinhead, the Dog-Faced Lady, the India rubber Gent, Bear Woman and the Mighty Midget? Or perchance it is our Learned Pig what takes your fancy, a hanimal what can select your card from a pack and tell the hexact time to the minute, blindfolded mind? If that ain't sufficient marvel for any man, there is also waxworks and a genuine Redskin within.'

'We are here to see the Aphrodite,' pipes Pure John, proffering a shilling.

'There ain't no Haphrodite,' retorts the showman.

'But it is wrote on your billposts,' insists Pure John.

'There never was a Haphrodite, young sir. 'Twas a thing called Hermaphrodite, to be sure, known as the 'mazing Man-Woman. But that creature is stone dead and never more for hexibition.'

169

'Hermaphrodite, you say?' I exclaim.

'Indeed, sir. In my experience these freaks of nature do not survive long. The Pin-headed curiosity is already on his last legs, which is why you must take my advice and enjoy the spectacle while you can.'

'Is the Hermaphrodite within?'

'It is, sir, laid out just so in a sealed tent and shut away from public view. Were it down to me I would make a spectacle of it, quick or dead, but Professor Socrates, him what owns the fair, he do indulge his freaks so.'

'May I speak with this Professor?'

'You will find him within. Engaged in discourse with our Learned Pig, but quick now for the showing has already begun.'

'Very well, Pure John, give the man his shilling.'

Pure John's bottom lip trembles. 'I was to see tits.'

'You may see all the tits you like on our Learned Pig. Being a sow, you will find she keeps twelve on 'em, and so you will be spoiled for choice,' advises the barker, holding back the tent flap.

Pure John and me enter a damp and narrow canvas corridor illuminated by a series of tin sconces tacked to the tent poles. We step carefully, giving our eyes time to adjust to the flickering candlelight. Ahead is a flap heralding the Bear Woman. I gingerly pull it to one side and we enter a gloomy pavilion housing a small cage. Enclosed by the bars is a colossal figure perched on a stool, surrounded by old gnawed bones. Her head and face are completely obscured by a matting of thick black hair. She wears a tattered dress, but a similar dense black fur sprouts from her arms, hands, legs and feet.

She growls at Pure John, who grips my sleeve. 'I do not like this place, Mr Samuel.'

The creature steps off the stool and advances, rattling at the bars.

I can feel Pure John trembling at my side. 'Come now, Pure John. 'Tis only a human woman, notwithstanding the pelt.'

The Bear Woman chuckles, a very human sound. 'This last season, I was only the Bearded Lady and not so very terrifying to the young 'uns.'

She smiles, I think. It is hard to tell.

'And what of all them bones?' squeaks Pure John.

The Bear Woman shrugs. 'Old beef bones, same as you will find on any of the vendor's carts. I do not think I have ate any young lads in a while now.'

Pure John releases my sleeve, stepping a little closer to the bars. 'I was not afeared, you know.'

'I am sure of it,' affirms the woman gently. 'Well, you may stroke my arm if you wish.'

'You have always been so?' I ask.

'I have, sir. A ball of fluff at birth, and much resented by my mother, who was bit by a mastiff when gravid. Stranger still is that our Dog-Faced Lady, though she has the face of a mastiff, tells of her papa being bit by a sailor's monkey. Which event occurring a good six-month afore she was even thought of.'

'And you are content to live in this way?' I ask, indicating the bones and bars.

'Why bless you, sir. 'Tis only for make-believe. The cage is not secured and for the most part I live as you do, I should imagine. Better, perhaps, for there is always a bite to be had and a roof over my head at night, albeit of canvas. And I have travelled the length and breadth of this country, taking in the wondrous sights of it, which is more than can be said for most.'

'And your master, Professor Socrates, what manner of man is he? I have a proposition for him.'

'A good enough sort, I suppose, though mercenary. You will find no satisfaction there without the prompting of tin. And even then, perhaps, only in the language of the Romans.'

I place my hand on Pure John's shoulder. 'I fear we are keeping you from your duties.'

'By no means. Our patrons are for the while distracted by the performance of the Professor and his Learned Pig. A four times daily showing and a welcome respite for the rest of us.'

'In that case, I will inquire of you, if I may, about the Hermaphrodite, as was.'

'To what end?' For a moment, she becomes guarded.

'The boy—my boy, had his heart set on the sight of it. He is somewhat inquisitive by nature.' I squeeze Pure John's shoulder, cautioning against contradiction.

'They most always are, at that age,' she says fondly, reaching through the bars with a hairy paw and chucking him under the chin.

'Well, there is little enough to tell,' she shrugs. 'She was called Bobby. Shortened from Robert or Roberta, I could not say which, for she was both man and woman in parts. She—I will say "she", as I believe there was more of the woman about her, though she dressed in the clothes of a man when not on display—she was known to us in full as Bobby Herman, though that was the name given by Professor Socrates as a kind of joke, a play on words, if you will: Her-man.

'Bobby Herman came to us a little over a year or so past, around sixteen years of age, having lived in London somewhere. She had been ill-treated and bore the marks of it, but that is scarcely unique amongst folk like us. Socrates made much of her, for she had a cutting wit and a quick tongue and she rubbed along well enough with the rest. But it was Stephen Florey, the India rubber Man, who took a proper shine to her. I do believe he loved her: following her about, making puppy-dog eyes, performing little acts of devotion and so forth. So, you see, young man, love is such a gift that even the least of us may live in hope of it.'

'It is a sad tale then,' says Pure John. 'What is become of the India rubber Man?'

'Why, it has quite broke his heart.'

'I am sorry to hear it.'

'And now, we will shake hands, for soon I must come it the savage Grizzly once again and were you to put your hand through the bars another time I should be obliged to bite it off.'

'I do not think so,' says Pure John, grinning, as he grasps her hand. 'I was never in the least afeared.'

We step back through the opening, dropping the flap, leaving the Bear Woman to her bones and her cage.

'Mr Samuel, I have shook the hand of a bear,' whispers Pure John gleefully. 'Just wait 'til I tell the rest on 'em. Thomas Lane will puke with envy.'

'I expect he is busy just now, puking with too much porter.'

'Not Lane. He can drink as much as any man, since he is at least thirteen years. And I should very much like to see this India rubber cove.'

'We cannot,' I say, leading him on down the dark tented corridor. 'I have urgent business with this Socrates and must speak with him.'

'We are here on my tin, Mr Samuel, and it ain't charitable in you to hurry me along like this.'

'You have the right of it, Pure John. There is no need for you to 'company me and so will leave you to your India rubber cove.'

'Oh, Mr Samuel, I wish you would not go. It is dark in here and what if I mislay my bearings? You would have to tell my brother of how you 'bandoned me to the gloom, 'mongst pinheads and dog-midgets.'

'Very well,' I sigh, 'we will inspect your India rubber cove, then I must straight to my affair. Agreed?'

'Agreed.' Pure John gobs on his palm, which I am obliged to shake in honour of this arrangement.

'And what is a India rubber Gent, 'zactly?' queries Pure John as we seek the entrance.

'I have not the slightest idea,' I reply.

CHAPTER XVII

A couple of inebriated but cheerful labouring coves share this cramped tent-space, passing a bottle while they wait for the sullen young man in tight-fitting spangles to begin.

The spangled performer takes a small bow, steps daintily into a small glass box and lowers himself slowly inside the container. Over the course of the next few minutes he somehow manages to pack his entire body into this tiny crate. Finally, a long, fluid arm snakes out and pulls shut the lid.

One of the labourers belches. 'Well, I never,' he says, 'I swear I could not put more 'an a dozen bricks into such a casket.'

'In course you could not, since you can never be persuaded to do any heavy labour above the lifting of a bottle,' says his mate.

'True enough,' agrees the man. 'Still an' all, it is a prodigious feat. And would trim the expense of a fumeral most handily.'

An odd sound emerges from the box. The lid is flung open, the young man briskly unpacks himself in a tangle of limbs. He steps out, hands on hips and glowers at the labourers, eyes blazing. 'Not ten paces from where you stand, one of our troupe lies cold. You think it proper to make light of this?'

The labourers back away, shocked by the outburst. 'There was no offence meant, we did not know, sir,' replies the one.

The cove with the bottle lowers his head. 'I had not heard of it and am heartily sorry for them ill-chosen words, which was only said in jest.'

There is a terrible silence, the labouring men inspect their boots, until the one holding the bottle finds inspiration: 'Jack, we should not miss the Bear Woman as I have set aside a piece of bacon as tid-bit for the creetur.'

'There ain't a creetur alive what don't approve of bacon,' agrees his partner. With that, the two men sheepishly shuffle away, retreating through the canvas flap.

''Cept the Learned Pig, most like.'

'Or any porker come to that, learned or no, for it don't take learnin' to know t'ain't right to gobble your own.'

We can still hear their debate as they withdraw along the canvas corridor.

'Well then,' says the India rubber Man, appraising us through narrowed, pale blue eyes, 'shall I bend in half backwards and propel myself crabwise, on hands and feet for you? I am not always so quarrelsome with our patrons, as you shall see.' The young man is tall and bony, almost consumptive but for the sense of barely constrained energy he exudes and the strange gleam in his pale eyes. His thin face tapers to a sharp chin and is framed by twin locks of mousey-coloured hair.

'They meant no harm, I'm sure of it,' I say.

'Are you very heart-sick, sir?' asks Pure John.

'What is it to you?' snaps the India rubber cove, coming upright.

'We have just now come from the Bear Woman since I was not afeared,' explains Pure John, stoutly. 'And had the tale from her.'

'So, it is not enough to twist myself into a clove hitch for the amusement of the public, but must have my doings exposed to all and sundry?'

'We have no desire to intrude upon your affairs, sir,' I say. 'It was the herm—Bobby, which had aroused my boy's curiosity. He has a soft heart and was much distressed to hear of her passing.'

'Was you now?' The young man lifts a foot, arching and stretching, as though his sinews were in a state of constant rebellion.

Pure John pitches in like a good 'un, plastering a gentle smile across his grubby mug, 'It is particular sad, sir.'

'Well, my heart is sore, to be sure, but you may wonder at the pitch of my feelings, which are not so close to grief as you might expect. What you observe in me, sir, is anger. Anger, I say.'

'How so?'

'Bobby Herman did not "pass", but was murdered most foully. I know it.'

I have become submerged in very deep waters here, my first instinct is to back away and have nothing more to do with this tainted corpse. But Facey and me must quit the metropolis in a day or so; we are all but penniless and no more than ten yards away, enclosed by nothing more substantial than canvas walls, lies a hundred sovereigns. For the moment at any rate, I resolve to stay the course. 'If that is true, then how does the law stand in this affair?' I enquire, this being something of a priority for me.

'The law,' he sniffs. 'There is no law for such as we, for we are poor and beyond protection.'

'This new army of Peelers is law enough for any man.'

'Well, at any rate, their law has done its work. And never a peep for justice. There was an inquest on the body and no notice taken of the signs of foul play. This, despite the presence of a very eminent man of science and medicine.'

It occurs to me that Stephen Florey has been driven mad with grief, which is a good thing, since this talk of murder is likely no more than the ravings of a deranged mind. 'Ah, it was ever thus. At least the poor creature will have a decent burial. I suppose you will lay the body to rest somewhere hereabouts?'

'Not 'til I have brought a Magistrate to it and had him confirm the marks of guilt.'

'What marks are these, that you can see and yet a man of science cannot?'

'I will tell you, sir,' he announces, seating himself on his glass box, grim-faced. 'At one time we had a Fakir from the continent of India in our troupe who informed me of a sect of men from that place known as Thugees—bandits who prey on the unwary. Strangulation, their preferred method of dispatch, and for the purpose will employ a silken cloth, weighted at one end with a coin. The cloth is flung around the neck of the unwitting victim, the ends drawn together, stopping up the breath. Though there is no obvious wound or deep bruising, an expert in such matters can tell the method by a red line around the throat and the bluish cast to lips and fingertips caused by lack of air. It is these exact marks I see on Bobby. I have said as much to the Magistrate.'

The mention of a Magistrate has decided me: it is time to give up the chase and go, while my own neck is still intact.

'Thomas Lane will spit cabbages that he did not 'company me,' announces Pure John. 'You will verify my account of it, Mr Samuel, for he will never believe it from me.'

'And that is not the end of it,' intones Florey with a strange smile on his face.

'Alas, it must be so for us, since there is much else to see.'

'You will allow me to finish, sir, since you have expressed an interest in the thing.' The young man bends back the fingers of his left hand, cracking the knuckles in a series of pops.

'I cannot, we must be away.'

'I must hear it,' pipes Pure John gleefully, 'and commit all to memory, for it is precious dreadful.'

'I see that your coming here was no accident,' says Florey, giving me a bit of a turn. ''Twas the will of God. I realize now, that the best chance in this case is for all men to hear of it. Commit the tale to memory by all means, young sir, share it with your Thomas Lanes. The dead cry out for justice.'

They don't. The dead are silent and cry out for nothing. That is the entire point.

I turn to go but Pure John grips my sleeve. 'One minute more, Mr Samuel, 'til the tale is done.'

'A minute then, Pure John. Not a moment longer.'

Pure John hugs himself with glee. Florey fixes us with his gaze, eyes burning with righteous zeal.

'Here is the remainder then, since you have the stomach for it. As you may know, our troupe arrived here five days ago from an engagement in Bristol. The instant we pitched canvas there was nothing for it but Bobby must be away, to look up some acquaintance in the metropolis, who she claimed owed her money. In the interests of her safety, I followed at a distance, though her course that night did not conclude at some humble workman's cottage as I imagined it would, but a grand villa in the West End. She was admitted to the place by a liveried servant and so, thinking all was well, I left. Now, I bitterly reproach myself for that error of judgment.'

'Aye, the London streets can be most vicious at night,' I say.

Florey looks at me meaningfully. He takes a deep breath before continuing: 'When Bobby did not show the next morning, Anton Whalen—that is the Mighty Midget—and me went searching. By this time her poor body had been discovered in the street and took for inquest. Those coddled nincompoops found nothing amiss and so the corpse lay cold and alone in some tavern cellar, awaiting kin who would never come. I could not allow that, sir. And so Anton and me returned in the dead of night and claimed it, Anton being sufficiently compact to gain entrance by the barrel chute.'

Pure John's mouth is a hoop, his eyes shining with delicious horror.

'It is my firm belief that Bobby was done to death in that very house on Poland Street and after, her body dumped outside like so much refuse. I have said as much and laid my complaint with a Magistrate.'

'I am sorry for it,' I say, taking a firm grip on Pure John's arm, hastening him towards the tent flap. 'And we shall be sure to share your tale, for, as you say, it is seldom that poor men such as we are able to command justice.'

'And that is all I ask,' replies the India rubber Man bowing us out, forehead touching the tip of his toes.

CHAPTER XVIII

Outside the sky has a bleak, forbidding cast and though it is only late afternoon, torches have already been lit. We each of us take a breath, savouring the sweeter air after the damp, stale fug of the tents. The crowd has thickened but Pure John is quick to spy a few of his confederates milling about a pastry cart, his brother amongst them, though I see no sign of Rosamund.

Pure John dashes over, bursting to share his news. I follow behind and throw Kak John a curt nod.

'Why, Mr Samuel, I am happy to see you here,' he says, 'though you appear a little out of sorts and I should not be surprised if it is down to the company of my brother, who can be a sore trial.'

Sleek, is how he appears to me. Different in every respect: face scrubbed and shaved pink, he wears a tolerably respectable black coat along with a clean red kerchief round his neck. Most telling is his wayward hair, which has been flattened and tamed by the application of oil, making it glisten in the flickering light of the torches.

'We have had a curious time of it, to be sure. But your brother is no trial at all, though he will have his way should he set his mind to a thing.'

'He will indeed, Mr Samuel. At any rate, you could use some refreshment I should think. What say I stand a round of ginger beer and you'll join us, for I am here with Rosamund, who has been, for a while, diverted by the sight of caged songbirds?'

'I have shook hands with a bear,' announces Pure John loudly to his fellows, eyes shining in the half-light.

'You never did, you mumping toe-rag,' retorts the largest of the boys: Thomas Lane, I presume.

'You will stand witness, Mr Samuel,' he pleads.

'True,' I say. 'Bold as brass, Pure John took a hold of a huge, hairy paw and shook it.'

'And where is Dillon?' Pure John demands of the admiring youngsters.

'Carried home, puking and blubbing,' replies one of the boys.

'Dammit all, I have a tale that would make his hair stand on end: a gang of Punjabi bandits have strangled one of the freaks, and are even now holed-up in a house in Poland Street, waylaying and murdering all in the vicinity and "kiss my arse" to the law.'

'You are talking gammon again,' objects Thomas Lane, visibly anguished at having his thunder stolen.

'Mr Samuel?' queries Pure John, grinning from ear to ear.

'It is all just as he says,' I confirm.

'Oh, Pure John, you will tell us and not leave out one single detail?' pleads one of the smaller boys.

'Certainly I will, for the India rubber cove who confided the tale has made me swear to share it with you. But only on the strictest condition that I say naught 'til Thomas Lane has brung me a bottle of porter and some gingerbread.'

'I will not.'

In short order a squabble erupts, angry piping voices raised, small fists flying. Kak John sighs and shakes his head. He takes my arm, steering me toward the ginger beer stall. 'He will have his way, Mr Samuel.'

'Well, John, you are looking decided spruce today,' I say. 'And do I spy the sheen of Makassar in your locks?'

'Oh, no, Mr Samuel, I can't afford such stuff. 'Tis only cheap lamp oil, for my hair can be every bit as stubborn as my brother.'

'Then you must take care to avoid the torches, John. I should not wish to see you become a Roman Candle.'

'Are you making fun with me, Mr Samuel? Have I done aught to offend you?'

Kak John halts and gazes earnestly at me. There is nothing but candour and concern in that open, uncharacteristically clean face, giving me cause to regret my facetious remark.

'Forgive me, John. Mr Facey and me have lately suffered some about-turn in our fortune, I am vexed and poor company, so shall not detain you further, having no desire to keep poor Rosamund waiting on your return.'

Kak John nods. 'I had heard about Mr Facey from my brother and I am sorry for it.' He grips my arm again, more firmly this time. 'But you shan't escape, Mr Samuel. I can't in all conscience permit you to slip away without at least a word to Rosamund. I should never be forgiven were she to discover that Mr Samuel Samuel himself was here and I didn't break my back to bring him to her.'

'It is kind in you, John, but I would only be the extra wheel that overturns your apple cart.'

'Whatever are you saying, Mr Samuel?'

With a tip of my head I indicate his natty appearance.

'Bless me, but you believe I have designs on Rosamund's affections?'

'I had thought so, since you present yourself so trim that—'

'Rosamund has always been assured of my regard but I wouldn't never think to press a suit on her. Why, she is quite venerable.'

'What? She is but four-and-twenty.'

'Almost twice my years. I am seventeen, I think. To me, four-and-twenty is a very great age.'

'I am pretty sure I am six-and-twenty.'

Kak John gives me a sly glance. 'Then you are ancient, Mr Samuel. 'Tis a wonder you can get about without the aid of a stick. Here, put a little more weight on my arm.'

'A stick would be a fine thing at the minute, but I should not use it to lean on.'

'Well, Mr Samuel, you are quite your former self, I find.'

'The notion of ginger beer has cheered me.'

'I had thought so.' Kak John grins. His teeth, which are surprisingly good, gleam in the waning light. I wait a while, feeling that he is on the verge of saying more.

'You know, Mr Samuel, age ain't the only thing stands 'twixt Rosamund and me.'

I do not think he requires an answer and so say nothing.

'Pure John and me had a elder sister. 'Bout of an age with Rosamund. No pa that I recall. Ma died birthing Pure John, so there was nothing for it but Jane, for that was her name, must stand in for both. Five years back we lost her to the pox and have missed her sorely since.

'You must know that Rosamund is very like her, Mr Samuel. Perhaps that is why Pure John has never taken to her quite. I reckon he cannot forgive her for surviving the pox when our Jane did not.'

'A sister to you then?'

'As like as makes no difference. And I will never see her harmed.'

'Nor I, John.'

'So you see, there ain't no applecart for overturning.'

Rosamund perches on one of the benches set near the Ginger Beer cart, little willow basket at her side, looking every inch the fine lady in a plaid shawl and her best green dress. The fabric's colour has perhaps faded a little over the years, and so she has artfully stitched new ribbons about the sleeves and waist to revive its gaiety. She looks up just as we hove into view, as though gifted with second sight.

A tiny smile appears on her face as she rises. 'Sammy,' she says, extending her arms, 'you decided to come.'

I take both her hands in mine and there we stand for a moment, grinning, well pleased with one another. 'I have shook hands with a bear,' I announce, for the want of something cleverer.

'Good for you, glocky,' she replies, withdrawing her hands to adjust her shawl.

'He has been with my brother.' Kak John appraises us a moment. 'I believe I shall fetch that ginger beer,' he announces, heading for the cart.

Rosamund settles herself back on the bench, indicating a space for me beside her. 'So, you had a time of it with Pure John?' she asks softly.

'The boy was afeared of the curiosities and so I resolved to keep him company.'

'You weren't along for a peek at the Aphrodite then?'

'I was not. There was no Aphrodite. Only a poor creature at one time known as The Hermaphrodite.'

'Ah, Pure John must be quite downcast.'

'There was some consolation. He is even now cock of the walk amongst his fellows, I believe.'

Rosamund chuckles. 'Well, you are no cock of the walk here for all your bears. Kak John and me have enjoyed the spectacle of trained monkeys in the arena and a pack of dogs, walking upright, which made me laugh some. Though I did not get to shake any paws.'

'I should like to have seen you laugh. You do not laugh enough, in my observation.'

'Don't eat in front of folk, neither,' she says. 'Nor smile much. My teeth were broke from a raving fall while insensible with the sickness. I do not like to have them observed.'

'A chip or so to lend character, but scarcely grim. Only yesterday we had a fellow with a set of wooden gnashers all blacker than the Earl of Hell's riding boots barge his way into our company and not even Facey could stop his yap, notwithstanding the truly disagreeable nature of his smirk.'

Rosamund chuckles, a raised palm sheltering her mouth.

'Rosamund,' I say, 'I am not a fine-looking man, as some are. Neither am I a man of—'

'Hexcuse the intrusion, but did you find satisfaction with Professor Socrates then, I'm wondering?' I peer up. It is the sly-looking barker cove leaning in over my right shoulder.

'I did not get that opportunity.'

'Then, you may wish to know that Professor Socrates is the grey-haired gent yonder,' advises the barker, indicating a tall, soberly-dressed, elderly man standing not five yards away, engaged in earnest conversation.

'It seems that an interview is no longer required. But I am, in any event, grateful to you,' I say, handing him a copper, to get him to clear off as much as anything.

At that moment Kak John returns with three leather mugs brimming with ginger beer. He joins us on the bench and we toast.

As I tip my head to drink, Professor Socrates gesticulates and shifts to one side revealing the other party.

It is Liston's toady, Phillip Trubshaw.

CHAPTER XIX

'If it does not wish to, a ape will not come when called, 'tis a good deal different from a dog in that respect,' declares Kak John. 'And I cannot fathom how they can be got to play the fiddle, since they are quite contrary, you know.'

'They are very like old gentlemen, I find, in their appearance and behaviour.'

'You have hit upon something there, Rosamund. I do believe old gents can be made somewhat agreeable when they are coddled, forgiven their temper, kept warm and fed on a diet of pap ... are you quite warm enough there, Mister Samuel?'

Rosamund chuckles.

'I am, John,' I reply, pulling down the brim of my hat. It is none of my concern, but I cannot help but keep half an eye on the young swell over the rim of my mug while Kak John and Rosamund blather. A travelling fair is not ordinarily a place for toffs so I can only imagine that Trubshaw's presence here is no coincidence. At length, Socrates bows, marking the conclusion of their business. With an expression of the greatest distaste, Trubshaw counts out a good few sovereigns, which he hands over before striding swiftly away. Socrates may well indulge his freaks but it appears he is not above the selling of their corpses.

Socrates circles the benches, casting about for someone. 'Calix meus inebrians. Wretched man,' he mutters. His eye falls upon me. 'You, sir, you and your companion seem a handy-looking pair. How should you care to earn a shilling apiece in return for a stint of easy labour?'

Kak John glances at me and then Rosamund; I have no doubt he could use the shilling. I shrug, reluctant to have anything further to do with the murky business of Bobby Herman.

'Qui tacet consentire. He who is silent gives consent,' pronounces Socrates.

'Then we are at your service, guv'nor,' replies Kak John, rising.

I follow, more from curiosity than anything else. Stepping through a complicated web of ropes and pegs, Socrates leads us to a secluded area at the rear of the pavilions. The opening at the back of one of the tents has been unlaced, flaps hanging open. Socrates enters and beckons us inside. I am familiar enough with the faint and particular odour of a three-day-old body to know what awaits.

Laid out on an old trestle is the corpse of Bobby Herman. It is small in stature, as I have heard; almost child-like, and has been packed around by large chunks of ice, which puddle the rough wooden surface. The body is clothed, not as a female, but in the style of a respectable young buck: good coat and trousers, clean linen and neck-stock. A faint, sweetish odour emanates from the flesh, not yet foul, for the ice, along with the mildness of the weather, has contrived to postpone corruption.

Rosamund, who has followed us in, is not violently disturbed by the sight but simply gazes wistfully down on the remains. 'How very sad. He is quite beautiful.'

To be sure, Bobby Herman has neat, pleasing features and a full head of dark flowing locks, which have been tied back in a tail. I understand how she could pass for a fine-looking young man or indeed, a pleasing enough woman.

'Sic transit gloria mundi,' intones Socrates. 'One of our troupe, alas passed. To be returned to the bosom of his family for the proper rituals. There is a tarpaulin,' he indicates a brown bundle by the entrance. 'You will oblige me, you men, by wrapping the corpus first, for I should not wish to discomfit our patrons with the sight. You will transport our brother to a conveyance close by, then you shall have your shillings.'

Kak John and I set about our work, first spreading the tarpaulin sheet on the ground. We lift the body, which is as light as a child, placing it carefully in the centre of the sheet, we replace the lumps of ice around the torso, and finally wrap the whole thing up nice and tight, like a long brown parcel.

We follow Socrates, toting our burden across a short stretch of grass to Rookery Road where an old but serviceable horse and cart await. The carter, however, is nowhere to be seen.

We gently place the package into the bed of the cart while Socrates paces anxiously. 'Tempus aestusque neminem manent. Time and tide wait for no man, except, it seems, that great drunken oaf of a carter.'

'Noooo.' A terrible, anguished wail pierces the night, outdoing even the steam trumpet for volume.

It is Florey, I know it. As we turn towards the sound, my instincts are confirmed by the sight of the India rubber Man staggering from the empty tent, clutching a lantern.

'Hell and damnation,' exclaims Socrates, 'that bloody man.' He hastens towards Florey, covering the ground at an impressive rate for an oldster. 'Florey,' he bellows, 'for God's sake, calm yourself now. Bobby is gone, claimed by his rightful kin.'

Punjab bandits, India rubber coves and the majesty of the law notwithstanding, here is one hundred gold sovereigns dropped into my lap, neatly parcelled, with a conveyance thrown in. I have never been one to look a gifted horse in the mouth. And this, being a cart as well as a horse, I don't.

I hop up onto the driver's bench, exhorting Kak John to climb aboard at back. He's such a biddable lad that he does so without the slightest hesitation. I lean over to Rosamund, standing there on the track. 'Forgive me, Rosamund. I will explain another time. For now, we must away with all speed.' I grip the reins, cracking them sharply against the pony's back. 'Wisht,' I exclaim, 'wisht now. Away.'

Nothing happens.

'Garn,' I say, giving the reins another crack. 'Garn with you.'

The pony takes a reluctant step.

Rosamund places her basket onto the driver's bench and stands, hands on hips, glaring up at me like I'm an idiot. 'Have you never managed a cart before, glocky?' Without waiting for answer she walks to the pony's head and removes the nosebag. She returns, hoisting her skirts with one hand, holding the other to me. 'Come on,' she orders, 'give us a hand up.'

She sets herself next to me on the bench. 'Shift up then, Sammy,' she orders, shoving me over with her hips, and takes the reins. She cracks leather, makes a clicking sound with her tongue against her teeth, and we are off at a fast trot.

A second anguished wail splits the night. I turn my head to see the figures of Socrates and Florey silhouetted against the pavilion rush lights. Socrates stands upright, attempting to administer consolation with futile words and gestures. Florey is on his knees, howling up at the sky.

CHAPTER XX

I grip the edges of the driver's bench, knuckles stretched white, as Rosamund urges the horse to a prodigious speed along the track. She avoids pedestrians and oncoming gigs with ease; in short order, we leave the common behind and are on to Clapham High Street.

I throw her a curious glance. 'My pa was a printer of handbills,' she bawls over the clatter of hooves on cobblestones. 'Kept his own conveyance for the delivery and collection of paper stock. I've had the trick of managing a horse and cart since I was very young, some eight years of age I believe.' She adds a touch of rein and takes us neatly round a pothole.

'It is a goodish distance 'twixt ourselves and the alarm, we may be safe for the while,' she announces, hauling in, slowing the beast to a more sedate walk. 'Perhaps you will tell me at least where we are headed?'

'Well, now …' I bluster. The fact is, I have no idea.

'Fond as I am of you, Sammy, I should rather not swing for you.'

'Nor I,' adds Kak John from the back.

'What are we about, Sammy, making off with a good horse and cart?'

I am not especially skilled in the art of dissembling and cannot bear to lose Rosamund's good opinion of me, so my mouth opens and closes once or twice but nothing of any useful substance emerges.

Rosamund reins in violently, hauling us to a dead stop before turning her piercing grey eyes on me. 'Sammy, we will go not one step further until you make some explication.'

'I ... the fact of the matter is ... '

She sighs. 'You must know that I have always been perfectly aware of your profession. I neither judge nor think the worse of you for it. Evidently this cargo has some especial value to you and, were you to confide its destination, we should resolve the matter a great deal easier than if you just sit there playing the guppy.'

'The cargo is worth one hundred sovs; it is a most unusual corpse,' I say.

'Mother of Christ,' breathes Kak John. 'One hundred sovs. And him but a scrap of a fellow too.'

Even Rosamund's narrowed eyes go wide at this.

'The destination is Great Marlborough Street, residence of one Joshua Brookes, a distinguished gentleman,' I announce. 'But we dare not go there.'

'Why ever not?' exclaims Rosamund.

'That is to say, we cannot go there now,' I explain. 'It is scarcely evening as yet, and so we cannot simply clatter up to the doorstep of a noted medical gent, hauling a corpse at this time. These things are best managed in the small hours.'

'Then where? There will be a hue and cry for the conveyance soon enough.'

'Somewhere solitary, where a few hours may be passed exempt from prying eyes.'

'If you'd be so kind as to allow me to make a proposition, I believe I have the means to resolve your dilemmon,' interjects Kak John from behind.

'By all means, proposition away,' I say.

'You will know I'm at the Bermondsey tanneries most days with my pure, but, in the main, reserve my finest for Bennett and Sons at Crucifix Lane. They have always been skrewplus fair with me in the matter of price and I have particular friends there.

'There is a small hut, no more than a hovel, set back from the yard where the working men find some degree of relief from the prevailing stink. We may go there now with your cargo, Mr Samuel, and wait out the hours of evening in safety and some degree of comfort. As for the watchman, I am well in with him, having done some small services in the past, and so may come and go as I please at all hours.'

'An admirable plan,' pronounces Rosamund, without a second's hesitation.

'And what of the conveyance? Is there means of concealment?'

'I do not think it right to keep Polly a moment longer than we must,' says Kak John hesitantly.

'Polly? Who is Polly?'

'Why the pony, Lady Rosamund. What you have took, along with the cart.'

'You know the beast?' I say.

'Course I do, for his master is in the leather and from up Bermondsey way. 'Twas Polly I reckonized, from the white socks on her. Her master is a oldish gent, like yourself, Mister Samuel, and a bit of a tippler, not 'alf. But a goodish sort on the whole, who we have, for the moment, misfortunately deprived of his livelihood. And him with a big fambly to provide for, tomorrow being a working day, he will sorely miss his Polly and be down a day's wages into the bargain.'

Rosamund makes a wry expression. 'You are in the right of it, John. We must devise a way to return this man's property just as soon as we have reached your sanctuary.'

'Ah, but ain't that the beauty of the thing, Lady Rosamund? We may ride Polly and her cart to Bennett and Sons like Lord and Lady Muckamuck. The instant we arrive, set her loose, give 'er a slap on the rump and off home she trots on her ownsome, knowing the particulars of that trip better than the backs of her hooves, I should expect.'

'Good, then it is decided,' announces Rosamund. As she collects in the reins, readying for the off, I reach across to stay her hand.

'Rosamund, I have no desire for you and Kak John to run a further risk. It is my business alone.'

'So,' she says, 'you intend to bilk us of our share?'

'That was never my—'

'''Twas meant in jest, glocky.'

'It is no game, Rosamund. If we are taken with the pony and cart they will surely scrag us. I should not allow you to run such a risk.'

'Let me remind you, Sammy, that you are not my keeper. It is my risk to run. Besides, that milk is well spilled and cannot be put back in the can. The cart is already took. And were you to put us off at the kerbside, how then would you transport your cargo?'

'I know the streets, I expect I could manage the conveyance.'

'And shatter a wheel at the very first pothole? That's if you do get the pony to move at all.'

She's right. At the reins I am likely to be the cause of a considerable catastrophe in these busy streets. There is nothing for it but to accept defeat.

'But, what of—' I say. Too late, Rosamund has gathered up the reins and we are off.

Kennington Lane and Newington Butts are behind us as we approach the busy confluence of the Elephant and Castle. At this hour the great junction teems with traffic coming and going from St George's, Great Surrey, Old Kent and the Borough Roads.

Ignoring the loud and noxious imprecations of an oncoming cabby Rosamund deftly weaves us into the stream and so we blend with the mass of lawful conveyances.

'Where after the Elephant, John?' I enquire.

'The Borough Road is the directest and most economic approach. Most days will find me beating this very path, a stout yoke of my own devising across my shoulders, twin pails dangling like a milkmaid. 'Cept I am no apple-cheeked charmer and you would not find the contents so refreshin' on a hot summer's day. One bucket is reserved for the canine stuff and t'other for the horses. Though it is all kak, there is a world of difference in the qualities. Edifying, is it not, Mr Samuel?'

'I am all agog,' I reply. He is quite oblivious to my ironical tone and so we must continue to endure this unwelcome lecture.

'The tanneries have no use for the doings of a horse, you understand, which is the reason for a separate pail. It is excellent stuff for growing and so I sells it to the fruit and vegetable men of Covent Garden. Now, the canine variety is for the leather men and can go to the bate pools along with pigeon droppings. Don't know why, since there is, to my mind, a considerable difference 'tween a dog and pigeon. But there you are.

'Pure is always in high demand for the bating of the hides and imparts a softness to the leather. How? I could not say. But it is all jumbled together into a watery pit, wherein the working men must stamp about in their bare legs for a good few hours. Then out comes the hides to be soaked in brine and dried. And there, Mr Samuel, is the story of your boots for you.'

'I will never after gaze at my boots in quite the same way again.'

'A smidgeon of learning is never wasted, Mr Samuel. That is my motto.'

'My thanks, and I believe that may be sufficient edification for the while.'

Rosamund has taken us past the thick of the traffic and I detect the sour tang of river mud once more as we approach the end of Borough High Street. There is a softening to the air and I spy the first delicate tendrils of a mist rolling in from the river. A London fog is always welcome to men of our trade and this night's work will go all the smoother for it.

'A jink down Saint Thomas Street will take us past the 'spitals and down along Weston. From there 'tis Snow's Fields onto Crucifix Lane,' advises Kak John.

While Kak John has been blathering, I have been mulling over the problem of how we might safely transport Bobby Herman's remains to Great Marlborough Street in the wee hours. Though she is light as a child, we cannot manage it on foot for fear of the law. It must be a carter but I am not sanguine about finding a willing hand at the Fortune of War. There are carters aplenty there but they are reluctant to stray from their own parish, being used to conducting an easy trade in the vicinity of Barts'. There is nothing for it but Shields. He is not a man to trust overmuch and yet I warrant the sight of me will not send him running to Pimlott and Chuffington, since he is tarred with the very same brush.

'Well now,' announces Kak John, indicating a painted sign over a works entrance, 'here 'tis. And since you've taken such a interest in the workings of a tannery, what a rare treat is now in store for you, Mr Samuel. What a treat, 'pon my soul.'

The sour river smell has been replaced by a more acrid odour, doubtless effluvia of the bate pools, which Kak John has so thoughtfully described for us.

We clamber down from the cart, Rosamund arranges her skirts while Kak John and me lower the parcelled remains of Bobby between us. It is so light I am able to hoist it over one shoulder without overmuch effort.

Rosamund hands her little basket to Kak John. 'There is vittles, should you have the stomach for it,' she wrinkles her nose at the stench. 'A little of baked meats, fruit and gingerbread, which I had purchased at the fair.'

'You are very good, Lady Rosamund, and will, some day, make a excellent wife for a 'septionally fortunate gent, I have no doubt,' replies Kak John, who is grinning hugely, enjoying the mischief he has stirred.

Rosamund fusses at the reins in an effort to cover the colour rising to her cheeks. With the reins firmly secured around the driving board, she gives Polly's hindquarters a sharp swat. To our consternation, Polly lurches a step or two but shows no inclination to head for home.

Kak John purses his lips. 'I 'spect I have gave old Polly too much credit for her wits. Either that or she has taken a liking to us.'

'Well, she cannot remain,' I say. 'There is no concealment for a cart and we will become a source of curiosity soon enough.'

'Then I must take her closer to home,' announces Rosamund, climbing back up onto the driving bench.

'Which being no great distance,' says Kak John, 'for it is only up Webb Street way, so I believe.'

'Rosamund,' I say, 'do not take it amiss, but there is no call for you to return. I hope you will retire to Nine Elms once safely free of the conveyance.'

'Sammy, do not take it amiss, but I should not be easy without knowing that you are both safe,' she retorts.

I grimace. Rosamund smiles to herself; I know very well what she is thinking: 'You are in the right of it, Rosamund,' I sigh, 'I do not know how I would have managed the thing without your assistance.'

'And how will you see it through now, left to your own self?'

'I am resolved to fetch a carter. A man well accustomed to this manner of work.'

Rosamund sniffs, unconvinced, before giving the reins a flick. 'Take good care then, Sammy.'

The cart trots off back up the lane and is soon out of sight, lost against the darkening skies, swallowed up by the enveloping mists.

Kak John grins, teeth gleaming surprisingly white in the dusk. He gestures me forward a ways. As we pass, I observe the glow of a guttering candle in the window of the watchman's cabin and so take care to land my boots without a racket. Kak John is remarkably unconcerned. 'Have no fear, Mr Samuel, Old Tom will have been at his bottle by now and would not stir for fire nor flood, and, for a certainty, will never start at the mere clack of heel on cobblestone.'

The two of us scurry past the cabin into the body of the works, which, from what I can make out through the gloom, is a large open area, bordered by a number of small buildings, the whole enclosed by a high brick wall. The reek here is almost overpowering. 'Follow me close and keep strictly to the pathways,' advises Kak John, 'else you find yourself in one of the pits and drownded.'

In a short while we are at the workman's hut, a fragile wooden lean-to affair propped by the farthest wall. Kak John creaks open the door and we enter. I hear him rummaging for something in a corner; a lucifer flares for a moment before the steadier radiance of a candle illuminates the room.

It is not much of a place, boasting only a few piles of leather off-cuts to sit on and an old straw paillasse on the floor, but it is dry and provides some relief from the prevailing stink.

I lay the body gently on the paillasse. 'Will you stand a watch here while I make for the Feathers and find my carter?'

'I will, Mr Samuel. The stench is naught to me and I have often passed entire nights here when the need arises.'

'If you are so immune you must help yourself to vittles then, it will help pass the time.'

'I will, Mr Samuel,' he replies, 'and you will have a care now and stick to them paths.'

I leave Kak John reclining on a pile of leather, humming softly to himself, untroubled by the reek of the pits or the company of a corpse.

CHAPTER XXI

Once across the river at New London Bridge the route is arrow straight; directly up Fish Street Hill, then on to Gracechurch. Even so, it is well that I know these roads as I do since the mists have now thickened to a proper London Peculiar. It is halfway up Shoreditch High Street when I gratefully perceive through the murk, the light of candles in lead-paned windows and the flaking gilt letters, which herald the Feathers. I enter with some trepidation, leaving the door a little way ajar lest Meathook or some other assailant lies in wait.

Happily, I can see naught amiss. Most all the faces here are known to me, though one or two of the tipplers shoot me curious sideways glances as I pass through in the direction of the counter. Fearon's eyes widen, he waves me over. Leaning forward, his head almost touching mine, he hisses into my ear. 'Samuel, I did not expect to see you here tonight. Nor any other night come to that. You and Mr Facey are sought by half of London and not the good half neither.'

'I know it, Fearon, but I must speak with Michael Shields.'

'You will not find him, he has skedaddled in fear of his life.'

'How so?'

'He was here last night in company with Jack Stirabout as he ordinarily is. Though I marked that Stirabout was most free with his coin, which he seldom is, inducing Shields to become staggering drunk. In his cups, he was less than discreet while Stirabout pressed him hard on a certain matter, plying Shields with sufficient rum to fell a frigate's crew.'

'What matter?' I ask, feeling a leaden weight beginning to settle in the pit of my stomach.

'The matter of a notorious hoist over at the Shoreditch. Your hoist, it would seem, Samuel.'

Fearon has confirmed my worst fears: there is no longer any doubt that those men, Pimlott and Chuffington, know us to be the culprits. I cannot imagine they will be merciful. 'Christ,' I mutter, 'you fool, Shields. You blind, blinkered, bloody fool.'

'You have been well and truly peached, Samuel. Strangers have been here inquiring after you both, hard looking coves who would not blink twice at cocking up your toes for you. Others too, in the same line of work as yours.'

'What others?'

'Teeth and Mutton were here likewise inquiring and have but shortly left. I should not dawdle, Samuel, was I you.'

'I will not. My thanks to you, Fearon.'

Fearon pushes a filled tumbler across the counter. 'Here now, you must take a bracer afore you go.'

I swiftly knock it back, savouring the rough brandy on the back of my throat.

Tendrils of mist are stirred to whirligigs by the wheels of slow moving carriages while pedestrians abruptly loom in and out of the haze as I trudge back to Bermondsey after my fool's errand.

I am caught on the horns of a dilemma: a resolute carter is all that stands between me and a hundred sovs tonight. Whilst such a one might still be found at the Fortune of War or the Rising Sun, even after the bracer I am too afeared to show my mug in any such places.

To be sure, I am no fearless brawler like Facey, but had always imagined myself a deeper file, a man of sensibility and consideration. I realise now that I am no such thing: no man at all, but a coward; a poltroon who must be swayed and cajoled into saving his own best friend; a weak, pathetic creature so debased and timorous that I will call a dog my master if it will save my hide. I have in my grasp a hundred sovs, yet lack the resolution to see the matter through.

By the time I approach London Bridge I have decided to return directly to Crucifix Lane. Kak John and me will cast about amongst the tanneries, glue works and vinegar manufactories in the vicinity and perhaps filch an untended pushcart or suchlike. It is a feeble, rickety plan at best and not without risks of its own, but it is all I have for the nonce.

In the murk, the roads are now almost empty of wheeled traffic, what conveyances are abroad have attached bull's-eye lanterns and crawl along, barely keeping pace with a fast-walking man. I have been lost in my thoughts but now over the past minutes, have slowly become aware of the sound of stealthy footsteps close behind.

It is rage that does it. Fury and disappointment at my own want of character that compels me to suddenly stop and turn. I cannot be certain through the muffling blanket of the fog, but it seems to me that the footsteps have also abruptly ceased.

'Who is there?' I shout.

The world is silent but for the lapping of the Thames against the Portland stone buttresses below and the faint creak and grind of carriage wheels on cobblestones.

'Show yourself,' I bellow.

Naught.

My fingers rootle in my elongated pocket, seeking the chisel. It is not much of a weapon, being neither long nor sharp, but at close quarters may give a good account of itself.

I can feel the rage beginning to burn itself out to be replaced by the familiar clammy grip of fear.

'I have a barker,' I announce, brandishing the short iron rod in the hope that, in the haze, it may pass for the barrel of a percussion pistol.

The sound of carriage wheels intensifies as the unseen conveyance approaches. Using the clatter to cover my retreat, I spin on my heels, turn west and run fast as I dare, along Upper Thames Street, hoping to double back, but the carriage wheels behind me are remorseless. The rhythmic slap of my own pounding feet and the frantic panting of my breath are loud in my ears, yet still I hear the sounds of close pursuit.

I know the streets of London a sight better than I knew my own ma, but find I have momentarily lost my bearings in the thick fog. In my headlong panic I have missed Southwark Bridge entirely and find myself now at Blackfriars. I scurry across, keeping an ear well cocked.

I cut down Holland Street, slowing only when I reach the relative safety of Bankside. Here are the cramped warrens of riverside wharves and warehouses where I may shake this harrier. I pause briefly, leaning against a timbered wall to catch my breath, I cock my head but the only sound is of the creaking wharf timbers shifting to accommodate the gentle swell of the river.

I step out briskly, taking a circuitous route through the narrow back alleyways though mindful to keep my bearings by following the line of the river. There is no use pausing to listen now since the ground here is a soft and silent churn of mud, factory waste, dung and rotting fish to judge by the smell.

As I pass along the blackened timber wall of a ramshackle tenement a stout figure steps from the shadows, blocking my path, sending my heart into my mouth.

'Well, here's a nice article,' grins a blowsy mollisher, flushed with liquor and swaying alarmingly. 'Here is comfort for you on a foul night. Tuppence for a short time,' she slurs, hoisting her ragged skirts. 'Come, for two coppers you may have my virtue in the doorway.' For an instant, a breath of wind from the river lifts the veil of fog in the alley behind her and I spy the hunched figure of her bug-hunter creeping around to take me in the flank. Grinning like a gulpy I reach to my pocket, knowing by the rapacious gleam in her eyes that the lushy act is all a put on. I whip out my chisel once again and take a half-step back. 'And here is your short answer, my dear.'

Her smile instantly disappears to be replaced by a look of consternation. 'No need for a row, sir. I was only askin'.'

'Have no fear, the ball will not be for you, miss, but your associate lurking in the alley, should he take one more step in my direction.'

"Vast it, Jackie, the mark has a barker on me,' she calls out to her accomplice. Turning back to me, she shrugs. 'You will not hold it against me, I hope, sir, that I took you for a bug, seein' as you have the appearance of being a trifle befuddled?'

'I will not, and have a proposition that will not leave you the worse for our encounter.'

'Try me,' she says.

Lowering the chisel to preclude closer inspection, with my free hand I dig for my last sixpence. 'I am hunted by a splitter. In return for my sixpence you and your associate might oblige me by detaining him.'

The woman grimaces. 'If 'tis a splitter we might detain him for good, and gratis. But I'll take your tanner and make the best of it.'

'Well, I suppose you will not take offence if I keep the barker handy until I am clear,' I say, backing away. I flip the coin into the air. As she flails for it, I turn and run, pocketing my chisel on the fly. I keep a straight path now, in the hope that my scrap of silver has purchased me some respite.

In short order I emerge onto a patch of waste ground, which I know to be the site of the old Clink prison, long since burned to the ground. Without the protection of the Bankside maze I must now rely solely on the murk to conceal my progress.

I give it a half-minute to be safe, then pelt hell for leather, headlong across the open ground, hoping that there are no unseen obstacles lying in wait to snag my boots or worse, run my skull into.

I continue at the sprint on into Winchester Street where I can just make out the monumental bulk of the cathedral itself looming above me, peeking out from the mist. Slower now I lope around the south side of the building, being sure to stay close to the buttressed wall, from here it is a short scamper across the churchyard to the fence line.

The building has been left in a state of some disrepair for the past twenty years and so the railing is no barrier. I remove my hat before squeezing through a gap in the rotten iron palings and am onto Bedale.

As I cross the Borough onto St Thomas's Street, I feel that I have at last achieved sanctuary of sorts. Despite the weather and lateness of the hour there are still some few folk going about their business at Guys' and Thomas's and I am on familiar ground here, knowing the backstreets as well as I do my own hands. I veer off into the sooty passages of Snow's Fields, work my way past the glue manufactories and am safely into Crucifix Lane.

Outside Bennett and Sons, I pause for a moment at the watchman's hut, gratified to hear the sound of harsh, rumbling snores from inside. I enter the works, carefully picking my way past the bate pools and creak open the door to the hut. I am not in the least surprised to find Rosamund present, indeed, I am somewhat relieved, given the meagreness of my only plan; no doubt she will help devise a better one soon enough.

She is perched on a leather pile with Kak John, who helps himself to the vittles by the flickering light of the candle. She starts at my sudden appearance, eyes widening in horror. 'What have they done to you, Sammy?' She leaps to her feet.

I extend mollifying hands. 'Why, nothing.'

'Half your ear is gone, and you say it is nothing?' she retorts, angry now.

I put my hand to the wound. My hair is all awry from the chase and without my hat clapped to my head, I can feel that the brown paper has come unstuck, most likely when I squeezed through the railings; it has set to bleeding once again.

'I did not come by it tonight and it is not so bad as it looks,' I say. 'It will keep, at least 'til I have told you all.'

'First I will see to your injury.'

'Sammy will do well enough without a bit of lug, lady Rosamund, for it don't signify and may be an improvement to his looks,' announces Kak John, attempting to make light of things. 'I knowed a cove once with no flapper at all on the left side. Had it bit away in a bare-knuckle brawl and reckoned his hearing was tip-top ever after. Though swore that some nights he would hear a strange voice whispering to him in the dark, soft as anything, the word "Jeremiah". Don't ask me why.'

''Stead of spouting nonsense, Kak John, you might make yourself useful and pass me a cloth from my basket.'

'You may use my kerchief, Lady Rosamund, for it has only been about my neck, which I swear was good and scrubbed last night,' offers Kak John.

Rosamund demurs, 'The cloth will serve, John. It is old and your kerchief is too fine an article to be made a bandage of.'

Kak John rummages in the basket and passes over the long white cloth in which Rosamund has wrapped her gingerbread, helping himself to a chunk in the process.

Rosamund balls up the cloth and begins to dab at my ear. 'Did you at least engage your carter, Sammy?'

'I did not. I gained naught by the hike but ill tidings. It seems Facey and me have been betrayed in our doings by Jack Stirabout, the sneaking blackguard.'

'Then it is well I did return since we must contrive a new stratagem,' says Rosamund, with that half smile of hers. She turns to Kak John. 'Is there clean water?'

'There is a butt just to the side,' he replies.

Rosamund shakes loose the cloth, opens the door a crack, careful not to spill too much light, and slips outside.

'You have been in the wars then, Mr Samuel,' remarks Kak John, scattering crumbs.

'A run-in with a bug-hunter and his mollisher, 'twas nothing.'

'Curious sort of bug-hunter to be employing the blade and not the Neddy,' he says, appraising me shrewdly.

I lower my voice. 'Fair enough, John, it was something more, but it is of no consequence and I have no wish to concern Rosamund further.'

'I'm with you there, Mr Samuel, and you will not hear another word on the matter from me.'

'Good lad.'

At that the door slowly opens to reveal Rosamund, near to tears, holding the sopping cloth in both hands. A man's hand rests on her shoulder.

She steps into the light to reveal Mutton at her back. With his other mitt he has a wicked-looking chiv to her throat.

CHAPTER XXII

Keeping a tight grip on Rosamund, Mutton enters the hut, followed by Teeth, who is forced to incline his head to come beneath the lintel. 'A merry dance, you have led us, Mr Samuel,' he remarks, the words clipped and precise as though bitten off then spat out through those prodigious enamels of his.

'Not so fecken merry was you the one running back and forth to bring on the Hack,' growls Mutton.

Teeth smiles, giving us the benefit of his shire horse grin. 'Ach, a little exercise is for the blood a fine thing. Not so, Mr Samuel?'

'I do not know,' I reply, 'but you will take that chiv from her neck or I will put a ball through your head,' I hiss, reaching to my pocket.

'Ah, yes, the barker. I will take it, if you please,' says Teeth, casually extending a hand.

Rather than releasing Rosamund, Mutton tightens his grip and pinks her with the point of his knife. A tiny red jewel blossoms and trickles down her white neck.

My bluff is called and so, reluctantly, I reveal my chisel. 'I have no barker,' I sigh, 'only the short chisel, along with a promise that should you do her further harm I will kill you with my bare hands, whatever the cost to me.'

Teeth's smile disappears, to be replaced by a grim nod. 'I respect you for it, Mr Samuel.'

'And if you are not already destroyed by Mr Samuel's hand, I will make certain of you after,' announces Kak John, baring his own teeth.

Teeth waves away the chisel. 'Well, I will not deprive you of the tools of trade but your threats are quite wasted on me since I have no mind to spill blood, but, like your Facey, my partner Mr Mutton has no such scruples. Is that not so, Mr Mutton?'

'For a certainty, Mr Teeth. I'll slice her gorge like a cutlet, should the need arise.'

'And so, what to do, Mr Samuel?' Teeth throws his hands in the air.

'You are here for the body, I suppose?'

'Naturlich, Mr Samuel, that is all I ask,' he says, glancing down at the bundle on the paillasse. 'Who else would have it? Bishop and Williams? Tremlett? What is left of the Borough men? I did not think so. We were certain it would be you who discovered it and so, we did not chase the corpse but you.'

'It was the merest chance I came by it.'

Teeth shrugs. 'Glück. Call it what you will. Though I find that men of attainment most often make their own luck. I have kept you in my eye, Mr Samuel, patiently waiting at your favoured watering holes, for I am a jaeger, a huntsman, and was always certain that you must be our quarry.'

'You hunt on Liston's behalf then?' I say with contempt.

Teeth shrugs. 'He holds the heaviest purse. You must forgive me for setting him upon you, but what better way to … how you say it, flush out the game? I took him for a gentler man and did not expect his methods to be so harsh,' he grimaces, gesturing at my ear. 'To your credit, Mr Samuel, you gave us a precious waltz in this grim weather and I was most especially amused by your bug-hunter stratagem—that gentleman will not be so bold again, I am thinking. And so, here we are. And we will have our prize.

To the victor, the spoils, Mr Samuel. All is fair when the dogs must feed on the dogs in this world of ours.'

'Take the prize and welcome, but you will release her, I beg.'

'By and by, Mr Samuel. But first, you will unpack your corpse for us and convey it to our Hackney.'

Mutton tightens his grip on Rosamund's throat, leaving us no choice in the matter. Kak John and me set to work unravelling Bobby from her tarpaulin sheet. The rigidity that comes with a fresh corpse has long passed. One final tug and out she rolls, sprawled across the paillasse, arms and legs awry, as though sleeping through a nightmare.

'A moment,' orders Teeth. He steps to the mattress and, crouching over the body, shoves a hand down the waist of Bobby's fine breeches, nodding thoughtfully as he rummages the nethers. 'Curious,' he announces.

He withdraws the hand, knees creaking as he hauls himself upright. 'A pimmel, but, where the stones should be, the parts of a woman. A true Man-Woman. Never before have I encountered such a thing.' He gives me a brusque nod. 'Bitte, if you please,' he says, indicating the corpse. Me and Kak John make to hoist Bobby by arms and legs like a sack, but Teeth demurs: 'No, no. I desire that you place his arms around you in the manner of a drunken English gent.'

We wrap an arm round each of our shoulders and hoist Bobby upright; I can feel the prodigious chill in him from the ice. Teeth now produces a small hip-flask from his coat, which he unstoppers to sprinkle a little brandy over Bobby's clothing. The man is no fool: given the fine togs and state of preservation, Bobby appears no more worthy of suspicion than any other whey-faced, liquored-up young buck after a good night on the town.

We drag her past the bate pools, head lolling, soles of her fine leather pumps dragging on the paving stones, Mutton and

Rosamund following close behind. In the mists at the gate is a waiting Hackney.

'You never said nothin' 'bout takin' on a lushy,' grumbles the sly-looking jarvey from his bench.

'Our young companion will be accompanying us. The matter is not open for dispute,' snaps Teeth, 'you are being well paid.'

'He don't look too 'ealthy. And what if the young gent pukes inside? Who's to pay the expense of cleaning out the compartment, is what I'd like to know?'

Teeth ignores the objection and flings open the coach door. I climb inside, hauling Bobby up with Kak John's help and settle her, slumped but more or less upright, on the bench.

I step down, glaring at Mutton through the haze. His blade has disappeared from Rosamund's neck, doubtless owing to the presence of the jarvey, but he keeps a tight arm around her, as though she is some dollymop. The chiv, no doubt, now pressing somewhere into her back.

'I'll be wanting extra for the intoxillated passenger,' demands the jarvey. 'For the risk of the thing. You have no notion of how the stink of a puke will infest a carriage and no amount of vinegar and water will extinguish it.'

'What will you take then?' hisses Teeth, losing patience.

'The 'spitals is only down the road and even on a night such as this will find myself another fare and happy to leave you high and dry, gents. But, seeing as you owe me already the sum of three shillin' for all the stoppin' an' startin', this way, t'other way and all that trailin' your man in the fog shenanigans, I will only ask a extra two bob for the risk.'

'You will have it,' concedes Teeth, through gritted gnashers.

'I will take it now,' demands the jarvey with outstretched hand.

'I do not have that sum about me,' replies Teeth, 'you will get it at our destination, along with the rest.'

'A precious rummy affair and no mistake,' the jarvey gazes about, appraising us all with a jaundiced eye, most especially me, with my bloodied ear. For a moment I think he might be about to throw the whole thing up and take off into the night, considering us all too unsavoury, even by his standards. Instead, he nods slowly down at Teeth. 'A extra two bob then, on your honour.'

'Done,' announces Teeth, flashing me a parting grin as he climbs aboard.

I turn to see what Mutton is about but can discern only the lone figure of Rosamund through the haze. In an instant she is wrenched sharply backwards into the mists. 'Oh,' she sighs softly, accompanied by the sound of her body hitting the cobblestones.

I pelt towards her, sensing Mutton pass me in the mist, racing for the growler. Crouching now, I feel my way towards the sprawled brown figure. On the road behind the Hackney rumbles and creaks away into the night.

My hands reach out encircling a worsted ankle. 'Sammy?'

'It's me,' I say, heart pounding in my chest.

'I am well, Sammy. He flung me down is all. I was not expecting it.'

'Thank God,' I say, groping for her hand, helping her to her feet. She grins at me through the swirling vapours.

The patter of running feet heralds Kak John, who slides to a halt before us. 'Well, that's us good an' fecked,' he announces breathlessly, 'saving your presence, Lady Rosamund.'

'We are all of us safe and sound, which is no small thing,' I declare.

'Not entirely sound,' replies Rosamund, indicating my bloodied ear.

CHAPTER XXIII

Led by Kak John, we make our way back to the little hut, taking good care not to misstep in the fog and so end up in a bath of pure to put the topper to this miserable night.

Rosamund sets me down on the leather pile, still clutching the wetted cloth after all she has been through. She employs it now to wipe away the worst of the fresh claret. 'The wound is beginning to crust over and is best left alone, other than to make a bandage for it.' With that, she binds the cloth across my head, failing to stifle a chuckle as she claps my old hat over the doings. 'A fine pair of matching bookends you and your Mr Facey will make now.'

Kak John chuckles.

Rosamund notices that I have not smiled. 'You are disheartened, Sammy. Yet you should not be since we are hale and above ground still.'

'It is the Stirabout business, Rosamund. You do not know the worst of it.'

Rosamund touches me softly on the cheek. 'It is never wise to disclose your dealings in a place like the Feathers. But truly, what harm can come from this Stirabout creature knowing your business?'

I stare into Rosamund's calm grey eyes and, for a moment, feel the strength in them, sufficient at least to lay out the catastrophe. ''Tis as bad as can be,' I say, 'since it was a crone by name of Ma Pimlott we took from the Shoreditch.'

Rosamund's hand flies to her mouth. 'Oh, Sammy. You do not say so.'

Kak John whistles.

'Then you must run. Gather the tin you have saved and quit the metropolis tonight; I wager you are already hunted by worse than Teeth.'

'There is naught to gather.'

'There is the shine for your Rig.'

'Gone. Another consequence of that ill-starred hoist.' I shrug. 'I have not a single sovereign to my purse.'

Kak John shoots his hands into the pockets of his keks and stares down at his boots, shifting his weight from one foot to the other before clearing his throat to speak. 'Mr Samuel, I hope you'll not take it amiss, but I've some few shillin's put aside 'gainst calamity, which I should wish for you an' Mr Facey to have since you'll not get far on a promise.'

'Kak John—' I say, but my voice has hoarsened, refusing to discharge further sound. I am appalled and ashamed that only some few hours past I was scathing and scornful of this young fellow for his sleeked down hair and natted-up toggery.

'My pa left me a timepiece, a hunter, which, if I am not rooked, will raise a few sovs at the least,' adds Rosamund.

For a moment, I do not trust myself to speak and hang my head, unable to meet the eyes of these two who have so little and yet are prepared to give up all they have. I am ashamed for Facey too, who has never even given Rosamund a kind word.

I swallow, finding my voice. 'You must know what kind of wretch it is that you make your offer to. I am not the man either of you believe me to be.'

Rosamund cocks her head, smiling softly. 'I know you, I think, Sammy.'

'You do not know me for the shameful poltroon that I am.'

'Are you so?' demands Rosamund, taking my jaw between her fingers, slowly raising my head back up. 'Then I must have taken you for another when you threatened that great white fellow with bare-handed destruction on the instant 'less he released me.'

'I am a coward, ever skulking behind Facey's strong arm and quick temper.'

'Then you are no fool,' says Kak John. 'I should do likewise, given the chance.'

'You do not know the half of it, Kak John.'

'I know the difference between kak and the stuff that glitters, Mr Samuel, and perhaps you will be amazed to know that I rate you in that very small basket of stuff that glitters.'

'You would not have found me glittering last night, John, were you to have seen me call a dog, "sir". And this night, should you have seen me scampering for my life.'

'And what is the dog's opinion on it?' queries Rosamund, still smiling.

'I could not say, for it was just a dog.'

Rosamund shakes her head. 'So, how can it signify?'

'It matters.'

'And us, do we matter at all, Sammy?'

'A great deal.'

'And what is our opinion on this fellow, Kak John?'

'We believe him to be a man of sense, ingenuity and resource. On the whole, a goodish, decent man, Lady Rosamund.'

'Well said, John.' Rosamund takes my hands in hers. 'And now, knowing our good opinion of you, I hope you will understand why we choose to conspire in your preservation.'

'Your good opinion is worth worlds to me,' I say, 'but I cannot accept your proposition.'

'Why ever not, Sammy?'

'I would not leave either of you without means, Rosamund, the world is never kind to those without either an arm of iron or a hand of gold.'

'Oh, stuff. We will get by as we always have done.'

'I do not think so.'

Rosamund releases my hands, arms dropping forlornly to her side. Her eyes glisten in the shaky candlelight as she gazes up at me. I realise in this moment that her estimation of me has always been so much higher than my own and find that I cannot now bear to forfeit even a shred of her regard. 'You will not be sad, I am sure, when I tell you that your good opinion, both, has given me something tonight more precious than sovs or shillings.'

'I should like to know what that is, Mr Samuel, for henceforth, I'll pursue it like a rat up a drainpipe,' announces Kak John.

'Resolution, John. I'll not call it courage for I have precious little of that. But a small measure of resolution in a man may sometimes be sufficient to pass for the genuine article.'

Kak John pops his lower lip and nods sagely. 'Resolution. I like the sound of that, Mr Samuel.'

'If I must leave the city, then so I must. But I will not quit empty-handed nor your purses of others, not when I have a commission outstanding.'

'You propose to reclaim your prize then, Mr Samuel?' grins Kak John.

'In this murk, a Hackney can make no more headway than a sprightly man afoot and so I may still run it down. They head north and will make for Blackfriars Bridge, I am certain.'

'Then what?' enquires Kak John.

'I have not one idea, John,' I sigh. 'It is a foolish notion, yet I cannot just lie down.'

'You are certain they head north?' interjects Rosamund.

'I know their destination, alongside every resurrectionist in London,' I shrug. ''Tis a toffken at Poland Street.'

'Then we shall not catch them,' she says. 'There is no need, for we will be there long afore them and may contrive some way to put this murk to our advantage.' Rosamund grins as though this were the easiest thing in the world.

'How so, 'less of a sudden we sprout wings and fly?'

'Ah, Sammy, you are forgetting London's greatest and most direct thoroughfare of all.'

My forehead puckers at this.

'We cannot wait for you to riddle it, glocky. 'Tis the river I am speaking of. Old Father Thames himself.'

CHAPTER XXIV

Despite my protestations, Rosamund and Kak John will not be put off from the venture, and so, together, we descend the slimy steps of Pepper Alley Stairs. Even through the haze, the aspect here is dominated by the shadowy, looming bulk of New London Bridge. Behind it, unseen, stretches the older crossing. The two conduits tethered in parallel like a pair of carriage horses; the one a young and glossy colt, the other ancient and clapped-out, fit for naught but the knacker's yard.

Down in the depths of Pepper Alley pier it seems that the wherries have thrown it in for the night on account of the fog, but a few penny-clinkers still ply for trade, prepared to risk life and limb to make the crossing.

'Where away?' hails a figure bundled in shawls and blankets at the oars of the nearest.

'Savoy Wharf or close enough,' calls back Rosamund.

In the smudged glow of a lantern fixed to a pole above her head I see now that it is a woman, albeit one built like an ox and of middle-years. Slowly she removes the clay pipe from her mouth to fix terms. 'I'll take a bob for that, no less,' she says.

'Sixpence,' counters Rosamund.

'Then you may swim for it, my girl, and good luck to you,' chuckles the oarswoman clamping the pipe back between her frayed gobblers.

'Come now, 'tis not so far a ways.'

'You do not pay me for the journey, but the distance I have oared these long years, which amounts to many a hard mile all told.'

'Gammon,' says Rosamund, 'why would we pay for crossings already made?'

'Only them that knows each watery mood, sly trick and sodden inch of this river might take you safely across with a rising tide in such a haar, and there are few enough of us abroad. The fare is for my knowing, not my pulling. But there are others you may try and they will take you for a tanner or less, to be sure, most like directly into the headway of a paddle steamer. If not that then you must face the fast-swirling currents of the Blackfriars pilings and there the river will take you anyways, pulling you under, brisk as thought.' She takes a philosophical puff on her clay pipe and gazes at the wavelets slopping around the sides of her little clinker. 'Save your sixpence by all means, girlie, 'tis not my place to dun the sense into you that will preserve your life.'

Rosamund treats her to a pursed-mouth, sceptical look but produces a shilling nevertheless. 'For your long years on the river, so,' she concedes.

The woman snuffs her pipe bowl with a thick, blackened ball of a thumb and lays it on the bench beside her. 'To the fore with you then,' she orders, stowing the shilling somewhere in those voluminous wrappings and extending a powerful hand.

Scarcely requiring the outstretched arm, Rosamund steps nimbly aboard, clambering around the oarswoman to seat herself at a tiny bench at the front of the boat. 'You, crack'd nob Jack, will join her at the fore,' the woman commands, indicating me with my bandaged head.

Though raised in a port city I have never mastered the art of natation and ordinarily avoid riverine transport. So it is with some trepidation that I step on. Instantly the little wooden vessel tips alarmingly, and for a terrible moment I'm aware of nothing but the dark, jagged waters of the Thames rushing up to devour me. Mercifully the crisis is averted by the woman's strong grip on my coat, she manhandles me behind her, all but hurling me to the pointed end of the boat where Rosamund makes room on the tiny bench.

'Dapper Dan, you will settle aft,' commands our Amazonian pilot.

Kak John steps off the pier with all the grace of a dancing master and settles himself happily in the rear, facing our oarswoman as she casts off the stinking, greasy rope and begins to pull.

'Where is your tiller?' enquires Kak John, impressing upon her that, unlike me, he is no clumsy, mumping landlubber.

'Bless you, young man, 'tis a only modest skiff and easy enough to steer by management of sculls alone should you have the brawn for it.'

Whatever she has just imparted seems to have assured Kak John. At any rate, he leans back on his bench smiling happily for a moment before another question occurs. 'And what of the tides?'

'Highish just now but already running strong this night.'

Instead of heading for the middle of the river as I expected, the oarswoman sticks close to the bank as she pulls upstream and, though I cannot quite see it, I sense the familiar odour of the Bankside ooze. At length we veer away into deeper water. From the haze an outline begins to form; an arced stroke of black that gradually begins to draw itself into the shape of an enormous iron span, the first arch of the Queen Street Bridge.

As we pass beneath, fat, oily droplets of water rain down, while the sound of our sculls rhythmically slapping against the surface echoes all around us.

'View halloo,' bellows Kak John, delighting in the sound of his voice, amplified, bouncing about within this damp iron grotto.

In a moment we are clear and I sense the slight change of heading as we veer back towards the southern bank, prompting another enquiry from Kak John. 'Why do we hug the Southside shallows still when we must be across to the far bank?'

The woman continues her steady pulling. 'No doubt you occupy some elevated position at the Board of Admiralty?'

'Not I.'

'And yet I must pass examination for a Master's warrant before you will let me be?'

Kak John grins. 'I make enquiry only since I have some small understanding of the river and its ways from acquaintances: larks and river men mostly. It's my belief that knowing the wherefore of things is seldom effort wasted.'

'No doubt you will go far with such a philosophy, if you are not first drownded for your constant what, whys, and whichevers.'

Kak John's grin broadens, clearly enjoying the woman's sour disposition. I, on the other hand, am terrified, wishing she had not mentioned the churning horrors of Blackfriars Bridge. To add to my discomfort I sense the vessel changing course, heading out into the depths of the river.

'If I do not miss my guess we should be passing Falcon Wharf just now, where we will quit these slacks and set a course for the second arch of Blackfriars.' She fusses with the oars pulling a little more on side, slewing us round a little way. 'And afore you vex me again, young man, I will tell you straight off that I must take especial care to align the vessel for a good straight rattle through. Since 'tis running brisk tonight, you will be so good as to hold onto the sides as we run, in the event of careen or broach.'

Both eventualities sound equally dreadful to my ears. I clasp the side of the boat with one hand, and, with the other, reach for Rosamund. Her grip is as tense as her face is tight. Only

Kak John seems to be enjoying himself, leaning back on his perch with a blissful smile on his face as though out for a stroll in the park.

Within a yard or two we feel our little tub gripped and mauled by the powerful eddies swirling about the colossal stone palings. The oarswoman heaves first to one side, then the other in an effort to right the boat, fighting the capricious power of the currents for every inch of headway. We hang on for life as the tiny vessel is tossed from side to side, Rosamund's grip tightens around my fingers as we shoot beneath the crumbling yellow Portland stone of the arch and then, with barely a moment to register the dank cavernous ceiling passing overhead, like the maw of some frightful leviathan, we are spat out to the other side into the calmer, stately waters somewhere near the centre of the river.

'And there is your shilling for you, young lady,' announces the oarswoman, twisting on her bench to reveal a complacent smirk.

Rosamund swallows, releasing my hand for the sake of propriety, white-faced but game enough to make a reply. 'Well spent, right enough.'

'Good lass,' acknowledges our pilot, 'and now you will be silent as the grave, 'specially yourself, Lord Admiral, for we are not quite out of the woods. We are mid-channel and must keep a ear cocked at all times for the sound of barges and paddle tugs. They will not give up right of way to such as me at the best of times, and, in this witches brew, will run us to the depths without a second glance. You will assist by keeping a sharp eye out for approaching lights.'

Slowly, ever so slowly, working against the tide, we creep across the water heading for the north bank. From time to time shapeless objects float past, dark and glistening from too long in the river. Occasionally something paler bobs up, gleaming foul and white. I have seen the dead in all their aspects, but on this night and in this place, these things, whatever they may be, seem somehow grimmer and more awful. The oarswoman, impervious, continues to pull softly, sacrificing speed and power for silence, stopping altogether every so often to listen out across the waters.

Finally, the bitter tang of Thames mud comes on strong again, signalling the proximity of the north bank.

The woman strokes with increased vigour as we approach the shallows. 'We approach Surrey Stairs I believe, and you may alight here for your Savoy Wharf to avoid a second buffeting at Waterloo Bridge should you so choose.'

'Then that is what we shall do,' says Rosamund quickly, to my intense relief and Kak John's evident disappointment.

'Fend off now, fend off,' barks the woman, as a decaying, ramshackle wooden structure looms out at us from the mists.

CHAPTER XXV

'The next time I cross the River it will be with the aid of a bridge and on my own two feet,' I say, breaking the strained silence.

'"Fend off" is hardly Greek nor no seaman's cant, Mr Samuel,' responds Kak John.

'I did not take her meaning quite, with her careens, broaches and aft currents. I am not a nautical cove, nor never have been. Mr Facey is your man for the boats.'

'Least said, soonest mended,' advises Rosamund wisely.

'Still, I have learned a good few new curse words on your account, the like of which I had not heard before.'

'Then I wish you joy of them, Kak John,' I retort.

A brisk, silent walk through the Liberty of the Savoy, across the broad thoroughfare of the Strand and up Bedford Street takes us onto St Martin's Lane. Though the narrow street is full of noisy, inviting boozing kens we do not tarry for even a quick bracer after our ordeal.

As we approach Long Acre Rosamund begins to slow. Up 'til this moment she has been setting the pace, mercilessly chivvying us along in this race with the Hackney. Now she treads carefully, like Kak John about his daily business, scrutinising each of the granite paving stones in her path for the leavings of Covent Garden Market. And there is plenty to occupy her, the pavements hereabouts being smeared and littered with pulped, rotten fruit and vegetables. Amongst decaying apples, oranges and slimy blackened onions are old stems, wilting and discarded by the flower sellers. It is these she collects.

'If it's blooms you want, Lady Rosamund, Mr Samuel and me will club together to buy you fresh and better.'

'Gather ye rosebuds while ye may, old Time is still a-flying and this same flower that smiles today, tomorrow will be dying,' she responds, grinning. 'You are very good, John, but for the moment, these will serve my needs.'

I gaze at the sad, drooping stems she cradles in her arm and wonder if we are to hear further discourse on the ephemeral. Instead, she bends to gather a last Iris, tucks it in amongst the rest and ushers us onwards into the fog.

We veer northwest up Crown Street, taking care to avoid Seven Dials and the Holy Land. We have little enough of value about us but should we trespass on the territory of the St Giles Rookery, the savage denizens of that place would certainly strip us of all, perhaps even of our very lives.

I soon catch the bitter, wheaty cattle stench of Soho Square; the wealthy and respectable having long since fled these venerable mansions for more fashionable parts. Now drovers and rustics have become accustomed to using the place for the penning of cattle before herding them to the morning market; the beasts are restive as we hurry past, perhaps conscious of their fate come the dawn. We cut through Carlisle and Little Chapel Street before preparing to cross at Wardour.

'Naught remains but the short stretch of Portland Street,' says Rosamund, 'and before we go further I will lay out my proposal: Sammy, I hope you do not imagine to oppose that great blanched spectre and his partner, given that one or both carries a blade?'

'No, we cannot win by force of arms,' I readily admit. 'Nor would I make the attempt.'

'Then we are of a like mind. Your best stratagem is to make a confederate of the mist and spirit the body away undetected. To that end you might wish their attention elsewhere before making the attempt. It is not much of a plan,' she announces, 'but 'tis better than nothing at all.' Rosamund pulls her shawl up over her head, cowling her face. ''Twill be the Lucifer Lay,' she explains, 'only carried off with blooms.'

The Lucifer Lay is a simple racket, much favoured by young ladies on the streets of the metropolis, wherein they contrive a collision with a well-dressed gentleman, spilling their wares into the dust. The young lady makes such a pathetic spectacle, piping her eye, rummaging in the dirt for her spoiled lucifers that the gent is invariably persuaded to part with a few coins to make amends. More often than not, the mark will be dipped by a Buzzer while his attention is diverted.

'There is too much risk in it, Rosamund, they will know you straight off.'

'Pish, Sammy,' retorts Rosamund, 'they don't expect us, never for a moment supposing us to have headed them. 'Twas in any case only the long white cove with the gobblers who has seen my face, the other was behind me with his arm about my throat.' She pulls the shawl closer about her face and hunches over her blooms. 'Besides, I intend to come it the crone,' she announces in the petulant warbling tones of an old 'un.

Kak John guffaws. 'Ah, very good, Lady Rosamund, and now you are of a perfect age for Mr Samuel.'

'It is no laughing matter, John,' scolds Rosamund, glancing at me. But beneath the shawl's shadowed cowl I cannot help but notice the gleam of a half smile.

'And what is to be my part?' enquires Kak John.

'You will keep crow; then should chance allow, add what you can to the confusion. If all turns out in our favour you will help carry away the prize.'

'Well then,' announces Kak John, 'let's be about it.' With that we head across Wardour and into the misty warren of Portland Street.

CHAPTER XXVI

We identify Glendale by means of a discreet but well-burnished brass plaque affixed to one of two square columns framing the entrance. Like the surrounding houses, Glendale is a fashionable residence of four stories, slim and angular, constructed from blocks of pale sandy stone. Candlelight illuminates the windows of the first and second floors but outside the pavement remains dark and obscured by fog.

Rosamund and me melt into the denser shadows on the other side of the empty street. Kak John trots to the corner of Broadwick, where he slumps, sinking against the iron railings, knees tucked under his chin, another of London's vagrants.

Rosamund is so close I can feel her quivering beside me. 'You are cold,' I whisper.

'Not so much,' she breathes, grinning in the dark, 'though my hands are somewhat chill.'

I take the flowers, lay them on the ground close by, and cover her hands with mine, chafing and blowing on them, our faces almost touching.

'You have uncommon sweet breath, Sammy,' she whispers.

'It is only liquorice,' I reply, 'I keep a stick about me for the purpose.'

'No,' she says, 'I think it is because there is a sweetness inside of you.'

For a moment I do not know how to respond, redoubling my efforts to warm her hands, rubbing away like a Bedlamite washerwoman. 'That cannot be the way of it,' I say, 'very often in the mornings Facey has a breath on him rank enough to stun an ox and yet there is a goodness inside of him, I believe.'

Rosamund grimaces. 'I will have my hands back now, Sammy, lest you wear them to nubs.'

Before we can further explore Rosamund's theorem a short, sharp trill cuts through the silence.

'John,' whispers Rosamund, dipping to gather her blooms.

Sure enough, it is not long before we hear the ponderous, grinding squeak of the Hackney's wheels accompanied by the muffled clop of the horse.

The vehicle emerges from the fog, trundling towards us with agonizing slowness, until finally pulling to a halt outside Glendale. The unmistakable figure of Teeth steps down from the cab followed by Mutton. There is a hasty, whispered discourse whereupon Teeth bounds up the steps to the front door and heaves at the bell-pull, leaving his partner to pacify the irascible jarvey. The door is opened by a stout footman who, despite white cravat, canary yellow breeches and wig, has the phizzog of a rough, brawling sort of cove. A short but heated exchange on the threshold is quickly brought to a close when Teeth simply barges past and enters. The footman, smarting at this affront to his dignity, makes haste to follow, but not before slamming the door behind him.

Mutton approaches the driver's perch, digging into the pockets of his coat, before offering up a handful of shillings.

'Now then, cocky, this is only three bob what you give me. Five was the agreed on sum,' insists the jarvey.

'And you will have the remainder when my partner returns. Meantime, you will wait and cease your mizzlin'.'

By way of answer, the jarvey hawks and spits over the side before withdrawing his head into the collars of his coat.

Beside me Rosamund adjusts her shawl, cowling her face. She sets off across the cobbles, hunched and doddering. I watch until she reaches the kerb before scuttling across. Using the vehicle's bulk for concealment, I crouch on the road beneath the Hackney's near side door and hear Rosamund's quavering voice: 'Buy my fair blooms, sirs, do. Fair blooms to buy.'

'Fuckoffoutofit,' bellows Mutton. I hear Rosamund squeal and catch the faint patter of her blooms scattering across the paving stones. I ease open the door above me and poke my head inside. Bobby is sprawled in the far corner of the cab giving off a strong odour of cheap brandy and just the faintest hint of sweetish putrefaction.

'Oh, sir, that's me livelihood you're clumping all over in yer great boots. How am I to pay for me wittles now?' wails Rosamund, her words punctuated by heaving sobs. She slumps heavily against the cab, setting it rocking on its great leather springs, the disturbance neatly masking my entry as I clamber aboard. Rosamund continues to press herself against the vehicle, raging at her ill fortune and Mutton's clumsiness.

'Now then, missus, mind the conveyance. That's *my* livelihood you're a mauling,' objects the jarvey.

'Shall I hold your hosses for you, sir, for they can be precious skittish in this fog?' I hear Kak John's voice now adding to the commotion about the vehicle.

'Leave off them harnesses, you damned rascal,' bellows the jarvey.

'I should only ask a farthin', sir,' pleads Kak John.

Bobby is a surprising weight for all her slight appearance and I am still struggling to get my arms properly around her when through the window I see Mutton brutally shove Rosamund aside, sending her sprawling. She screeches and sets up a dismal keening, distracting Mutton for a few more precious seconds.

The sound of boisterous laughter echoes from across the way. It ceases abruptly, to be replaced by a young man's drawl, heavily laden with entitlement, though somewhat slurred by drink: 'What the devil are you about, sir? You, sir. I am addressing you.'

Mutton ignores the interruption and prepares to launch a kick at Rosamund's cowering figure.

'Stand away from the hag or you shall receive a thrashing. Do you rob an old woman, do you, sir? Is that what you are about?'

'The crone accosted me with her wretched blooms,' objects Mutton.

'And so in consequence, you see fit to cast her down and trample her wares into the stones?'

'Whip him, Poppy,' urges his companion.

'Be off now, before I have the Crushers on you.'

'I have business here, sir,' wheedles Mutton.

'Step away this instant, or I swear I shall take my stick to your back.'

'I will step away, if it makes you happy. The hag may go hang, she is nothing to me,' concedes Mutton.

I hazard a peek through the carriage window and it is a pair of young bucks who swagger into view as Mutton retreats from the vehicle. Their evening dress is askew and it is evident that they are both somewhat the worse for strong drink.

'Now then, old mother,' advises the more sober of the pair, the one I take to be Poppy, 'collect yourself and be on your way. Here is something for your troubles.' Poppy produces a few coppers from his silk waistcoat and, with a flourish, scatters them onto the pavement where Rosamund crouches, gathering her crushed stems. She scrabbles for the pennies, bobbing her head, careful to remain concealed within the shawl.

'Bless you, sir,' she croaks.

'Poppy,' groans the other young buck, 'I should be very happy were we to take the Hack, the night is foul and I cannot quite make my feet work as they ought. What do you say?'

'A public Hack, Edward?' objects Poppy.

'Oh, Poppy, my legs are all at sixes and sevens. I must sit.'

'Very well then, Edward, needs must when the devil drives.' He bellows up at the cabby on his perch, 'Jarvey, here is a fare for you.'

Inside, I am caught betwixt and between, with Bobby as yet no more than halfway off the bench. I remain quite still, awaiting the cabby's indignant refusal, but it is Mutton who makes objection. 'The Hackney is not for hire, gents. It is yet under obligation to myself and partner.'

'You don't say so?'

'I do, your honour. As I have said, there is unfinished business here.'

'Thrash him, Poppy, and have done with the fellow.'

'If'n you don't mind, gents,' interjects the jarvey, 'this here vehicle is my property and I am the one says who rides and who does not.'

'Five shillings, jarvey, if you will run us to Berkeley Square,' announces Poppy briskly.

Without awaiting a reply, Poppy flings open the door. His refined young face registers a mixture of shock and consternation at my presence inside. 'And now you, fellow. What do you do here?'

'We are on our way elsewhere, sir,' I reply, stupidly.

'And who is this?' he demands, indicating Bobby.

I decide to fall back on Teeth's ready-made flummery: 'It is my master, a young gentleman like yourself,' I reply, 'though all insensible with brandy.'

Poppy, still on the point of entry, cranes his head to the jarvey on his perch. 'It seems there is a gentleman already ensconced here with a prior claim on your services. I should not wish to inconvenience him.'

I hear the jarvey's voice reply, 'I only know that I have not been properly settled with for this here trip to this here street.

I am gipped two shillin' and cannot now say who wishes to go where, and for why. Moresomever, I am certain that you are all intoxillated and so I should rather every man-jack of you quit squabblin' about my conveyance afore I do call the Crushers meself.'

'The gent in the Hack is indisposed and I must see to him,' insists Mutton.

'Stand off, you brute,' retorts Poppy, raising his cane, 'the young gentleman has his man to see to him and requires no assistance from the likes of you.' He glances up to the jarvey. 'Very well, seven shillings then, that should cover whatever you are still owed.'

'Well, I will do it for seven, but it is to be a extra five bob should anyone hurl the cat in my cab.'

'Done,' agrees Poppy. Ignoring my weak protestations, he settles himself on the bench facing us; extends a languid hand to Edward and hauls him aboard before slamming the door and rapping twice on the ceiling with his cane. There is a sudden jerk as the horse strains at the traces and we are away.

I see Mutton through the window, marooned on the pavement in an agony of indecision. Rosamund, still shrouded and hunched, totters away without a second glance, vanishing utterly into the mists. As we trot past, Mutton finally turns, races up the steps and begins to haul frantically on the Glendale bell-pull. Kak John leans against the iron railings, raising a hand in stealthy salute. Even through the haze I can detect the gleam of his delighted grin.

Edward is already drooling and snoring, head lolling against Poppy's shoulder as Poppy reaches to pull down the leather window blind. The cab is now almost pitch black, though I can see the glint in Poppy's eyes as he turns his attention to me and I realise that this young Mohock is not quite so drunk as I had supposed. 'Well now, it seems that the Hack is mine and so you and your master must ride along with us for the moment.'

'So it would seem, your honour.'

'You say your master is a gentleman, and so I should not like to have turned him out on such a night, abandoning him to the tender mercies of such a man as that: no doubt some species of cutpurse or cozener. I did not much like the cut of him, nor his bugger's grips, the wretch.'

'Oh, sir, you have the right of it. That rogue and his confederate have tonight plied my young master with strong drink and carried him to this residence with the intention, I believe, of fleecing him at cards. It is a blessing that my master has no head for liquor and was made utterly insensible by it. Elsewise, who can say what calamity might have occurred?'

Poppy considers this for a moment, eyeing Bobby shrewdly, who, despite my firm grip on her arm, rolls with the motion of the cab, giving, for the moment at least, the illusion of life. 'I had supposed as much. And so, who, precisely, is your young gentleman?'

'We are fresh up from the country, sir. You will not be acquainted.'

'That he is not from the metropolis is evident from the cut of his clothing. It is not what I enquired of you.'

'We are just only come to town today, sir.'

'And already the worse for it. Well, well, it was not so very long ago that I was, myself, a callow young fellow newly arrived and come face-to-face with the wicked snares of the capital.' Poppy sighs like a battle-weary veteran. 'It does you credit that you are anxious for your master. And does he play Hazard at all, your young fellow?'

'Alas, he enjoys all games of chance, as he does the bottle. Both, I should say, a good deal more than is good for him.'

Poppy's eyes gleam with what I imagine to be avarice, though perhaps it is only the trick of the murky gaslight occasionally peeking in through the gap in the blind as we trot along the West London streets. 'Excellent fellow, he shall be my protégé, my project, while he is in Town. His people are well-founded, I suppose?'

'A thousand acres, sir, of the finest Hampshire pasture, no less,' I reply, recalling the renowned Garrett Estate, half a day's tramp from Portsmouth, and a place where me and Facey happily poached fowl as youngsters. From what I can detect of Poppy's expression, I feel I may have over-egged the pudding a little.

'Indeed?' he purrs and grins broadly, nudging his companion awake.

'Wha … wha … whoya?' Edward peers about him like a ruffled parrot.

'Ain't it prime, Edward? Unless I miss my guess we share our Hack with a young Staunton sprig.'

Edward sniffs, grimacing. 'Has someone let a fart?'

Bobby is on the turn now, the strong stench of brandy insufficient to mask the faint odour of putrescence coming off his corpse in this enclosed space.

'I am to blame, sirs, and humbly beg your pardons for it,' I say, quickly.

Poppy's eyes narrow. 'You remain inside with us for your master's sake and that alone. In other circumstances I would require that you ride postilion or to run alongside the Hack. Do you understand the dispensation I make on behalf of your master?'

'I do, sir. And am grateful for it.'

'Then if you wish to keep company inside you will not be saucy, nor will you give free vent to your disgraceful bowels. Is that clear?'

'It is, sir.'

'Well then. You may tell me, do I miss my mark, or does your master enjoy some connection perhaps to Leigh, the Garrett Estate as was?'

'I see I cannot withstand a man of your perception, sir. He is indeed the very gentleman you speak of and heir to the estate.'

'Thought as much.'

'But, sir, now that you have done us such a service and prised my master from the clutches of those rogues I would ask that you do another, greater service and shortly set us down. I would not wish you to trouble yourselves on our account since I shall manage my master quite well enough in these kinder regions, intoxillated though he is, me being much used to his ways.'

'Do not even consider it. How should I live with myself were I to offload young Staunton, green and insensible, into the predatory arms of the unforgiving metropolis at this late hour? No. Such a thing cannot be done, at least not by a gentleman of any feeling. In such a condition he must pass the night with us, we shall make up a couch for him, eh, Edward?'

'Just so, Poppy. And tomorrow, he will join us at supper and make a fourth with Cavendish at the pasteboards.'

With a final, emphatic jerk, the Hack comes to a halt. Poppy flips up the leather blind to reveal a newish house in a fashionable square. Poppy leaps out and quickly settles with the jarvey before rapping hard, three times, with his cane on the imposing front door of this residence.

Edward trips clumsily down from the Hack, very nearly tumbling, as the door is opened by a diminutive, sharp-eyed steward holding an oil lamp. All smiles, he gives Poppy a crisp bow, nodding dutifully as his master peppers him with instructions.

I cannot flee with Bobby's corpse, nor do I have the readies to remain with the Hack, so, for the moment, I must go where the winds have blown me. I take Bobby's arm and fling it round my shoulders, hauling her up off the bench. Of a sudden Bobby's dead-weight burden is eased; I find that Edward has draped Bobby's other arm round himself. Between us it is a simple matter to drag Bobby into the house, notwithstanding Edward's erratic, crabwise gait.

The steward gives me a friendly grin as we pass into the hallway. 'Ah, I feel it would take the crack 'o doom to wake this 'un, stupefied, so he is, I can smell the reek of brandy from here,' he announces with a broad Scotch accent. 'Young gents, eh?' he sighs, rolling his eyes.

I cannot put my finger on it quite but there is something discomfiting about the man's willingness to please. At any rate, I have no wish to make an enemy, so I make no reply, merely returning the smile.

'I am Gunn,' he announces, opening one of the doors leading immediately off from the hallway.

Between us, Edward and me convey Bobby into a dark and tiny parlour furnished only by an old Chesterfield couch, draped with what appears to be a frayed candlewick. As we lay Bobby down I am careful to turn her facing the wall, covering her quickly with the old bedspread in order to avoid closer inspection by the household.

Edward and me retrace our steps to the hallway, where Gunn awaits with his lamp. 'Mister Popplewell has this moment retired, sir.'

'Likewise, Gunn, likewise. I will bid you all a good night,' slurs Edward, claiming the oil lamp before staggering off in the direction of the master stairway.

Gunn retrieves the candlestick, from an alcove by the door. 'Your master will be comfortable here I am sure, while you yourself shall have the truckle in our attic. You will find our household a modest one, my friend. Myself, Euphemia the cook, and our slavey, Hannah, the sum total of us.' Gunn smiles broadly, exposing overlong front teeth, his tongue slithers out, gliding from side to side as he moistens them.

'My thanks to you, Gunn,' I reply, extending my hand. 'My name is William.'

Gunn takes my hand, grinning in the guttering light of the candle flame. His grip is soft and clammy and I do not like it at all. 'Well, William,' he whispers, 'you are welcome here.'

He leads me down the hallway indicating the narrow wooden back-stairs. 'My own room is down a flight and so you will not mind if I leave you now to shift for yourself and make do with what you find about the attic. It is something of a climb.' He hands me the candlestick. 'Well, a good night to you, William. I trust you will be comfortable and not stir.'

'Obliged to you, Gunn,' I reply, beginning the ascent.

CHAPTER XXVII

I make my way up the wooden staircase, taking care to discover any creaking step, which might later serve to betray me. Fortunately, the house is of a recent construction and the timber well seasoned, so I ascend without undue alarm.

On the top floor is a compact landing. A single squat door gives onto a cramped single-windowed garret in the eaves. The room is dusty, with little by way of ornament or furniture other than the ramshackle canvas truckle bed, a cracked chamber pot and, propped against the wall in the far corner, a faded portrait marred by a deep gash.

I set my hat and candlestick on the bare boards before gingerly unfastening the cloth bandage from around my head, it sticks a little at first then comes away easy enough. I prod at the wound, gratified to note that it has scabbed over and there is scarcely any pain. I lower myself gingerly onto the truckle's sagging canvas, swing up my legs and slowly recline, testing the ancient material to see if it will bear my weight. It does. For the moment, there is naught to be gained while Gunn remains alert, so I resolve to enjoy a couple of hours repose before attempting to steal away with my prize.

Gunn I cannot catch the measure of. I do not care for him and cannot quite put my finger on the why of it, since he is amiable enough. Certainly, his master Poppy is no puzzle; his type are to be found all over our West End: young men with little or no fortune, often the disinherited, or second and third sons of reputable families, presenting a respectable appearance to the world yet, in reality, living from one day to the next on their wits along with their luck at cards: dowry-hunters and sharps, preying on the callow and gullible. Chancers, but no more wicked than the rest of us, to be sure.

Poppy's household is a façade: no more than a fashionable address; leased no doubt, and likely much in arrears. Indeed, there are no articles of value anywhere to be seen about the hallway or parlour room. His companion, Edward, is a typical flat, perhaps already tapped out as a source of ready money, and so a pigeon of Staunton's fortune and expectations just now falling into Poppy's lap must seem like a gift from heaven.

Well, I do not begrudge a man his bread, but there is naught to be gained from Bobby's expectations. With that grim thought I close my eyes and rest my weary carcass for a few moments.

It is a full bladder that wakes me; I curse myself for my own lethargy and weakness whilst availing myself of the piss pot. The candle is burned out but I do not think I have been asleep for more than two or three hours. By my estimation it must be somewhere around four or five of the morning, even so, it is closer to sunrise than I would have wished. The house is still silent but soon, no doubt, the slavey will be up and about for the water.

"More haste, less speed," as Pounds used to say of my careless letter formations. I do not think he would have taken much pride in his handiwork now as I creep, swiftly as I dare, down these back stairs like a common cracksman. Mercifully, the stairs remain true and do not protest my weight and so I reach the hallway on the ground floor without incident. Curiously, the door to the parlour is now somewhat ajar though I would swear that it was closed when I took my leave of Gunn.

My heart is thumping in my chest as I enter the room. A shaft of moonlight spills across Bobby's recumbent form, at the same time, to my horror, illuminating the stealthy figure of Gunn looming over her. Sensing my presence, the man freezes for a moment before slowly tilting his head towards me with his customary smile. He moistens his front teeth with his tongue and nods affably as though our meeting here at this hour was the most natural thing in the world.

Advancing softly on stocking feet, he waves me back from the threshold. I duly retreat and it is only when we are both in the hallway, parlour door safely closed, that he speaks and then only in the faintest of whispers. 'Ah, William,' he murmurs, 'did I not say to myself that there was something of the weasel about you? Gunn, I says, now there's a tricksy fellow if ever I saw one.'

I do not return his amiable smile and make my reply in a low but forceful growl. 'What is your business here, Gunn?'

'Now, isn't it me the one should be askin' you that very question?'

'It is my master sleeps here. I am come to see to his comfort and just as well I did.'

'And isn't it my own household that I am protectin' from a vicious night prowler now? A wee, sleekit cracksman, inveiglin' his way into my ain master's good graces. Into his very home, forsooth. All I need do is raise the hue and cry and you will be instantly taken up, so mark well what you say to me next, young William.' He smiles, tongue darting out to flick back and forth over those slimy front teeth of his.

I am no hand at horseflesh but reckon my circumstances may be somewhat likened to the driver of a runaway coach: I might cut and run this instant, bailing for my very life, or I might stay aboard, risking all, taking a firm grip of the reins and hope to play the thing out to a happy conclusion.

'I must see to my master,' I announce, spinning on my heel and flinging open the parlour door. In a few short steps I am at Bobby's side, crouching over the body, giving it a vigorous shake. Gunn stands at the threshold, leering.

I rise instantly with a horrified expression on my face. 'Good God, man, what have you done?'

The smile on Gunn's face collapses. 'Whatever do you mean?'

'He is quite dead, Gunn. My master is killed.'

'What?' squeals Gunn. 'I did not a thing.'

'It is murder, Gunn, and you will hang for it.'

'But I did naught, never even came near him, I swear,' Gunn moans in terror, wringing his hands. 'You are certain of it?'

I lift Bobby's lifeless arm, raising it high before releasing. The limb flops, bouncing off the floorboards with a meaty thump.

Gunn goggles in terror. 'You must believe me, William, I meant no ill to you or your master. Just a little dipping, which is my only perquisite in such a house-crumbs from a mean table. But I never filch more than a couple of shillin' and so where's the harm?'

'There is the harm,' I say, pointing down at Bobby's corpse in the manner of a fire-and-brimstone preacher. 'That harm is done and cannot be undone.'

'William, I beg you. My hands were not yet even about his pockets when you came upon me; I never touched a hair on his head, I swear to you.'

Gunn looks so forlorn now, wringing his hands, with tears in his eyes that I cannot bring myself to lay on further torture. 'Well, well, I am inclined to believe you, Gunn,' I say. 'It may be that my master has drunk hisself to death.'

'Bless you, sir,' sighs Gunn, deflating, cuffing his eyes. ''Cordin' to Mr Popplewell he is the Staunton heir, is it so, William?'

'It is.'

'Christ. At the very least there will be a scandal that will bring my master down and may yet see us all at the rope's end.'

'The finger of suspicion will not rest on you alone. Our fates are bound in this, and so you must calm yourself, Gunn. All is not yet lost. It is clear that the body must first be removed from this house while it is not fully light.'

'And what then, William?'

'It must thereafter be disposed of in as thorough and speedy a manner as we can devise.'

'How so?'

'There is a sort of fellow in this metropolis who is always pleased to receive a fresh corpse and will pay cash money for it to boot.'

'You mean to say a resurrectionist?' he shudders.

'I do, Gunn. It so happens I am acquainted with some such.'

Gunn throws me a foxy, appraising look. 'Then you are a bolder fellow than I took you for, William.'

I fear now that, with his disposition somewhat restored, he means to haggle with me over the value of our body. 'Listen to me, Gunn,' I hiss. 'My master is dead; my livelihood gone. I have nothing further to lose and must now look to my own welfare. If I might make a few shillings out of this I will think myself fortunate enough and you will be content to have shot of us both, and none the wiser. So, mark me well, when I quit this house our connection is quite at an end. There will be no further obligation between us. Is that understood?'

Gunn has the grace to look a little shame-faced. 'It is, William, it is. And so, what would you have me do?'

'No doubt you keep a laundry hamper somewhere in the bowels of this house?'

'We do, though it is but half-filled as yet.'

'So much the better. You will fetch it here and rouse the slavey to call for a carter. Quickly now as there is not a moment to lose.'

Gunn disappears about his tasks while I set to preparing Bobby for what I fervently pray will be her final journey. I spread the coverlet across the boards before dragging the body off the couch. Next, I tidy her sprawled limbs, drawing the spindly legs together and crossing her arms over her breast before rolling her tightly into the bedspread. From the hallway I catch the sound of the slavey's yawning protestations, followed by the clatter of the front door being unlocked.

In short order Gunn reappears, dragging a sizeable laundry hamper behind him. Between us we hoist the parcelled corpse and lower it into the receptacle before covering it with sundry articles of soiled linen.

We drag the hamper into the hallway, over the threshold and out onto the street, where we wait a while. It seems that I could not have cut it finer: dawn is breaking, the birds roosting among the eaves have already begun this day's long chorus whilst fragile wisps of spectral vapour are all that remain of last night's fog. Even these will quickly burn to nothing as golden fingers of sunlight reach out for them across Berkeley Square garden.

'Mr Gunn, sir, I 'ave brung 'im for you,' bellows the slavey, as she approaches, accompanied by a red-faced cove pushing a handcart. Her harried awakening evidenced by her slovenly appearance: dress and hair askew, without even a cap on her head. She has a pale, undernourished look and is all sharp pink elbows, prominent ears and goggling eyes. 'He was a right bugger to rouse an' all.'

'Good lass, Hannah, and now you may go for the water, if you please,' Gunn waves her off, though she continues to stare, slack-jawed and gawping.

'But laundry day ain't 'til Thursday, Mr Gunn.'

'Laundry day is when I say it is, now get you about your duties,' snaps Gunn, sending her scuttling back inside.

'What's all this about then, Mr Gunn?' enquires the carter. 'I never knowed laundry needed doing so urgent that good Christian folk must be roused from their beds afore sunup for it. Has someone shitted the bed linen?'

'Must I explicate the inner workings of my household to you, Wombwell, afore you will take my commission? If so, I should certainly see about another carter in future.'

'No, no, Mr Gunn. I am roused from my pit now and may as well be about it as not.' With that he reaches for the hamper.

''Tis heavy, I warn you,' advises Gunn. Instead, the three of us pitch in and up it goes, right enough, onto the bed of the handcart. 'It is our good plate inside, to be hocked by the offices of this gentleman. But I should not like it known abroad that my master is in such straits,' explains Gunn, proving by this stretcher that he is every bit as tricksy as he considers me to be.

Wombwell grins and taps his ruddy nose. ''Tis ever the same with them fast young gents. But do not trouble yourself on that account; I am the very soul of discretion, Mr Gunn. Though, given the circumstances I should ask to be paid up front, if it don't give offence. Or, to be honest, even if it do.'

Gunn looks at me expectantly. I shrug, patting my empty pockets. Gunn glares before rummaging in his own breeches for a couple of silver shillings. 'Well now, William,' he announces, handing the coins to Wombwell, 'I do not expect our paths will cross again and earnestly pray they do not. And so, I will not shake your hand.'

'You have my thanks, Gunn, at any rate,' I reply.

Wombwell tilts his cart and begins to push, following behind as I set off in the direction of Brook Street. 'Where we off to then, yunker?'

'Not so far,' I reply. 'Not so very far now'.

CHAPTER XXVIII

I am poor company for a man of Wombwell's talkative disposition, sunk as I am in an agony of trepidation while we cover the final mile or so to our destination. Fending off all enquiries as to my line of business and the likely value of Popplewell's silver plate, I grunt and shrug and grimace until he gives up entirely and diverts the remainder of his energies into propelling the cart.

Stepping a few paces to the fore I hunch my head deep into my jacket collar, keeping a sharp eye out for any acquaintance, assuming all now to be of ill intent following Pimlott and Chuffington's recent discovery.

We cross at New Street, now called Regent, with its brand new columns and porticoed splendour; it is almost deserted at this time of day but for a handful of early vendors calling out their wares: the cowcumber cove, wicker basket on his head; a water-cresses woman wheeling her tiny barrow; and a stout, gap-toothed milk maid. We turn onto Argyll Place and Great Marlborough Street where I breathe a small sigh of relief. It has been a mere four nights since Facey and me were last here but we have been through a deal of strife in that short time.

I direct the carter to the narrow lane running up the side of Brookes' residence, where I commence hauling at the tradesmen's bell-pull, praying that our principal is at home and not indisposed, nor gone to the country or other suchlike catastrophes.

In a little while there is a heavy clunk followed by a sharp metallic scraping as the door is unbolted and unlatched from within. It opens but a few inches to reveal the sharp nose and suspicious eyes of Brookes' elderly manservant. He peers out for a moment, his gaze moving swiftly betwixt me and the pushcart at my back. 'You have come then?' he says finally.

'I have,' I reply, 'with the goods expected by your master. They are of some value and were best brought inside without delay.'

The manservant nods without expression, throwing wide the door.

Wombwell and me manhandle the hamper over the threshold into the vestibule and I note that, despite the hour, the manservant is already primped out in his livery and perfectly alert. Though elderly, this one is clearly no dotard.

'You will be pleased to wait without, while I inspect the contents,' he says, addressing Wombwell. 'Never fret, the hamper will be restored to you in due course.' Wombwell meekly does as he is bid, stepping back out to the alley, doubtless awed to silence by the grandeur of his surroundings. The manservant shuts the door behind him, securing it with the hefty iron bolt before turning to me. 'Is it the one?'

'It is the oddity, be assured of that.' I reply, raising the hamper's lid on a tangle of bundled linens. A sharpish odour briefly wafts up from the contents, a mixture of sweetish putrefaction and the tang of stale sweat. I shove the soiled laundry aside to reveal the tightly wrapped candlewick bundle nestled inside like the cocoon of a butterfly.

'Thank heavens. You have done my master a great service. Greater than you know.'

I reach down inside taking a good hold of the head, the manservant secures the legs and we haul the body out. I bend my knees, taking the strain, as the manservant settles the full weight of the burden across my shoulder. He gives me an approving nod. 'It is but one short flight,' he announces, indicating the backstairs.

'It has been naught but one long and fearful flight thus far,' I respond. I do not expect him to understand my quip but, to my surprise, he smiles and bids me follow.

We make our way up to the first floor of the house passing the cluttered rooms where Facey and me met previously with his master. He shows me into a smaller, connected room in which there is a long, stained wooden workbench cluttered with papers and apparatus of scientific enquiry. On the wall is a good-sized engraving of some misfortunate party with his innards all exposed. On the floor below it, an open chest containing more books and instruments.

The manservant clears a space, returning the paraphernalia to the chest, in order that I might deposit my burden onto the long workbench. Between us we carefully unwrap the body from its candlewick shroud and set it to rights. The manservant collects the coverlet under his arm and the two of us stand for a moment gazing down at Bobby's remains. She, or perhaps, he, is rather beautiful in repose, long curling black hair frames a pale, finely featured face. The eyes are closed but furnished with long, lustrous lashes. Only the mouth, with its full lips, gives any hint of former character, set as it is in a vaguely petulant pout.

The manservant breaks the silence: 'If you would be good enough to attend here I shall rouse the master and settle matters with your carter. I should ask that you remove your hat if you please, and you may take what refreshment is to hand in the meantime,' he announces, indicating a half-finished decanter of deep red port wine and a discarded plate of Sally Lunns on the mantelpiece.

I realize that I have not eaten in a good while and am ravenous. I grab one of the little buns and cram it into my mouth. There is no glass to hand and so I simply upend the decanter. In a few urgent swigs I have drunk off the lot and quickly feel the restorative glow of the rich ruby liquid warming its way into my belly. With nothing else to occupy my attention I step over to the wall to make closer inspection of the engraving. The anatomised cove has a curiously blithe expression on his dial, as though he has not yet twigged to his misadventure. And, to be fair, the guts of him are all set out neat and tidy as you like while the flaps of his belly are turned back on themselves like the petals of a flower.

I scoop up the remaining Sally Lunn and make short work of it.

'It is true then, Mr Samuel? You have brought it off?' Brookes arrives in undress and a state of some agitation, iron-grey hair all skewwhiff, still tucking his shirt into his breeches.

'I most earnestly pray so, sir. Though the doing of it has been a precious sore trial to me and my partner,' I reply through a mouthful of bun.

Brookes is decent enough to ignore the discharge of crumbs spattering all around him. He leans over the body, peering closely into Bobby's face and tenderly brushes a stray lock of hair from the forehead. A strange choking sound escapes from him, whereupon he shakes his head vigorously, like a wet dog, straightens and composes himself before clearing his throat. 'It would certainly appear so, but we shall shortly see for certain.'

All business now, he prises apart the eyelids and inspects the cloudy orbs. Once blue, they now have a milky opaque sheen, the whites blackened and engorged with blood. Brookes carefully closes them once more before loosening the shirt collar. He briefly inspects the neck, nodding grimly to himself. At length, he reaches down into the wooden chest, withdraws a hefty leather bundle and unrolls it to reveal a terrifying array of sharp-edged brass instruments. He selects a wicked-looking long brass scalpel.

I swallow, forcing down the remnants of my bun. 'As you well know, sir, I have never been one of those men who quail at the sight and odour of mortal flesh, but I should far rather not remain for your procedures, if it be all the same to you.'

Brookes grimaces, wielding the scalpel. 'Fear not, Mr Samuel, you shall not be forced to endure a lesson in anatomizing. I merely wish you to observe whilst I examine the body. Stay, I beg you.'

'I am relieved to hear it, and so I will, sir.'

Brookes moves to the feet and slits the cuff of Bobby's trouser leg, slicing upwards with the scalpel, running the blade all the way up to the waistband. He repeats the procedure with the other leg; the trousers fall open, neatly as the belly of his engraving, revealing slim, marble-white legs. At the meat of Bobby's calf I notice a shiny circular cicatrix, shaped like two irregular halves of the waning moon.

Brookes pulls away the remaining material covering the crotch. Whoever has dressed the corpse has seen no necessity for nether-garments and so Bobby is quite exposed, the manly part naught but a tiny thing, nestled in a clump of downy brown hair, curled and pale, like a slug after the rains. Sure enough, there is neither sack nor stones below, but a cunny.

I have dragged, hauled and lifted this creature across half of London, but it is only now that I perceive the humanity of him. I say "him" for I now see him to be a man of sorts. Observing his vulnerable, naked flesh, I find myself pitying what he was and what has become of him. Despite the repugnance I feel at his peculiarity, I sense a mortal kinship, as though I myself am in some way diminished by his extinction. Rosamund was right, it seems: here is a sad, ephemeral creature, and my heart aches.

I withdraw, stepping back from the workbench, unwilling to conspire in this final indignity. Brookes appears to have no such scruples and is avid to make closer inspection. He parts the legs, and delicately lifts away the prick to further expose the womanly part.

He shoves the tips of his fingers a little way up inside the crack of the cunny, carefully probing, before pressing apart the soft folds of flesh on either side. 'There now, do you see it, Mr Samuel?'

'I do not wish to look, sir,' I say, staring fixedly up at the engraving. 'It appears somehow … wrong to me.'

'I understand your sensibilities, Mr Samuel, and they do you credit, but I will tell you, you do not pry into God's work here, but my own.'

I glance down at the body. Brookes holds back the twin pleats of flesh, prising them apart with his fingers, to reveal not the delicate folds of a woman but merely a shallow indentation enclosing a long, jagged scar.

'It is not a oddity then, sir?'

'It is not. 'Tis but a young man for all his want of stones. There was little enough of the flesh remaining to stitch closed the terrible wound and that all tattered and mauled. The scarification here has contracted inwards to form a small concavity and puckered to produce a superficial similarity to the parts of a woman.'

'And so, not Bobby?' I ask, feeling my heart descend.

'No, not Bobby, though perhaps more rightly Bobby, since that is the name he took for his own.'

'I cannot understand you, sir. You speak in circles.'

'I am sorry, Mr Samuel. I have not been fair to you. The young man you see here is Robert. Robert Templeton. I am quite certain of it,' announces Brookes, setting Bobby's legs together and covering him once again.

'But how can you know this, sir?'

'Because,' he replies, a curious, tight expression on his face, 'this young man was my own son.'

CHAPTER XXIX

It has been a queer and troublesome commission from the first and now here is the mazer to cap all. I stare back at Brookes, my trap opening and closing like a guppy, unable to put a voice to the manifold questions now swirling about my canister.

Brookes smiles sadly and places a gentle hand on my shoulder. 'Well now, Mr Samuel, we must see to the business between us.'

We are interrupted by Brookes' manservant who appears at the door, expressionless and unruffled. 'May I enquire, sir?' he says, addressing his master.

'He is somewhat changed, but now that I have seen my own work, I am certain of it. It is he, Crick, without a shadow of doubt.'

'Then I am sorry for it, sir. But rejoice that he is, at last, in your care.'

'My care? Shame on me for such tender solicitude,' replies Brookes bitterly, indicating the body of his son. 'I trust you will make the necessary arrangements with Marsden's and St George's at all speed. I should like to attend to the matter today.'

'I will, sir. I have set a fire in the lady's music room according to your wishes and there is a bottle of good Madeira wine laid out.'

'My thanks, Crick. You are very good.'

Crick bows gravely to his master, followed by a brief, but approving nod to me.

I follow Brookes along the passageway to another of the rooms on this floor, small but more comfortable and, uncommonly for this house, bearing the sure signs of a woman's touch. Indeed, the portrait of a pale, fine-featured woman, of about my own age, hangs above the fireplace where a modest blaze warms the room. There is a small pianoforte at one wall, shrouded against the dust, which would account for the room's former purpose. A delicate side table of some fine, dark wood supports the afore-mentioned bottle and two crystal glasses. There is a bookcase furnished with slender, leather-bound volumes, their spines embossed with gilt lettering. Knick-knacks and daintily filigreed ornamental fripperies abound. Yet, even the ardour of a good fire cannot overcome the air of stale musty neglect that hangs over this room like a transparent shroud.

Brookes indicates that I take one of the two armchairs set out by the hearth, while he sees to the wine. He offers me a glass before settling himself. As always, I am anxious lest I snap the stem or allow this beautiful object to slip through my clumsy fingers and shatter. And so I drink with two hands.

Brookes holds his own glass at the stem betwixt finger and thumb, raising it aloft against the glow of the flames before sipping. 'It is my wife, Leanora,' he says at length, nodding up at the portrait.

'She is ... '

'Dead. Many years past now, Mr Samuel.'

'I am heartily sorry for it, sir.'

Brookes dips his head in acknowledgement before continuing. 'When she passed it was not easy for me. She was taken young: at the age you see her now in point of fact. I find scant comfort in the likeness and so do not come here often.'

I cannot think what reply to make and so I remain silent, nodding sagely.

'We were not so fortunate as to have been blessed with offspring of our own. Robert was my natural son, born out of wedlock.'

'Sir, there is no need to ...'

Brookes cuts across me, some indefinable compulsion driving him onwards. 'Leanora was never robust in health and so Mrs Templeton, Robert's mother, had been, for some years, my dear wife's nurse, companion and confidante. You will not judge me too harshly, I hope, when I tell you that when Leanora passed I sought comfort from those closest to me—closest to her. It was improper of me to keep Mrs Templeton on, I know, and yet in my weakness, I could not bear to part with her. It was here we sat in the evenings, together, talking of Mrs Brookes. Sometimes, she took a turn on the pianoforte. And so, we became close. In a moment of weakness I allowed that intimacy to become something ... more.'

I finish my wine. The little table is too far from me to return the empty glass and I dare not set it down on the floor for fear of my great boots. I nurse the delicate receptacle betwixt my paws and notice that Brookes is staring at me expectantly, awaiting some kind of response. 'Sir, it is not my place to pass judgment on any man. There are far too many shortcomings and weaknesses in connection to my own character for me to come it the canting hypocrite.'

'I do not require your judgment, Mr Samuel, I have estimated my own conduct and found it quite wanting. No, nor do I require your pity.'

'I understand, sir,' I reply, unsure whether I am expected to pass further comment or perhaps begin an account of our trials. Certainly, I have pressing concerns of my own, not least of which is to see to the whereabouts and wellbeing of my confederates without delay. But I can do nothing until we have come to the matter of the bounty and so, I must, for the while, comply with Brookes' whims.

'In truth, I did not love her, nor she, me. She would not, in any case, consent to be wed, our stations being so far apart the scandal of such a union would have ruined us both,' adds Brookes.

I see now that he is determined to run his course. It is a most curious fact of human nature that, though we live our lives immersed in deceit and lies of all description—we exaggerate our virtues and make light of our vices, passing off half-truth and distortion as good coin, and the absolute truth is seldom freely given—yet, once a man has determined to unburden his soul with an unvarnished veracity, there is almost no power on earth that will stop him.

I carefully shift my hands down the stem to reveal my empty glass. If I must remain, I might as well do so with some comfort.

'I observe your glass is empty, Mr Samuel. Allow me to fill it for you.'

'I will take another drop, sir, despite the early hour. It is not every day that I am able to enjoy a wine of this quality.'

'You have earned it, I'm sure,' he says, gesturing to the lobe of his ear.

I adjust my locks, covering up the wound. 'Indeed, sir. It has been a most troublesome hoist—forgive me, a hoist is our cant for the removal of a ... '

'I take the meaning of it, Mr Samuel,' interjects Brookes, returning my recharged glass. 'To split a hair, you have in this matter, as on other occasions, strayed beyond the boundaries of the law. But morality is never absolute to be sure, and the law, far too blunt an instrument to accommodate all our requirements to a nicety. Rest assured, you have carried off a righteous enough deed here.'

'I feel certain of it, sir. He is ... home, at the least.'

'Home? No, this was never Robert's home, just as I was never a father to him, though I made every provision for him and his mother's comfort, settling a sizeable sum on them. Following her confinement I secured for them both a comfortable cottage in Richmond but I never saw her again, nor had commune other than through the offices of my man of business. I do not censure myself for this. It was in accordance with her own wishes.'

I nod attentively, wishing he would but finish and settle the sizeable bounty on me.

'I received a brief report each year from my man of affairs, following the dispensation of the monies. By all accounts, Robert was a wayward, difficult child and a source of little pride or comfort to his mother. In his fifteenth year, she died of the cholera and, within a matter of days, Robert was gone, subsequently presenting himself but once, on Lady Day, at the offices of Bamfield and Sons. There he expressed a desire to exchange his settled annuity for a capital sum. A prodigal son indeed.'

I shake my head in disapproval, hazarding this to be the required response having no particular notion of the vantages of annuities versus capital sums, but quite certain that I should be content with either. I have decided not to reveal what I know of Robert Templeton, nor of the debts he left, since it would serve no purpose here and would only add to Brookes' misery.

'I had not seen the young man in the flesh until one evening almost two years past when I received an urgent communication from an address not so far from here in locus but so very, very far in situation: a dismal, comfortless place, grim beyond words. There I found Robert, sprawled on a stinking mattress, soaked in his own blood, life hanging by a very thread. I had him taken up and carried here at all speed, where I ministered to him, labouring through the night with all the skill I possessed, and was able to preserve his life only by means of the chirurgical work you have observed.'

'What in God's name should be the cause of such a savage injury, sir?'

'Why, a savage beast, Mr Samuel. Indeed, there were bites all over his body, but the injury that you have observed, the worst of them by far. The testes had been quite torn away in the violence of the attack and what remained of the scrotal sac, a mere scrap of flesh.'

I am conscious of an icy chill about my own parts as I gaze at Brookes, unable to disguise my horror at such a thing.

'Your pardon, Mr Samuel, these terms of anatomy are the cant expressions of my own profession. What I mean to say is ... '

'If you please, sir, though not familiar with those exact words, I catch the meaning of them well enough.'

'Just so, just so,' murmurs Brookes. He gazes at the dying flames for a time. 'Throughout the period of his recovery I was able to come to know his character a little. It grieves me to say so, but I found in him a vain, petulant, begrudging soul, though not without charm when he wished to make himself agreeable. And, as you have seen, he was not devoid of physical ornament.'

'No, sir. A well-looking young man, to be sure.'

'He had run through his small fortune in fast living and ill-advised speculation and so I desired to set him up in a small way in the colonies. But he would have none of it, on the contrary, issuing threats to reveal our connection, thereby hoping to extort further sums from me. Can you credit it, Mr Samuel? Blackmail, 'gainst his own father?'

'I cannot, sir.'

'I stood firm though I wish I had not. But angry words were spoke; he quit my roof in high dudgeon and I never saw him in life again.'

'A sad and sorry tale, to be sure, sir. Though not, I imagine, a singular one in this wicked metropolis.'

'Indeed not, Mr Samuel. You will have observed his eyes, I take it?'

'His eyes, sir?'

'Engorged with blood, along with other small signs I had noticed at the inquest but could not confirm 'til now.'

'I am a man of meagre learning, sir. I do not take your meaning.'

'Meagre learning perhaps, but a man of surprising perspicacity I have found, Mr Samuel.'

'I thank you, I hope, sir,' I reply, setting myself to remember this new word to Rosamund.

'There is a faint band of bruising around the neck, which I take to be the imprint of a ligature, moreover, there is bruising to the wrists and arms: signs of a struggle, which lead me to conclude that Robert's life was forcibly taken, by means of strangulation.'

I cannot deny that I am full of admiration for Brookes' learning that he is able to read a man's body like a book, deciphering the events of a prior chapter from but a few small marks. Yet, I hold back, considering how to reply, fearful now lest Brookes means to bring in a Magistrate. What more is to be gained by revealing Florey's suppositions, since it is not only our bounty that hangs in the balance here, but perhaps our liberty too? I swallow, moistening my tongue.

'I tell you all of this,' continues Brookes, 'so that you know how matters stand between Robert and myself. If there is any useful intelligence, you will hold nothing back when you relate your own tale. And perhaps, between us, we might contrive some clearer picture of what has brought my own blood to this sorry pass.'

'I can offer little enough by way of information, sir, and what there is will certainly bring no comfort to you.'

'I do not ask for comfort.' The rigid, expressionless mask is beginning to slip now. Tears dew in the corners of his eyes. 'Forgive me, Mr Samuel, I would not have you see me like this for worlds; I have made too free with the wine. It is stronger than it appears and has fuddled me.'

'It is strong, sir.'

'I will take no more, but you will have a further glass?'

'I will, sir, with thanks,' I reply, passing across my glass. Brookes fusses with the wine, taking time to compose himself.

I accept the recharged glass and toss it back for the resolve in it. 'Well, sir, on gaining entry to the Coach and Horses, there we discovered that the body had already been removed.'

'Impossible. It cannot have been claimed; there is no extant family but myself.'

'Not lawfully claimed, sir. The body had already been hoisted the previous night. After making certain enquiries we followed the trail to a travelling fair on Clapham Common, where we were able to secure it.'

'A travelling fair? Surely the brutes did not mean to ...'

'They meant no ill, sir. The body had been respectably dressed, laid out with all possible care and readied for burial as you noted. It seems that Bobby ... Robert, had been among their number this year past and more and was much loved by the troupe.'

'A troupe? What manner of troupe?'

'Men and women of all descriptions, decent enough souls, but each of them manifesting some particularity of nature.'

'Curiosities you mean to say?'

'Indeed, sir. He was of them, known amongst them as Bobby Herman, the Man-Woman.'

'I see it, Mr Samuel,' nods Brookes, gazing into the fire, as though conjuring the image of his son. 'The removal of the stones at such a young age will inhibit the body from achieving its full manly condition. Poor Robert.'

'Well, sir, that is all I know.'

'You believe this travelling troupe had aught to do with it?'

'I do not, sir. Else why would they go to such trouble and danger to retrieve the body? As I say, sir, he was treated by them with much care and tenderness.'

'Perhaps I should have left matters well alone and Robert would have been put to rest by those that loved him best in life.'

'We are all on us blessed to be wise after the event, sir.'

'Indeed, Mr Samuel. What's done is done.'

'May I enquire, sir, as to why you did not raise suspicion as to the manner of your son's death at the Coroner's Inquest?'

'Oh, but I did, Mr Samuel. Those cloth-heads are not men of science and gave no weight to my suppositions, for as you have observed, the signs are very subtle. Those kind of men have no desire to extend themselves over the demise of yet another anonymous pauper of no family from the London streets. They were sharp set and waiting on their suppers; in great haste to conclude matters, remarking only upon the unusual nature of his … affliction, making light of it for their immodest amusement. You will understand that I could not press the matter for fear of revealing my connection.'

'So, you will not pursue this line of enquiry through the channels of the law?'

'I cannot. I had hoped to learn the circumstances for his sake alone.'

I am relieved to hear it. 'Well, sir, as I have said, it has been a most arduous commission and … '

'You are anxious to come to the matter of your bounty, I imagine.'

'I am, sir. Though it is not the genuine rarey aviary that I have brought, I believe—'

'Calm yourself, Mr Samuel, I have no desire to cozen you. Certainly it is not the rara avis; I should have been most surprised if it had been, since that was never the true object of your task. Let me assure you that you have fulfilled your commission as I imagined you would.'

'Then … '

'Then you are to be paid in full, Mr Samuel.'

'I rejoice to hear it, sir.'

'No doubt. But you will understand when I tell you that I do not keep such a large sum in sovereigns to hand, and I daresay you would prefer not to take my note of hand for it.'

'I should rather it be in ready money, if it please you, sir.'

'Well then, I shall impose upon your patience for but a few hours more. I am determined to lay my natural son to rest this very day. It is to be St George's Church at Hanover Square where Crick has already gone to make all ready. There lies the Brookes family mausoleum where Robert will be interred. It will be a very small affair, with but myself, Crick and my Mr Bamfield in attendance—none else knows of the matter. But it will be properly carried off by Marsden & Sons. The thing will be handsomely done, sir. I will recognize my own son in death though I did not do so much in life.'

'Very right in you, sir.'

'Mr Lionel Bamfield is my man of business, and should you present yourself at St George's by, say, three o'clock, he will arrange to settle with you in full.'

'I shall be there, sir. You may be sure of it.'

'For the moment though, Mr Samuel, you have my very great thanks. And I will shake your hand if I may.'

'An honour, sir,' I reply, rising to my feet along with Brookes. I manage to fumble the empty glass, just saving it from catastrophe, whilst extending a grimy paw.

'Well, Mr Samuel. I rejoice to see that you have not broken anything on this occasion at the least,' he smiles gently. 'Crick is otherwise engaged; I trust you will not object to showing yourself out.'

I retrieve my hat, leaving Brookes alone to sit and stare into the dying embers. But I do believe he is mistaken here: for certainly it is his heart that has been broke.

CHAPTER XXX

It is but a short distance from Great Marlborough Street to the Coach and Horses and I should feel naught but jubilation, yet I am curiously low. Certainly, I sympathise with Brookes for his wayward, troubled son and am uneasy at my own part in the shadowy affair, moreover, though a hundred sovs will certainly ease our flight from the metropolis, I cannot be sanguine, since my departure must entail the losing of Rosamund.

Owing to the early hour there are few patrons as yet. Thankfully, the counter is unattended and so, for once, I am not required to endure Ned's nonsensical babble. I make my way up the backstairs to the spare chamber. My knock remains unanswered and so I enter to find the room empty but for Facey, who lies, quite still, under a single sheet.

For a heart stopping moment, I fear he has karked it, 'til I catch sight of his great chest slowly rising with the intake of breath. I slump down on the seat by the side of his bed, so drained of vitality that I can barely remove my old hat. Now that I have a moment for contemplation, I find I am, in truth, much affected by Facey's final words to me, fearful that they might be his last in life and I cannot escape the notion that I have turned my coat against my oldest friend. More than a friend: as boys in Portsmouth, we both of us having absent, undetermined fathers, put it about that we were connected by blood and so half-brothers.

Though never vain of his appearance, Facey has always relied upon his quick hands and eyes. And, should he recover, I wonder if it will only be to find himself but half the man he was.

I am by no means certain that this decision to irredeemably mangle him was a necessary one. If not, then the error can only be mine. By hinting at my lack of courage, Tom was able to inveigle me into this uncertain course of action, thereby exposing a woeful defect in my character: this wavering of spirit. I am always so effortlessly persuaded to take the easy road and so despite the protestations of Rosamund and Kak John, I know myself to be a man of straw. It is most vexing.

I awake, barely refreshed, to find myself still in the chair, though I have meantime been draped with a rug. A few hours must have passed and yet it seems that Facey has barely stirred. Conscious that I am shortly to conclude our business with this Bamfield, I briefly make myself presentable with the jug and ewer, retrieve my old hat and seek out Tom.

Finding the door to Tom's private room downstairs already open, I enter to see Tom seated at his table accompanied by Trench and Pure John, the makings of his tea between them. Tom leaps to his feet. He grips my hand in his and pumps away with his customary enthusiasm. 'Sammy, it is gratifying to see you returned and in one piece.'

'Forgive me, Tom. I was detained; it is a long and intricate tale.'

'I have no doubt of it. Seeing the condition of you this morning, thought it best to leave you to your slumbers alongside Facey, who has passed a quiet night at the least.'

'Thank 'ee, Tom.'

Trench rises and gives me a brief nod, which I return. 'Lieutenant Trench, how do you do?'

'Well enough, Sammy. I came for tidings of our friend upstairs and to accompany the lad who is troubled by the absence of his brother.'

Pure John sits quietly in his chair, swinging his legs, which do not even reach the floor. Ordinarily, he is such a boisterous, irrepressible lad that it is easy to forget how very young he is. 'I have not seen hide nor hair of him since the fair, Mr Samuel.'

'That is on my account, Pure John,' I say, 'and I am heartily sorry for it. Never fret, for I last saw him, and not so many hours ago, in company with Miss Rosamund.'

Pure John brightens, rubbing his eyes. 'Then I am content to hear it, Mr Samuel. To be sure, many a time he beds down at the tanneries if the hour is late. It is quieter there and he is used to the stink. I am somewhat accustomed to shifting for myself.'

Tom rubs his hands. 'Now then, since all is in order, I shall send out for a bite and perhaps we might even broach a bottle while you recount for us your tale.'

'I cannot, Tom. I have pressing business.' A glance at Tom's clock reveals that there is an abundance of time as yet, but in truth I do not care for company since my low spirits have not much improved.

Tom places a gentle hand on my shoulder. 'I see there is a good deal on your mind, Sammy.'

'There is, Tom. It is an impossibility and yet I had somehow hoped to find Facey back to his old self and none the worse for it.'

'It is no easy thing to stand aside and watch one dear to you mauled and mutilated. I well know it from my days at the scratch; your feelings do you credit.'

'What eats at me is that I cannot say if we have acted for the best, Tom.'

'Nor I, Sammy. But in life we must act as we find, decisively, on what intelligence we have to hand. If the outcome of all our doings was known to us beforehand then what use courage, what purpose virtue? It is life. How we face the unknown is the measure of us.'

'I cannot deny it,' I say, not much comforted as I smooth the brim of my battered old hat.

'Is it wise to show your face, Sammy?' inquires Trench. 'You are hunted most assiduously.'

'I have an appointment not far from here to collect a bounty; it cannot be postponed.'

'Allow me to send the boy, in your stead. You well know how he can be trusted with a purse.'

'I have never doubted it, but a messenger will not serve.'

'Then I will go myself. You cannot be seen abroad, the hazard is too great.'

'My principal will never see you. He is a cautious, private man and will have dealings with no other.'

'You are resolved to it then?' inquires Tom.

'I am, else what kind of partner would I be to Facey, should I remain cowering here, incapable of concluding our affairs? How we face the unknown is the measure of us. You have said it, Tom.'

'You have me hoist on my own petard. But you will at least go cautiously and return to my roof, where you may remain for as long as is necessary.'

'I will, and my thanks to you all.' I clap Pure John on the back. 'You shall see your brother soon enough, never fear, and when next you do see him I hope you will direct him to this house. I should like to give him some small token for the service he has done me.'

'Just as you say, Mr Samuel.'

I nod to these good souls and quit the room with a heavy heart. At the foot of the stairs, I don my hat, pulling the brim low and raise the collars of my coat to cover as much of my face as it will. The can acknowledges me with a knowing leer and wink as I enter the public. I pass through without a word and am quickly onto the pavement outside.

It is the peal of St George's clock some few hundred yards ahead, striking the hour of two, which informs me that there is yet a full hour until my rendezvous. Better though to be early and far better to be abroad in this gentle sunshine than fretting in an oppressive, frowsty room.

Though Brookes resides but a stone's throw from this hallowed ground, he has arrived, it seems, with due ceremony, in a mourning-coach, which waits at the steps of the church. It is accompanied by a black lacquered hearse drawn by a matching pair of Flemish draught horses decked out in mournful equipage, the tall black plumes affixed to their headpieces bobbing gently in the breeze.

Having no desire to intrude my shabby presence on the ritual within, I slip directly into the churchyard via the George Street gate. The churchyard is empty but for a lone, distant figure loitering under a yew close by the sexton's hut. Taking him to be the sexton, I give a friendly wave but rather than returning my hail, the figure swiftly vanishes behind the tree.

Curious now, I make for the hut, stepping around a fresh-dug, open grave in my path. I catch a breath of it in passing: a mixture of grass, damp earth and decay. As I approach the hut, I see that I am not mistaken: the figure of a man lurks in close proximity to the great gnarled trunk, partially concealed by the shadows. He starts, alerted to my presence; swings around and I see that it is no lawful officer of the church but John Bishop. 'Why, Mr Samuel, you gave me a right turn. I did not recognize you with your face all muffled like some bleedin' splitter.'

'What do you do here, Bishop?'

'Same as yourself, I imagine, Mr Samuel. Only I am here first and so me and Williams will have the dibs on this night's work. Besides, I have already paid out the sexton's man.'

'You will have no quibble from me on that score, Bishop.'

'Very right in you, Mr Samuel, and you will inform Mr Facey that we have shook hands on it like gents?'

'Certainly I will,' I say, taking his grimy paw.

'A young 'un they are putting to rest, Mr Samuel,' he announces, through his murky grin, 'and a toff, and so worth the extra trouble, though we shall have to crack a morseleen for him. Which one ezactly I am waiting to discover.'

'I have no wish to tell you your business, Bishop, but should you attempt this hoist, at best you will have naught but your own sweat to show for it.'

'Ah, Mr Samuel, they do say you are a downy bird. But you will not throw me off the scent as easy as that.'

'The flesh you are set on is almost a week gone and best left where it is laid.'

'You are a caution, Mr Samuel, but I was not born yesterday. Williams and me will have the dead 'un away for all your wiles.'

'Surely a less troublesome prospect awaits,' I say, indicating the fresh-dug hole behind me, 'one that would not require the cracking of a mausoleum?'

'Would that it were so, Mr Samuel. But that hole will not be filled; not today at any rate. Today's dead 'un is not for this ground, not good enough for him, it seems: though he bears no particular name, he must be placed in one of them grand morseleens in the necropsilis. Most irregular and the sexton's man was wery indignant on the subject, having already digged out the six foot here.'

'I have information on this matter, Bishop. And I will tell you there is to be a sharp watch set about your mausoleum. Trust me, that hoist will not be worth the candle.'

'No gammon, Mr Samuel?'

'God's truth.'

Bishop considers me for a moment, his head cocked to one side, like a Covent Garden pigeon. 'Well then,' he announces, 'since I have always held you in the greatest esteem, I will take your word for it and sling my hook. Thank'ee, Mr Samuel.' He tips his hat to me, blithe as you please, before ambling away in the direction of the George Street gate.

I have never mistaken Bishop for a man of good sense and so am somewhat taken aback by his easy capitulation. Much as I should like to credit my persuasive tongue, I believe it was simple sincerity that swung the thing. Certainly, not one word of a lie has passed my lips and, living as we do in a world of stretchers and outright deceit, on occasion the light of truth is able to shine out all the brighter for it. At any rate, I am well pleased with my efforts. After all of Bobby's trials and peregrinations it is only fitting that he be permitted to rest undisturbed. I feel too an obligation to Brookes, and cannot help but recall his pain when I left him and so would not see him further anguished.

I take Bishop's post in the shadows of the yew's spreading branches, settling myself on the grass to wait. It is not long before a small, sad procession emerges from the church: a pair of mutes precede a French polished oak-wood coffin carried by four stout bearers. Behind them I can discern the Ordinary, Brookes, his man Crick, and another fellow; a squat, florid-looking cove who I take to be Bamfield, Brookes' man of business.

The group slowly wends its way down the path towards the necropolis where our betters rest in state, in their grand stone edifices and mausoleums, set apart from the rest of us, even in death. I soon lose sight of the cortege as it passes amongst the jumbled landscape of angelic statuary, plinths, sepulchres, monuments and suchlike. It will be a while yet before I may approach this Bamfield: there will be further observances at the family mausoleum, thereafter the masons will begin the lengthy business of sealing up the stonework.

Should one discount the decaying architecture of mortality, it is a pleasant enough spot to wait; the grass is soft and lush, there is a gentle breeze, while the golden sun is warmly tempered by the shade of these branches. I am still fatigued from the exertions of the night, and so I place my hat over my face and close my eyes.

It must be a good hour or so later when I am brought sharp awake by the soft voice of John Bishop. 'Well, well, Mr Samuel. Still here, I find.'

I whip the hat away from my face and leap to my feet. Bishop leans idly against the trunk, the charcoal slash of a smile creasing his dial. 'You are returned, Bishop,' I say stupidly, fixing my old tile firmly back on my head.

'I am, Mr Samuel, and you must take me for a most uncommon flat.'

'All I have told you is true, Bishop,' I reply.

'Then why do you remain?'

'I have legitimate business here which is none of your concern.'

'Legitmit, is it? You do not afright me with such a menacing word, Mr Samuel. Whether you have tried to cozen me is of no account, since I would as soon take a bounty for the living as for the dead.'

'There is naught for you here, Bishop. And I wish that you would leave me to my business.'

'Ah, but there you are mistaken. For you are here, Mr Samuel. You are the real prize today and a precious fine one at that.'

For a moment Bishop's gaze flits from my face to a point over my right shoulder; instantly I understand that he has been keeping me occupied whilst some stealthy confederate approaches from behind. I whirl to face this interloper just in time to catch sight of the mud-crusted, pitted iron blade of the sexton's shovel as it swoops down. I hear the dull clang of it as the flat surface connects but strangely, no pain. There is a sudden sharp, metallic taste in my mouth. Then all is darkness.

CHAPTER XXXI

There is no sudden awakening as though from a dream. For a good while I have been conscious, though without true comprehension. Gradually, my recollection returns, and with it, a fuller awareness of my self. I can recall the pitted, pitiless shovel blade with perfect clarity; I know that I am Samuel Samuel and that I have been betrayed by this man Bishop. My primary senses are not yet fully restored, but there is pain: a dull, black megrim thudding at the canister.

I wait as the agony subsides to a nagging ache.

I become aware of a strongish odour: a stale, though not entirely unpleasant yeasty scent. It is my own sweat.

I am lying on my back, I cannot say precisely where. My eyes, though wide open, detect nothing. This is not the darkness of a room with the odd gleam or chink of moonlight to provide relief but terrifying blackness, deeper and more profound than pitch. I realize that it is not the dark but the absence of sight, which afflicts me.

I am blind.

I squirm struggling in panic only to find that I am utterly incapable of movement other than the slightest tweezing of my right index finger against my thumb. There is a fragile, gritty substance caught between the flesh of the pads, which crumbles as I rub and twitch.

I gasp, straining for air. It is like inhaling a thick cloth. A shocking weight pushes down on my chest; I cannot wholly catch my breath and what air I can snatch is stale and foul. My breath comes only in short, sharp sobs. The life is slowly being crushed out of me as though I were being pressed by stones.

There is another pervasive odour too, a clammy, earthy stench not entirely masked by my sweat: the stink of the grave.

It is a thing from my nightmares made real.

I scream in the dark.

CHAPTER XXXII

I think for a while I must have lost my wits. I do know that at some moment my bladder has loosed. I feel the warm wetness of it about my nether regions but am past caring. I thrash against the great weight of soil pressing down on my body but it is futile, I am fixed more firmly than a fly in molasses.

I had always seen myself as a father of children, and now it will never be so. It is anger rather than regret that I feel: I had, in fond imagination, at some indeterminate point in the future, envisioned myself steering a young Samuel Samuel, or even a Samantha, onto the correct path. It is only now I realise that I have naught to impart that would not be tainted: how to lift a latch; how to tickle a bloom; how to skin a flat; how to lift a slab; how, where and when to hoist a corpse. It is but a long and shabby receipt for my own unworthy life. I should not have made a proper parent and it is well that I am not to be graced with such opportunity.

I consider though, the application of Rosamund's influence on any such progeny and believe that she, at the least, might have been the making of them.

I ought to have made my intentions clear to her when I had the chance. But a lack of courage has ever been my failing.

It occurs to me that this is God's judgement on my doings. Though I have endeavoured to live a goodish sort of life, I am not a fellow for overly strict observance of the scriptures. I have rousted the dead from their rightful rest and now, for my sins, must take their place while I yet live. There is justice here and it gives me a curious sense of peace to think on it.

I recall the other portion of my existence: my friendship with Facey. Though we were both from Portsmouth sprung, we were not ideal bedfellows, to be sure. Like me, Facey had no pa to speak of and, though a year or two older, was far my superior in physical stature. He was at the baccy and booze way before the rest of us scallawags, being so overgrown from an early age. And so, on the whole, I did not encounter him overmuch, other than when he was forced to repeat his letters at John Pound's School, when he could be made to attend. I took to sitting by him and whispering the corrections under my breath. But it was not that which made us close.

When not at my chores or letters I liked to sit at the Gunwharf wall and watch the comings and goings. Invariably, there would be Facey, in the midst of it all, loafing, on the lookout for an unguarded bale or barrel. On this occasion he was spied by a ship's Master in the act of shoving a sack of purloined tea down the waistband of his keks.

As he scarpered, the sack fell, unobserved, to the cobbles, whereupon I, following close behind, kicked it smartly into the sea.

Running into him that afternoon, I observed that he bore the signs of a good beating. I told him what I had done and, grinning, through broken lips, he replied, 'It explains why they did not bring me to a beak. Your good swift boot doubtless saved me from Van Diemen's land or a scragging. In any case, that tea had passed along the coarser regions of my keks on its journey to the cobbles, and so I cannot not imagine who should ever have desired a single ounce of it.' With that, he roared with laughter.

And that is Facey. Ever since, he has loved me like a brother, as I love him.

I chuckle and lay still. I wonder that I yet live at all. My breath arrives in shallow, insubstantial gasps. It is the only sound, the last I will hear. I am no longer afeared, only filled with deep regret that my dear friends will think the worst of me, believing me to have skedaddled, looking only to myself.

I feel a solitary tear trickle from my left eye and, without thinking, make to wipe it away but, of course, I cannot shift my arm. I blink rapidly, puzzled that my eyes, though sightless, are quite free of mud and soil. Indeed, there seems to be a cavity of some kind above my face. Some small movement is possible and I am even able to raise my head an inch or so, feeling a softish, greasy texture against my cheek. The odour of my sweat is more pungent here. I cannot fathom it, nor can I say whether my discovery is for good or ill since this meagre alcove has undoubtedly been the sole means of prolonging my life.

What air remains in this tiny space is becoming fouler and tainted, I breathe but it does not satisfy. I begin to cough and choke; my senses reel and I feel my consciousness beginning to drift once again.

The burrowing creatures that live below the earth and feast on human flesh have already begun their desperate work. I feel them scrabbling at my limbs, tugging, fighting for a greater share of the meal. I only wish they could have left me in peace for just a little longer …

'Mr Samuel, Mr Samuel.' Strange. Pure John is here with me now.

'What, Pure John,' I whisper, 'are you dead too?'

It is though I have lain abed far too long and the curtain has been ripped back of a sudden to admit a harsh daylight. The brilliance of it scorches my eyes. I blink to find Pure John's grubby face looming over me. 'I feared you was a goner, Mr Samuel.' His lower lip trembles as he fights back tears. 'I am sorry

I could not come to you sooner. I had to wait 'til them buggers had mizzled afore I could begin to dig you out.'

I raise my head, emerging an inch or two from the earth surrounding me. I cannot say in all certainty if this is a dream or no. Pure John squats above, my old hat clasped in his muddy hands. 'Why, Pure John, you have saved my hat at least.'

''Twas over your face. And a good job too, it being the thing what preserved your life.'

'Am I truly alive, Pure John, or are you come in a dream?'

'A bloody nightmare more like, Mr Samuel, were that so. No, 'tis me right enough, in the flesh and here at the bidding of my Lieutenant and Mr Tom Canon.' Pure John sets my hat aside and continues his excavations. As he scoops away the soil I find the strength to raise my right arm. I feel it breaking through the thin layer of earth, emerging from its bed like some strange sapling. I reach out to him, whereupon he takes my hand in both of his, sets his heels firmly into the ground and heaves. Gradually, my shoulders come free along with my left arm. It is sufficient. I let go his hand and, with both arms am able to dig for myself.

At last, I emerge from my hole, plastered in clods and filth; drenched in my own piss. I do not care. I stand for a moment and gaze up at the sun, breathing deep and greedily. They say that the London air is tainted and noxious from the sea coal, and the fumes of industry but to me at this moment, London air is the purest thing on God's green earth, fresher by far than any mountaintop.

I gaze at Pure John, no less caked in filth than I am, straw-coloured hair plastered to his forehead with perspiration. He grins, his begrimed dial beaming back at me. It is the face of an angel.

CHAPTER XXXIII

'My Lieutenant and Mr Tom Canon was not quite happy with you being out and about on your ownsome and so I was excused regular duties; they bid me follow behind most discreetly to see you safe and sound. And as well I did, sir.' Pure John prattles away ten-to-the-dozen as we make our way back down Great Marlborough Street. It is no surprise to find the elegant pedestrians hereabouts giving us a wide berth and many a curious glance. I am enveloped in filth and stink, while Pure John is scarcely much better. But even Pure John, grubby as he is, places a little distance between the two of us. 'You will not be offended, Mr Samuel,' he explains, 'when I say that you reek most shocking of piss.'

'No, Pure John, I am not offended. There is naught you can say to vex me after the service you have done.' Pure John grins broadly as we reach the doors of the Coach and Horses. We enter and the raucous crush of patrons in the Public is swiftly brought to silence by our shocking state; the throng instantly makes way, clearing a broad pathway for us as we pass through to the backstairs. I am somewhat concerned for the damage to Tom's reputation but there is naught else to be done, since there is no back alley to this establishment.

'Dear Lord,' says Tom Canon, ushering me into his room upstairs, 'it is the golem, which the Shoreditch Jews prophesy: a creature all of clay with the stench of the grave about him.'

Trench occupies the chair, clay pipe in his hand and a leather mug of porter at his feet. He acknowledges my return with a nod and a puzzled frown.

'I am only the same Samuel Samuel as left some hours previous,' I reply, 'and naught to show for it but a lump on the canister the size of a duck's egg.'

'I will have the kettles put to boil,' says Canon with a critical eye, 'but I cannot say that this profession of yours offers much by way of ease and prosperity. No, nor good health neither,' he adds, indicating Facey tucked up in the bed behind him.

Facey is no better, nor worse, breathing like an old bellows though calm and regular. His face, in sleep, is composed in an expression of contentment, which to my mind, bodes well for his recovery. There is nothing for it but to submit to Tom's ministrations as he removes my old coat.

'This must be sponged and steamed, Sammy, as will your unmentionables.'

I divest myself of my keks and stand in shirt and undergarments, which are of themselves, a terrible disgrace.

'I should very much like to remove those things for burning; they will never be saved by any amount of scrubbing,' says Tom.

'Then you must have them, Tom. I have come back from the grave a better man than I went in and would wish to begin all afresh.'

Tom raises an eyebrow as he gathers my clouts, handing me a scrap of linen to preserve my modesty. 'You will excuse my curiosity, Sammy, but I had understood that you were out to collect brass and not soil. Or did I mishear?'

'As to that, Tom, you may have the tale of it from Pure John since he enjoyed a far better vantage point than I.'

Pure John grins. 'Well, gents, I did follow directly after Mr Samuel as you bid, nor did he ever clock me at his heels since he was in a strange sort of reverie all the way to St George's. Once at the churchyard it was a simple matter to remain out of sight behind all them pediments. There I spied a sly-looking cove skulking about by the sexton's hut with a gob on him blacker'n a gypsy's curse. Mr Samuel approached to have words and I kept 'em in my eye all the while they yarned. At length, this cove slings his hook and I see Mr Samuel settle himself for a nice nap in the sun. All is peachy for an hour or so, and there I am just thinking to meself, "Well, John, this is an easy afternoon's business and whyn't I take a little snooze meself," when what should I see but that hell-gobbed creature come a slinking back. In company with him is a stocky, darkish fellow, this one with a butcher's awl hanging at his belt and a look on him that says he has used it for more an' just beef.'

'Meathook,' I interject.

'If that's his moniker then he's well named, Mr Samuel, and no doubt of it.'

'He is Pimlott and Chuffington's man.'

'You must thank God for your great good fortune, Sammy, since it is well known that those men seldom miss their mark,' adds Trench.

'I thank God and the lad, both.'

Pure John barely acknowledges my thanks, so desperate is he to complete his account. 'At any rate,' he continues, breathlessly, 'this Meathook splits away and makes around the back by way of the sexton's hut where he collects a shovel. 'Twas plain to see from all this sneaking about that they meant you ill but what to do? I daren't reveal myself and so dabbed a good few pebbles in your direction, but it wouldn't serve since you was too deep asleep and snoring fit to wake the churchyard residents. Meantime, t'other, the shite-gobbed villain, steps up and, well, the rest you know better 'an anyone else can say. This Meathook gives you a clang across the noggin to beat the Clements' clapper and down you go like a hod full of bricks. Then the two on 'em slings you into the empty hole like an old sack and sets to burying you alive.'

'A wretched, evil act,' gasps Trench.

'Not above 'alf, sir. But not afore the shite-gob runs through your pockets, then picks up your titfer what had gone for a tumble, and finding it not much to his liking, flips it in after you, where it lays across your dial. And so it was that which kept you in breath 'til I could dig you out.'

I stroke the beaten, crushed old stovepipe in my hands. 'I have always reckoned my tile to be a grand 'un and now I know it for a certain.'

'No question about it,' grins Pure John, 'you are not your proper self without your busted-in beaver, Mr Samuel. Though now it is dented on both sides.'

'So it is, Pure John. Though it is never for the slop shop yet; I will have it fixed up with stiffened paper afore I buy another,' I announce, setting the battered old tile to my head.

'And a very fine figure you will make, Mr Samuel, coming it the Hotentot in only breechcloth and hat.'

'It is no use, Pure John, you will not vex me.'

Canon attempts to conceal a smile. 'I shall see about those kettles and I daresay I may find a shirt that will do for you, though it will be on the large side.'

'You are very good, Tom. I am much in your debt all of you, most especially you, Pure John.'

The boy beams as Trench squeezes his shoulder. 'You are a tolerable fine lad, though somewhat disreputable-looking just now.' He fumbles in his pocket. 'But I am right proud and you will take a shilling for your fortitude.'

'I did not ask for no reward, sir.'

'And that is precisely why you shall have one.'

It is a curious but affecting aspect of human nature, that those who have done you a small good turn will often become even better disposed towards you on account of it. And though I should prefer not to further impose on Lieutenant Trench I am most anxious to have news of Rosamund.

'Lieutenant, I am grateful for all you have done but there is one further service, which you might render me.'

'Name it, Sammy.'

'I should like to send a message. Though it must be on tick, for as you know, I was not able to collect my tin.'

'As well you were not since that mumping villain would have had it off you.'

'True enough, and that must keep for the moment. For now I should like to send most urgent to Vauxhall.'

'Rosamund Pitface ... ' blurts Pure John, instantly catching himself, slapping at his own forehead, 'Ah bollix, Mr Samuel, I did not mean to say that for I know you are soft on the lady.'

'Well, I should not say so much, but it is true that I hold Miss Rosamund in some regard. I must speak with her urgently and, since I cannot go to her, you will see if she will be good enough to come here to me.'

'You will dress yourself first I hope, Mr Samuel?'

'Certainly I will. Never fear.'

'And you, lad, must scrub, before you venture out,' Trench commands his subordinate, 'lest you are taken for a sweep's brush and thrust up some chimney.'

'The matter is urgent, sir. I should welcome news of my brother,' babbles Pure John as he makes for the door, 'and Miss Rosamund will never be offended at a spot of grime.'

'Now, Pure John ... ' insists Trench.

But it is no use. The boy has skedaddled.

CHAPTER XXXIV

It has taken no fewer than three full pitchers of good, hot water and soap to scrub the grime from my body. By the time I have shaved and scoured the gnashers with Tom's excellent compound of salt and ashes, my coat, weskit and keks are back from the laundry shop. Tom has laid out for me in his dressing room an old but serviceable shirt along with a blue spotted neckcloth, which I believe is rather natty. My keks are yet damp from steaming and sponging but for propriety's sake I put them on. The coat may air a while longer. The pitiful contents of my pockets, dust bag, twine, liquorice twig and my precious letter are laid out on a small side table, though my crowbar, tin box and remaining coins have gone, doubtless filched by Bishop.

At my disposal on the washstand is Tom's matched set of tortoiseshell comb and pair of brushes, so I take the opportunity to attend to my hair, taking good care to mind the painful lump, combing it back from my forehead and over the ears where it hangs, black and damply glossy. The length of it serves to conceal the wound to my lug, which is healing well enough, though I will ever be short of the lobe's end. As the finisher, I dab a little of Tom's orange blossom scent about my neck. The shirt is somewhat capacious for a man of my stature and so I must pull the excess folds behind me and tuck them down into the back of my keks.

After thumping out the dents in my old hat, I present myself to the long mirror. Though I am somewhat long-faced and on the shortish side and my eyes now reveal a wary, haunted aspect, it is not by any means a dreadful prospect. Indeed, I doubt I have ever cut such a dandified figure. I have returned from the earth cleansed; a new man, filled with fortitude and determination, prepared in both mind and body to make my proposal to Rosamund.

In the passageway outside this room my ancient boots await, scraped and freshly blacked. I put them on and step across to Tom's bedroom, knock gently at the door and enter.

Trench is absent but Tom remains seated in the bedside chair, watching over Facey. He rises, places a finger to his lips and whispers, 'He woke for a moment and knew me; I believe the fever has broke.'

I gaze across at my slumbering partner: indeed, there is a healthier pinkness about his complexion; his skin is dry, no longer sheened and clammy. 'I am relieved to hear it. He seems a little improved,' I reply in a low murmur.

'As do you, Sammy. He should not be disturbed for the moment and so you may have the use of my private rooms downstairs. It would never do to meet with your good lady in the public,' advises Tom, stepping back out into the passageway with me.

'We are already so much in your debt, Tom,' I reply with feeling.

'Sammy, I tell you, one man can only drink off so much tea, stuff his belly with so much beef and sleep in but one bed and so what else is an excess of fortune good for if not to share with friends in need?'

'If all men thought as you do this metropolis would be a good deal better for it.'

'Ah, but 'tis only that I have had the wits pummelled out of my noggin that I speak so. We old pugilists are all a little glocky; notorious for it we are.'

'I do not think so, Tom.'

'Get on with you, lad. You would never wish to keep your young lady waiting. I shall remain at the bedside and keep a watch.'

I do not need to be twice-told. Now that Facey appears so improved, my concern is now for my meeting with Rosamund. Moving soundlessly for such a considerable man, Tom slips back into the bedroom, leaving me to fetch my coat and few possessions. I head for the backstairs, descending with a spirit of cautious optimism: if all goes well I am shortly to become a man of means and, dare I say it, perhaps even of settled and respectable estate. To be sure, I am somewhat anxious over Facey's opinion on matters, but I cannot imagine that, lacking a glim, he would wish to continue at our former profession. Besides, he has but little choice: though Pimlott and Chuffington may imagine me dead and buried, they will not have abandoned the hunt for Facey. Nor will they any time soon. One way or another my partner must come to terms with a life outside the metropolis; besides, I do believe that the happy conclusion of our commission will surely sweeten the pill.

With that thought in mind, I enter Tom's private room downstairs, followed closely by the can. 'Might I be so bold as to observe which it is a more distigwiched figure you presently cut than when you entered prewious. And how fares our one-eyed gent what is not hereabouts present, sir?'

'Well enough, and I should take it kindly if you would remember to avoid his mention howsomever slantendicular.'

'I have it, sir. I take your meaning 'zactly. The one-eyed gent will no more be discoursed upon, though I hope he is well in himself?'

I sigh heavily and, though I am required to endure another round of winks and leers, it appears that the can has taken the hint: 'Since you are a personal guest of Mr Tom, you will make free with this here room; there is a decanter of port wine to hand, which is of the wery finest, though I should not be the one to say so.'

'A young lady will shortly arrive for me accompanied by the running boy. I should be obliged if you will show her to this place directly.'

'I will, sir. And not a word about it to no one, no, nor of the one-eyed gent neither,' he announces with a parting wink.

I wonder that Tom puts up with such a vexatious dolt as I sit and pour myself a glass of the port wine, which is indeed very fine. I catch myself thinking thus and smile, marvelling at the nature of things: how I come to be here, so titivated; quaffing good liquor from this delicate receptacle; finding fault in the help like the most tremendous swell, when not so many hours past I was the most abject of creatures, entombed in mud and utterly without hope. Tom has the right of it, I believe: it is life. How we face the unknown is the measure of us.

I have barely taken half a dozen sips at the wine before I catch the clear, piping voice of Pure John from without. I leap to my feet. There is just sufficient time to adjust my neck cloth and arrange myself in a pose of calm, manly resolution before the door bursts open to admit Rosamund and the boy. I clear my throat.

'Oh, Sammy,' cries Rosamund, rushing into the room, 'it is a joy to see you well, but I must tell you straight that John is not to be found.'

The words I had ready prepared are dashed from my throat, I can only gawp like a guppy in the face of this unwelcome information. Rosamund bustles past me, takes up my half-finished glass from the side table and dashes off the wine in a single swallow. 'Last night when you rattled off so sudden in the Hackney I did not know what to think. There was naught to be done but to collect ourselves and away home, trusting to your good fortune. And so I concealed myself in the mists not so very far from the premises. For a while there were raised voices and the sounds of alarm; there I waited, biding my time, until venturing back across the street where John had earlier stationed himself, but he was nowhere to be seen.'

'Oh, Mr Samuel, I had never imagined my brother about such a frightful business,' adds Pure John. 'I fear for him.'

'Hush, Pure John,' I say, placing a hand on his shoulder, mindful of his trembling lip. 'Last night's affair was never so bad as all that: naught but a little fakery and pantomime in the murk, hardly a desperate venture. Never fear, your brother will turn up out of some lushing house, right as a trivet.'

'He has never taken to liquor, Mr Samuel. Only small beer and a little porter.'

'Well, well, there will be something, mark my words, some simple explication. In the meantime, you must return to your Lieutenant, I believe he has need of you for what remains of the day.'

'I will, sir. But you are quite certain that my brother is sound?'

'I am, Pure John. Your brother is such a gentle, good-natured soul, it is impossible to imagine anyone could wish him ill.'

Pure John considers this, brightening. 'Yes, I do believe you have the right of it, Mr Samuel.'

'You have your shilling yet, Pure John?'

'I do, sir. Safe in my shoe.'

'Well then, you will keep it so and give it to your brother. And when I have come into my bounty I will add to it by another five sovereigns.'

'You never will,' replies Pure John, wide-eyed.

'I shall, Pure John, for that is the esteem in which I hold your brother and his service, and not a word to the contrary from Mr Facey.'

The boy beams, his grubby face exhibiting all the trust in the world for my superior understanding of the way of things.

'Off with you now to your duties, Pure John. Come back in a few hours and you shall have news of your brother just as soon as we come by it.'

'Thank'ee kindly. Mr Samuel, Miss Rosamund.' With that, the urchin is away with his customary haste, heading out for Trench's offices in Albemarle Street.

As the door closes, I turn to face Rosamund, from whom I expect condemnation but, contrariwise, she is full of self-censure: 'Forgive me, Sammy, I was overmuch concerned when John did not come to see me at my pavement today, I quizzed his brother too closely on our way here and in so doing revealed much of our doings and unwittingly stoked the lad's fears.'

'We cannot know for sure how things fell out, Rosamund. Kak John may have come upon fresh employment or bedded down at another establishment.'

'It is not his way, Sammy. He is a steady young man and much attached to his young sibling, only once in a while choosing to doss down at the tannery if the hour is very late.'

'Well then, so it was.'

'I returned to the tannery this morning; the watchman gave me leave to look about in view of the regard they have for John. The shack has not been occupied since we left it last night.'

'Then another spot entirely? He dossed at a crib we do not know, perhaps?'

'He would never have slept so late.'

'True enough,' I say, 'I do not think he was one to lie slug-abed long, even at his own best place.'

Rosamund gazes up at me, blinking back tears. Before I know what I am about I have gathered both of her hands in mine. 'Well then, tell me, what is to be done?'

Rosamund meets my eye with her penetrating, grey gaze. 'After the brouhaha. I believe that those men, understanding that they had been rooked, discovered John outside and so took him up.'

'For what purpose? Even if he was took last night, they would not have got so much from him.'

'Perhaps it was not information they required, but recompense.'

'Recompense for what? I do not follow.'

'For the vexation we have caused them; for revenge, Sammy. You have never understood how the world works, though you imagine you do: despite your unlawful profession you rub along well enough and, by a squeak, remain on the right side of the ledger; you believe all men to be so, more or less; a little good here, a little mischief there, but on the whole, decent sorts. Poor Sammy, you do not understand how truly vile the world can be. You have never confronted true wickedness, which needs no excuse to exist.'

'I do not see why you would say such things to me, Rosamund.'

'You do not. And it is a part of your character, which, make no mistake, I have the greatest admiration for, but at this moment, would instantly exchange for a particle of fortitude.'

I release her hands and take a step back, lifting my chin and arranging my features in what I believe to be an expression similar to that of the face on the statue at St George's. 'I am a changed man, Rosamund. Surely you have heard what passed this day?'

'I had it from Pure John, but, Sammy, I—'

'I was preserved by a whisker and have returned to the world a better man by far, with fortitude enough for the both of us. Tell me what it is that you require and I will see it done.'

Rosamund nods vaguely, a scant acknowledgement of my appalling trials. 'I believe that John was took by those villains. We must hazard all to see to his return.'

'I will then … I will. I will go this instant and lay a complaint against that household.'

'Pish, Sammy. And that is the extent of your resolve? You, a man of no fixed abode and no profession to speak of, or would care to admit to, intend to approach the Crushers or Magistrate to lay a complaint against a West End swell—most likely a lordling or a justice himself? That will never serve.'

'He is a swell, to be sure, but none of those other things to my knowledge.'

'You are acquainted with the master of that house then?'

'I am, though I wish I was not. A vicious, debauched fellow and a toff, right enough; it was his mastiff had the flesh off my ear.'

Rosamund grimaces. 'Then I am ever more persuaded that John is in the greatest danger.'

'And so what would you have me do?'

'Why, we must beard the lion in his den of course. We will go there this instant.'

'We will not get past the tradesman's entrance.'

'Then we shall not go by the tradesman's entrance.'

CHAPTER XXXV

In short order, Rosamund and me find ourselves once again before the twin columns framing the entrance to Glendale. The ground floor windows are already shuttered, albeit the sun is only just beginning to set. The house gives off a silent, somewhat sinister air, though I cannot say if this is because I can sense the taint of wickedness or that I already know it to be the case.

Set into the beautifully polished brass nameplate is the bell-pull. I give a good few hauls on it and from within we hear a series of solid thumps as the bolts are drawn. The door is opened part way by the brutish, bewigged and liveried servant, who glares at the sight of us.

'I am here concerning the Man-Woman, Bobby Herman,' I announce.

'This ain't no thrupenny crib, nor common gin palace, you scoundrel. What do you mean by showing your selfs at this front entrance?'

'Your master instructed me to bring word of this matter most urgently; I must have an interview without delay.'

'Then you will kindly take your selfs round to the side, there to wait in your rightful place,' snaps the servant, pushing the door to.

'Come, Sammy,' announces Rosamund, pulling at my sleeve, 'we shall leave this lackey to inform his master that he saw fit to turn us away without so much as a hearing.'

We turn about, making to leave.

'Stay,' growls the servant, 'I shall not split a hair with you since you are so obstinate. You had best come in then and quickly, but I am no lackey to the likes of you, Miss Sharp, and you would do well to remember it.' With such admonishment he widens the door and ushers us inside.

We find ourselves in a vestibule of fine milk-white marble but are given no time to admire our surroundings before we are chivvied up the grand central staircase to the first floor. The servant bustles us into an anteroom. The place is exquisitely decorated in a lilac striped wallpaper punctuated here and there by framed miniatures and fashionable silhouettes. A row of finely carved mahogany chairs line the wall. On a small side table is a very fine beaver of a condition and gloss way superior to my own, and so I set my battered old remnant upon the seat of one of the chairs.

'You will be good enough to wait here,' announces the servant, scratching at the door to the reception room.

We catch the hum of raised voices from within.

The door is opened a little way, enabling us to hear quite clearly now the sounds of a violent disagreement. A deep bass voice bellows objections over Liston's languid, composed drawl. Trubshaw's face appears in the doorway; a hasty, whispered conversation takes place with much gesturing in our direction on the part of the servant. Trubshaw nods brusquely and the door is slammed to again.

The servant, without expression, sets himself before the entrance, arms akimbo, as though Rosamund and me had it in mind to make a rush for it.

Of a sudden, the door is flung wide. Instead of Trubshaw, it is a thickset, purple-faced, clerkish-looking gent all in black.

Still bellowing, he shoves the servant aside, striding angrily across to the side table to reclaim his beaver. 'I will not wait a month, sir. No, not a week longer. You will pay me what is due or I shall see about it.'

Liston appears from within, clad in a long blue silk gown over breeches and linen shirt. He leans languidly against the doorframe. 'And what will you, sir?'

'Why, I shall call in your paper, every scrap.'

'Then you will gain nothing.'

'I have nothing now, sir.'

'You will give yourself apoplexy, Bamfield. Calm yourself, man, surely a little in a month or two is better than nothing at all?'

'I shall proceed against the surety.'

Liston chuckles. 'My father? He would not speak with a man such as you, nor even admit you to his house. Certainly his name is on the paper, but not his true hand. You will get no satisfaction by that means, I assure you. I am cut off.'

'Then it is a fraud, sir.'

'Call it what you will, but you will wait. Sink me and you sink yourself, Bamfield.'

'You are an infernal villain, sir, a sponger and a rogue. Yes, I do say that.'

Liston merely shrugs. 'I daresay I have been called worse. You are becoming tiresome, Bamfield. There is nothing more to be done, and, as you can see,' he nods in our direction, 'I have other business to attend.'

Bamfield, seeing the futility of further discussion, jams his beaver emphatically onto his head and turns on his heel. 'You will hear from me, sir. Good day to you. Do not trouble to show me out.' He nods, barely acknowledging Rosamund and me, before stamping away down the stairs.

Although it was some distance across the churchyard that I spied him this afternoon, this Bamfield is doubtless the very same gentleman. I find myself torn: on the one hand desiring to follow and claim the bounty I am owed, on the other, there is my most urgent duty to Kak John.

'So,' Liston's languid drawl interrupts my thoughts, 'it is the wretched double bastard, and he has brought his drab too. Well, well, we must not keep them waiting, Cobb.'

The servant, Cobb, steps towards us, inclining his head towards the reception room. Rosamund and me enter. I find myself helped on my way by a swift shove in the back.

The room is expansive and exquisitely furnished. The upper storey shutters have not yet been put up; four immense casement windows admit the waning light of the setting sun, which casts a soft golden glow across the scattered Ottoman rugs and gleaming chestnut-coloured floorboards. The walls are of a delicate eggshell blue, studded with portraits of distinguished personages as well as horseflesh. The room is decked out with couches and high-backed armchairs upholstered in a pale-blue velvet of a somewhat deeper hue than the walls. Trubshaw reclines in one of these chairs by the window, legs outstretched and crossed, a glass of some rich ruby wine to hand. A marvellously pleasant odour of beeswax and lavender infuses the room.

Cobb enters behind us, closing the door emphatically. There he remains, arms crossed.

By the far wall stands another servant, in his hands a salver bearing wine decanter and glasses. Like Cobb, he is liveried and powdered, yet he is not the kind of man I would have marked for such service, having all the appearance of a footpad or bug-hunter.

Though it reeks of fashion and refinement, there is something unsettling about this place: something not altogether right, like a chunk of rotting flesh in a good meat pie.

Liston has stationed himself at the huge marble fireplace, elbow resting on the mantle, utterly composed, master of his domain. 'Well, Mr Samuel Samuel,' he announces, eyeing Rosamund sourly. 'I had required from you the Man-Woman, instead you bring me a poxed drab. And a live one to boot.'

'I am no drab,' retorts Rosamund, 'nor poxed. And were you any sort of gentleman, you would not speak so.'

'You will curb your shrew's tongue, Mr Samuel,' warns Liston quietly, 'or else.'

'Have Cobb thrash her into the street,' drawls Trubshaw, 'such insolence is not to be borne in your own home. This is an uncommon fine Madeira, Harry.'

I grip Rosamund's arm, feeling her tense with barely restrained fury. 'She is neither shrew, nor drab, sir, and the matter at hand concerns us both. We are here with information concerning the Man-Woman, Bobby Herman.'

Liston nods. 'Speak then, man. Out with it.'

'The body you so urgently seek is quite safe, its whereabouts known only to me, but first, I would have something in exchange.'

'Indeed?'

'Information concerning a friend of ours. It is a young man, no more than sixteen or seventeen, fair of hair and of modest, though respectable, appearance.'

'You believe me acquainted with such a person? Whatever gave you that notion?'

'He was here last night in the street outside and has since disappeared.'

'Ah, and now we come to it, eh, Philip?'

'Indeed, Harry,' says Trubshaw, firing up a slim cigar.

'The body of the Man-Woman was brought last night but snatched away from under our very noses by persons unknown. You would know nothing about the matter, I take it?'

'I know what became of it,' I say.

'Well, that is something.'

'I will tell you where the body is to be found, but I cannot say how it came to be there.'

'And what if I were to tell you that you were seen, Mr Samuel? The Mutton fellow insists that you were present in their carriage when the Man-Woman was snatched.'

'That is between you and your informant; I cannot account for it.'

Liston chuckles. 'Mr Mutton was most adamant. I admit, I should not have thought you capable of such a ruse. And yet, here you are, bold as brass.'

'The hows, whys and wherefores of the thing are of no account. I have the information you desire and you may keep your thirty sovs.'

'That is generous in you, Mr Samuel Samuel, but in truth I am no longer interested in the matter.'

'How so, sir?'

Liston shrugs. 'I am, as you know, mindful of your profession; doubtless you filched the body only to sell it on for a higher price to some curious anatomiser?'

'I did not.'

Liston smiles. 'I cannot see how it would profit you else. Whether it is you, Mr Teeth, your Mutton Head or Uncle Tom Cobley takes his profit from it is all one to me. It has been a nuisance to me but I had no real wish to possess the body myself, desiring only its disappearance. No doubt it is by now reduced to a hundred pieces on some slab. And so, although you have disregarded my express instructions, you have, I should say, achieved my ends. For now, our business is concluded.'

'It is not. We yet require information in regard to our associate.'

'Associate, Mr Samuel Samuel? Associate? A nice description for one of your gang of degenerate night crawlers.'

'A crossing sweep he is and as honest as they come.'

'Now that you mention it, perhaps I do recall a young man on the pavement outside.'

'Then will you tell us what became of him?' pleads Rosamund.

'I do not know, much less do I care.'

'You must tell us if you know aught,' insists Rosamund. I grip her arm, anchoring her for a moment as she tears at me in desperation.

'"Must", you say?' Liston's expression of amused malice alters to one of genuine surprise. He sweeps his arm from the mantle and, stepping a half a pace forward, strikes Rosamund's face with the full force of his open hand, slapping her to the floor. 'You will make no demands of me, slut.'

I lurch for him myself, my hand outstretched for his neck; I manage to grip an edge of his silk gown which only glides through my fingers before I am overpowered by Cobb and his liveried partner.

'What is the commotion, Harry?' pipes a scared, pale-faced young man peeping round the door to the inner chambers. From what I can see of him he is a well-looking fellow, about fifteen years of age and similarly attired in a silk robe, but his face is bruised, his dark curls mussed and his eyes red from weeping.

''Tis a matter of business, Freddie. None of your concern. Off with you now.'

The lad goggles as I struggle with the servants; Rosamund collects herself from the floor, her mouth leaking blood from a split lip.

'Do as I say, Freddie,' barks Liston. In a trice the young lad disappears.

Despite the violence Trubshaw remains sprawled in his chair, languidly sipping at his wine. 'Shall I call for Hodges, Harry?'

'Do not trouble yourself, Philip. Cobb and Miller here will suffice,' replies Liston, fastidiously smoothing his robe before settling himself again at the mantle.

'It is plain to me that you are no gentleman, whatever your station, aye, nor even a proper man,' announces Rosamund, getting to her feet.

Liston glares at her, his mouth thinning to a pale slit. He makes no retort to her jibe, directing his gaze instead to the burly servants who have an arm of mine each locked behind my back. 'Should this filthy jilt open her poxed hole again you will be so good as to break a finger for each word uttered.'

'Very good, sir,' replies the man Cobb, grasping the little finger of my left hand, forcing it up against the joint. The pain is so intense as to bring instant tears and I pray that, for the moment at least, Rosamund is able to keep mum.

'There is nothing further to detain us and you will not come here again, I hope,' Liston flaps a limp hand, imperiously ushering us from his presence. 'Put them out; you need not be gentle about it neither,' he orders.

Though there are children's rhymes on the subject, it is no laughing matter to be kicked down the stairs. And, as we pause at the topmost step, my arms pinioned by the two servants, for a dizzying moment I fear I am to be hurled headfirst down the flight. Instead, Cobb releases my arm, takes a hold of my collar and drags me down at considerable speed, like a felon, tardy to the gallows.

Rosamund, having collected my old hat, has preceded us and awaits silently in the vestibule, dabbing gingerly at her lip with a balled up fogle.

Miller throws wide the door and Rosamund steps out. The two servants encourage me on my way with shoves and sharp punches to my back and ribs.

'There is no need to show me out,' I say, echoing Bamfield's words in an attempt to preserve my dignity. I slowly descend the three steps to the pavement and receive a colossal kick to the seat of my keks, which sends me sprawling to the dust.

As Rosamund helps me to my feet we turn to find Liston now framed in the doorway between his two servants. 'You should take more care,' he says, addressing Rosamund. 'I fear you have done yourself quite an injury.' He produces a kerchief from the pocket of his robe and flings it in our direction. 'Here is something for it, my dear.'

The door slams and we hear the bolts being shot as the kerchief flutters to the ground at our feet.

It is a square of bright red cotton.

CHAPTER XXXVI

'It is John's,' says Rosamund, carefully folding the red kerchief, 'I know it.'

'You do not know that for certain. One red kerchief is very like another.'

'He wore it at his neck all last night, Sammy, and was most proud of it. You cannot have missed it.'

I did not miss it.

I know that she is right and I am utterly at a loss, unable even to offer a single word of comfort. I take her arm in mine and, for want of a better plan, head us back to the Coach and Horses. From time to time she dabs at blood and a beck of tears with her little fogle. The other, Kak John's red kerchief, she has stowed in her sleeve. We cover those few yards in silence. So downcast are we that it comes as something of a surprise to find the place full of noise and warmth and good cheer.

The can is not at his usual post by the counter and so I do not have to endure his tomfoolery. Tom stands yarning at the fire, holding court amidst admiring patrons, tankard in his huge, scarred fist. Being somewhat larger than most he is quick to spy us over the throng. With a nod he gestures us to his private room. I steer Rosamund past the curious patrons and have her settled in Tom's easy chair before the man arrives bearing a jug of water and a small cloth.

'What's this?' says Tom. 'Claret spilled 'mongst men don't trouble me overmuch but I will not happily see it in a lady.' He extends his great hand to Rosamund. 'Well, miss, Tom is my name and right sorry I am to find you so distressed.'

Rosamund's tiny hand disappears for a moment into Canon's mighty paw. 'Rosamund,' she replies.

'It seems I am to be nursemaid to all your acquaintances today, Sammy,' observes Tom, dipping the cloth into the jug. 'Your Facey has not stirred and now, miss, you will pardon the liberty, I hope?' he says before dabbing clumsily at Rosamund's broken lip.

Rosamund hesitantly takes the cloth from him, giving Tom a rueful smile. 'You are very kind, sir.'

Tom frowns. 'I have been too long a mauler not to know the signs of a dunt. The mark on your cheek is yet livid. Well now, Sammy, the lady has been struck to tears and I will know the circumstance.'

'Tom, there is more to this than a single blow. He who struck it has took our friend and may yet do him some injury. But it is a person of standing and property, a high gentleman, who is way beyond the reach of the likes of you and me.'

'Then he may be touched by the law, Sammy. It is assault at the least. Who is it stands so high that he may strike out at womenfolk as he pleases?'

'His name is Liston, a gentleman who resides in Poland Street, not two hundred yards from here.'

Tom rises. 'I have heard something of that name; not a bit of it good. But you are in the right of it, Sammy. He would happily use his elevated station to avoid culpability. I cannot easily have satisfaction from him, but I am not without influence as you will see.' With that he strides purposefully from the room.

Rosamund's lip has stopped bleeding; she rinses the cloth in the jug before carefully folding it and placing it on the side table. 'Can your Tom do aught?'

'Tom is well regarded by the Fancy and has friends and patrons both high and low, so perhaps there is something to be done.'

'I would not wish to make it worse for John. You do not think that Liston would truly harm him?'

'I cannot say what he is capable of, Rosamund. The man is an abomination.'

'Though a brute and a molly, he has his station to preserve at least.'

I gawp at her. This is news indeed to me.

'You did not twig it?'

'I see nothing carefree and bawdy in him like those boys of Catherine Street, only a vicious cur, cossetted and disguised by wealth and status.'

'He is a mandrake for certain, Sammy, but of a vicious, predatory nature. The poor young man Freddie, his latest Ganymede. It is why my barb about him not being a proper man found an easy mark.'

'Oh, good Christ,' I slap my head, 'then here is the answer to the riddle of the Man-Woman.'

'How so?'

'The corpse never was a true hermaphrodite. Bobby Herman, as he was known, was the natural son of Joshua Brookes.'

Rosamund's forehead puckers. 'You say that you have the answer and yet here you are speaking conundrums of your own. Who is Joshua Brookes?'

'My principal, the anatomist and man of natural science who first set us on Bobby's trail.'

'Your anatomist was father to the corpse he sought? That is a chilling tale, Sammy.'

'No, my principal is blameless, desiring only the return of his son's body for a Christian burial. Still, the story is grim enough when I tell you that Bobby Herman, or Templeton, more properly, was much abused in his short life, most likely by Liston.'

'How so?'

'Bobby Templeton had been at one time Liston's companion. I believe it was Liston's treatment of him, which rendered him half a man.'

'You are speaking in riddles again, Sammy.'

'I cannot mention the specifics for decency's sake.'

'Oh, pish, Sammy. I am no high-strung dame.'

'In his earlier youth Bobby was savaged by a hound and thereby deprived of that which would have rendered him a complete man. I cannot put it any clearer.'

Rosamund blushes. 'I take your meaning, Sammy. And you think that Liston's work?'

'There were scars elsewhere on the body from the jaws of a mastiff. I am certain that Liston set his hound on the boy as he did to me.'

'Liston is not the only man in all of London to own such a creature.'

'Indeed not, but I have not told you all. Bobby Templeton was murdered: he died from strangulation.'

'How could you know this, Sammy? How could any person know?'

'His father showed me marks, unmistakable to a man of science, likewise observed by Stephen Florey. It was this Florey we took the body from at Clapham Fair.'

'You returned the boy to his father, Sammy. We did right, I hope?'

'We did, though perhaps Florey had a claim right enough, since he loved the boy in his own way. And it is Florey who connects Liston to this murder. 'Til this moment it has all been scrabblings in the mind, scraps and impressions like your chalk markings on the street: a little shading here, a little there, until from nowhere the full picture comes suddenly all into view.'

'How so?'

'Shortly after the travelling fair came to London, the man Florey followed the boy at night to a certain house in Poland Street. It was the last time Bobby was seen alive. And there was another, at the fringes of Liston's world, who may have been present that night, for he knew of the existence of Bobby's corpse before all others. A notorious mandrake, pipe addict and most likely, I believe, Liston's procurer, he sought to profit from the information and so his mouth was quickly stopped. Likewise by Liston's hand, I am certain.'

'You knew this and yet have said nothing?'

'What could I report, and to who? As I say, it has only been scant lines and tracings in the ether 'til now.'

'You did not inform the father?'

'I did not wish to add to the burden of his sorrow.'

'I see the picture clearly and cannot bear it. Our John is in the hands of such a man.'

'Now then, now then.' A brisk, portly, oldish gent in dark coat, matching breeches and pure white stock enters, followed by Tom bearing a good crystal goblet and a bottle with a dark green wax seal.

Rosamund and me rise, for it is clear from his appearance and Tom's deference that this is no common or garden patron.

'Sit ye, sit ye,' orders the gent, settling himself in the chair nearest the fire, 'no need for ceremony here; we are not at formal session.'

Tom uncorks the bottle and fills the man's glass. 'Here is Mr Justice Roe, of the Great Marlborough Street Office to speak with you, Stipendiary Magistrate, no less.'

'Thank'ee kindly, Tom. It is not every day that I can get you to part with your Green Seal. And so here I am, all ears. Ordinarily, you must wait your turn for a Constable at the offices of justice, but I hold Tom Canon in some esteem and so he is a good man to have in your corner, so to speak.'

The man's ears are certainly worthy of note but only for the prodigious quantity of hair, which emerges from them. He examines the dark red liquid in his receptacle, his eyes soft and glistening and with an alarming tendency to bulge from his head like a pug dog. He closes them briefly before downing the wine in a single swallow. Tom chuckles dutifully at the pugilistical squib, before refilling the glass.

Roe blinks at us, now somewhat fortified. 'Well, well, let's to it. You have some complaint to voice, I believe?'

'As you may observe, the young lady has been subject to an assault,' prompts Tom gently at the Magistrate's shoulder.

'I see a mark on the young lady's face, certainly,' responds the Magistrate with a deal of complacence. 'I am sorry for it, my dear, but there must be evidence and the like before it can come to a proper legal complaint.'

Rosamund swallows, raising her head to look the fellow in the eye. 'Well, sir, I was struck by a gentleman I know to—'

'I should wish to hear a little something of you first, my dear. Are you old friends with this lady, Tom?'

'Alas, not old friends, Mr Justice Roe, sir, I have only tonight met her.'

'Then how are we to know who she is?'

'My name is Rosamund Howlett, sir.'

'Very well, Rosamund Howlett. And where do you commonly reside at?'

'Nine Elms, sir.'

'Nine Elms, I see.' Mr Justice Roe repeats the words as though he just drank cat piss instead of Tom's Green Wax stuff. 'And this gentleman is?' he asks, indicating me.

'Witness to the assault, if it please you, sir,' advises Rosamund.

'My name is Samuel Samuel,' I say.

Roe frowns as though my name displeases him. 'And your own place of residence?'

Not knowing what answer to make I blow out my cheeks, gazing about me a little.

'I take it then that you are of no fixed abode?'

'At this time, sir,' I acknowledge.

'And what is your profession?'

'I am a mechanic and labourer.'

'So, no especial skills then?'

'None to speak of, your honour, though I have my letters and can enumerate well enough.'

'Tush, it will not do. A man of no fixed abode and a denizen of Nine Elms, forsooth.' The Magistrate peers round at Tom who waits with the bottle. 'Forgive me, Tom, but should this complaint be 'gainst any person of respectability it would never stand, despite the excellence of your bottle.'

'Your honour, it cannot be denied that the lady has suffered injury.'

'True enough, Tom, but for two such as these the metropolis is a rough and tumble place, we cannot turn every knock into a matter of jurisprudence, more especially on the word of an itinerant. Indeed, this man is only fortunate to be under your roof without I call a Constable and lay a charge upon him under the Vagrancy Act myself.'

'We are all Englishmen here and subject to the same protection, I hope, your honour.'

'Well, well, charge my glass and I will give the young lady a hearing. I should not see a good bottle wasted.'

Tom does as he is bid, whilst Rosamund hesitantly attempts to complete the tale. 'Your honour, I was struck a blow to the face by a gentleman by the name of Liston, residing at Glendale House in Poland Street.'

'And where did the event occur?'

'Why, at this Glendale House, sir.'

'You were at Glendale House then. And what did you there, young lady, at the home of this gentleman?' he asks with a significant look.

'I had gone to look into the disappearance of my friend, John.'

'You were not present by invitation?'

'No, sir.'

'Then you were there through trespass or at the least, on sufferance?'

'I do not understand these legalistic terms, sir.'

'You were not in that house by legal admission, young lady.'

'We had been admitted by a servant.'

'The gentleman himself had not invited you in to his home?'

'He made no objection, sir.'

'Until he struck you a blow?'

'Yes, sir, but I do not see-'

'And you were accompanied by this vagrant?'

'It is Mr Samuel Samuel, sir.'

'That is no proper name.'

'It is my only one, sir,' I interject, seeing Rosamund becoming somewhat flustered.

'You invade the home of a gentleman accompanied by a vagrant of no proper name or address and desire the law's protection when the gentleman makes objection and turns you out? To my mind it is the gentleman himself who is the more sinned against.'

'Sir, we believe that this "gentleman" has abducted our friend and means to do him some harm.'

'You have proof of this?'

'I have our friend's kerchief, sir, which the gentleman had about his person,' says Rosamund, producing the item from her sleeve. She holds it out to Roe who examines it, watery eyes bulging out from over the rim of his glass.

'And how is this significant?

'It was the property of our friend, your honour.'

'It is a scrap of cambric to be found in any slop shop. And how did you come by this article?'

'It was given me by the gentleman.'

'And that is before or after you were struck?'

'After, sir.'

'Surely then the giving of a kerchief was only the natural act of a gentleman in solicitude of your injury, an act of kindness and scarcely a matter for complaint?' the Magistrate blithely drinks off the wine remaining in his glass. Tom hovers at his shoulder with the bottle. 'Come, Tom, I will finish it to the lees and then I must be about my supper.'

'The man is a mandrake, sir. And not above –'

'Now you go too far, Miss. Not another word now. A man's reputation is vouchsafed under the common law; character and good fame must be protected. I give you warning, young lady, you are perilous close to an actionable slander.' Rising swiftly, Roe quaffs the remaining wine and makes a hasty bow to Tom. 'Tom, I know you to be a worthy sort but it is your good nature that makes you an easy mark for such a pair as these. Take care lest they draw you further in to their schemes; better you do not suffer them a minute more under your roof; I shall send a Constable should you require it.'

'No, no, your honour,' says Tom, taking the man's arm and steering him to the door. 'I do not believe it is malicious instinct, which moves them. You have given a fair hearing and I ask your pardon for the trouble I have put you to. You will take a bottle of the good stuff home with you as a mark of my esteem.'

'Well, that is decent in you, Tom. And you and I will part friends with no harm done.'

The door is closed leaving Rosamund and me to the sounds of the fire crackling in the grate like a crone's laughter.

'There is the law for you,' I sigh. 'I did not ever expect to find much virtue in the opinions of Pimlott and Chuffington, but when they speak of two worlds—a higher and lower—I believe they have it right. The law's only purpose being the protection of those above from those below.'

I don't think that Rosamund hears my words; she remains quite still, solemnly cogitating, chin deep in her hands. At length she gazes up. 'The law will never act lest it is held by the nose and shoved directly into the business like a naughty puppy. But now all trace of villainy is gone; the proof squared away. We have done Liston's work for him, Sammy.'

'How so?'

'This Florey was the one we left howling at the moon?'

'The Man of India rubber he is called but his tale will carry no more weight with the law than ours. Less, I imagine, since he is so inclined to rave, crying assassination to all and sundry.'

'The ravings of a madman it would seem to most, yet even a broken clock rings true two times in a day. A cracked bell he may be, but this Florey made sufficient clamour to cause Liston alarm. It was why he wished the body beyond reach and was content to believe it anatomized.'

'The body is away right enough. It was today entombed by a proper mason.'

'Liston does not know that. Though we have no hope of bringing the man to justice we must have some lever, Sammy. Every minute that passes places our John in further peril.'

'But how to begin? At every which way I see naught but obstruction.'

'There is one powerful connection you have not yet pursued in this matter, Sammy.'

'I cannot think of it.'

'It is the boy's father. And I believe you owe him the truth.'

'Forgive me, young lady, I am somewhat abashed,' announces Tom, entering the room.

'Do not be, Mr Canon. I should never have put you to such trouble were I not so fearful for our friend,' replies Rosamund, adjusting her shawl for the streets.

'I hope you will not think too badly of Mr Justice Roe, he is a decent enough sort for all his finnicking. Though I admit, I had expected something more from him after all the thunderings of Mr Peel.'

'Mr Peel has made the law no kinder than it has ever been and his new breed of constables merely the same old watchmen but with finer brass buttons to their coats. Expect naught from great men and you will never be disappointed,' I reply.

'I pray that is not true,' says Rosamund, 'since our last final hopes now reside in one.'

'Then we shall see, by and by,' I reply, clapping my old stovepipe to my head.

'You have had one near shave today, Sammy, surely you do not mean to hazard another foray into the streets?' says Tom.

'I would as sooner keep you out of it, Tom, but what Rosamund has said is true. A young man stands in harm's way on my account; I know you will agree that I cannot look to my own safety in preferment to his. You have seen the kerchief; trust me when I tell you that it was certainly the property of our friend John.'

'Then I am truly sorry that Roe could not be persuaded to give it more credence.'

'The fault is not yours, Tom. But never fret on my account, it is dark enough outside and our destination but a short way from here.'

'That's as may be, but if you are taken up by Pimlott and Chuffington's creatures what would you have me tell Facey? Some amends are due you both and so I will fetch a cudgel and walk alongside if you have no objection. Where are we bound?'

'To the residence of Sir Joshua Brookes on Great Marlborough Street.'

Tom nods and leads us out into the noisy taproom. Dipping behind the counter he emerges with a stout billy club, which he tucks into his jacket pocket. He gestures for the can, exchanging a few brief words with him before ushering us out onto the pavement.

I take Rosamund's arm and head us down Great Marlborough Street. It is full night now but, this being a prosperous thoroughfare of great mansions, new cast-iron gas lamps have sprouted every few yards giving it the appearance of permanent dusk. In consequence, the streets are still well populated, in the main by respectable folk in their evening finery on their way to the Pantheon Bazaar, the Princess's Theatre or the suchlike amusements. Tom keeps a sharp eye out for any ill-looking sorts who might reveal themselves to be the underlings of Pimlott and Chuffington. Despite my earlier bluster, I am relieved to know that he is alongside us with his truncheon and good right arm.

We come without incident to the imposing mansion that is Brookes' home and rather than risk giving offence by presenting myself at the front door, I steer us to the side entrance. Tom produces his cudgel as we step into the pitch-black alleyway.

It reeks of piss, but other than for an indignant, hissing tomcat, which flees at our presence, the alley is empty. I discover the doorknocker by feel, and, giving it a smart rap, I am rewarded by the sound of slow, heavy footsteps from within. The Judas hatch is slid aside; the harsh yellow glare of a lantern shines out through the grate. I raise my face to the light. 'It is Mr Samuel,' I announce.

'I see you, Mr Samuel. But you should not be here. You must settle your accounts with Mr Bamfield at Berner's Street.' It is the voice of the tough old retainer Crick.

'It is not for mercenary motives that I have come, Mr Crick, but on an urgent matter concerning your master.'

'My master is indisposed.'

'It is information concerning his son.'

'His son is dead and well buried, Mr Samuel, as you must know above all people. You will kindly leave my master to his grief.'

'It relates to the manner of his son's death. There are new facts come to light.'

'Then they will keep. There is nothing to be done for the son and I would not have my master further troubled. Your commission is at an end, Mr Samuel.'

'You are aware that it was no natural death, Mr Crick?'

'I was not, Mr Samuel. And should far rather you did not bellow it from the rooftops like some Penny Blood hawker. 'Tis against my better judgement but perhaps you had best step inside and I will inform my master that you are here.'

The door is unbolted. As we are let into the small vestibule, Crick frowns at the sight of us. 'I did not expect a congregation neither, Mr Samuel.'

'This lady is intimately connected with the business, Mr Crick; I believe your master would wish to hear her.'

'I am the fifth wheel on this cart,' announces Tom in his easy way, 'and only alongside to lend protection, which I can do just as well from without and so I will wait in the alley.'

Crick turns up the oil lamps set about the place before dousing his lantern. He catches sight of Tom's face in the radiance of the lamps. 'You are Tom Canon, the pugilist, if I'm not mistaken.'

'The very same, sir. Do you know me?'

'Only by sight and reputation, Mr Canon. I had the very great pleasure of observing you 'gainst West Country Dick in '17. A singular honour if I may say so,' adds Crick, offering his hand, which Tom cheerfully seizes.

'Thank 'ee kindly, Mr Crick.'

'I will inform my master and, if he will meet with Mr Samuel and the lady, you will perhaps consider remaining as my guest in the parlour here,' he says, indicating a small but comfortable-looking cubbyhole to the side.

'I should like nothing better, Mr Crick.'

With that Crick bows and begins to ascend the stairs to the upper floors.

Rosamund peers curiously at Tom. 'You have kept your light under a bushel, Mr Canon. I did not know you were a man of notoriety.'

'I am naught but an old mauler, long past his prime, Miss.'

'You are a most gentle man and yet a somewhat fearsome one, it seems.'

'Well, Miss, it is my earnest wish that you come to a happy conclusion and your friend returned to you safe and sound, peaceably by means of this gentleman's influence. But should it come to stronger measures you will not find me a wilting violet.'

Rosamund nods. 'Let us hope it does not come to that, Mr Canon. I would not see you hazard your good name for our mistakes.'

Before Tom can reply, we hear Crick's steady tread on the stairwell above. He makes his stately way down the stairs illuminated by the lamp's yellow glow. He halts at the foot and hands me his light, for which I exchange my old beaver. 'He will see you, Mr Samuel, with the lady. You will find him in the Music Room, where last you met with him.' He nods at Tom before placing my hat on a ledge. 'Kindly take your ease in my cubby here, Mr Canon.'

The upper corridor is dark and silent, the lamps set in wall sconces have been left unlit and so Rosamund and me find our way by the lamp in my hand. Once past Brookes' work place it is a simple enough matter to find my way to the Music Room. I knock once before entering.

This room, like the corridor, is gloomy, illuminated only by the embers of the hearth, which flicker still, though the pile of wood in the grate is now much reduced. Brookes is seated in the same armchair staring up at his wife's portrait. A half-drunk glass of wine sits on the side table next to him. I doubt he has stirred since the mournful proceedings at St George's.

He nods in acknowledgment of my presence. 'Mr Samuel, I had not expected to see you again.' Catching sight of Rosamund, who stands hesitant in the doorway, he rises, offering her the briefest of bows.

'Forgive me for disturbing you, sir. I would never intrude but for the most pressing reasons. May I introduce Miss Howlett, who has a connection to this matter?'

'You are welcome, Miss Howlett,' says Brookes, inclining his head. 'And you will forgive this doleful reception, but it has been a long and cheerless day. Please be seated,' he instructs, indicating the armchairs. 'And set the lamp down, sir. Pray do not stand there like some gawping link boy.'

I set the lamp down on one of the delicate little tables, brightening the place a little before seating myself. Brookes remains standing before the small fire, facing us, arms behind his back. 'Well, Mr Samuel, I had hoped that this sorry tale was closed and yet it seems I am mistaken.'

'We would not trouble you, sir, but you will recall this morning that you inquired whether I possessed intelligence as to the fate of your son?'

'Certainly I did.'

'I informed you then that your son had lately spent time with a travelling fair. There it was that I discovered the body in the possession of a certain Stephen Florey, otherwise known as the India rubber Man. He passionately believed that your son had been victim of foul play, observing in him those very same signs of strangulation, which you yourself remarked upon.'

'Indeed?'

'To cut a long story short, sir, this man Florey had followed your son one night to a house not far from here, where he fervently asserts that Bobby met his end. Moreover, I am certain the gentleman of this house had a prior connection with your son.'

'Continue, pray.'

'I think it was to break off that connection that this gentleman set his hound at the boy. I know him to possess such a creature, a mastiff, which he set upon me a few nights previous,' I reply, turning my head, brushing back the lock of hair from my wounded ear. 'My partner, Mr Facey, believes him to be of a twisted, vicious nature; one who takes gratification in the pain of others,' I add.

'It is no great thing that a man should own a savage dog, however brutish his own inclinations.'

'True, sir. But there is more to this.'

'How so?'

'This same gentleman went to very great pains to take possession of your son's body, issuing the promise of a bounty to all and sundry of my profession for that purpose.'

'Perhaps an anatomical gentleman then?'

'By no means. He is a scapegrace and a rakehell—'

'A mandrake,' interjects Rosamund.

Brookes seems to deflate. 'I wish you had not put it so direct, young lady.'

'Forgive me if I am blunt, sir, but with what is at stake I cannot daintily step around the subject.'

'It was not our intention to imply that your—'

'Come now, Mr Samuel. You think a father does not know his own son? Or his inclinations? I was hardly a doting father but I am not blind. I take it that the gentleman you refer to is Henry Liston?'

'The very same, sir. Then you were aware of this connection?'

Brookes pauses for a moment before replying, I imagine lost in some remembrance. 'I was. From time to time I received information that Robert had been seen about the metropolis in that man's company. I never heard a good word said of him and when my son was left so horribly mauled and lying close to death in that rookery, I always believed it to be Liston or those of his circle at the bottom of it.'

'Now you know it for a certainty.'

'I know nothing for a certainty, except what my heart tells me. But that will never stand in a court of law. You have provided me nothing of substance here, only further dismal conjecture.' Brookes stoops to rattle the embers with a poker, fostering a hesitant flame or two. I wait until he turns again to face us.

'Sir, Florey sought to raise a hue and cry and, through his loud and strident protests of murder, may ultimately have caught the ear of the law. Certainly, he claimed to have laid a complaint against Liston, which I believe panicked him and would account for his urgent desire to obtain the body, and why he raised such a bounty on it.'

'Well, well,' says Brookes, 'it confirms that Liston's hand was somehow in it, but it is still no proof in law. What's more, I cannot fathom why the boy should return to a house where he was so badly used.'

I have given this some thought and am quite certain of the reason, though I doubt Brookes will relish the hearing of it. 'Sir, will you allow me to state my feelings frankly on the matter?'

'I am all ears, Mr Samuel.'

'You intimated that your son was not above the practice of extortion?'

'Regrettably, you know it to be the case.'

'I had it from Florey that your son went to that place in the expectation of money.'

'You suggest for the purpose of blackmail?'

'Well,' I say, not wishing to discomfort the man further, 'perhaps it was only to seek recompense for the injury he had previously suffered.'

Brookes grunts, slapping a palm down on the mantle in agitation. 'Mr Samuel, the young lady has it right: let us not pussyfoot about the thing and say it straight out. My son threatened to expose this gentleman for a mandrake; that is what you mean to say.' Brookes glares at us, daring us to contradict him, though it is, in truth, we who have led him to it. 'But why is it only now that you come to me with this?'

'I have told you that the commission was a most troublesome one, sir.'

'And you have been well recompensed, I believe.'

'Indeed, though I have not yet completed the business with your Mr Bamfield, sir. The task became both arduous and perilous on account of Liston's bounty. In consequence of which, your son's body was last night snatched by others in my line of work. I will spare you the details of its retrieval but it was desperate work, in the course of which an acquaintance of ours was abducted. A good and decent young man, innocent of any wrongdoing, who was only pressed into service to keep a watch for us.'

'Abducted, how?'

'We do not know the essentials, sir,' interjects Rosamund, 'but certain it is to be Liston's work.'

'Why do you say so?'

'He flung the young man's kerchief at me as a parting gift to go along with the injury he had already given,' she says, indicating her broken lip.

Brookes peers intently at Rosamund's face in the lamplight. 'It is the mark of a blow right enough. I would dearly wish to pay the man out for all his wickedness, but I cannot see how I am to intercede.'

'You are a gentleman of influence, sir,' I point out.

'I cannot involve the law; you well know this, Mr Samuel. The evidence, such as it is, has been consigned to the ground and it would serve no purpose to bring a scandal upon my house. You forget that Liston is shielded by his own wealth and connections. His uncle, I believe, holds very high office. If I felt able to bring the man down, do you not think I would have done all in my power when my son was first harmed?'

'So, you will not help us then, sir?' sighs Rosamund.

Brookes brings his hands together, allowing his long, tapered fingers to form a kind of steeple. 'I would do anything to settle the score with that creature, pay any amount, aye, even my entire fortune to see him brought to account, but I would not part with my good name. I will not have a scandal.'

'I had thought, sir, that you being a man of science, might easily convince Liston that you had observed on the body these signs of foul play,' I say.

'And what of it?'

'And that you intend to reopen the coroner's inquest in the light of this and Florey's testimony,' adds Rosamund, leaning forward in her chair.

'Surely you understand that the coroner's inquest cannot be reopened since the body has been lawfully interred.'

'Liston does not know that,' continues Rosamund quickly. 'He is ignorant of the precise whereabouts of the body, sir, believing Mr Samuel to have sold it for anatomizing. If he imagined the body to be in your possession, then you would hold sufficiently powerful a threat to induce him to release our friend unharmed, at the price of your silence.'

Brookes suck his teeth, considering. 'It is an exceedingly rickety stratagem, young lady, since we possess no evidence.'

''Tis the only one we have, sir.'

Brookes shakes his head emphatically. 'You ask me to stoop to blackmail myself, child. You talk prettily of inducement and yet it is blackmail, pure and simple.'

'But not for mercenary gain, sir. For righting a great wrong, surely—'

'You expect me to play fast and loose with the truth and the law, and worse, to bargain with this villain for my silence?'

'For the preservation of your good name, you have already chosen to make that concession, sir.' Rosamund sinks back in her chair, seeing her last hopes for Kak John's safety crumble at Brookes' moralising.

'Neither have you always been so exacting when it comes to the boundaries of the law,' I interject.

Brookes inhales sharply. He has been so subdued and easy with us that I have allowed my emotions to get the better of me and have assuredly crossed a line in challenging him so. 'Mr Samuel, you forget yourself. I will not bandy words with you.' With that, he turns on his heel to face the fire and I fear we have been dismissed.

Rosamund, however, is quick to leap to my defence. 'Forgive him, sir. You have been so sympathetic and graciously condescending that we have, indeed, forgot ourselves. Mr Samuel is not a man who ordinarily considers his own thoughts before airing them and tonight, out of overmuch concern, his tongue has even less a curb to it than usual.'

Brookes turns and looks at her for a moment as she gazes up beseechingly. His stony expression softens. 'Young lady, there is something about you of my dear wife. I marked it at the outset. Not in looks or station, of course, but in your demeanour, and a certain facility with words that would put many an attorney-at-law to shame.'

Rosamund gazes down at her shoes, modestly. 'I believe that to be a compliment of the very highest order, Mr Brookes. And I thank you for it.'

'Well, well, I will consider your scheme and will sleep on it, gossamer thin though it is.'

'Sir, it is a construct fragile as a snowflake,' insists Rosamund, 'and you will forgive me when I say there is no time for consideration, since each moment that passes melts more of the edifice away, turning all to water.'

Brookes pauses before clapping his hands together, startling us both. 'Indeed it is. You press me to have it done tonight, young lady. Well, "If it were done when 'tis done, then 'twere well it were done quickly".'

Rosamund smiles. '"Screw your courage to the sticking-place, and we'll not fail".'

Brookes goggles at her for this retort. For a moment I fear that he has somehow been offended again, but finally he nods, acknowledging Rosamund's learning.

'My father was a printer, sir,' explains Rosamund simply. 'I was weaned on India ink and my cradle lined with Quarto pages.'

Further discussion is interrupted by a soft scratching at the door, followed by a respectful cough from without.

'Enter,' orders Brookes.

It is Crick and Canon standing side by side. But it is Tom Canon who speaks rather than Brookes' man. 'Forgive this intrusion, sir. I am Tom Canon from the Coach and Horses Inn. My can has come to the door with news concerning Mr Samuel and Miss Howlett. It cannot wait, I believe.'

Brookes inclines his head. 'Please.'

Tom bows at the courtesy before speaking: 'Sammy, Trench is arrived at the Coach along with the young'un. It seems the body of a young man has been brought in off the river at Hungerford Stairs.'

CHAPTER XXXVIII

Rosamund is first to recover herself. She rises, briefly dipping her head to Brookes. 'Sir, you have been more than kind, but you will understand that we must depart this instant.' I am astounded by her composure, but as she adjusts her shawl for the night air I notice that she is unable to keep her hands from trembling.

'Surely you do not intend to walk to the river, Miss Howlett?'

'We have no other means, sir.'

'You have prevailed upon me to assist in this matter and so must continue to allow me to be of service,' responds Brookes, assisting with her shawl. 'I shall not call for my carriage since it is an age to prepare but Crick will summon a Hackney and I will accompany you, if you do not object.'

'You would be most welcome, sir,' replies Rosamund.

With a bow, Crick withdraws, along with Tom, to be about his allotted task.

Brookes gathers himself. 'I am not dressed for the streets. You must excuse me and we shall meet downstairs in a moment.' He quits the room leaving us alone together.

I gaze at Rosamund, conscious of her welling tears as they glisten in the firelight. 'Forgive me, Sammy, I had hoped to maintain my fortitude.'

'There is naught to forgive and I pray those tears are wasted. We do not yet know that it is John.'

'I feel it must be, Sammy. I ought to have sent him home when at the tannery.'

I place my hands on her shoulders, feeling them tremble. 'Rosamund, I had thought to bring you happiness and, even dared to imagine, companionship. Instead I have given you naught but sorrow. The fault is mine for drawing you both into such a foolish, hazardous venture. It is myself I cannot forgive.'

Rosamund gently places her hands atop of mine for a moment. 'Whatever the outcome tonight, I would wish you in a more honourable occupation, Sammy.'

'I am done with the resurrection game, you have my word on it.'

Rosamund dabs at her eyes and attempts a smile. 'Then that is some small thing.'

I pick up the lamp and we retrace our steps along the upper corridors, descending to the small side vestibule on the ground floor. I reclaim my beaver from the ledge just as Brookes emerges from a connecting hallway in a heavy Garrick overcoat, gloves, gleaming stovepipe and cane. He ushers us out into the alleyway, closing the street door behind us with a heavy thud.

We emerge from the alley's deep shadows and piss tang to the muted yellow glow of streetlights and a more pleasing waft of London coal smoke and horse manure. A soft drizzle hazes the air; at the kerbside stands a Hackney, accompanied by the silhouetted, but unmistakable, figures of Tom and Crick.

Crick directs the beam of his bull's-eye lantern at the coach step for the convenience of his master. 'Sir, Hungerford Stairs is by no means the gentlest of districts at this hour and I should feel a deal easier were I to accompany you. Mr Canon here has been good enough to give me the loan of his billy club.'

'Has he indeed? Well, I thank you, Mr Canon. I trust we will not require the use of it,' says Brookes alighting.

'Always better to be safe than sorry, sir,' replies Tom in his bluff way, before bowing.

As he turns to leave, Rosamund stays him, laying a hand on his arm. 'Tom, I must beg a favour of that gentle man in you.'

'Name it, Miss.'

'Will you see to the lad, the messenger boy? He is due to return shortly for news of his brother; he has no other family and so will be utterly distraught.'

'Have no fear, Miss, I shall do what I can and will, at any rate, keep him safe beneath my roof. It is quite wrong to wish ill fortune on any man and yet, for your sakes, I do pray that it be some other party they have fished up from the Thames.'

'Likewise, Tom,' I agree, shaking his hand.

Rosamund and me climb aboard. Brookes raps on the roof with his cane and the Hackney lurches away. Tom waves us off as we clatter past into the night.

We trundle quickly through Argyll Place and head down Regent Street. The novelty of flying through the metropolis in a horse-drawn conveyance has now paled for me and so I am not much troubled when Brookes pulls down the leather window blinds. The lantern in Crick's lap casts sufficient light for us to discern one another well enough.

We are all of us silent, none wishing to speak ahead of Brookes. For a while he appears lost in cogitation, until finally he says: 'Forgive me, young lady, I believe I heard you mention that your friend is without family?'

Rosamund smiles sadly. 'Indeed, sir.'

'Though I hope that it should not be so, if it be your friend, should you wish to claim the body?'

The carriage rattles into longish bend, most likely Regent Street Quadrant, throwing us against one another. 'I had not thought of it, but yes, I would, sir, since there is no one else,' replies Rosamund.

'Then I might at least be of service to you in that regard. There is little else I can do.'

'You are very good, sir.'

Brookes nods before addressing himself to me. 'And you, Mr Samuel, you say you have not yet had your bounty off Mr Bamfield?'

'I was detained, sir, and unable to meet with him this morning, though now I come to think on it, I am certain it was your Mr Bamfield I saw later at Glendale House.'

'Very likely. Mr Bamfield manages the business affairs of a great many West End gentlemen; he is utterly scrupulous in all his dealings and much in demand. I shall send him a note tomorrow to add a further sum of twenty sovereigns for the hardships you have endured.'

'I do not ask it, sir.'

'You shall have it nevertheless. You will find him at his place of business in Berner's Street.'

'That is most generous in you.'

Before Brookes can make a reply we feel the carriage jerk to a halt. Crick raises the blind and cranes his head to peer out of the window. We hear the sounds of muffled conversation before Crick's head reappears. 'We are by Hungerford Street market and must alight here since there is a gated slipway ahead.'

'Very well then, light the way, Crick,' orders Brookes, as he disembarks.

Crick clambers out with his lantern at the ready, followed by Rosamund and me. The road behind us is mean and narrow up to this point where it widens to accommodate a market area. The stalls are mostly shuttered now, though one or two still do a little trade, mostly in the line of oysters and whelks by the indolent flickering of candle stubs and tapers. The people here are not desperate, like the men and women of Devil's Acre, since most are able to make a living of sorts from the river. But they are poor enough and there is no shortage of surly, watchful eyes upon us; a fact not lost on Brookes in his gleaming topper, which, despite the voluminous Garrick, instantly marks him for a gent.

Brookes addresses the driver, 'You will be good enough to wait for us here and you shall have ten shillings.'

'I shall, your honour.' The man touches his forehead with the handle of his whip. 'The Stairs is yonder at the end of that there passage. Straight ahead. And should you find your feet wet, you has gone too far.'

The way is very dark once we quit the dubious lights of the market; Crick leads us by the beam of his lantern through the narrow passage formed by a pair of tumbledown, three-storey brick buildings. The edifice to our right is most likely a blacking factory to judge by the smell of rancid tallow; the other, to our left, resembles a shadowy hedgepig from the many washing poles projecting out from it. Crick plays his beam against the frontage to reveal a hanging sign displaying the image of a running fox. Sure enough, a modest, grimy banner proclaims it to be The Old Fox tavern.

We enter and what low conversation there is abruptly ceases. It is a dingy, squalid place, lit by blackly smoking tallow candles; the ceiling is bowed with age, stained from old tobacco smoke, supported by rotting wooden beams. The floor is formed from damp grey flagstones, stained and worn to ruts with years and tread. There is a rough counter boasting a single ale cask with a leaking wooden tap set in the bunghole. A group of men and women huddle around a low trestle smoking clay pipes and drinking from leather mugs or dented tin cups. The focus of their attention is a shrouded corpse laid out before them.

A squinting, bewhiskered fellow in a bluff waistcoat and stained Nankeen trousers detaches himself from the group and approaches us. He bows deeply to Brookes. 'Welcome to The

Old Fox, sir. Jonathan Trimble is my name. How might I be of service to you?'

Brookes gazes at him imperiously. 'We are come about the corpse.'

'Taken from the river, sir. Not three hours previous. For a gawp, is it?' leers Trimble, assessing Brookes' worth before naming his price. "Tis sixpence, your lordship, and a ale apiece, gratis.'

Crick produces a silver sixpence, which he hands the fellow. 'There is your fee, Trimble, and you may save your ale.'

Trimble slips the coin into a waistcoat pocket and turns to address his patrons before wading in to the huddle. 'Come now, make a hole for the gentleman and his party. Let the dog see the rabbit, ladies and gents, come now, make a hole there.' The assembly grudgingly parts to reveal the corpse on the trestle. It is unclothed, partly covered by a scrap of old canvas, leaving the head and shoulders visible. Long fair hair flows across the wood, draping the edges. The corpse has not long been in the river, since there is no sign of bloating, but the skin is remarkably white. It is heartbreaking to see Kak John so clean.

I turn to find Rosamund at my side. She is quite still, her face bearing a look of utter weariness.

'It is our friend,' I say to Brookes.

'Then I will arrange for you to take possession of the body. Might I examine him first?' he inquires.

I gaze at Rosamund, who nods briefly. 'By all means, sir.'

Crick holds the lantern over the body while Brookes steps to the trestle. He gently pulls down the canvas a little way, and hunches over the corpse, beginning the examination with the head. There are bruises to the face and arms, and curious, bloodless gashes across the ribs. Brookes presses down on the ribcage two or three times.

''Tis just another poor lost soul puked up by Old Father Thames, your honour,' cackles one of the hags, her mildewed bonnet askew, ale gushing from her toothless, grinning gob.

'You may shove him all you wish, sir. He will never repay what tin he owes you,' adds a leering, greasy-faced cove, raising a gust of mirth from the congregation.

'Now then, now then, what's this, sir. A tanner don't buy you the right to go poking and proddin' about the corpus,' interjects Trimble, forcing his way through the onlookers.

'Stand off, fellow,' growls Crick, brandishing the cudgel in his free hand.

'You threaten me? In my own tavern? I will have the law on you.'

'You may bring the law by all means, Trimble. I take it you have already summoned a Constable as is your bounden duty?' replies Brookes.

Trimble halts, unsure of himself. 'It is not … ' He raises a placatory hand. 'You are quite right, sir. And I was just this minute on my way to do so.'

'Then perhaps you will also explain to the Constable how it is the garments come to be missing.'

'Surely your honour would not begrudge a man turning a few coppers from what comes out of the river? 'Taint as if he needs them clouts now. And 'tis but the custom of things hereabouts, sir, with the drownded ones. The boatmen dredge 'em out and brings 'em in to me and I lays 'em out 'til the relatives come to claim 'em or the parish. I only takes what profit I can for the service, sir.'

'Well, Trimble, I will save you the trouble,' announces Brookes, replacing the canvas. 'Here is the boy's sister, come to claim the body.'

Rosamund removes the red kerchief from her sleeve and steps to the trestle. Gently raising Kak John's head, she ties the scarf around the lad's neck and plants a kiss on his forehead.

'And where would you wish it conveyed, my dear?' inquires Brookes delicately.

'Why, sir. I had not thought … '

'I believe Tom Canon will have it at the Coach and Horses, sir, since the brother is most likely there,' I suggest.

Brookes throws me a look. 'The very premises we began at, Mr Samuel.'

'Indeed so, sir.'

'Well I must tell you straight out, I believe your misgivings to be justified,' announces Brookes. 'There is something amiss here and I should have liked to make further inspection in a less public setting.'

Trimble gapes in horror. 'Sir, for the love of Christ. I have done nothing irregular but lay out the drownded corpse as any decent Christian would.'

''Twas in any case Big Nose Greggs snagged 'im with his irons and brought him in off the river,' insists the hag.

'Calm yourself, Trimble. You are not implicated here. But you have taken profit from another's misfortune, and so will make amends. You will have a carter convey the body to the Coach and Horses Inn at the corner of Poland Street and we will say no more about the business.'

'I will, sir,' replies Trimble with relief.

'Here is something to defray your expense.' Brookes rummages in his coat for a shilling.

Trimble accepts the coin, raising a finger to his forelock. ''Twill be done, just as you say, sir.' He addresses Rosamund: 'And I am right sorry for your loss, Miss. The river can be a harsh and unforgiving master at times.'

'He was always a little afeared of it,' says Rosamund sadly.

It is with some relief that we climb aboard the waiting Hackney, which sweeps us away at a good clip. Brookes lowers the blinds before addressing us. 'I have no wish to add to your distress, young lady, but the news is not agreeable.'

In the lantern's light, Rosamund's face is calm and determined, her hands perfectly composed, resting in her lap. 'Nevertheless, I would hear it, sir. Spare nothing.'

'It was only a cursory inspection, but your friend did not meet his end by drowning.'

'How do you say so?' she asks.

'You will have observed me press on the chest, which has the effect of compressing the lungs. There was no water inside them, which tells me that the young man was dead before he was put into the water. Moreover, there was bruising about the head and arms. The bruising round the upper arms corresponding to the marks of fingers, tightly clenched. There was a bluish cast to the lips signifying suffocation, though no sign of ligature marks around the neck.'

'And what of those wounds to his ribs, sir?' I ask.

'The lacerations of the grappling irons. There was no bleeding from those wounds and so they were made after the heart was stopped; post mortem, as we say. They would have been inflicted when the young man was fished from the water: you may discount them. My opinion is that the young man was forcibly held, pinioned by at least two strong men and beaten about the face and head to unconsciousness. Like Robert, he expired as a consequence of asphyxiation, or lack of breath. Judging by the fainter marks around his lips, I would say a compress was used, perhaps a piece of fabric, then a hand or hands were clamped about the nose and mouth.' Brookes shakes his head. 'I would estimate the event took place last night, Miss Howlett. If it be any consolation there was naught you might have done to save him.'

'My consolation will be in holding that man to account, sir.'

'As would mine, but Liston will never be held responsible for this. Moreover, it is always possible that your friend fell victim to footpads.'

'That is not so, sir. I know it, as I think you do. The compress you mention, would a thick kerchief do it?'

'It would.'

'Then it pleased Liston to fling at me the very means by which poor John's life was taken.'

'It is no true evidence. There is nothing to be done.'

We clatter along in silence, bumping and swaying against one another as the conveyance jolts along the many potholes and humps of London's streets.

Abruptly, Rosamund's head comes upright. 'Sir, you have said you would part with any amount to see Liston brought to account?'

'It was a figure of speech, young lady. I will not countenance any rash proposal or action outside of the law.'

'But if there was a way to bring the law to bear on this matter, would you then consider it, sir?'

'Certainly I would.'

'Then I believe I have something,' she announces, her face a picture of grim determination in the lantern's glare.

CHAPTER XXXIX

'Bless my soul,' says Brookes, 'what an extraordinary young woman you are.'

Rosamund briefly dips her head in acknowledgement. ''Tis no great thing, sir. I am well enough versed in matters of debt.'

'How so?'

'I have mentioned, sir, my pa was in trade, and though I was but a child it was his habit to use me as confidential secretary in his dealings since he himself schooled me in my letters and I have always had a fair hand. I penned his correspondence and kept his accounts. He was a good, sober man, sir, though overly lax with his creditors.'

'Indeed.'

'In consequence his enterprise was much burdened with debts of its own; our modest cottage was lost to a lien; in the end my father's press, his precious trays of types and inks and all the sundry articles of the trade were carried off by the bailiffs. When my father passed, it fell to me to meet his obligations. And so I understand as well as any the power of paper to bring dismay and ruin.'

'The law can be remorseless in these matters. It fell to you to make settlement of all?'

'Each and every penny, sir, by means of another kind of paper: everlasting blooms, manufactured by my own hand and sold in the street. There is no man now can say my pa left him the worse off in his dealings.'

Brookes nods soberly. 'That you are sensible of these weighty matters I have no doubt, and I applaud your reasoning. But Liston is another kettle of fish entirely. There is a powerful family and a very great estate that must be brought down before the man is even scratched. It cannot be done. I have not the means for it. Aye, nor another ten like me.'

'I am mindful of it, sir, but you must know that Liston is cut off from that great source; estranged from his father's protection. This we had from his own lips and you may confirm as much from your Mr Bamfield.'

The Hackney trundles to a snail's pace before finally lurching to a halt as the cabby applies full rein. We hear his strident call from without: 'Here is Poland Street, your honours, Coach an' 'Osses as was directed.'

Rosamund remains seated, hands demurely in her lap. Brookes reaches across to pat them with his long, elegant fingers. 'Then there may yet be some chance for this scheme of yours; tomorrow, I will hear what further detail Bamfield may be persuaded to furnish. Crick shall arrange for a visit in the morning—let us say ten—and we may drop two birds with the one stone, since Mr Samuel will receive his monies. You will both of you attend, I hope?'

'I would not miss it for worlds,' replies Rosamund with that selfsame grim expression.

'Well then, sufficient unto the day is the evil thereof. You must see to your poor friend's reception and I will leave you for the while to your doleful business. To be sure, I am heartily sorry for your loss.'

Rosamund and me clamber out, I raise my beaver to Brookes before taking Rosamund's arm. 'I will bid you good night then, sir,' I say as we turn for the doors of the Coach and Horses. The Hackney clatters off to deliver its remaining occupants to their beds.

Within, the public is silent and all but empty on account of the late hour. Tom is sat by the guttering fireside, idly perusing old broadsheets; he leaps to his feet at the sounds of our entry. His hopeful, eager expression instantly crumbles at the sight of us and so he stands, respectfully, awaiting the news he has already divined.

Rosamund sighs. 'Tom, it is good of you to wait on us. Is young John here?' she inquires.

'He is above. The young'un was adrift on his feet, so I fetched him a posset of warm milk and brandy and some while ago put him to my own bed.'

'Poor Tom,' says Rosamund, 'between us we are jouncing you from your own home, one room at a time.'

'No matter. I do not sleep so much and it is a small thing to offer since I fear the news is grave.'

'It is, Tom. The very worst.'

'Then it will do no harm to delay the particulars of it 'til the morning. We shall all of us be better able to endure for a night's rest. It is late and I hope, Miss, you will not object to sharing the lad's bed. Mr Samuel will make shift where Facey stays. And you will be pleased to know that he has woken near enough his old self tonight and taken nourishment: pap and a little wine.'

'I am overjoyed to hear it, Tom,' I say. 'But I must tell you I have taken one further liberty with your generous nature.'

'Name it, Sammy.'

'We could not let our poor friend lie where he was found, so for want of aught else have directed the remains to be carried here.'

'Quite right too—and when are we to expect him?'

'Some time in what remains of this night or early morning, I would hazard.'

'Then I shall keep a watch here in my chair to receive him. The two of you must take some rest and leave all to me.'

'Is my brother here?' inquires a tiny, hesitant voice. Past the counter in the shadows at the foot of the stairs stands Pure John in his stockinged feet, rubbing sleep from his eyes. He is a heartbreaking sight, all skin and bone, gossamer pale hair mussed from the pillow and a tiny white toe peeping out from one of the much-darned worsted socks. 'I heard voices,' he explains.

Rosamund hastens towards him set to gather him up. 'Hush now, young John.'

The boy takes a step backwards seeing the grim in Rosamund's face. His own features appear to collapse inwards on themselves before she sweeps him up in her arms. Tom and me catch his muffled, heartsick wail as Rosamund bundles him back up the stairs.

'Well now, Sammy, I can observe a grown man go a hundred rounds and take his knocks in the squared circle with perfect complacence, but this, this is a precious hard thing to abide.'

'True enough, Tom,' I reply, as Tom fills us both good beakers of brandy from the cask at his counter.

'You will not tarry over that,' orders Tom, indicating my beaker, 'down it quick smart to ease your sleep. Do not think to keep me company tonight. I reckon you will have much else to occupy you tomorrow. The dead are in no hurry and can afford to wait a while on the needs of the living.'

'Thank'ee, Tom,' I say, swallowing a good half of the measure, 'you have been more than obliging to us. More so than two such as me and Facey have a right to expect, even from even a decent, upright gent such as yourself.'

Tom slowly sips his brandy before eyeing me over the black rim of his leather beaker. 'I am gratified that you came to me again, Sammy. Our parting was rancorous but the years have cooled hot blood and I see the matter different these days. It was I forsook young Facey and not t'other way round as I always had set in my mind and my words. I let him go and so failed him on account of my own ill temper and that's the truth. Had I used a modicum more patience on him, who knows how he would have turned out?'

'He is what he is, Tom. I have known him all my life and he will shape himself for no man.'

'Even so, that clay might have been moulded with a gentler hand.'

'I could not say, Tom, but I do not believe he was ever apt for prodding or shaping.'

Tom chuckles and throws back the remnants of his brandy. 'Well, at any rate, happy as I am to be of service to the pair of you, now I am drawn into the young lad's circumstances and will do as much for his part as I am able.'

'I could not ask for more,' I say, raising my beaker, draining it to the dregs.

I take my leave of Tom Canon and slowly climb the stairs with an effort that surprises me. I had no idea I was so fatigued, though, to be sure, it has been a prodigiously long day. Before I make my nest on the floor where Facey sleeps I decide to look in on Rosamund and the lad who occupy Tom's own room at the head of the corridor. I turn the handle and open the door a crack. It is a simple room as befits a man of simple tastes, boasting only a plain nightstand with pitcher and ewer, a solid, but comfortable-looking bed. The bed is empty though coverlet and pillows are awry. Rosamund dozes in the stout wooden armchair at its side. Her eyes flutter open and, catching sight of me at the door, she gives me a weary smile. It takes me a moment to see that beneath a covering of shawl and blanket her arms still enfold Pure John. The lad is fast asleep in her lap.

What with all his insolence, contrariness, bantam pride and readiness to dispute a point, I had never reckoned him so very, very small.

CHAPTER XL

It is long past dawn when my eyes open. Though I made my bed on the floor, wrapped in an old rug, I slept like a babe, notwithstanding the gale of Facey's snoring.

And it is the absence of that very sound, which alerts me to the fact that I am late to rise. To my delight, Facey's bed is empty.

I take up the piss pot for my necessary evacuations and thereafter cross the hall to Tom's dressing room. The water in the ewer is cold but fresh, and, though I have no pressing need for it, I treat myself to a cat's-lick about the pits and nethers. Tom's folding razor is to hand and, finding a good edge on it still, I apply it carefully to my wet chin and cheeks. It is not so often that I have the opportunity to titivate myself in this manner and so I dampen my hair, carefully smoothing it to glossy tresses with Tom's set of brushes. A dab or two of Tom's toilet water about my face and I am sweet as an earl. Finally, I scour the gnashers with my little stick of liquorice root, having no desire to ruin these efforts with a breath on me that reeks like the Fleet ditch.

'And here is old slugabed, looking like the cat what got the cream,' announces the can as I arrive downstairs. 'They is long since up and out, all but One-Eye Jack who is at his breakfast in the parlour,' he says, jerking a thumb over his shoulder in the direction of Tom's private snug. 'There may be scraps remaining if you make haste.'

'It is Mister Facey, you are speaking of,' I reply, refusing to allow this oaf to sour my joy at the prospect of Facey's resurrection.

'There is so many comings and goings under this roof that I cannot keep all in my noggin and must name as I see.'

'And me? What is your moniker for me?'

'I calls you The Mourner, sir, on account of your long-faced dismal countenance and fumeral airs. Speaking of which, there is another dead 'un in the cellar, brung in this very morning. You will take no offence, I hope. In course, you are most likely a most jolly fellow I imagine. 'Tis often the way, I find, when a gent ... '

I cannot bear his prattle a moment longer; I turn on my heel and head for the parlour. Despite my best intentions the fellow has set me aback with this reminder that poor Kak John lies in a cold, dark cellar below.

I fling wide the door to find Facey seated at a small table surrounded by the remnants of his breakfast: cold slices of mutton, fatty pork and some cheese along with the end of a loaf. He looks up from his plate and grins at the sight of me. 'Sammy Boy, it does me good to see you.' He impales a slice of cold lamb on the twin prongs of his fork and waves me over with the instrument. 'Come. Dig in, Sammy. Tom Canon has ever been open-handed in the matter of vittles.'

I pause for a moment taking in the sight of him. He is dressed in his accustomed coat and keks but while formerly they were tight about the thighs and arms, now they bag around him. Though still an imposing sight he is diminished in bulk and white as a turnip. The black cloth binding across his eye gives him a sinister, sordid air. Still and all, it is good to see my friend again.

'Facey. You are sight for sore eyes.'

The words are scarcely out of my mouth before I wish them unsaid. Facey glares at me with his one remaining peeper and

I see that his fiery nature has in no way been extinguished. At length a slow smile steals across his face. He chuckles. 'It is no matter, Sammy. I must learn to be content with one less glim than I was born with. And for suchlike mischance does God, in his wisdom, give us two on 'em. Here, take my hand.'

I shake my partner's hand and sit beside him at his little table. 'It seems you have performed prodigious feats while I have been at my ease.'

'Though not without some cost.'

Facey's grin disappears. 'So I have been told and I am sorry for it. He had the makings of something, that young lad. It is a wicked world we live in, to be sure.' He reaches for a half-broached bottle at his feet. 'Here now, have a little of this good port wine to rattle the blood.'

I take a good swig and reach for a chunk of the cold mutton.

'The lad now rests below. Rising early, I found Tom already up and about and had the tale of it from him. It is a bad business, Sammy.'

I sigh, steeling myself to break the news of my promise to Rosamund. 'It has been a most unlucky commission through and through, though all but at an end.'

Facey gazes at me before taking a swig himself. He wipes his mouth on his coat sleeve. 'And there are others of our acquaintance under this roof,' he says shrewdly.

'You mean to say Rosamund, no doubt. She has risked much for our enterprise and, in truth, I could not have succeeded without her. No, nor for that matter without Kak John.'

'And the pipsqueak?'

'It is his only kin who lies below. I owe him my concern.'

Facey shrugs. 'He would not be the only young stray in the metropolis. But I will not make a quarrel with you on that account.'

'We are under some obligation to Lieutenant Trench also.'

'I can recall sinking a few bottles with that one, who is not such a bad stick. It is my last clear recollection.'

'That day our chickens returned to roost; Pimlott and Chuffington's creatures were set upon us. He it was brought you safe to this roof. You must know that we are in mortal danger on account of that ill-starred Shoreditch hoist.' I take the bottle from him and fortify myself with another swig.

Facey still has that shrewd look on him, gazing at me intently. 'And what of us, Sammy?'

'I believe we are as we ever were.'

'I should say you are a mite closer to that bint now than before I was took insensible.'

'I have promised Rosamund that I will no more go resurrecting.'

'And is that all you have promised though?' Facey sucks at his teeth. He waves his fingers, indicating that I should pass him the bottle; he takes a great swig, finishing it to its dregs. 'Ah, Sammy, do not fret. We are brothers, or close enough to make no odds. Do you think I would choose to stand between you and your sweetheart once your mind is made up?'

I shake my head.

'Then, you shall have your Rosamund if that is what you wish, and with my blessing.'

He slaps his great paw on my lowered head, like some kind of pugilistic pope. I twist myself out from beneath his dubious benediction. 'Facey. I do not require your blessing to do that which we have always agreed. We will buy an inn with the tin from this commission and will be partners in the enterprise as was always planned.'

'A man may only have one true partner, Sammy,' he says, mournfully.

'By no means. A man may have a partner in his affairs as well as a companion of the heart,' I reply. 'Besides, you presume too much. I have not asked Rosamund for aught so far.'

'But you will,' insists Facey.

'I will,' I admit, knowing now how I wish my life to unravel from this moment onwards.

'And where is this inn of ours to be found, Sammy? I take it you do not wish to try for Edinburgh now?'

'I do not. That great stinking sinkhole full of red-faced, bewhiskered brutes, mistaking the bellowing of sheep for proper converse.'

Facey wheezes with mirth. 'Aye, well, that tallies my own feeling on the subject right enough. So, what do you propose?'

'I have given the matter little contemplation, having plenty enough to occupy my attention these past days, but I should say perhaps Portsmouth, given our knowledge of the place. At dusk we might set out for the Angel where the Post departs a little after seven.'

Facey finishes the bottle. 'The notion of a life with you, your bint in one ear and John Pounds' dismal sermonology in t'other does not 'zactly fill me with glee. But I do suppose there are worse outcomes for a one-eyed fellow without useful occupation.'

'Then we are agreed,' I say, jubilant that my partner has so easily fallen into the comfortable life I have somewhat imagined for myself.

'It may be the best of a bad job, for the while,' says Facey, giving me his hand.

We shake mightily.

'What day is this? I am still all at sixes and sevens,' he asks.

'Why Tuesday,' I reply.

'Ah, then it is the day of the Rig,' he says with a great sigh.

'Facey, do you recall aught that has occurred this week past?'

'Some, though much of it is mazed.'

'Then, you will know that we cannot show our mugs out of doors without a deal of caution.'

'I know it, but if we are to slink away with our tails between our legs I should like to know how our final stroke might have fared in Bloomsbury.'

'We do not need it. Brookes is to give us one hundred and twenty sovs. That is how your final stroke fares. You need concern yourself with naught else.'

'There is curiosity, Sammy Boy.'

'Which did for the cat.'

'I am not so easily snuffed.'

'I cannot debate this with you now. What is the hour, do you reckon?'

'I should say somewhat before ten.'

'Then I must go. Facey, you must promise me on your word, that you will not quit this roof.'

At that he smiles, but there is only sadness in it.

CHAPTER XLI

The church clock has already struck a quarter after ten as Crick ushers me up the main stairs and into Brookes' formal receiving rooms.

I have not come to this part of the house before and these quarters, though spacious, are somewhat austere compared to the rooms housing his collections. There is a simple varnished screen against the far wall, a solid oak secretary and chair by the window. In the far corner stands a square, upright clock made of some light brown wood, its dial numbered in the manner of the Romans. Twin alcoves frame the fireplace, above which is a portrait of a bewigged, hard-faced gent. A few urns occupy the alcoves but there is little else by way of decoration or frippery. It is undoubtedly a room for business.

Brookes, Rosamund and Bamfield already occupy a group of wing chairs set before the hearth. Breaking off their conversation, Brookes and Bamfield rise as I am ushered before them.

'Forgive me for my tardy arrival,' I say.

'Never fret, Mr Samuel,' replies Brookes smiling. 'I should like first to name my man of business Mr Bamfield here. Bamfield, here is Mr Samuel Samuel.'

Bamfield eyes me grimly from under wild, grey bushy brows, like an indignant badger dragged out from its burrow. The intensity of his glare puts me in mind of Facey, though he is otherwise quite portly and of rubicund complexion. The man is already perspiring somewhat albeit the room is mild and the fire unlit. 'Honoured, sir, honoured,' he insists, though it clear that the converse is true. He offers me the very briefest inclination of his head before resuming his seat.

Brookes indicates an empty chair; I catch Rosamund's admonishing glance as I settle myself.

'Now then, Mr Samuel, we have somewhat broached Miss Howlett's stratagem but let us conclude our commission before returning to the other,' announces Brookes with a nod to his man. Bamfield reaches across to the low boy at his side for a capacious leather satchel. He rummages within, producing twin, heavy leather bags, which he hands to me.

'One hundred and twenty gold sovereigns. It is a very great deal of money, sir,' he states, as though chiding me for some imagined prodigality. 'Yesterday, it was but a hundred when you failed to collect. Today it is twenty more. Better than any three-per-cent consol, I daresay. I may press you for your secret to acquiring wealth, sir.'

I make no reply, having none to make, and simply take the bags. Though the temptation to rip them open and revel in my new wealth is strong, I thrust them deep into the capacious inner pockets of my coat.

'You are wise to keep mum. And so you will not count it, Mr Samuel?' inquires Bamfield.

'There is no need, sir.'

Bamfield sets his head at a slantendicular angle and eyes me curiously. 'Put it this way, sir: there is always a need to enumerate when it comes to the matter of money. That is the entire point.'

'Enough,' intercedes Brookes, 'I take it very kind that Mr Samuel reposes such trust in us, nevertheless, the other matter is pressing. And so, Mr Bamfield, what do you say?'

Bamfield settles back in his wing chair, cogitating, steepling his fingers beneath his lips. 'Put it this way, sir: it is to my mind a fool's errand, from which you will derive no pecuniary advantage. Indeed, quite the converse.'

'But can it be done, that is the question?'

'Why, certainly it can be done. It may be done by any man should he wish it so. The question is: should it be done, sir? Should it be done?'

'And if I say it should?'

'Then as your man of business, I would do it. I can do no other, though it does present somewhat of an ethical dilemma.'

'How so?'

'Why, sir. The pecuniary advantage of such a transaction would be mine and so, in fine, I would not be acting in your best interests, nor with my accustomed impartiality.'

'Then what this young lady has said is true, this Liston is deeply indebted?'

Bamfield considers the question, tapping his steepled fingers against one another for a good while. 'Well, sir, as you have had it from another party and not from my own lips, I believe I do not transgress the boundaries of confidentiality when I so affirm. Put it this way: that individual's pockets are very much to let, sir.'

'That is not precisely what I have asked. There is a considerable obligation outstanding, I believe?'

'Ah, as to that, I may not say. You will understand, sir, that discretion is, not to put too fine a point on it, my stock in trade.'

Brookes turns in exasperation to Rosamund. 'Miss Howlett, pray continue.'

'I fear that yesterday you were somewhat intemperate, Mr Bamfield. Mr Samuel and myself were waiting in the room outside and able to overhear much of the exchange. A significant obligation exists and you possess notes of hand and other such paper from Mr Liston affirming such.'

Bamfield nods. 'I do not deny it, though I cannot approve the manner of its revelation.'

'Come now, Bamfield. Do not play the coy maid, it does not suit you. What is the extent of Liston's obligation to you?'

'I should not wish to say, sir.'

'Much of the debt has come due, though. You do not deny this, for Miss Howlett has heard as much?'

'Again, I do not deny it. It is a significant sum and I must go to the law to press for its return.'

'Then I wish your grandchildren joy of it, for Miss Howlett has given me to understand that a good deal of the paper is falsely backed and will be disputed. You will never see the conclusion of such a suit in your lifetime.'

Bamfield's rigid, indignant posture sags; he slumps back in his chair. 'You have it exactly, sir. Old man Liston's signature was counterfeit, and so he does not stand guarantor as I imagined. It is a very great sum and I am a proper fool for having been so taken in.'

'Then you must surely consider my proposal, Bamfield.'

Bamfield raises his head a little way, his badger eyes squinting. 'I will, sir, though I cannot fathom its motive.'

'Then we may proceed. I will not press at your integrity in regard to the detail, but you will acknowledge the substance of the matter as I lay it out.'

Bamfield nods.

'The debt is large, this we understand, but how much of it may be ... '

'Sixteen thousand, three hundred, seven pounds and twelve pence, is the exact and total sum. There, I have said it,' announces Bamfield. 'I had no desire for the world and his wife to know that I have been so rooked. A proper flat I must appear to you, sir.'

There is a silence in the room, punctuated only by the ticking of the brass pendulum from the corner clock.

'Good God, man,' says Brookes, both amazed and appalled at the same time. 'That is a small fortune.'

'Put it this way, sir: he baited me like a haddock, and it was neatly done. At first it was only trifling sums paid against notes of hand. Once he had me on the line, his demands became ever greater. He inveigled me to part with larger amounts by means of promissory notes indorsed by his father, redeemable in three years at a handsome twenty-five per-cent.'

'And according to this young lady,' says Brookes, with a nod of acknowledgement to Rosamund, 'those indorsements are, in effect, counterfeit.'

'It would seem so, sir. That ... that ... blackguard is long cut off from his father's grace. The promissory paper is all but worthless,' says Bamfield in a very great passion.

'And the notes of hand for the smaller sums, what of them?'

'Those, at least, are redeemable.'

'They are signed by the principal alone, not backed by a disputed guarantor?'

'They are, sir. Signed by Liston in the presence of my clerk and witnessed.'

'And does Liston propose to repay those smaller sums?'

'I do not believe he can, sir. He is without means until he finds another like me to bleed dry.'

'And what is their value?'

'There are eight of them, sir. Seven at five hundred pound, the last at eight hundred and seventy pound, all long past due.'

Brookes pauses a moment to tally the figures in his noggin. 'Somewhat over four thousand pound.'

'Four thousand, three hundred and seventy pound to an exactitude, sir. Should you wish to see them? I had thought to offer them at Garroway's, discounted, for whatever I might get for them.'

'Certainly, Bamfield, certainly.'

'I cannot recommend them, sir, though it does me a disservice to say so. I fear that Liston will not stir himself to redeem them, even had he the means. You would still be obliged to go to the law.'

'And that is precisely what I intend,' says Brookes. 'But your scrupulousness does you credit even now.'

'Mr Brookes does not wish them redeemed,' says Rosamund, 'he desires them in order to place the principal under a legal obligation.'

Bamfield's expression changes, his creased and anxious face softens into the semblance of a smile. 'Then you may have the paper, and with my blessing,' he rummages once again in his satchel before producing a slim packet neatly wrapped in paper, handing it to Brookes. 'I should let you have them gratis, was I able.'

'There is no need,' says Brookes unwrapping the packet and carefully examining the notes. 'And so, what are your terms, Bamfield, for all of these?'

'Well, sir, I laid out four thousand pound cash money for them; three hundred and seventy being the premium on top, that is to say, my profit on the transaction. Though in all honesty, I would get but half that figure at Garroway's, and that if I should find a buyer at all.'

'Then I will give three thousand for 'em. What do you say to that?'

Bamfield nods acknowledging Brookes' generosity. 'I should say, Mr Brookes, as your man of business, that it is a most reckless investment and I should not advise it. As the antipodean party to this transaction, I should say you are most gentlemanly, sir.'

'So, we are agreed are we then? I cannot tell, Bamfield, for all your obfuscation.'

'By all means,' says Bamfield, 'I shall sign these notes of hand over to you this instant and be glad of it.'

'Come then,' says Brookes, rising. 'I shall prepare an instruction for the withdrawal of the three thousand from my account.' He turns to address Rosamund. 'And you, miss, will be good enough to append your name to the notes of hand as witness?'

'I should like nothing better, sir.'

We cross the room, gathering around Brookes' secretary where he takes up a finely wrought silver penner, dipping it into the matching inkpot, before handing it to Bamfield. One by one, Liston's notes are duly signed over and witnessed; the signatures carefully sprinkled with a little pounce to prevent their smudging. Finally, Brookes pens a receipt for his man of business and gathers up the notes.

'Use them well, sir,' says Bamfield offering his hand.

'I shall, Bamfield. I intend to send for my attorney the instant we are finished, and, though I must employ the law, I shall not hide behind it. I shall set a meeting with Liston this very day, since I desire the fellow first to know who is prime mover in his downfall and for what reason. God willing, I hope we may see this villain in the King's Bench before the month is out.' Brookes turns to Rosamund brandishing the notes. 'So, young lady, though it will not bring back your friend, here is a modicum of retribution at least.'

CHAPTER XLII

I cannot pretend to comprehend all your promises of this and notes of that but it appears that you have given Brookes some powerful legalistic hold over Liston,' I remark, as Rosamund and me head back down Great Marlborough Street together.

Rosamund smiles, taking my arm in hers. 'The law, whilst it will not stir itself overmuch for cold-blooded murder, will never suffer a debt to remain unpaid. Mr Brookes now owns a portion of the smaller debts incurred by Liston. They are past due and may be strictly enforced through the workings of the courts. If Liston cannot or will not pay, he will be consigned to a debtor's prison, the Fleet, King's Bench, or some such. It is justice of a sort, I believe.'

I nod, conscious of the weight of gold tugging at my coat. My commission is at an end and we have done all we can to square our accounts with Liston. I believe that Rosamund, like me, desires to know how matters stand betwixt us.

We are both silent a while.

'I was thinking …' I say, at the exact moment Rosamund speaks. 'What do you … ?'

There is a spell of confusion as we disentangle arms, halting in the street only some ten yards from the doors of the Coach and Horses.

'What is on your mind, Sammy?'

'This morning you were gone with the lad and Tom, I am curious to know what you were about.' It is not what I had meant to say, but my courage has deserted me.

Rosamund seems relieved at such a practical question. 'We set out to find a proper resting place for poor John in the churchyards hereabouts,' she replies. 'Though none of the churchmen will take him since he is not of their parish.'

'I could pay handsomely for a funeral, cash money,' I say, rattling my heavy coat, 'no doubt that would change their outlook.'

'It might at that,' acknowledges Rosamund, 'but I cannot see why any Christian soul should be denied a Christian burial in a churchyard by a man of God. It should not require the greasing of a palm to make it so.'

'It is the way of the world, and perhaps of the world to come, Rosamund.'

'In any case, it may be too late. One of those saintly gentlemen we encountered intends to inform the Parish Office of John's presence in the tavern cellars. The Parish Men will come for him, Sammy, to bury him in common grave, and that I cannot bear on top of all. Not after the same was done to my pa.'

I clasp her hand, patting it gently. 'I will not let it come to that, I swear it,' I say.

She gazes up at me. 'And what will you do?'

'I do not know, but I will not let it come to that. Come now, we should get ourselves inside since it is still hazardous for me to be seen abroad.'

'Forgive me, Sammy, I had forgot,' she says, taking my arm as we set off once more.

We enter the Coach and Horses and wend our way through the now busy Public, heading towards Tom's private snug.

Rosamund pushes open the door to find Tom and Pure John at their vittles.

Pure John has a tumbler of brandy in one hand, a cigar in the other. He inclines his head to us, unsteadily. The ruin of a cold pie sits on the table before them. Tom gives us a wink over the rim of his own tumbler. 'This fine young man has been expounding most edifyingly on the virtues of the London messenger service and how it might be improved, particularly with regard to the exclusion of one Thomas Lane, a disreputable young rogue by all accounts.'

Pure John nods in approbation, head slowly sinking to his chest, hands dropping to his sides, spilling brandy and tobacco. Tom rises, whispering, 'A sleep will do him a power of good and so I will carry him to his bed. You are welcome to the vittles here and the remainder of the bottle.' He scoops up the lad and whisks him out of the room, leaving Rosamund and me to our own company.

We seat ourselves while I pour out the remnants of the bottle. Rosamund takes up the tumbler and sips a little. 'Will I cut you a slice of this pie? I shall turn away while you eat,' I say, digging in with the knife.

'I will take a little as we set out so early and missed our breakfast,' replies Rosamund. 'And I should not ask that of you, since you do not appear to find my broken mouth so repugnant.'

'I do not find any aspect of your appearance so,' I say. 'Quite the contrary in point of fact.' I am amazed at my own audacity, having no clue from where these bold, insinuating words arise. Perhaps it is the brandy. I pass across a slice of pie to hide my discomfort.

'You are kind to say so,' she replies, crumbling a little of the pastry in her fingers before popping a morsel into her mouth. 'And what of you now, Sammy?'

'I had considered Portsmouth. There is sufficient shine for a good tavern on Pembroke Street, and I would dearly wish to see John Pounds' school again.'

'And your Mr Facey, what of him?'

'He is a great deal improved. I sat with him this morning in this very chair while he ate a hearty breakfast.'

'That is not precisely what I meant.'

'Though as hale as can be expected, he is out of sorts with the world. He is ... bleak. I fear he believes himself only half the man he was, having now but a single glim. And there is something more.'

Rosamund takes a small sip from her tumbler. 'What more?'

'He is loath to find himself third wheel on a cart.'

'Meaning?'

'I had ... I had thought ... it is my wish ... in short, I ... ' My temporary courage deserts me.

'Sammy,' sighs Rosamund. 'I am no great beauty, I well know it, and so I have never learned the arts of the coquette. Nor am I practised in casting my line for empty compliments. Perhaps you would be so good as to be plain with me.'

Coquette is a new and baffling word for me but, from her manner, I do not think it wise to ask for explication. 'Have you ever been to Portsmouth, Rosamund?'

'I have not, though I hear it is a busy, bustling sort of place, with some charm and the clean air off the sea to breathe.'

'Then should you desire to visit?'

'I should, though it is a good way off and a short visit would scarce be worth the candle.'

'Oh,' I say, crestfallen.

'Perhaps I might travel in this cart you mention?'

I gaze at her a moment. She grins, unmindful of her chipped tooth. 'You are making fun with me now.'

'I am, Sammy, since you will not say what you mean.'

'There is no cart, it is merely a manner of speaking; Mr Facey believes that you and me have become somewhat close.'

'That is true, I hope.'

The brandy has imparted a warm glow and I know it to be one of those moments when to say naught is to hazard all. I reach for the bottle. 'Should you take a little more?' I inquire.

'I am not so accustomed to spirituous liquor, but would not resent another drop to mark the success of your commission.'

I rise, moving to her side. She holds up her tumbler and, as I stoop to her with the bottle, I see it tremble in my grasp. She places her other hand upon mine to steady it. Her touch is warm and dry and our faces but a few inches apart. I can feel her breath on my cheek. Amazed at my own audacity, my head moves of its own volition towards her. Her eyes close, and slowly, ever so slowly, my lips press upon hers.

Her breath is sweet with the aroma of the brandy, my free hand strokes her cheek, and, though scarified, her skin is soft as damask. After what seems an age she pulls away, her eyes opening wide. She holds up her tumbler. 'Well, Mr Samuel, I do believe I shall take that drop now.'

I pour a little of the brandy as I am bid, my hand, if anything, trembling even more. 'Forgive me, Rosamund. I am fuddled with the liquor and do not know what I am about.'

Rosamund smiles before taking a little sip. 'There is naught to forgive, Sammy.'

'I have trespassed on our friendship,' I say, filling my own tumbler. 'And I would not have offended you for worlds.'

'I was not offended, nor even discomfited,' replies Rosamund with a little secret smile. 'On the contrary.'

I drink deeply from my tumbler, the brandy now harsh in my gullet. 'Then I believe I may now speak plain to you.'

'I wish you would, Sammy.'

'I should very much like you to accompany me to Portsmouth.'

'You have already said as much. And I should very much like to visit one of these days.'

'What I have in mind is longer than a mere visit.'

'Is it now? You give me no especial reason for such a journey and so I do believe you have placed your cart before your horse.'

I gaze up at the ceiling for inspiration, noting how the moulded patterns around the edges are studded with plaster roses. It seems somehow a favourable sign to my mind. 'You are right to say so. What I had meant to say, what I feel I must ask of you … what it is … I have always had a great respect for you, not to say … and that being so … might I … Rosamund … in short, I should take it very kind were you to be wife to me.' I lower my gaze, scarcely daring to breathe as I await her response.

To my surprise, she laughs, not troubling to cover her mouth at all. She rises, holding out both her hands to mine. 'Sammy, you are no silver-tongued lothario, to be sure,' she gathers my outstretched hands in hers, 'but I believe I should like that above all things.' For an instant I find myself grinning like a Bedlamite. 'I must tell you though, there is a matter,' she continues, serious as a bailiff now, 'that may give you pause to reconsider.'

'Those words were hard enough got out, I cannot imagine aught that would make me wish to take them back.'

'I have made an undertaking which precludes my leaving London.'

I stare, wordlessly. Her hands slip through my fingers. 'But … '

'I am not prodigal with my affections, Sammy. Rest assured, there is no other.'

'Then what is it?'

'It is young John. He is a mere infant and without kin. I promised I would not leave him. Nor should I wish to, promise or no.' She lowers her head.

I reach out my hand and slowly raise her chin so that we are once again eye-to-eye. 'And I should certainly think the worse of you were it to be otherwise.'

'I am sorry, Sammy. I know you cannot stay.'

'I cannot. Facey and me must Post the Sailor's Highway this very night. But do you imagine the boy might care for Portsmouth at all?'

Rosamund's eyes widen, she smiles up at me. 'I think he would like it very well.'

'And so, this final impediment being removed, will you now tell me that you consent to come?'

'I will, Sammy,' she cries, embracing me.

CHAPTER XLIII

We break apart abruptly as the door is flung wide by the can. He stands a moment, winking and leering at the sight of us. 'Well, ain't you the dark horse and no mistake. I needs to give the snug a once over seeing as how my master has with him a wery important personage by name of Sir Josiah Box. For the moment, he asks that both of you remain present here.'

Rosamund and me back away from the little table as Ned sets about his duties. He carries off the remnants of the pie, placing it on the dresser by the wall before producing a little horse-hair brush from his apron, employing it to flick away pie crumbs from the table cloth. Likewise, he removes the platters and tumblers, replacing them with a set of fine green glass goblets and a decanter of what appears to be Madeira wine.

No sooner has he completed the room's transformation than Tom appears, ushering in Brookes. 'Miss Howlett, Mr Samuel, Mr Brookes has honoured my house with his presence, desiring first a moment with us all.'

Brookes removes his beaver and topcoat as he enters, handing them to the can. He settles himself at the table, while Tom fusses with the decanter, pouring glasses for all. I note that one additional goblet remains empty.

'Thank you kindly, Mr Canon,' says Brookes, raising his glass to Rosamund and me. 'I have not been idle this past hour or so: even now a writ is being drawn up against Liston by my attorney and I have sent a summons to that gentleman. Having no wish to beard the rogue in his den, nor desiring to invite such a creature across my own threshold, Mr Canon has allowed me the use of these rooms for the purpose. I gave no clue as to my reason, only requesting that we meet, at the half hour past midday.'

'You believe he will attend you, sir?' I inquire.

'I dearly hope so, Mr Samuel.' Brookes produces a hunter from his vest pocket and thumbs it open. 'Since you are already present you may wish to remain, but I understand if you do not.'

'I will stay,' announces Rosamund firmly.

'As will I,' I say.

Brookes dips his head in acknowledgement.

As Tom turns to leave I tap him lightly on the shoulder. Keeping my voice low, I say, 'Tom, I have my bounty at last. It is monstrous heavy on the pockets; heavier indeed on my nerves, being such a deal of tin. I ask that you give it to Facey since I can think of no safer place for it.'

'I wish you joy of it, Sammy. He is resting upstairs; I shall be sure and take it to him shortly.'

I hand over the heavy bags to Tom. 'I shall leave you all to your business then,' he announces with a bow. 'You must call for me should you require anything further.' He gives me a meaningful wink before closing the door.

We each of us take our seats around the little table. Brookes sips at his wine with a nod of approval. 'Very fine; a Malmsey Madeira, I believe. I had not expected a wine of such quality here.'

'I understand Mr Canon keeps a reserve for his more esteemed guests,' I remark, raising my own glass, for all the world like some well-heeled buck at Almack's. And, it occurs to me that, though I am no swell, I may now be described as a man of certain means, and an affianced one at that.

Brookes inspects his hunter once more, frowning. 'He is late, if indeed he comes at all.'

As though to give him the lie, the door is flung open by the can, who announces, 'Here is Mr Henry Listers come at your pleasure, your honour.'

Liston barges past the can, cane in hand, stopping short in the doorway at the sight of us, a puzzled frown upon his face. Brookes calmly rises, offering only the slightest inclination of his head.

Liston ignores the courtesy, offering none in exchange, nor even troubling to remove his glossy beaver hat. 'What's this?' he says. 'I had received a summons from what I took to be a gentleman, but find here instead a fine parcel of rogues.'

'It seems I have the advantage of you, Liston. I am Mr Joshua Brookes.'

'Brookes, I have heard something of you.'

'And I you.'

'Though I had not heard that you had sunk so low in society, sir,' says Liston, indicating Rosamund and me with his silver-topped cane.

Brookes settles back in his chair shifting it alongside Rosamund and me, as though drawing up a line of battle. 'A man may very well be judged by the company he keeps, sir. I have found these to be honest, good-hearted individuals and so am well content with what they may reflect upon me.'

'You may choose your company as you wish, it is none of my concern. I will not stay to bandy words with you.' He eyes the empty goblet on our little table with a sneer. 'Aye, nor stoop to drink with your creatures.'

'Then I shall offer naught, but you will stay, sir, and hear me out. It is a matter of some consequence to you.'

'Yesterday, these scoundrels gained entrance to my home, where they made free with insults and vile calumnies, I'm damned if I'll give them another hearing.'

'You are damned for what I know you to have done, sir.'

'You know nothing of me, for if you did you will apprehend I will not suffer to be disparaged and libelled by some scrofulous doxy and her dray-faced pimp.'

Rosamund bites her lip, glaring at the man, her gaze darts to the heavy decanter; I believe she has it in mind to hurl it at Liston's head and so I reach beneath the table for her hand, holding it steady.

'Then you will let me speak, sir,' snaps Brookes.

'I will not, sir.' Liston turns on his heel, reaching for the brass doorknob. 'I wish you good day.'

'I am shortly to lay a writ upon you for the sum of four thousand pounds. I wish to know how you intend to pay.'

Liston releases the doorknob and turns to face us, amused now. 'I see it. You have set these wretches upon me with their libels and now intend to cozen me. Blackmail is it, sir?'

'It is not.'

Liston leans against the doorframe, a slight smile on his face. 'Then what, sir? What is your game here?'

'No game, Liston. A more serious matter cannot be imagined. Those notes of hand, which were formerly Bamfield's property, are now mine. I well know you have not the means to make good and so I will see you broken and in the King's Bench by the month's end. God willing, there you will rot and we shall see you no more.'

'Great heavens, Brookes,' chuckles Liston, fingering his cane. 'What on earth can I have done to earn such disapprobation from a man I never before met?'

'We have not met, and yet our paths have crossed.'

'How so?'

'Robert Templeton was the only son of a good friend and somewhat dear to me.'

'That name means nothing to me. Another of your verminous followers perhaps?'

'A young lad, taken up by you and your disreputable crowd some two years past. You will not deny it, since he was seen in your company at the tables and suchlike often enough.'

Liston cocks an eyebrow. 'Ah, yes. Young Bobby Templeton, I do recall him now. A fine-looking lad. And so, what of him?'

'You led him to his destruction, Liston.'

'He was never a one to be led, but rather embraced on his own account the many pleasures of the metropolis with open arms.'

'Debauchery, vice and dissipation you mean.'

'Cards, wine and a little fast living is all. The young man ran through his money at a precious good clip, and, when there was naught else forthcoming, we dropped him. Scarcely a hangin' offence, I should hazard,' says Liston, smirking.

'You did more than fleece that young man, I know it.'

Liston tilts his head, peering down his finely chiselled nose at Brookes. 'You know naught of the matter, sir.'

'I know the marks of a hound well enough. I know that the boy was brought to me near to death, with the flesh torn from his body.'

'A one time acquaintance I will not deny, but you should know that the young man was, in truth, a wretch; a mewling, pouting popinjay. In short, a tiresome bore and light-fingered to boot. He stole from me, sir. Three guineas he had from my purse.'

'When you had tired of him, after you had fleeced him of all, he tried to take back some of what had been his. And so you set your hound at him.'

'I closed my doors to him is all. What befell him after has naught to do with me.'

'I have it that the young man came to you again, a week or so past.'

Liston appears to examine the silver head of his cane as he rotates it slowly between his gloved fingers. It is a finely wrought head of a wolf. 'Then you have been misinformed, Brookes. I never saw him again.'

'He was followed and observed entering your home.'

'As I say, you have been misinformed.'

Brookes shakes his head, sadly. 'He is dead as you well know, murdered by strangulation, and that is why I will do all in my power to see you brought down.'

Liston peers up from the wolf's head, a curiously malevolent expression upon his face. He grasps the cane with both hands, gazing intently now at Brookes. 'Really, he was the most aggravating creature, Brookes. But do you know, he had the slenderest neck? Had I been the perpetrator, as you so insinuate, I might have enjoyed placing both hands about his throttle, thus.' Liston tightens his two handed grip around the cane. 'But he was always precious fond of silk and so, more likely, the thing would have been carried off with a scarf or some such, perhaps wrapped twice or thrice around that fine throat. I imagine the boy's soft white hands frantically scrabbling, his merciless adversary hauling ever tighter until that light in those fearful, fluttering eyes was quite extinguished.' Liston's head drops, almost coyly. 'Of course, that is only supposition, you understand.'

Brookes glares at him, white-faced. Beneath the table I feel Rosamund's hand quivering in mine. 'You are a monster,' she says.

Liston raises his head, his upper lip curled in derision. 'And the other: the crossing sweeper. Should you wish to hear how I fancy his last moments were spent?'

'Get out, this instant,' roars Brookes, rising. 'You are beyond despicable. I wish I had the means to see you hang, but of a certain I will see you rot.'

Liston smirks, fixes his glossy beaver more firmly to his head, offering us a brief ironical bow. 'It is true that my father and I are not on the easiest of terms but do you imagine that he would see his own son in a debtor's prison? He does not care for me above half, nor never did, but he cares for a scandal less. Do your worst, sir. I daresay you shall have your few thousand before I am much inconvenienced.' With that, he turns on his heel, flings wide the door and strides away through the busy public.

We gaze mutely at one another for a moment or so until finally Brookes breaks the silence. 'I confess, I am quite set aback. I had never imagined that: a man so depraved and brazen he all but admitted to the deed to my face.'

'It gave him pleasure, sir,' says Rosamund, 'both the act and its retelling, just as it pleased him to deprive our friend John of life. He believes himself to be untouchable and I do not imagine he will stop at these offences, if indeed, they are the first of their kind.'

Brookes sags as though all the air has been pressed from his body, his hands tremble as he reaches for his glass. 'I scarcely thought to find contrition, but it is no easy thing to hear the barefaced substance from his own lips. I see now that it will be no easy matter to bring him down, no, nor even touch him. I cannot say if I should have the heart for the struggle.'

'You may touch him right enough, sir,' I insist. 'Liston is well-practised at the tables, skilled in the art of high stakes play, his complacency is likely bluff and bluster.'

There is a polite cough. Tom stands at the open door with a grim expression on his dial. 'Forgive me, Mr Brookes, Miss Howlett. I must beg a word with Mr Samuel.'

I approach Tom, who inclines his head to my ear. In a low voice he says, 'Sammy, I could not earlier intrude, but Facey is gone. Ned, my can, informs me that he slipped out an hour or more ago, though the mutton-head saw no reason to remark it.'

'Gods, Tom.'

'It may be he has only stepped out for a breath of air.'

'He heads north, to Russell Square, I know it. The one place in London where Pimlott and Chuffington are sure to be found today.'

'Why ever would he do such a foolhardy thing?'

I sigh. 'To show that he is still a man to be reckoned with.'

CHAPTER XLIV

Certainly, it would have been easier to lay low until dusk, awaiting the cover of darkness so that I might scuttle away to the Strand, there to take the Night Post for Portsmouth. In a day or two I would have sent for Rosamund and the lad. But the quiet, contented life I had imagined for us would have been forever tainted. I should have come to despise myself and, like Nero's dead dog in the ditch, that obstruction would have festered and become a vile Moloch corrupting and, ultimately, extinguishing us all.

Instead, I clamber down from a Hackney at the corner of Southampton Row on Russell Square. I tender the cabby two shillings from the few that were thrust at me by Tom. He offers no change, nor do I have time or inclination for a dispute, so I let him on his way.

I hold out little hope that I have beaten Facey to Bloomsbury. Though he is in a weakened condition, I do not think it can have taken him above twenty minutes to get here on foot. Nevertheless, I loiter for a while, strolling back and forth along the Square to glance down Montagu Street and Bedford Place in the hope of sighting his distinctive figure and great clumping gait.

At length, I turn back to number Fifty-Two, the great mansion at the corner. A liveried servant stands at the open doorway. Unlike those brutes of Glendale House, he is a more proper example of his kind: sharply togged, clean shaved, with an open, honest face, though with the nose of a toper. He winks as I approach. 'Well, my old cock, if you have come for crockery, you may be sore disappointed.'

'How so?'

'The affair within has been most shockingly disrupted with a deal of damage and consternation caused. Not half a hour since, some crackbrain found his way inside; instantly began to make the most excessive of bids, hooting and uttering oaths and imprecations, throwing the auction into confusion. It took no fewer than four on us to restrain the lunatic and a quantity of the better porcelain was smashed to particles in the process. Still and all, good order is now restored and there is copper pots and pans, fine silverware and a good few sticks of fine furniture still to be had by the discerning.'

'It is a Rig,' I say.

'Begging your pardon, sir?' he replies, all innocence.

'I am no pigeon and so you may set aside the gammon. It is a lay to which I am party.'

'Now, cocky, you might of said so at the outset, 'stead of wasting my patter. I am not privy to the ins and outs of this caper, being paid only by the hour to make a respectable appearance on account of my decent bearing and sturdy calves.'

'A most respectable bearing indeed and I would not have twigged it. But tell me, what is become of this crackbrain?'

The man licks his lips and darts his gaze to the cellars beneath us. 'The two principals have him stowed safe below. I duresn't like to say what may become of him.'

'It is the two principals I must see. I take it they are within?'

'They are, cocky, having made a counting room of one of the empty chambers on the first floor.'

The cove steps aside and I make my way into the great entrance hall. If anything, it is even more imposing than Brookes' residence. A vast, glittering chandelier hangs from the ceiling; the gleaming floor is tiled in a complicated interlocking pattern of dark red and blue tablets, the walls adorned with dark-wood panelling and, looming upwards, is a great carved staircase. There are trestles installed about the place, adorned with white linen, boasting what appears to be precious silverware and jewellery, but which I know to be only plate or pinchbeck. The hall gives off to a series of high-ceilinged rooms crammed with wooden furniture and sundry household items for sale. Despite the earlier commotion, the place is packed with folk of all classes and description: from West End matrons to the lowliest of skivvies out on the spree. I hear the hoarse cries of the auctioneer in full spate from one of the far rooms as I push my way through the throng towards the roped-off stairs. Of a sudden I feel the weight of a heavy hand upon my shoulder. I turn, fearing the worst, to find Teeth, in his customary black coat, beaming down upon me with his great gnashers.

'So, it is not my eyes that make tricks with me. I was hearing you was dead and buried, Mr Samuel, and thinking to hoist your corpse, but ... well ... the grave was empty. A little premature, I believe.'

'Out of my way, Teeth. I have no wish to speak with you.'

'Ach, no hard feelings. You are a fine adversary, Mr Samuel. The prize was rightly yours; I make no grudges with you.'

'That night a young man lost his life on account of your dealings and you think it all a game?'

'The man Liston paid us something for our troubles but I did not much care for him. After you had made off with the body, there was no reason for us to remain. True, a young man was taken into the house but, forgive me, that was none of our concern.'

'They killed him, Teeth.'

'Then I am sorry for it. We knew nothing of that.'

'You swear it?'

'We are hard men, Mr Samuel, but we are not savages.'

'Well then, I will shake your hand, for I am no longer at the business.'

'Efreut, Mr Samuel.' As I take his great white paw he draws me closer and bends his head to speak softly in my ear. 'They have taken your Mr Facey, you know.'

'I know it,' I reply, 'I hope I may bargain for his life.'

'Do not look around,' he hisses, 'but it seems you have already been observed. Meathook, Bishop and others approach. What should you wish me do?'

'Delay them a moment. I cannot let them take me 'til I have spoke with their masters.'

'Very well, Mr Samuel,' says Teeth, stepping behind me. 'Viel Glück.'

I dash towards the staircase, conscious of the sounds of a small commotion behind me, taking the stairs two at a time. Near the summit, a gaggle of ponderous ladies obstruct my way and I briefly lose my footing. I collect myself, taking a moment to glance behind. A ruckus has commenced in the hall below, all heaving, shoving and oaths flying. True to his word, that great white-faced apparition stands sentinel at the foot of the stairs, long, powerful arms holding Pimlott and Chuffington's murderous brutes at bay.

I barge the ladies from my path, oblivious to their disapproving tuts and twitters, and, trusting to fortune, make for the less congested left hand corridor. I jink and twist past parties of gawpers and bargain hunters, ignoring the stately chambers filled with cheapjack furnishings. At the end of this passageway is a door, which declares itself off-limits to the hoi polloi by virtue of a braided silk rope suspended betwixt twin brass uprights. I head for it at a run, praying it is the counting room.

I step over the rope, fling open the door and enter. It is only a modest room, but it seems a haven of noiseless industry, quite removed from the hubbub without. The floor is bare board and there is but a single window overlooking Bedford Place. Over by the wall stands a counting desk and high stool, where perches a spindly clerk, tallying piles of coin. Occupying most of the space in the centre is a library table with a green leather surface. And it is here that I find Pimlott and Chuffington, for all the world like monstrous spiders, at the heart of their great metropolitan web.

CHAPTER XLV

The pair are identically attired in their customary garb of black coats, breeches and Geneva collars; they peer up at me from their ledgers at the same moment. Pimlott blinks owlishly, a look of consternation on his dial, as though I am some riddle he can find no answer to.

I close the door and remove my hat, standing upright and respectful at the table's edge, like a felon before the bench.

Chuffington carefully sets down his penner and takes off his spectacles, proceeding to polish them with a clean white fogle. 'Why, bless my soul, Mr P. We have an unexpected guest.'

'No ordinary guest, Mr C., but Lazarus risen,' quips his companion with a complacent smirk.

'Or are you a spectral being, Mr Samuel, a phantom come to reprove us? Should we be much afeared?'

'I breathe yet, Mr Chuffington. No thanks to your underlings.'

'A man of flesh and blood then, still bound by the trials and tribulations of this mortal coil. It would seem that our resurrectionist has resurrected himself,' remarks Chuffington with a snort.

Pimlott grunts with displeasure, before extending a fleshy paw toward the pile of Bath buns set close to hand, doubtless peeved that his partner has topped his quip.

'You are bold as brass, Mr Samuel. I will grant you that. We had been assured by certain parties that you was safe beneath the sod in just and condign reckoning for the affront you dealt us.'

'Though, to be sure, I never did care for that woman overmuch,' pipes Pimlott, spattering crumbs.

Chuffington sniffs, fixing his spectacles to his face. 'I cannot imagine how you extricated yourself from those circumstances, though better you had quit the metropolis with none the wiser than to present yourself here, turning up like a bad penny.'

'It cannot be helped, Mr Chuffington. I have no wish to aggravate you gentlemen further but my purpose here is the preservation of my associate.'

'Certainly your Mr Facey has been amongst us. His intent, we can only suppose, was to cause mischief and mayhem; a deal of property was lost and with it a considerable profit, not to mention the general disruption to our commerce.'

'Then we are even on that score, since, if you recall, our own crockery was broke by your fellows.'

Chuffington pours a tiny glass of sherry from the decanter beside him. 'You speak as though we were on an equal footing to begin with, Mr Samuel. We were not. Your Mr Facey has compounded his earlier sin with this latest transgression and so must face the consequences.' He sips delicately, closing his eyes to better savour the liquor before continuing. 'There have been ructions in our world, Mr Samuel. Great matters you will know nothing of, but for a good while, certain other parties have eyed our enterprises with envy. We have cunning enemies who only now begin to show themselves. They have nipped at our heels, and undermined our interests. In short, they have sought to step into our shoes. It will not do, Mr Samuel. It is not to be tolerated. Examples must be made.'

'As you say, sir, I know naught of these things, being but a simple man with modest ambitions. I seek only to preserve the life of my partner and should never trouble you after, nor should our paths ever cross henceforth.' I believe I know these men and what it is that drives them and so it is with some complacency that I deliver my trump card: 'Gentlemen, I am in possession of a very handsome sum, which I should be content to make over to you by way of exchange, in cash money, this very day.'

Pimlott reaches across the table for the decanter and pours a tiny glass for himself. 'Would that it were that simple, Mr Samuel.'

'Once again, Mr Pimlott has the nut of it,' announces Chuffington with a sigh. 'It is not so straightforward as all that. As I have said, our many enterprises have been disordered; our trusted associates bribed and suborned. A firm hand is required.'

'An example made,' remarks Pimlott, reaching for another bun.

'An example, Mr Samuel, to show that we are not to be trifled with,' says Chuffington, with a friendly nod as he tips back his dainty glass of sherry. 'You must understand that your partner cost us dear today, not only in the destruction of our property but through the damage to our reputations. It has been a most public affront and so your Mr Facey must, likewise, be made example of. This is no time for weakness, nor forgiveness, Mr Samuel, it is a time for vengeance and a show of strength.'

'Mr Facey meant you no harm nor is he an enemy. He is scarce recovered from a fever and his wits are quite addled.'

'I do not doubt it, Mr Samuel, only a fool would have done as he did. But his transgressions, if not severely dealt with, would show us in a precious poor light.'

We are interrupted in our dealings by a scratching at the door.

'Come,' intones Chuffington.

Meathook's head appears at the crack. Instantly spying me, he flings wide the door and rushes in, followed close behind by a pair of bruisers. I observe the small marks of affray upon them and so believe that Teeth has given a good account of himself.

The bruisers roughly pinion my arms. I make no objection, nor move to throw them off, knowing the futility of such attempts. 'Forgive me, gents,' says Meathook, 'I cannot for the life of me fathom how this scoundrel comes to be here; I assure you, I saw him dead and buried not a day ago.'

Chuffington shrugs. 'And yet here he stands, right as a trivet, for all your assurances.' He glances at the elderly clerk who continues to scribble away at his elevated desk, obdurate and unmindful of the events surrounding him. 'Mr Crockford, you may wish to take a breath of air.'

Crockford instantly drops his quill, stepping down from the high stool and adjusting his coat. 'Most kind, Mr Chuffington,' he replies with a short bow, before leaving the room.

'Shall he be put with the other rogue in the cellars, sir?' inquires Meathook.

'We may carry him off through the servants' passages to the rear and none shall be the wiser. I mean to finish the job this time, good and proper.'

'You are hasty, Mr Meathook. The fellow has not yet had a fitting hearing.'

'Proposition away, Mr Samuel,' adds Pimlott, 'for we are busy men and these ledgers will not balance themselves.'

'Gents, it is one hundred and twenty gold sovereigns I will give for my associate.'

Chuffington cocks his head, like a startled sparrow. 'I am astounded, Mr Samuel. I must say, I had imagined a fruitless attempt with a few paltry shillings but that is a very handsome sum. Much may be forgiven and forgot for it. What is your opinion on it, Mr P?'

'A most tolerable sum indeed, Mr C.' Pimlott turns his beady gaze upon me, assessing my coat and pockets. 'I take it you do not have that quantity of tin about your person?'

'Forgive me, but I am not such a flat as that, sir.'

'Then how are we to have it?'

'It is close by. I shall return here in a Hack accompanied by a most sturdy, determined fellow and you shall bring Mr Facey to the conveyance. Once safely inside I will deliver up the monies in exchange.'

Chuffington nods his approval. 'A fair plan, Mr Samuel.'

'Then you consent to it?'

'I believe we may consider it.' He smiles thinly, flapping a hand at the bruisers who instantly release me. Meathook chivvies them from the room, though he himself remains close at my back. Even so, I am elated. I have stepped into the lions' den and may emerge none the worse for it. Though penniless once more, we remain unscathed and may yet make a new life for ourselves at Portsmouth or some other place.

Pimlott coughs softly.

'A moment,' announces Chuffington, 'I believe Mr Pimlott has a further word to say on the matter. Mr P?'

Pimlott brushes a few crumbs from his black coat and settles back in his chair, the wooden joints emitting squeals of protest. 'There is a conundrum here, Mr C, which, I confess, I have been racking my brains at.' His forehead puckers in exaggerated consternation.

'How so?'

'By my reckoning, two lives were forfeit, were they not?'

'They were indeed, Mr P.'

'And yet two lives remain.'

Chuffington purses his lips.

'By my estimation, a hundred and twenty sovs is a fair price for a single life,' continues Pimlott, holding up a pudgy finger, 'but not for two.' With that he links his soft white hands, reposing them complacently upon his ample belly.

'What a mind. What a prodigy of reasoning you are, Mr P,' exults Chuffington. He raises his tiny glass to his partner, who acknowledges the gesture with a nod, beaming like a vast, milk-sodden babe.

Chuffington sips, before returning his gaze to me. 'A wonder is he not? As always, he has winkled out the meat of the matter. In a nutshell, Mr Samuel, you have escaped chastisement. It is two lives owed us and, as you know, the books must be balanced.' He gestures at Meathook. I sense a rustle of movement behind me, aware that he has taken something from his coat, most likely a weapon of some description, which I earnestly pray is not the butcher's hook.

I gape in consternation. 'Surely you have had your revenge of me. I have been buried alive; there can be no worse a fate.'

Chuffington pauses before placing the glass back on the table. 'Well, that is fairly put and there may be some merit to it. Mr P, you must bring that great mind of yours to bear upon the issue. I shall defer to it, as always.'

Pimlott regards the ceiling for a moment, cogitating; I can hear his breath wheezing like an old bellows. Finally, those tiny, pouched, remorseless eyes return to me. 'Your life was forfeit, Mr Samuel. The manner of its taking don't hardly signify. That the job was half done,' he frowns at Meathook behind me, 'is of no account. The reckoning must still be paid.'

'And yet,' interjects Chuffington, delicately sipping now, 'forgive me, Mr P, and yet, I cannot help but recall the very ancient tale of "Half-Hanged" Smith.'

'What of it?'

'Twice at Tyburn they jigged him but since he would not be topped it was considered the will of God that he was preserved. Justice had been done and there was an end to it.'

'As I collect, 'tis not a principle. For 'twas not the law made it so, Mr C., only the howling will of the mob.'

'Was it so? Well, we cannot have that. Order must be preserved and so our law must take its course.'

'There you have it, Mr Samuel,' pipes Pimlott, 'one hundred and twenty sovs is only sufficient for a single pardon. Now, which of you is it to be?'

Meathook claps a heavy paw on my shoulder, gripping me tightly and I see now that they have been toying with me. Even should I send for the tin they will never let either one of us go. My gamble has failed. Whichever choice I make, I fear I have done for us both.

CHAPTER XLVI

Whatever passes from hereon in, I resolve that I shall never send for the coin. My sole consolation is that those sovereigns are safely preserved for Rosamund and the lad.

'Come now, Mr Samuel, you must speak. We do not have all day,' says Chuffington.

'You have heard the gent. Out with it, man.' Meathook raps the back of my head with his knuckles. The blow gives land at the site of the great clump I took from him in the churchyard and brings a prickle of tears to my eyes. Nevertheless, I remain standing in stony silence.

'You must choose, Mr Samuel, for if you do not, both your lives will be forfeit to no account,' says Pimlott.

Chuffington inclines his head; Meathook deals me another, more powerful blow, this time to the side of my head. A multitude of tiny lights flash before my eyes and I feel my knees begin to buckle.

I must have fainted off for an instant, for when I collect my senses I find that my eyes perceive only the glossy whorls and knots of the polished brown wood floorboards. From somewhere above I believe I can detect the hesitant tones of the liveried doorman.

I haul myself to my feet to find that I am not mistaken: the liveried cove with the tippler's nose stands uncertainly at the open doorway, but he is not alone. My heart sinks when I see that he is accompanied by none other than Rosamund. I dare not catch her eye, staring steadfastly instead at the floor, preferring not to give these men an inkling of my connection to her.

'To the devil with you, Gilpin. Your business is downstairs, the doings here are none of your concern,' snaps Meathook, brandishing the implement he has just used on me—a sand-filled leather cosh.

Gilpin swallows nervously. 'You will forgive the intrusion, I hope, Mr Meathook, but the young lady was most insistent I carry her directly to these gentlemen's presence. Nor would she brook no refusal and I feared a further commotion. I hope I did right.'

'Are we to have no peace at all today?' pouts Chuffington. 'Young lady,' he says, addressing Rosamund, 'it is an open auction you attend, and, as with all sales of this kind, the principle is caveat emptor. Your complaints will butter no parsnips here.'

'Caveat emptor is the language of Romans,' declares Pimlott, 'it means that should you regret what you have bought, then you must learn from your error and take more care in future. Good day to you now.'

The liveried cove gently takes her arm. 'There. You have had your moment, now come away, Miss, if you please.'

'I will not,' says Rosamund, extricating her arm. 'I am not come to mither about your gimcrack goods, I am here for Mr Samuel,' she announces, boldly stepping across the threshold.

Chuffington frowns. 'Then I regret you have had a wasted journey, Miss, since Mr Samuel has important business with us, which will detain him for a good while longer.'

'I know very well the nature of your business and believe I might be of service.'

The two men exchange knowing glances across the table. 'Very well, Miss. You may remain and we will hear you out,' announces Chuffington at length.

'Back to your station with you, Gilpin,' snaps Meathook, waving off the tippler, who bows briefly before closing the door.

Chuffington rises from his seat, all civility now. 'You will forgive our makeshift accommodations here, miss. Please,' he says, indicating the recently vacated clerk's stool.

Rosamund demurs. 'You are kind, sir, but I shall remain as I am. I do not believe I shall be here long.'

'As you wish,' replies Chuffington returning to his own seat. 'Now, Miss,' he says, eyeing the drawstring bag she carries, 'I take it you have with you these sovereigns Mr Samuel has spoke of.'

'I do not, sir,' replies Rosamund.

Pimlott slams a meaty palm onto the desk, startling us all. 'Then why have you come? Why waste our time, woman? We have nothing to further to discuss. Meathook, you will turn her out into the street.'

'With pleasure, sir,' he replies.

'You will not lay a hand on her,' I bellow, ducking and turning at once. I launch myself at Meathook, hands outstretched for his throat. I hear Rosamund scream before those same myriad stars appear in my vision and I find myself falling once more. This time I am not deprived of my senses entirely; I am conscious of the rustle of fabric and the waft of rose water as Rosamund settles herself on the floor beside me. She lifts my head, cradling it in her lap.

'Bless my soul, Mr Samuel, I confess, I had marked you for a far more timid sort,' remarks Chuffington.

'I believe it is on account of he is sweet on the doxy,' sneers Meathook.

'So much the better,' pipes Pimlott. 'Young lady, if you have any feelings for Mr Samuel, you will fetch us the hundred and twenty sovereigns we have been promised. And quick smart about it for my patience wears shocking thin.'

Rosamund glares up at him. 'I am come here with a far better offer. Had you not been so brutish and ungentlemanly you would have had it from me by now.'

'Then make it, by all means,' says Chuffington.

Rosamund rises. Meathook stoops, gathers the folds of my coat in his powerful fist and hauls me to my feet. He is not gentle about it neither, no doubt feeling the need to compensate for his earlier neglect. His heavy left hand remains on my shoulder, the leather cosh at the ready in his other paw.

'Gentlemen, I must first have your assurances that Mr Samuel and Mr Facey will be safely delivered up,' says Rosamund firmly.

'You cannot have both parties,' declares Pimlott flatly. 'One hundred and twenty sovs ain't sufficient for it.'

'I do not offer one hundred and twenty sovereigns but four thousand pound,' replies Rosamund, without hesitation.

The pair are stunned to silence.

Rosamund reaches into her little reticule to retrieve the wrapped packet of notes. 'Not cash money, to be sure, but instruments, properly and lawfully indorsed by a gentleman of wealth and substance.'

Pimlott extends a fat hand, clicking his fingers. Rosamund duly passes across the packet; he tears impatiently at the wrapping in the way that old Sausages used to go at a package of rashers.

'You need not explain their merits to us, young lady,' says Chuffington. 'Mr Pimlott will confirm whether they are good or no. There is no one to compare with Mr P. when it comes to an instrument.'

Pimlott carefully inspects each of the notes, setting them down before him, one by one. 'These are notes of hand, indorsed by one Henry Liston of Glendale at Poland Street, 'gainst funds drawn on Lionel Bamfield. It would appear that Bamfield made 'em over only yesterday to a Mr Joshua Brookes.'

'Just so,' confirms Rosamund.

'We have had some past dealings with Bamfield and Sons,' says Pimlott.

'Then you know his paper to be good,' says Rosamund.

'It is Bamfield's hand right enough,' confirms Pimlott. 'This Joshua Brookes has had the paper a day only and yet has set his name again to these notes consenting to their transference. It is most irregular to my mind.'

'You will see, sir, that Mr Brookes has made them over to the bearer.'

'I see that quite well, young lady. I cannot fathom it though. Nor can I imagine how they came to be in your possession.'

'I am not at liberty to say, sir,' replies Rosamund, artfully.

'Never mind about all that,' interjects Chuffington, 'are they proper or ain't they?'

Pimlott rests a great paw on the neat pile. 'Indeed they are, Mr C., good as banknotes, so far as I can say, and right as rain. The paper is past due and so the bearer of these notes may dun Mister Henry Liston of Poland Street, a gentleman of property, for the full four thousand pound or see him answerable to the law.'

'We will not require the law for that,' sniffs Chuffington.

'You may have them,' announces Rosamund, 'but you will, upon this instant, release Mr Samuel and Mr Facey and never more hold them to account for their past actions nor in the future attempt to seek them out. You will swear to this and you may keep those notes with my blessing.'

'Well, Mr P., and what do you say to that?' inquires Chuffington rubbing his hands.

Pimlott reaches for the remaining bun. 'I should say it is a most satisfactory outcome, Mr C. The books have been balanced and, though I never did care for my old ma above half, she has been good for something at the least.'

'Well, well, you have heard the conditions,' says Chuffington, addressing Meathook. 'You will leave hold of Mr Samuel and fetch up Mr Facey from the cellars.'

Meathook clumps to the door, a sour expression on his dial; he pauses and turns, addressing me through narrowed eyes. 'You have more lives than a cat, Mr Samuel. But take good care that our paths do not cross in the future.'

'You have heard him, Mr Samuel,' remarks Chuffington. 'Whilst we shall not attempt to seek you out, you would be wise not to come under our scrutiny from this time forth.'

'You may rely upon it,' I say with a brief nod.

'Well then, I wish you both good day,' says Chuffington, picking up his penner once more.

And with that, our business is at an end.

CHAPTER XLVII

'Say what you like, Sammy Boy, it was worth the candle if only to see Spicer with a phizzog on him like a slapped arse as the crockery flew about,' chuckles Facey.

We are gathered in Tom's snug, regaled by a steaming bowl of punch and a couple of still warm fowls.

'How many went at you would you say, Mr Facey?' inquires Pure John, his eyes shining with admiration and strong drink.

'I am not my old self, young snot-nose, and so not such a number as would ordinarily have done,' replies Facey gesturing with the greasy duck leg in his hand. 'There was three on 'em to begin with but they was added to by Meathook, Bishop and two others, which would make it ...' Facey attempts to tally the figure by the fingers of his left hand but finding his right hand occupied by the fowl, gives up the task.

'You are quite incorrigible, Mr Facey,' remarks Rosamund.

Here is another mighty word, which I do not know the meaning of. But should it describe a fellow who is beaten, bruised and bloody, yet still prideful and mulish after such an ordeal, then it is a prime one, and I shall be sure and add it to my store.

'At any rate, it was a fair set to with the raws, the place in uproar and the trestles flying. They was two on my back while the fellow Bishop paid attention to my legs with the notion of tipping me arse-over-teakettle but I settled his business with a good hoof to the fruits and laid another of the brutes out with a fair flattener on the razzo.'

'And will you learn me the art of pugilism, Mr Facey?' pleads Pure John.

'Ah, Mr Canon is your man for that, young snotty, my methods are all brute strength and no science.'

'True enough,' says a thin-lipped Tom. 'It is to her credit that there is one amongst you with the wit to think afore rushing to precipitate action, else where should you be now?'

'Hear him,' I say, raising my tumbler to Rosamund.

Rosamund blushes. 'Mr Canon, you are too modest of your own part.'

'I had naught to do with it.'

'Come now, Tom,' she chides, smiling gently. 'You left so quick, Sammy, leaving me and Mr Brookes with no notion of what had occurred, and, though uneasy, Tom was swift enough to reveal all.'

'Forgive me, Sammy,' says Tom. 'I had no wish to betray a confidence but believed it for the best.'

'Certainly it was that, Tom; we should not be here else,' I say, raising my tumbler to him. 'But what of Brookes, how came he to part with his precious paper for your enterprise?'

'Sammy, you must know that Mr Brookes was much downcast by that interview. In truth, the man is quite broken in spirit and Liston had played upon his fears like a master at the pianoforte. Brookes believed that Liston would turn circles and squirm and twist, employing his high estate to evade the workings of the law until he was exhausted unto death. In truth, I think the poor man had not the spirit for such a contest.'

I nod. 'He has endured much, I believe.'

'That being so, I prevailed upon him to consider that another, more determined party might take ownership of the debts.'

Rosamund sips her punch, that same grim expression on her face. 'And what better home for Liston's paper than that vile, grasping pair? Were you not already in their power, I should have handed the instruments to those men, gratis.' She shrugs. 'Mr Brookes was most content to sign them away, making them over to "the bearer" since he had no desire to know what manner of man ended up with them, nor particularly, how those debts would be enforced. He was, at any rate, much relieved to come it a Pontius Pilate and has washed his hands of the matter, as we all have.'

Facey, oblivious to this fine point of morality, has gnawed the fowl's leg to the bone and gristle. He now extends his empty tumbler, which Pure John rushes to fill from the punchbowl. 'Sammy, are you still for Portsmouth?'

'I am, Facey, though you should know that it is not alone I go there.'

'Indeed you do not, for I shall accompany you. We are men of wealth and I should not like to split that substance. Far better to invest the entire sum into an inn for seafaring types with shore leave and a prodigious thirst.' As an exemplar of his vision, he takes a brimming beaker of punch from the lad and throws it back. 'I do not pretend to understand all that the young lady has expounded upon but I do believe that she has been of great service to us in preserving our hides, and so I have no grounds to resent her company, 'specially since I perceive that you desire it so earnestly.'

'I do at that,' I say.

'You are most kind to say so, Mr Facey,' remarks Rosamund with a quiet smile.

'Facey, I must insist that the lad accompany us also,' I declare.

There is a moment's silence whilst Facey cogitates upon this. Finally, he cuffs Pure John lightly about the back of his head. 'Well, it is a young snotty, who is pretty much the same as all the rest of his age: good and bad in equal measure. I shall learn him the brute flinging of the raws and he may amount to something. Mayhap Tom Canon will visit from time to time and learn him in the science.'

'I should like that very much,' announces Tom, raising his own tumbler to us all.

Pure John beams, hugging himself with glee.

'You will also attend the school that John Pounds founded and learn your letters, as well as to enumerate,' I advise, causing the boy's face to fall.

Facey grins. 'Then it is agreed. We shall pass an hour or two and take the Night Post for Portsmouth.'

'We shall not,' I declare. 'At least not tonight.'

'How so?' inquires Facey.

I note that Rosamund's expression is now as glum as Pure John's, but there is no help for it: 'Forgive me, Rosamund, I well know that I have sworn off our previous profession, but there is one last piece of night work that I believe you will forgive me for.'

CHAPTER XLVIII

He did twist and turn.

It was as we thought: those men who took our paper were not so fastidious about the law, nor were they in the least forgiving of the debts to be repaid.

They dunned him. They threatened, cajoled and squeezed him. They deprived him of his horseflesh and then his portable goods. Liston had only a lease on Glendale, so there was little to be gained from his property. They stripped him of everything he had. In the end, his father did not intervene, being utterly estranged from a son who had brought him naught but grief and humiliation.

And so, that remorseless pair, who were out to make examples, set a fine example of a gentleman from a most elevated station. They hanged him from a bridge for their unpaid notes of hand, from the middle arch of New London Bridge, with those remaining, unpaid notes stuffed betwixt his teeth, stopping up his deceitful mouth. There he twisted and turned in the breeze, suspended from that edifice, and there were few, if any, to lament it.

I imagine that John Pounds, should he have been exposed to this tale, would have found it impossible to relate to his youthful congregation. I know it, and so does Rosamund, for we are teachers at his school and there are certain lessons which are not worth the giving.

Instead, we teach our pauper charges their letters and the skills of enumeration; it is none of our business to explicate the pitiless workings of the world; they already know that well enough.

Facey slings sacks about at the docks, loading and unloading cargo destined for all corners of the globe. In the evenings he can be found at our tavern regaling the seafaring men with tales of London Town, or out at the fields showing the young'uns how they might throw the raws. I know he is not quite contented though, believing that with his single glim, he is but half a man. He chafes under the yoke of a settled existence, lamenting that he must endure the bonds of a marriage with none of the benefit.

Those joys, of course, are reserved for me and Rosamund alone. She steadies me and provides me with not courage—for I will never be a courageous man—but resolution. And if Facey rubs alongside like a fifth wheel, then Pure John seems happy enough to be upon this cart of ours. At least for the while. He is no saint, to be sure, and must be kept away from the stronger spirits in our cellars, but has taken to his learning well enough. A ship's Master of our acquaintance has put his name upon the books of his vessel and he will go to sea in a year or so. The name so inscribed is John—John Samuel.

And there is still a cold blank slab in the Shoreditch where no name is written, for the whole world believes it to be an empty grave. And yet on a particular day of the year, the twenty-fourth day of June, the site is memorialised by a single rose. None knows why, or who it is that lays it.

It is a rose that does not wither, nor does it decay.

For it is made of coloured paper.

And that is all I have to say on the matter.

ACKNOWLEDGEMENTS

I'd like to thank Tanya Morel and Alan Warner for their advice and encouragement along the way. Special thanks to Angel Belsey for her unfailing enthusiasm, insight and faith, without which this book would not have seen the light of day.

ABOUT THE AUTHOR

Siôn Scott-Wilson writes short stories, novels, plays and has won many industry awards for his television work, including a BAFTA nomination. His debut novel, *The Sleepwalker's Introduction to Flight*, was listed for the CrimeFest Last Laugh Award. He won the Yeovil Literary Prize for Best Novel in 2013 and was a runner-up for the Fish Publishing Prize in 2008. Siôn holds an MSc (Distinction) in Creative Writing from the University of Edinburgh.

ABOUT DEIXIS PRESS

Deixis Press is an independent publisher of fiction, usually with a darker edge. Our aim is to discover, commission, and curate works of literary art. Every book published by Deixis Press is hand-picked and adored from submission to release and beyond.

www.deixis.press

Lightning Source UK Ltd.
Milton Keynes UK
UKHW040046180921
390735UK00011B/106